WE NEVER TOLD

WE NEVER TOLD

A NOVEL

DIANA ALTMAN

SHE WRITES PRESS

Published 2019
Printed in the United States of America
Print ISBN: 978-1-63152-543-8
E-ISBN: 978-1-63152-544-5
Library of Congress Control Number: 2018956264

For information, address:
She Writes Press
1563 Solano Ave #546
Berkeley, CA 94707

Interior design by Tabitha Lahr

She Writes Press is a division of SparkPoint Studio, LLC.

Names and identifying characteristics have been changed to protect the privacy of certain individuals.

For Dorita Imperio

No one ever keeps a secret so well as a child.
—Victor Hugo

CHAPTER ONE

· · · · · · · · · · · · · · · · · · · ·

While cleaning out my mother's files after she died alone at her secluded house behind a locked gate near the Catskill Mountains, her five cats yowling from fear and hunger, I came upon an alarming letter. It was from a caseworker at Children's Services in Louisville, Kentucky. Its tone was tender but firm. Of course the case worker could understand Mrs. Adler's reluctance to admit to the birth of a son she gave up for adoption but the birth records show that she was, in fact, the Violet Adler admitted to Central Hospital and was the mother of a baby boy given up for adoption immediately after his birth. If Mrs. Adler did not want contact with the adopted person, she had to sign the enclosed contact veto form. "If we do not locate and identify the birth mother," the letter said, "then the adopted person is notified that they may search for the birth mother on their own without further restrictions. Children's Services had been trying without success to find Joan and Sonya Adler, Mrs. Adler's two daughters as stated in the hospital records. If they did not want contact with their half brother, they too had to sign the forms." The caseworker could not give advice, could only set out the facts as required by law. The contact veto form was still there. My mother had not signed it.

I couldn't believe what I was reading. My heart was thudding against my ribs. He had tried to contact her? He was alive? I picked up the phone and called Leo. When I finished telling my husband, I called my sister. "Are you sitting down?"

Had I been in a movie, the screen would become wavy signaling a flashback to the time when every family on Avon Road in New Rochelle had a maid and all those maids had Thursday nights off. Ours did too so we went out. The blurry screen of the flashback would become crisp and there I'd be age twelve, sitting in the back seat of the car worried because my mother did not drive to the train station to pick up my father. We had never gone out to dinner without him so I knew something heart-stopping was about to happen.

Ebersoles Restaurant catered to children in a respectful way. The tables were set with white cloths and good china and there was an air of elegance though many of the diners were in grammar school. Sticky buns were a specialty. Usually Joan and I got one of our own and another donated by each parent. This night, we got only our own and half of our mother's, and it was after she set the halves on our plates that she announced in a light and misleading voice her decision to divorce.

The very fineness of the place made bad manners impossible. There could be no display of emotion. I thought it cowardly and cruel to make this announcement in public. I sat there cursing my chin because it was trembling. What right did my mother have to ruin my home? I was sorry that my parents fought about money and had little in common, but much of my life had nothing to do with them. While my parents' lives were going on, so was mine. The boy who sat next to me liked the girl across the room and I thought he liked me, but my friend who sat behind me passed me a note that said he liked that other girl. My life included a secret rivalry with the boy who sat in first chair in the school orchestra. He had the unfair advantage of a mother who was a violin teacher, so I would probably never be able to move up from second chair. And I was writing a novel entitled *Tippy Adams* about a girl who gets invited to the prom by the handsomest boy in the class and goes shopping for a dress with her mother.

I knew only one person in my sixth-grade class whose parents were divorced, a perky girl who did not deserve to have a blot on her. Now there would be a blot on me. I'd have a blot on me the way kids do who have a dead parent. They were set apart even as they sat among us in class, apart because of their dark and secret sorrow. I would have to enter Albert Leonard Junior High next year at a disadvantage. I whispered, "What will I tell my friends?"

"There's no need to live with so much tension," my mother said. "You see how pleasant it is when Daddy's not here. Here we are having a lovely time. It can be like that all the time. There's no need to live with all that fighting and fussing. I have to do this now while I still have my looks. You two have your whole lives ahead of you." She was forty and always aware, even now, that both men and women were drawn to her beauty, kept their eyes on her or turned around for another look. That man at the table across the way had flicked his eyes toward her when we entered then turned back to his wife and now he was sneaking more peeks.

Joan said, "But where will Daddy live?"

"I don't know. In an apartment some place, probably."

"But he doesn't like apartments." Joan opened her mouth wide, stuck her finger in and readjusted one of the rubber bands on her braces. "Will we ever see him?"

"Of course you'll see him."

"When?"

"I don't know when. The court will decide that."

"What court?"

"I don't know. I don't know. Just eat your dinner. I don't know. He'll have visitation rights."

We would have to *visit* our own father? He would have to *visit* us in his own house? A frozen silence descended upon me, as if a traffic cone had been put over my head. Dinner finished, cloth napkins folded correctly and set neatly next to plates, we went out to the lobby. On the floor in the lobby was a pirate's treasure chest full of Tootsie Pops, treats to take home after dinner. Joan and I knelt on the floor in front of a mound of colorful lollipops to select either cherry, lime, lemon, or chocolate. I took two, a breach of Ebersoles etiquette. Joan saw me do it but didn't tell.

Turning into the driveway, I could see that my father wasn't home. There was only one window lit up above the kitchen where Ruby slept. She was back from wherever she went on Thursday nights. Had my mother confided in Ruby? Would Ruby lose her job?

Our house in New Rochelle was a white Dutch colonial with a black roof that hung down like bangs. The apple tree in the front yard burst with white blossoms in the spring. The forsythia that edged the house flared yellow, the rhododendron had fluffy pink blooms. Daffodils and crocus made what seemed a yearly mistake, showed themselves too soon. Ours was a narrow street without enough traffic to endanger our cat. Bordered by antique stone walls left over from the days when the neighborhood was somebody's farm, giant elms canopied Avon Road as it curved pleasantly past woods that contained a brook where Joan and I swished sticks among the pebbles. The land behind our house was a small farm owned by an unmarried old man who refused to sell out to the Wykagyl Country Club. He kept chickens in coops and never objected to our using his field as a shortcut to grammar school. The golf course came right to the edge of his land.

Every Fourth of July, the Club held its annual swim meet. Loud speakers broadcast metallic applause and shouts of victory. The hysterical enthusiasm of an announcer carried for miles right into my bedroom window that had to stay open because the weather was so hot. The revolving fan on my bookshelf blew hot air and was no relief. I tossed and turned all night as the roars of excitement came like waves into my room. This was not fair, here was injustice. I was kept awake by a place that excluded Jews—we were not allowed there.

Our shortcut to school included crossing the golf course. Joan and I often stopped to take revenge by slamming our heels into the velvet green saying, "Take that! And that!" leaving in our wake chunks of dirt like dead hedgehogs.

In the back seat of the car as Mother maneuvered the car into the garage, I worried. What would I say to my father when he got home? Did he know she was going to tell us that night? Had they planned this? Mother turned off the ignition and we edged our way out avoiding wheelbarrows, rakes, and bags of peat moss. Inside the dark house, we flicked on light switches as we went from kitchen to back hall to living room where there were sofas and wall-to-wall carpet and a breakfront displaying hand-painted plates. The fireplace hearth held an antique brass samovar and a log holder made of woven rope. A Steinway grand piano dominated the far corner of the room. My violin case was on the bench. The music stand held Ravel's *Pavane for a Dead Princess*, my teacher's notes in the margin, bow up, bow down, more vibrato here. This music made me swoon, and I planned to play it at the audition for the junior high orchestra next year.

A white cat ran to greet us. "Rinso, Rinso," I said and rushed toward him and scooped him up and hugged him for so long and with such desperation he wiggled out of my arms and sat with his back to me grooming himself. "Where's Daddy?" Joan wanted to know.

"I don't know," my mother said in a weary voice. Her walk in public was proud and full of thrusting bosom but at home she often drooped and walked as if her feet were heavy. This difference between the public self and the private interested me. Now Mother, using her weighted down steps, climbed the carpeted stairs and walked along the upstairs hall and shut the door to the bedroom she did not share with her husband. It was a feminine retreat with a canopy bed so high it required a footstool, a satin chaise lounge, and wallpaper covered in roses. There was nothing of her husband in her bedroom, not a shoe, not a half-read book, nor a glass of water on the bedside table.

My room, on the other hand, was full of Seymour Adler. Tacked to the wall were glossy autographed photographs of movie stars. "To Sonya, best of luck, Jimmy Stewart." "Dear Sonya, be a good girl," Greer Garson. Joan Crawford wrote, "To Seymour's little girl with fond wishes." Jimmy Durante and Mario Lanza smiled down at me as I sat on my bed making my boy doll kiss my girl doll, absorbed but also ashamed because I was too old to play with dolls. I was proud that my father was a famous movie producer, but I didn't really want all those strangers on my wall. I put them there because each photo was presented as a gift and I didn't want to hurt my father's feelings. The portraits were so fake. Studio lights made noses less bulbous and cheekbones more chiseled. I understood what lighting could do by the glamorous portraits of my parents done by Hollywood photographers. It went against my sense of Truth to see my parents flawless, lovingly shadowed. Violet and Seymour, heads tilted just so, looked like the happiest and best-looking couple on earth.

From my mother's bedroom came the sound of Beethoven's Fifth Symphony. Ta Ta Ta Taaaa. She was probably in her velvet robe reclining on her chaise lounge, knitting. A car whooshed by outside, its headlights illuminating my bedroom window for a moment. When would my father get home? Would I already be asleep?

A distinctive burning smell came from Joan's room. She was in her pajamas on the floor peering into a miniature kiln surrounded by bags of enamel dust and wires. She squinted into the oven, it was about the size of a cantaloupe, and said, "Done." With a spatula, she removed the piece and set it on an asbestos pad.

I thought her work was beautiful. "How did you get the yellow to do that?"

She looked up and moved over so I could sit next to her. "I don't know. It just did."

"Is it a pendant? Are you going to wear it?"

"I don't know. Maybe. Do you want it?"

"Yes."

"You can have it."

"Really?"

"Sure."

"Want me to make one for you?"

"If you want to."

"A pendant or a pin?"

"Pendant."

Just a few minutes before I was dangling off the earth but now some calm returned. My parents might be two battling creatures but Joan and I were one, at least right then. We sprinkled the copper pieces with enamel dust, inserted them into the kiln where the dust melted, then took the pieces out and examined them as they cooled. "Put a drop of yellow on that one," Joan said, "and put it back in." I did as she said and peered into the oven to watch the yellow dust merge with the other colors. When I took it out, I was glad I'd followed her advice.

"Oh, you know that girl Barbara Sandowsky?" Joan said as she drew a design on her new piece with a toothpick.

"With the mole?"

"She tried to take Kenny Fallon away from Susie Weber."

"How?"

"She called him up and asked him if he would go out with her."

"What'd he say?"

"Susie was at his house."

"So she knew Barbara called him up?"

"She was sitting right . . ." We both froze as we heard the back door open and close. He was home. He usually bounced up the stairs, but this night he seemed to take a long time walking along the downstairs hall and into the living room where he turned off the lights. Sometimes he brought cashews or chocolates from Grand Central, but this night he held only movie scripts as he appeared at the top of the stairs in a three-piece suit. Short and alert, his posture was erect and energetic. He was loosening his tie and opening his collar button. He paused when he saw me. "We went to Ebersoles." He acknowledged me with a forced smile, said in a weak voice, "Carry on, Kewpie," and went into his bedroom. As he closed his door I said, "Where were you?" When he had a sinus headache, we were not allowed to go into his room but one time I did and found him in the dark on his back pinching the bridge of his nose.

I sat down again next to Joan, who had not stopped her work to greet him. If he had come into her room, she would have looked up to say hello. But Joan was no tail wagging Golden Retriever available for hugs at all times. We never talked about how we felt. There was no need because we could read each other's faces, but this night I couldn't tell if she was even thinking about the divorce. Was she wondering how the house would be without our father in it?

Suddenly there was a loud thump, Seymour's fist against his desk where monthly bills were piled. I heard him shout, "What? What? Is she crazy!" We heard him yank open the door to Mother's bedroom. Did she think he was made of money? Did she think money grew on trees? She didn't know the value of a dollar! How could she spend that much on that thing? Was she out of her mind? She couldn't be trusted with charge accounts. Usually, there was no response to his tirades, but that night she screamed, "God! How I hate you!" and he slammed the door of her bedroom, the bang reverberating through the house, the force of it, the anger of it echoing within me.

CHAPTER TWO

....

L aid out on the platform next to the Twentieth Century Limited at Grand Central Station was a red carpet. Only those boarding the luxurious train were allowed to walk down the red carpet. Mother had turned up the collar of her mink coat to frame her face, and as I hurried along next to her I saw both men and women do double takes as if checking to see if that woman really was that good looking. Mother kept track of the attention with quick eye flicks here and there, and each glance was a victory that showed as satisfaction on her face. While she was absorbing what amounted to a standing ovation, she seemed unaware of Joan and me, and I felt unsafe in that chaos of bellhops pushing dollies heaped with luggage, crowds of passengers pushing forward, and loud speakers broadcasting train tracks and departure times. My socks kept slipping down into my shoes, and I had to stop to pull them up. If Joan hadn't stopped to wait for me, I might have lost sight of Mother altogether. "Sonya! Come on! Hurry up!" Joan too thought the train might pull away without us and our mother wouldn't even notice.

Mother showed her ticket to a conductor, and we climbed up onto the train and found our compartment. A red cap came in, swung the suitcases up onto the overhead racks then stood waiting for a tip from the woman in a full-length mink coat. My mother seemed startled as if she'd forgotten that she had to tip him. She peered into her coin purse as if the answer about the appropriate amount might be in there. Her face was a mixture of embarrassment and anger, anger I assumed, at Seymour who put her in this position, a woman alone on a train with two children. It was the husband's job to tip. Her fluster annoyed me. She was old enough to know how to take care of things. Why didn't she? She should have more poise in the world. Taking a plunge, she put some coins in the man's palm. He looked at them as if they were candy corn, touched his cap in a mocking way, and looked up as if asking God to help him endure such idiots. After he left the compartment, my mother sank down into the corner of the seat, pulled her coat around herself like a blanket and muttered, "They're becoming so arrogant."

The Red Cap had violated some rule. Maybe he was supposed to be grateful for whatever was given to him; maybe he was supposed to pretend to be grateful even if he wasn't. I knew my mother's attitude wasn't the only one because my father's was so different. She came from the South and he came from New England. When his friend Ossie Davis, the actor, tried to buy a house in New Rochelle and was turned down, I overheard outraged conversations between Seymour and the real estate broker. Most of the black people in New Rochelle lived downtown where the houses had no yards and were close together. The baseball player Willy Mays lived down the street from us, and I always wondered when I rode my bike by his mansion how he felt surrounded by white neighbors. One evening I met Ossie Davis and his wife Ruby Dee in our living room. They came to say hello to Seymour and to thank him for his help, but I never found out what he did that made it possible for them to buy the house they wanted. I was proud that my father's voice had weight in the world.

From our compartment window, we could see the hustle and bustle on the station platform, people rushing here and there, men with briefcases, women holding the hands of children, a man slumped in a wheelchair being pushed by a nurse. Mother erupted with one of her alarming sighs. It was the very sound of her, three fast inhales that sounded like sobs then an exhale that sounded like a moan. "What's the matter?" I asked.

"What?"

"What's the matter? How come you sighed like that?"

"Like what?"

"Like how you just sighed. Are you sad?" I hoped my question would show my mother that I loved her and cared about her happiness.

"Sad? Don't be silly."

But I wasn't being silly. In private, I imitated my mother's sigh so I could understand if it was a normal adult woman sound. No matter how I mimicked it, it always came out sounding like something from deep within, a sigh that spoke of despair.

"Hey! It's starting!" Joan announced. We watched the station platform recede as the train hurtled through a tunnel. The window turned black, became an unflattering mirror. Then our ghoulish faces evaporated and we could see into the windows of apartment buildings close to the track, old brick buildings with fire escapes like vines. Some of the people were just sitting at the window looking blankly out, smoking a cigarettes. There were long stretches of not seeing much but empty station platforms lit up as if for no reason because the train just sped by, and there were towns with rows of street lamps and lights at the windows of the few houses and always the sound of the wheels on the tracks, chuck-a-chuck, chuck-a-chuck, chuck-a-chuck and the pleasant feel of forward motion.

Joan dealt out Crazy Eights with intense concentration, placing the cards before our mother and me in neat little stacks. Then we played the drawing game. Mother made a scribble on Joan's sketchpad and another on mine and we had to make a picture out of it. We had high standards. If our mother drew a circle we did not turn it into a face. That would be too easy. We didn't turn rectangles into houses, either. Glad to be occupied, we took our time. When we finished, Mother burst out smiling and said, "That is so clever! I can't believe you made that out of what I drew!" Without Seymour, Mother was a good companion, easy to talk to, easy to make laugh. She told us our favorite story: When she was a child in Texas, climbing the water tower was forbidden, but a boy did it anyway and fell in and couldn't get out. She ran to the nearest farm and the farmer hitched up his wagon and galloped his team to the water tower, fished the boy out, and put him in the wagon. The water bounced out of the boy as the horses trotted along. "So he didn't die?"

"No. The water bounced right out of him."

"How did you know it got out of him?"

"Because he sat up." It was as if Mother was on a dimmer switch and was only fully bright when her husband wasn't there.

The dining car was a fairyland, white table cloths, silverware, martini glasses, flowers in vases, men in suits and ties, women dressed up, all hushed and sparkly. A small pewter bowl of water was set before each person. Years before, Joan lifted hers and drank it. Now we knew to dip our fingers in the water and wipe them in a dainty way on our napkins. My mother, in her beige cashmere sweater with a paisley scarf tied cowgirl style around her neck, sipped Harvey's Bristol Cream and wrote our menu choices on a card with the pencil left on the table for that purpose. She wrote roast lamb with mint jelly for herself, hot turkey sandwich for me, and egg salad sandwich for Joan. We buttered rolls and ate them, then asked for more and ate those too. We ate our dinner with the pleasant clinking of ice cubes in cocktail glasses at the other tables, soft conversation, and the perpetual sound of wheels on track. Time was suspended, we were being carried along. For dessert, chocolate cake and vanilla ice cream. Then chocolate covered after dinner mints on a pewter plate. We ate every mint. Mine was the only mother I knew who was not bothersome about sweets. Our kitchen cabinets at home were stocked with Mallomars and Oreos. She expected me and my friends to help ourselves when we came home from school. She liked candy too, and hot fudge sundaes, and pies and cakes. It was our good luck that Ruby at home was an excellent baker.

When we returned to our compartment, it was no longer a sitting room but a bedroom, the seats now converted into bunk beds. The porter made the bed so crisply I had to wedge myself in. As I lay there sandwiched tight between top and bottom sheet, I worried. Would the sound of the wheels on the track keep me up? Did my aunts and uncles know Mother intended to divorce? Did my cousins know? What could be more embarrassing? I was in a mess, and they'd all know it. Would they look at me with pity?

We were saved from the chaos of LaSalle Street station by Grandpa Greenstone's chauffeur, whose bearing was so regal I didn't dare hug him though I wanted to. Jordan led us through the crowds and out to the street where a black Cadillac limousine waited at the curb. When the Red Cap finished heaving the suitcases into the trunk, Jordan tipped him and I wondered if one black person tipping another black person was different from a white person tipping a black person. Did the Red Cap resent Jordan? Did Jordan look down on the Red Cap?

Sunk in soft gray upholstery, we felt the car glide smoothly out into traffic. People on the sidewalk stopped to watch the car swim by with its tinted windows and chauffeur at the wheel in black cap and uniform. I thought of rolling down the window and waving to the people on the sidewalk with my hand backward like the Queen. My sister, on the other hand, was not impressed by money. She didn't seem to appreciate that Grandpa, who only went as far as eighth grade, was once poor and because of his struggles and perseverance could now buy himself a Cadillac limousine. Joan might as well have climbed into a taxi. She collapsed the jump seats, set them up, collapsed them, set them up. Mother snapped, "Stop playing with those things for heaven's sakes!"

We drove through the streets of South Chicago where black men were idle on the stoops of brick buildings. Dressed in winter jackets, they followed the car with sullen faces. Did they envy Grandpa Greenstone's chauffeur? Did they hate him for driving white people? Did he care about their opinion?

When my mother withdrew her warmth from us, I could see it in her eyes. Her gaze turned shallow. She looked at Joan and me as if we were objects in a shop and she had to decide if we were worth the price. That we were not worth the price was evident in the impatient way she brushed aside Joan's bangs. "Get your hair off your face," she said. I knew from previous visits that her tension would mount the closer we got to her mother. Her mother was the harsh judge who lived inside her head. My mother was about to present her daughters, and we were not perfect. She spit on her hanky and wiped a mote off my cheek. "Yuck!" I rubbed the spot again and again trying to get the saliva smell off.

In the elevator, the other people had to get off on floors with numbers. Only we were allowed to go all the way up to PH. The elevator man, wearing white gloves, pulled back the brass gate and Mother, Joan, and I stepped out into a private vestibule. My grandparents' apartment was like a house perched on top of a building. Mother rang the doorbell and chimes made a melody inside. A mechanical bulldog stood guarding the door, a toy that Grandpa lugged home from China. It made raspy squawks when I pulled its leash. I saw the toy as Grandpa's twin, a stocky fellow with jowls and a turned down mouth. I pulled the leash again and again. Joan said, "Let me do that," and she pulled the leash and while metallic snarls ruined the quiet of the exclusive foyer, Mother said, "She always does this. Keeps us waiting. Makes us stand here."

When we heard footsteps behind the closed door, Mother said, "Finally," as if we had been standing there for hours. The door opened. A tiny woman, barely five feet tall, was so shy the force of our presence impelled her backwards. Instead of drawing toward us for an embrace, Grandma Greenstone was so overwhelmed she went backwards and might have continued on forever except that she was stopped by the first step of a grand staircase. She stood there helplessly and batted at her gray pompadour with the back of her hand. She was perfectly groomed in a tailored dress and low-heeled pumps. I was continually impressed by how tiny and insignificant Grandma Greenstone was to me and how gigantic she was to her daughter Violet. "Hello, Mama," my mother said in a dead voice.

I went forward and gave Grandma Greenstone a hug. As always she said, "Is that all I get?" As I squeezed her harder, I wondered why she would expect more? This final hug was phony; the first one was appropriate to what I felt for her. "Ah," she said, "that's better." Then Grandma Greenstone turned a critical eye on me, took my chin between her thumb and forefinger and gave it three firm tugs. Grandma believed a child's face could be molded. She wanted us to have strong chins. It was important for a girl to be beautiful and there was a danger that Grandma's offspring might inherit her receding chin. It was part of her duty to uplift her family in every way possible. I appreciated Grandma's effort to make our lives easier than hers had been. I could appreciate this effort because I saw its contrast in my father's family. The old ways were the best ways with the

Adlers in New England. Here in Chicago, in everything Grandma Greenstone did, I saw the struggle to leave behind the girl she used to be, a poor girl living in a shack on the plains of New Mexico with five sisters and immigrant parents who barely spoke English. Grandma's penthouse overlooking Lake Michigan was the dusty green of sagebrush, the tan of tumbleweed, and the brown of mesquite. The carpet was sagebrush and so were the walls. I moved aside so Joan could have her turn. She gave Grandma a hug. "Is that all I get? Ah. That's better." Then three firm tugs to Joan's chin. To her daughter, Grandma said, "Violet, where is your hat?"

"I didn't wear a hat, Mama."

"No hat? Why not? You must wear a hat. The weather is cold."

"Okay, Mama. I'll wear a hat."

"Do you have a hat?"

"Oh, for heavens sakes, Mama."

"Your hat should be on your head, Violet, but I do not see it on your head."

"Okay, Mama. Enough."

"If you do not have a hat with you, then we must get you one."

"Fine, Mama. Fine. We'll get me a hat."

As Grandma took our coats and hung them in the downstairs closet, she refused help even though she was obviously struggling with the weight of the coats, I hurried to the den where Grandpa Greenstone was beached on his Barcalounger, watching the only color television I had ever seen. Color television, everyone knew, was experimental and expensive. Shoes off, feet raised, belt buckle undone to allow for maximum pooch, Grandpa Greenstone took his cigar stump out of his mouth, waited for my sincere kiss on his jowl, and rewarded me with the music of his chortle. "Hello, honey," he said and we looked into each other's eyes long enough to say what we meant, we loved each other. He was such a character with his snakeskin belt, pointed-toe pumps, socks with swirls on the cuff, and a silk shirt custom made in Hong Kong with his initials over one plump breast. His watch was a solid gold Patek Phillippe. On one plump pinky was a star sapphire ring. Did he know his daughter intended to get divorced? Was he secretly seeing me as a helpless little victim?

Joan entered the den. "Hello, honey," Grandpa said, "Com-mere and give your ole grandpa a smooch." Joan thought Grandpa Greenstone was a bully. She came to the side of his chair, planted a dutiful kiss on his cheek then retreated immediately behind the heavy sage green drapery that Grandma kept closed over the windows so the sun wouldn't fade the sage green slipcovers and the sage green carpet. I joined Joan hiding back there behind the drapery. Hidden by yards of heavy fabric, we looked out at the rooftops of Chicago and the expanse of Lake Michigan stretch-ing to the horizon like an ocean. Lake Michigan was unreliable. It got all churned up and sent waves crashing over Lake Shore Drive. Like an ocean, the far shore was invisible but if you sailed across you wouldn't come to Sumatra but Indiana or Wisconsin. I thought the lake should be more humble with such a pedestrian shoreline. We stood gazing out at tiny cars below and seagulls flying not above but beneath us. We heard our mother come in. We couldn't see her through the thick fabric. "Hello, Daddy."

"Hello, honey," he said and chortled.

"What's this you're watching?"

"Wahl now, less see. That fella he's the detective. Seems some woman turned up dead. Set and watch with me."

"Mama wants us to unpack so we can give our dresses to Willa."

With a lowered voice he said, "How's everything, honey?"

"He says no. It's a flat no. He will not. Period." Were they talking about the divorce? "Hey you two, come upstairs and unpack." We thought we were invisible behind the curtains. "Did you hear me? I said come upstairs and unpack."

"We will," Joan called.

Mother whispered, "This could get expensive, Daddy. He'll drag it on for months."

We couldn't go upstairs and unpack before greeting Willa in the kitchen or before sniffing in the living room like puppies getting reacquainted. Across the hall was Grandma's version of the front parlor, a showroom for guests. Not trusting her own taste, Grandma hired a decorator to fashion a sophisticated living room. Here was Versailles, brocade upholstery on stiff sofas and chairs that demanded straight posture. Grandpa Greenstone played cards with other men at the Standard Club in downtown Chicago, but Grandma had no friends. The room just sat there with its hair combed.

In the kitchen was Willa, skinny and cringing as a coyote. Her maid's uniform hung on her skeleton like skin molting. Embarrassed by her buck teeth, she hid them with her palm when forced to smile. This she did when we burst into the kitchen and ran to her calling, "Hi Willa! It's us!" She made a singsong sound, um hmm, um hmm, a special kind of hum that never came out of white women. Grandma's relationship with Willa was more intimate than Mother's was with our maid. I didn't know much about Ruby, but I knew that Willa had six children and that Grandma Greenstone made sure they had warm winter coats and kept the appointments Grandma made with the pediatrician. When Willa went home at night to somewhere in Chicago, she carried bottles of vitamins, boxes of detergent, and food. She depended on Grandma to make the necessary appointments with the telephone company and the plumber. Willa, so whispers said, got involved with the wrong man and Grandma paid for Willa's abortion. Before we had Ruby, we had a series of maids, each one lasting one or two years, all of them quitting in an acrimonious way. Willa and Grandma had been together for more than twenty years. I had no idea what to say so I said, "How are you?"

Willa whispered, "I be fine." She never said our names, probably because she couldn't tell us apart. The kitchen was large with several pantries and sinks. Eggplant slices were sweating in colanders, potatoes were waiting to be peeled, and Willa's famous Monkey Bread was rising in its pan. "Willa, what's for dessert?" This was a set up. We wanted to hear her say it wrong. "Sherby ice cream."

The guestroom, also carpeted in sagebrush with sagebrush walls, was at the end of the sagebrush upstairs hall. I was aware in Grandma's apartment of the influence of interior design because it felt so different being here than it did being in my home. My house was obviously home to someone who thought about color, arrangement, and texture and spent a lot of time in stores looking for the perfect item. There was something pleasing to look at everywhere in our house. My mother loved decorating rooms, and it made me sad that she expressed this passion and talent in a negative way. She said, "You're a slave to a house." In Grandma's home, there was almost no color and almost nothing beautiful to look at. It worked upon my body in a different way from the rooms in my house in New Rochelle. It felt less demanding, like a note that was muted.

My mother was standing at the window in the guest room. She often stared off into space, went someplace else, was not even really in the room anymore. It was frightening and peculiar. To bring her back to me, I said something silly. "Why can't she come up and get them?" Mother didn't seem to notice that I'd come into the guest room with its twin beds and a cot set up for either Joan or me, whichever one lost the coin toss. "Why can't she come up and get them?" No answer. "Mommy, why can't she come up and get them?"

"Who?"

"Willa."

"What?"

"Why can't Willa come up and get the dresses."

She turned from the window and I could see her adjusting, gathering strands together as she focused on me and came down from wherever she went in those moments of absence. "What?"

The bureaus, tumbleweed tan, had been emptied for our use, but we couldn't hang our dresses in the guestroom closet because it was kept locked. It contained Grandma's private treasures and no one was allowed in. Aunt Dovey Lee, my mother's younger sister, called the closet Fort Knox. It held riches brought home from Europe, Japan, and India. Only upon Grandma Greenstone's death would we know what was in the closet. I wondered how long we would have to wait to know what was in there.

Wrinkled dresses in hand, Joan and I found Willa in the dining room taking gold-rimmed plates out of velvet envelopes and wiping each one with a dishcloth. We, the family, were the only ones who ever saw the china, crystal, and silver brought home from Europe. Grandma and Grandpa never had dinner parties for friends. My own parents had many dinner parties but the friends were all my father's. He liked filling up our living room with the hum of conversation and ice clinking in cocktail glasses and bursts of laugher. Grandpa, on the other hand, liked being by himself in his home. When they were alone, my grandparents ate in the kitchen at a Formica table and watched the six o'clock news on a small television. The dining room, this evening, would come out of its coma. "Here's our dresses," I said hoping Willa understood that it wasn't my idea that she should stop whatever she was doing to iron my dress.

I was changing into my party clothes in the guest room when Grandma Greenstone, wearing only her slip, her hair in dozens of pin curls held in place with bobby pins, came into the room full of purpose. The straps of her slip were held to the bodice by safety pins and part of one seam had become so threadbare it could no longer hold stitches so it too was closed with a safety pin. The slip was silk and Grandma could not throw away silk. When she came downstairs for dinner later the tattered slip would be hidden under an expensive dress designed by Hattie Carnegie. The extent of Grandma's frugality gave me a glimpse of how poor she once was. On the outside, she was a lady with servants living in a penthouse but underneath, privately, she was still an impoverished girl at a one-room adobe schoolhouse in New Mexico. Her parents spoke only Yiddish when they fled Russia and arrived at the port of Galveston, Texas. Grandma was four and remembered seeing the Tsar's soldiers marching through the streets shouting, "Kill the Jews!" She remembered feeling seasick on the boat. Everything she now owned, every eggbeater, towel, and pillowcase was a miracle.

She said nothing as she came into the room with a jingle of keys. Head down, not acknowledging our presence, as if not seeing us made us invisible, she selected a key, unlocked the closet door, opened the door, quickly ducked inside, and shut the door.

She came out, at last, holding some things wrapped in tissue paper. She set them on a table then hurried back to the closet and quickly locked the door as if bandits might be coming down the hall. "This," she said picking up one of the wrapped things, "is for you, Sonya. See that you take good care of it." Heart beating with excitement, I tried to open the tissue paper carefully but ended by ripping it off and there it was, another doll I couldn't play with, a French sailor six inches tall in a beret. I already had a milkmaid from Switzerland, a matador from Spain, a Hungarian bride, and an English Bobbie. "For your doll collection." But I didn't want a doll collection. All those miniature native people presented to me one by one, lifted out of a suitcase at the Waldorf Astoria when Grandma and Grandpa were in New York or brought forth from Fort Knox, all of them stood in a row on metal stands taking up space on my bookshelf because I was afraid Grandma might show up unexpectedly in New Rochelle. "Thank you, Grandma," I said and gave the required kiss but couldn't help resenting her for making me feel like a spoiled brat. It was always like this. Nothing really good ever came out of Fort Knox.

Joan's turn. She unwrapped her French sailor and said "Thank you, Grandma," in her insincere singsong. Grandma said, "No kiss?" Joan's miniature French sailor in a beret that couldn't be taken off would get tossed in a box in Joan's closet there with all the other inflexible dolls in native costumes.

My mother's present was always the same. Fabric. This time Thai silk. "There is enough, Violet, for a skirt and a jacket." Dutifully, and in her dead voice, my mother said, "Thank you, Mama." Perhaps Grandma wanted a more enthusiastic response. "Fabric, my dear," she said, "is not unimportant. The quality of the fabric one wears expresses more than you know. The feel of it and the look of it. Fine fabric has a distinctive voice. Take this silk to Frau Waldman, your excellent dressmaker." Her veneration of fabric came, I thought, from the olden days when women laid out patterns and sewed their own clothes. Perhaps as a child in New Mexico, her mother had to make clothes out of flour sacks. That she could give, and easily too, such beautiful fabric to her daughter was a thrill. Feeling bountiful, her walk was buoyant as she went out of the guest room and down the hall to finish getting dressed for dinner. In her wake was a pall of disappointment.

My mother became more and more agitated as the hour grew closer to the arrival of her sister and brother. She wanted us to look adorable in the twin dresses she had chosen. Joan stamped her foot, said, "Oh, who cares?" and flounced away when Mother tried to tie her sash more evenly. When it was my turn, I stood as still as I could so at least one daughter's sash would make an attractive

display. Soon the doorbell would ring and there would be Uncle
Alan and his family arriving in their Cadillac from a big house in
Highland Park and it would ring again and there would be Aunt
Dovey Lee and family arriving in their Cadillac from a big house
in Evanston. My mother, once known as "the pretty one" in the
family, would be judged as a failure by them: she had no career and
her marriage was a mess. That thought, I imagined, was what made
my mother's hands brush thoughtfully against the nap of the bow
as she tied it, giving it a final desperate tug before she pulled away
to examine it. "It will have to do," she said.

The first to arrive was her brother Alan Greenstone, a gentle
man in steel rimmed glasses, an unassuming person most comfortable when others took the lead. He was his father's right hand
at Greenstone Enterprises. He often said he would have no friends
if it weren't for his wife Dolly, but that was only because he was so
modest and didn't know how appealing his softness was. When
I was four, I asked him to marry me. Instead of laughing at me,
he said, "Ask me again when you're twenty-five." He arrived with
his wife and three children, one still asleep in a portable cradle.
I hugged him sincerely. Did he know my parents were getting
divorced? "How's the violin coming, honey?"

"Good."

As he was helping his children out of their coats he said, "You
had a solo, I hear. How did that go?"

"Good. It wasn't really a solo, Uncle Alan. It was a
competition."

"You played with others?"

"No, I had to play by myself but there were judges there."

"At school?"

"No. At Steinway Hall. That's in New York City." I wanted to
tell him that I won that competition, that I came in first and beat
out all the other sixth graders from all over the city but we were
interrupted by Aunt Dolly who handed him the portable cradle
she could take off her mink coat.

Aunt Dolly was short and top heavy with a gravely voice ruined
by cigarettes. She placed her cheek next to mine and hummed like
a mosquito. It was the sound of discomfort, and I wondered why

Aunt Dolly was pretending to be happy to see me. She was wearing a mink coat that was the genesis of my mother's mink coat. I had heard the arguments at home, heard my father say there was no reason for such ostentation, there was nothing wrong with Violet's storm coat, wasn't it warm? My mother complained on the phone to Grandpa Greenstone. Her brother Alan worked for Grandpa so really it was Grandpa who gave the coat to Dolly. It wasn't fair. Why should Dolly have a mink coat and the real daughter not have one? That was how we got our Cadillac too. My father refused. Said there's nothing wrong with a Dodge. My mother complained to her father and soon afterward a Cadillac was in our driveway.

Aunt Dovey Lee's family burst into the apartment, husband, wife, and three boys. Uncle Jack in a greatcoat such as a Russian prince might wear, fur collar and fitted at the waist, lifted me off the floor and twirled me around, and when I said, "More!" he did it again and when I said, "More!" he did it again. This was what it was like to have a young father. He could toss you around. Jack was testosterone incarnate, smelled of cigarette smoke and maleness. Joan hated roughhousing, backed away out of his reach.

Jack grabbed my mother, lifted her off the floor, and swung her around while she laughed. "Put me down! Jack! For heaven's sakes! Put me down!" She was discombobulated by that contact with him, blushed and fixed her hair. He bopped her on the head with one of his gloves. In his presence, with his cleft chin, his dimple on one cheek, his full lips, green eyes, thick curly dark hair, and friendly gap between his front teeth, I felt sorry for my mother being married to a man twenty years her senior. Here was what my mother was missing, this boisterous sexuality.

As masculine as Uncle Jack was, his wife Dovey Lee was feminine. Slender and cheerful in a red coat and red beret she said, "Here, Cutie Pie," and handed me a monkey puppet with long dangling legs and arms. She gave one to Joan too and showed us how to work them, made them dance in a funny way. Her voice was musical. She was four years younger than my mother, capable, confident, light-hearted. She said to me, "Daddy couldn't come?" Didn't she know? "Tell him hi from us, okay?" No one else mentioned him, as if he were a child hidden away in an institution.

Cousin Wiley was a grade ahead of me. I looked forward to seeing him because he was so affectionate and daring. On a previous visit, I saw him attach a rope to the top of the bannister at his house, yodel the Tarzan yell, and swoop down to the foyer. He could dive, play tennis, ice skate, ski, lift weights, and was the only person my age I couldn't beat at Ping-Pong. He looked very much like his father, cleft chin, gap between his front teeth, green eyes, full lips, dark curly hair. He grabbed my hand and said, "Hi, Cuz," and led me to the den. I was attracted to Wiley, felt his masculinity. We joked that he was my kissin' cousin but all we did was hold hands and sit close to each other on the sofa. Sometimes I wished I had a brother but the one I imagined was older and appeared in my imagination heroic in an Army uniform.

Grandpa Greenstone, still beached on his Barcalounger, greeted us all as we gathered in the den. A two-year-old grandson climbed up on Grandpa's lap and stayed nestled against him. Uncle Jack poured Harvey's Bristol Cream into Grandma's delicate cordial glasses that only came out of the cabinet for family gatherings. Holding the glasses up like Olympic torches the adults toasted, *Aproveche!* Not *L'Chaim* the Jewish toast, nor Cheers the assimilated toast, but a Mexican toast meaning enjoy. My mother and her siblings spoke Spanish fluently, having grown up in El Paso surrounded by Mexicans.

It was Willa's job to announce dinner. Might as well have asked her to address a stockholders' meeting. She entered the den in her gray uniform and stood trembling by the door. She hid her mouth with her palm and said, "Dinner be served." Grandma, her cheeks pink from the ice she pressed into them while sitting at her dressing table upstairs, so much less expensive than rouge, her eyebrows now arched by gray pencil, her expensive dress perfectly tailored, said, "Thank you, Willa." Aunt Dovey Lee and my mother looked up from their gin rummy game at the card table in the corner as we all shouted, "Thank you, Willa!" not in a mocking way but sincerely because we saw how uncomfortable she was.

Willa had transformed the dining room into a banquet hall. Here were Grandma's treasures on display: Rosenthal, Wedgewood, Steuben. Everything was precisely set, the white linen tablecloth and matching napkins, the silverware glinting from the light of the crystal chandelier. Grandma, dressed in pink lace, sat at one end of the table, her back straight. Grandpa sat at the other end with his snakeskin belt now buckled, a brown silk jacket open over a silk shirt, a short wide man whose head seemed to come directly out of his shoulders.

Grandma, in her deliberate way, picked up a small ceramic bell, held it for a second in the air, then tinkled it. Willa came in and stood abashed at the kitchen door. "We are ready, Willa." Willa shrank back into the kitchen. Grandma Greenstone's mission in life was to elevate her family, to protect us from being outsiders as she had been and this meant teaching us to subdue Jewish mannerisms, no cheek slapping and exclaiming oy yoy yoy, no gesturing with hands while speaking. It was her duty to teach her offspring what spoon to use at a row of spoons dinner party and to know the difference between the ping of crystal and pang of glass.

Grandpa's chauffeur Jordan, now in the role of butler, came in holding a tray of sliced roast beef, as if the bad fairy had turned him from prince to servant. Part of him, maybe the best part, just wasn't there. He held the tray down next to us as we tried to be careful to not drop a slab of meat onto the carpet. Wiley did all right with the roast beef and eggplant but he did drop a green bean. I saw Jordan pretending not to see as my cousin kicked the bean under the table. When Jordan moved on to the other side of the table, Wiley maneuvered the bean with his shoe, bent down quickly, and set it on my lap. I put it back on his lap. He broke it in half and kept half on his leg and put the other half on my leg, and so we flirted while Dovey Lee and Dolly got up from the table and went to cut up meat for the children who were too young to do it themselves.

Coming down from the ceiling like mist, coming up from the floor like bubbles from clams, was the ghost of Sebastian. He was in the air hovering over the basket of Monkey Bread, the decorative platter of radishes and celery, the pads of butter stamped with a flower design. My mother often told Joan and me the story of her two-year-old brother who died when she was four years old. She never, since the day it happened, spoke about it with her mother or father, and she warned us to never mention Sebastian's name in front of our grandparents. When Mother told us the story it was as if she could still see her mother in the house in El Paso cradling Sebastian in her arms as he was convulsing, could still hear her scream, "Get Señora Rodriguez! Get Señora Rodriguez!" and my mother, age four, running next door and standing in the neighbor's kitchen unable to say anything. She was supposed to have been looking after Sebastian. Her mother was busy packing, they were moving. She could still hear her father screaming at his wife, "I warned you! I warned you! I said be careful with them rat pellets. I said be careful with them pellets. Didn't you hear me? Didn't you hear me?" Grandma was twenty-four when that happened and Grandpa Greenstone was twenty-nine.

Aunt Dolly said, "We saw *South Pacific* Saturday. We loved it, the singing, dancing. What a wonderful evening!"

Mother said, "Without Ezio Pinza and Mary Martin, *South Pacific* is nothing." Her sister-in-law withered. "By the time the show gets to Chicago, the original cast is long gone. It's just the touring company."

"Sometimes those touring companies are as good if not better than the original," said Dovey Lee, who was not cowed by her sister's life in New York City.

"Don't be ridiculous. They're amateurish." This was what Mother had that they didn't: she'd seen every show on Broadway, sat center orchestra. She'd been to the Oscars, sat across the table from Elizabeth Taylor. She'd had the dancer Jacques d'Amboise at her dinner table.

"Say, Violet," said Uncle Jack tilting dangerously far back on his chair, "you ever meet Ezio Pinza?" He smiled, showing the gap between his front teeth.

"Yes. Seymour made a test of him."

"What was he like?" asked Aunt Dolly, brave in the face of Violet's scorn.

"Like? Like all the rest of them. Me, me, me."

"Mama," Aunt Dovey Lee said. "Tell us about the time you rode for the doctor when your sister broke her arm. Didn't you see Pancho Villa that day?"

"Yes," said Grandma batting at her pompadour with the back of her hand. "I saw Pancho Villa many days. He played poker with my father."

"What did he look like, Grandma?" said cousin Mike though we all knew the answer.

"Without his sombrero," she said, "his head was shaped like a bullet."

"Was he a bad man, Grandma?"

"He was a very bad man. But a gentleman when he played poker. When he lost, he paid his debt."

"But he's dead, right?"

"He is very dead."

"He's not coming over here, right?"

"He couldn't come over here," said Wiley's older brother Mike. "After he died, his enemies dug up his grave and chopped off his head."

"Mike!" said Dovey Lee, glancing at the younger children.

Mike, undeterred by his mother's scolding wanted to show us that he'd read up on the bandit. "When he was alive, he had a cruel mouth and bulging eyes."

"Why did they bulge?" Wiley wanted to know. "Did you ever see them bulge, Grandma?"

"Yes, indeed. He often came into Uncle Rovel's general store. One day, the feds came in and warned Uncle Rovel. Told him that if he sold guns to Pancho Villa he would go to jail. I sometimes helped in the store. I spoke Spanish better than my uncle did. I didn't learn English until I went to school, age six." She took a sip of water and dabbed her lips with her napkin. "I was there when Uncle Rovel told Pancho Villa that he could no longer sell him guns. That, my best beloved, is when I saw Pancho Villa's eye bulge."

"Why, Grandma?"

"Because he was furious."

"Tell us the story of when your sister broke her arm and you rode for the doctor."

"My sister," said Grandma, "was not an obedient child." She sent a meaningful glance at her grandchildren. "She was told not to play in the barn. She liked to balance on the wooden beams that—"

"Started with nothing," said Grandpa from his end of the table. "Had nothing. They called me the vitamin nut."

"Dad!" said Dovey Lee. "Don't interrupt Mama. She's telling a story."

"Aw," said Grandpa. "Go on, honey. Tell your story. Go on."

"No," said Grandma sniffing. "Never mind."

"Do, Grandma," Wiley said. "Tell us!"

"Aw, go on, honey. I'm sorry. Go on."

"No. Never mind."

"Please, Grandma!"

"Dad, promise you won't interrupt her."

"Go on, honey. Go on."

Grandma sniffed and batted at her pompadour. "As a result of her disobedience, Sally fell from the beam. My father was not at home. He was in Deming getting a harness fixed. My mother was home alone with the five of us. We lived two miles outside of town. Now today you could just phone the doctor, but then we didn't have phones and we didn't have doctors. We had Muley. He was a natural born doctor."

"Who was Muley, Grandma?"

"Muley was a freed slave. He came west and joined the Cavalry when he got freed. The Cavalry was stationed in New Mexico to protect our border towns from Pancho Villa's bandits. Our house was one mile from the border, and there was only a barbed wire fence between us and Mexico. No one paid much attention to that fence. It was easy to snip. Part of Muley's job was to ride the border and mend the fence. Muley was a natural born doctor. He had no training whatsoever, but he could cure people. He was the Cavalry vet. When my mother said I should ride for the doctor, she meant Muley so I—"

"Built the whole thing from scratch," said Grandpa. "Now we have plants in India, Belgium, Japan. Them Japanese fellas, they don't shake hands. Darndest thing you ever saw . . . aw, what's the matter honey? Go on. Go on. Tell your story."

"Never mind."

"Daddy," from Dovey Lee, "let her finish. You're always interrupting Mama."

"Go on, go on, honey. Go on."

"Never mind."

"Finish the story, Mama."

"You bow to them fellas," Grandpa said. "They got this whole system of bowing. Depends on your status how low you bow down. Now the Chinese, they don't do business that way. But you got to be careful with a Chinaman. When I started, I didn't have nothing. I built it up. Wasn't easy. Last year, we did twelve million dollars in the western states alone and that's not counting California and it ain't counting western Canada neither. Opening a new plant in Vancouver. They got a favorable exchange rate up there. Makes sense to do business with them. They don't all speak French you know. Some of them ain't French at all."

"Daddy!" said Dovey Lee, "You interrupted Mama. She was telling a story."

"Go on, honey, go on," he said looking across the table in a contrite way.

"Never mind."

"Nah. Go on, honey. I'm sorry. Go on. Tell your story"

"Never mind."

"Mama!" said Dovey Lee. "Tell your story. Daddy, be quiet."

Grandma pinched her lips together, wouldn't even say never mind anymore.

"Going to open a plant in India come March. We got plants in Italy, Greece, Hong Kong. Tell you how I started. We lived in cattle country. Them dairy farmers threw out the whey. I says to myself that whey must be chock full of vitamins. I had it analyzed. Full of vitamins. So I says to myself, what happens if you put them vitamins in animal feed? Why not collect what the dairy farmers discard, reduce it in a laboratory, and mix it in with feed. Most of them live-stock fellas called me the vitamin nut. How I'm smart? I surround myself with smart people. Chemists. We got the best chemists you can buy. Cattle and chickens fed with Greenstone Mix are healthy as heck. I got people working for me all over the world. Can't even speak the same language as most of them. Hire translators. Aw, honey. Don't be mad. Go on, you finish your story." He took a cigar from his breast pocket, lit it, and sat back in his chair, a pasha.

Grandma picked up her ceramic bell and tinkled it. No use begging her to continue. Her lips were pinched shut as if she was determined to be silent for the rest of her life. Willa and Jordan came in from the kitchen and cleared the dishes.

"Delicious as usual, Willa," said Uncle Jack tilting back on his chair. Mortified at being noticed, Willa hurried back to the kitchen.

"Yes, Willa, it was delicious!" everyone said.

"I got a little something here," said Grandpa.

"Is it money, Grandpa?" asked Wiley.

"Wahl now, you're going to have to come see for yourself."

"Now? Should I come up now?"

"Wahl now," Grandpa said, "Now, less see. Let's do youngest first. Dolly, bring that baby up here."

Dolly looked in the portable cradle. "She's sleeping, Dad."

"Wahl then you just come on up here yourself." Grandpa presented her with an envelope. "Now that there's for the baby. You put that in the baby's bank account." Dolly took the envelope and hugged him.

"Now, less see. Who's next? Chuckie. Come on up here and give your grandpa a big kiss. Come on. Atta boy. You come right on up here and give your grandpa a big kiss." Chuckie toddled up to him, put the envelope in his mouth to taste it, reached his arms up so Grandpa could lift him to his lap. Grandpa said, "What a big boy. What a big boy." As each child went forward, my heart pounded harder with excitement and stage fright. My turn. I didn't want to go back to my chair without thanking him. So I took a peek at the bills inside the envelope he handed me and flung my arms around his tummy. No one ever gave me money for no reason to do with as I wished. Grandpa's generosity was unsettling because it threw into contrast my own father's parsimony. Was this a difference in attitude or a difference in bank accounts? "Thanks, Grandpa!" I hugged him so intensely that he patted my back and whispered, "That's awright, honey, that's awright."

Joan's turn. She hated being in the spotlight. She did not want everyone watching her nor did she want to kiss Grandpa nor did she like this ritual, what she called this beggar's parade. "Your turn, Joanie," said cousin Mike who wanted her to finish because it would be his turn next. She pushed her chair back and walked slowly to Grandpa who said, "What's the matter, honey? You come up here and give your Grandpa a big kiss." She took the envelope and said, "Thank you, Grandpa," in her insincere sing song, pecked his cheek, then carried her envelope back to the table and sat there with her mouth twisted way over to the side nibbling the inside of her cheek.

"Now, less see," Grandpa said lifting jewelry boxes from the carpet next to his chair. "This here's Violet's. Commere, honey." My mother took the oblong box from her father, kissed him on the lips with a fast peck, and went back to her seat where she opened the box. I saw pearls nestled on peacock blue silk.

"They are perfectly matched and graduated," Grandma said. "You must care for them properly. Never store them without wrapping them first in a soft cloth. Never let them scrape against any other jewelry in your jewelry box. Never, and this is most important, put them in water. Pearls need to be worn to glow. Do not save them for special occasions. After dinner I will show you the proper way to care for them."

"Yes, Mama."

"Dovey Lee, come up here, see what I have for you." When Dovey Lee sat down she held the pearls up to her neck then turned to her husband Jack for help with the clasp.

When Grandpa handed Dolly the same oblong box he'd given my mother, I saw Mother frown as if she couldn't stand the thought that her sister-in-law merited the same gift. Mother had withdrawn into herself and for the rest of the evening, while we children played and the other adults talked, she was a brooding presence.

CHAPTER THREE

·······················

Joan and I overheard that there had to be "grounds" and in this case there were none. Seymour had to "grant" Violet a divorce and he would not. It was as if the trees were swaying, the air was chilled, the sky was dark, but there was a chance the storm might miss us.

Though we were living in a threatening atmosphere, I still practiced violin accompanied on our piano three times a week by Eliot, a delicate, musical teenager hired for that purpose. I still worked on my novel, was up to the part when Tippy Adams' boyfriend drives up to the front door in his jalopy and honks the horn and she runs down the front path to leap into his convertible. Joan still painted and made elaborate designs using colored pencils; our friends came over and we called up boys we liked and hung up the minute they answered. Mother still drove us to our lessons and orthodontist appointments, still tended to her seeds germinating in cold frames, still knelt with spade in hand putting in the yearly annuals. Seymour still went to work after eating corn flakes in the morning while reading the *Herald Tribune*, still stood before the full-length mirror on the back of his bedroom door practicing card tricks and rehearsing patter. Ruby still went to church every Sunday, sat eating a solitary lunch at the kitchen table while looking out the window at the golf course in the distance, and served us dinner most nights in the dining room.

One evening, while we were in the dining room, the doorbell rang. The food was hot on our plates. "Who could that be?" my father said. Dressed in his maroon velvet dinner jacket and paisley ascot, he got up from the table, opened the front door, stood there for a moment as if listening to someone on the front porch, and then closed the door. He was a nervous, fidgety person, and I'd never seen him stand so still. I heard a car door slam shut, then heard a car drive away. "Daddy! Who was it?" He turned and looked at his wife as she sat at the table in her long skirt and silk blouse. He seemed horrified as if someone had just thrown mucous at him. His lips were parted, his eyes were terrible to see. "Daddy! What happened?" He said nothing. He just turned and walked across the living room and went up the stairs, and we could hear his bedroom door shut. "Mommy? What happened?"

"It was a subpoena."

"What?"

"He got served a subpoena."

"What?"

She looked frightened and guilty. "It just means he has to appear in court."

"Why?"

"I don't know. That's how it's done."

"How what's done?"

"Just eat your dinner, please. Just eat your dinner."

Just as I would never go to him for consolation so did I know not to try to share his unhappiness. I did not seek him out after dessert.

At spring vacation, my mother refused to visit her husband's family. She despised his family, only went with him to Woodbridge out of wifely obligation. "What am I supposed to say to them?" I heard him ask.

"I don't care. Say whatever you want." Even when she did go with us, Mother showed her distaste for her in-laws by staying upstairs in one of the bedrooms. I would find her dressed in her cashmere sweater and slacks, laying on her back on the sagging bed staring at the bare bulb that dangled from the ceiling, the voices of her in-laws coming up through the grate in the floor.

I didn't want to go to Woodbridge either. "Other kids go to Florida on spring vacation."

"Aw, quit your bellyaching."

Seymour sat behind the wheel, started the ignition, sang out cheerfully, "We're off!" He was greeted with sullen silence by his

daughters. He backed the car out of the driveway by opening the
door and looking out rather than by turning his head to see behind.
He bumped into the hedges, pulled forward and tried again. My
mother was an excellent driver, had been driving since the age of
eleven when she drove herself to school in Texas. My father's lack
of skill, I thought, came from his being old. Since I didn't know
when cars were invented, I thought he wasn't good at working them
because they weren't around during his youth. After bumping into
the hedges, he backed out onto the street and came to a full stop
before turning the wheel not hand over hand as my mother did,
but by feeding the wheel from his left hand into his right. At North
Avenue, he braked for the red light but got lost in thought so Joan
said, "Daddy. It's green. You can go."

"Aw, hold your horses."

In Connecticut, we drove past tobacco farms where acres of
gauze covered the plants. Sometimes we stopped to explore old
cemeteries, the gravestones listing and fuzzy with moss. Some were
works of art, angels weeping with long hair, skulls with wide eyes.
Seymour made up a contest and gave a quarter to whoever could
find the oldest gravestone. Sometimes we had to brush back overgrown weeds to read the stone's inscription. It was fun and eerie
too. In Massachusetts, we drove through towns with quaint town
centers, a white church with a spire, an inn dating from the days
of the American Revolution.

We visited general stores that sold peanuts in barrels, wheels
of cheese, penny candy in jars, pickles in barrels, hunting vests
and fishing boots. I thought the proprietor, dressed in his white
apron, didn't know that now people could buy candy bars wrapped
in foil. I thought his place was so old-fashioned because he lived
far away from New York City. He didn't know people could buy
peanuts already out of their shells. My father always engaged the
proprietor in conversation, seemed to crave hearing a New England
accent. "They have no pretentions," he said. "They're real." His
conversation with the general store proprietor always led to a magic
trick, Seymour taking a coin out of the man's ear or elbow. Then
out came a deck of cards, my father fanning them in front of the
proprietor and saying, "Take a look at this. Pick a card, any card.

Don't show it to me." Then continuing the patter until the proprietor exclaimed, "Hey! How'd you do that?" It embarrassed me to see my father trying to be liked by the general store proprietor. Maybe he was telling himself that he could make friends with anyone. But this wasn't true.

What seemed true to me was that he wasn't good at talking to people or listening to them and had to resort to card tricks to make encounters possible. Joan and I went out to wait in the car. And wait. We sat inside the car, we got out, we paced, we snapped on the radio, we changed stations, we played with whatever dog wandered by. We were in the middle of nowhere, no stores next door, nothing but the road and in the distance a red barn and pasture. Then I couldn't stand it a second longer. I flounced into the store, stood glaring at him and said, "Daddy! Come! On!" He sent me a withering look. But he did come out. I was riding shot gun now and could feel his annoyance vibrating in my direction. I'd done him an injustice, from his point of view. This had happened before. It happened on every trip to Woodbridge. In the car, he said nothing and I said nothing. Maybe his stomach was in a knot, too. Joan and I pinched open peanuts and threw the shells out the window.

We arrived in Woodbridge through a canyon of red brick and my whole self seized up. I hated it here. It was as if the minute I saw those abandoned red brick mills on both sides of the road, windows bandaged with plywood, For Sale signs on their roofs, the seedy downtown with its Strand movie theater that showed films I never heard of, and the dress shop with a mannequin missing her arm, my very soul hid. My father, on the other hand, perked up. He loved Woodbridge.

He burst into song but not with words. He hissed a tune through his front teeth. It sounded like steam escaping. All that came out was the rhythm of the song. I knew which song he was hissing because he played them on our piano at home while I sang them. I felt an intimate connection with my father while he sat at the piano and I sang "Shine on Harvest Moon", "Bicycle Built for Two", and "All I do is Dream of You". He was hissing "By the Light of the Silvery Moon" when he turned onto the gravel driveway of a three-story wooden house next to a brick mill that was dark at the windows. "Dahlinks," I said mocking his mother, "come in. You must be starved." Seymour sent me a scolding look.

My haughtiness in Woodbridge cascaded upon everything, starting with the sparrows. Why feed such riff raff? I expressed my distaste for my father's side of the family by kicking pebbles at the birds. They flew up, a cluster of brown, then came down again, turned their backs on me, and continued pecking in another part of the driveway.

Chipped cement stairs led to a screened porch. The screen was so coated with soot it was hardly transparent any more, blocked the view of the mill next door like a black curtain. There were three chairs on the porch, two straight back with caned seats and one a bentwood rocker that I knew was a wedding gift to Grandma Adler when she married at age fifteen. I knew that she carried that chair with her on the boat from Austria to Ellis Island. Graceful in its rounded edges, the chair lived with her and Grandpa Adler in a tenement on the Lower East Side of New York where, at age seventeen, she gave birth to my father.

The doorbell was a bronze crank in the middle of the door. As my father took hold of it he said, "Just say your mother isn't feeling well." He wound up the crank, released it and a shrill twinggg! resounded inside. So, he hadn't told his family. He already had a lawyer named Clement Monroe, but he hadn't told his family. Did he plan to never tell them? Divorce to him was as shameful as bankruptcy or embezzlement. It was something that Jews just didn't do.

Again he twisted the crank and released it. Twing! "Maybe she's not home," from Joan. "Let me do it," I said and twisted the crank but my hands were too small to wind it tight so the sound was a feeble, twink. "She's probably in the kitchen," my father said. There was a window in the upper half of the door shaded by a lace curtain. He rapped. "Ma?" No answer. "Ma?" If there was one name that was forbidden in my mother's rules of assimilation it was Ma. The very sound of it made her shudder. To torment her, Joan and I sometimes called her Ma. She fell into the trap every time, got furious and said, "Don't call me Ma!"

"Let's go home," from me.

"Oh pipe down," from him.

The door opened and there was Grandma Adler, short and wide at the waist, with an apron tied around her house dress, prison matron shoes, and tightly curled gray hair. "Dahlinks, come in, you must be starved."

I prayed some miracle would happen so I could get past her into the front parlor but I couldn't. She let me know how happy she was to see me by pinching my cheek. It was a nasty pinch that ended with a twist. I backed away from her and stood waiting for the pain to ebb with my palm over the sting. That was her greeting, every visit, and it made me understand, through my fury at being hurt for no reason, that Grandma Adler had endured a rough life. My father was probably not the recipient of much tenderness in his childhood. He did not go toward his mother but stood holding the suitcases as he said in a cheerful way, "Hello, Ma, how are you?"

"How am I? How should I be? My beck. My beck is killing me." Grandma Adler touched the small of her back then said, "So where's your wife? Tell her to come in already."

"She couldn't come, Ma. She's come down with something. Is that chicken soup I smell? No one makes chicken soup like you, Ma."

"Oy yoy yoy," Grandma said, slapping her cheek and looking in a suspicious way at her son, "if it ain't one thing it's another. Come in, come in, you'll eat."

"No thank you, Grandma," Joan said. "We're not hungry. We just ate." This was true. We were full of peanuts.

"Listen to her," Grandma said. "Come in, come in. You'll eat."

"No thank you, Grandma," Joan said in a louder but polite voice, because she thought Grandma was deaf. "We just ate."

"I wouldn't give it to you anyway."

The staircase behind us was so steep it was almost perpendicular. There was no bannister to hold for balance. Each stair was covered in speckled linoleum that had probably once covered the whole stair but now was frayed at the edges and stained from years of use. Lugging the suitcases, Seymour went up and Joan and I followed him down the upstairs hall, also covered in speckled linoleum, to the bedroom where he slept as a child. I never saw how my mother lived as a child. She didn't grow up in that penthouse in Chicago. In Woodbridge, I got to see my father's beginnings. A bare light bulb hung from the middle of the ceiling over twin beds with iron headboards and drooping mattresses. In the corner was a massive Empire dresser with drawers that stuck. Heat came up through an iron grate in the floor. The view from the window was the bar across the street where a curtain was always drawn across the window. Sometimes at night Joan and I would see some drunk staggering out, the only person on the sidewalk.

Joan and I went, as we always did when we first arrived at Grandma Adler's, to explore the exquisite horribleness of the bathroom. The toilet flushed with a pull chain, the bathtub stood on claw feet, and the shower was a rigged up pole in the middle of the bathtub with a shower curtain around it that closed you in like a shroud. Instead of toothpaste in the medicine cabinet we found tooth powder. On a shelf was a red enema bag. Corsets the color of Grandma's flesh, contraptions made of stays and held together with laces, were draped over a drying rack. For as long as we could, Joan and I delighted in how repulsive everything was, including the smell, then went downstairs to face the music.

The front parlor was also from bygone days. The speckled linoleum was covered with a braided rug. Lace doilies were pinned to the arms and backs of chairs to protect them from wear. Grandma's radio was the size of a jukebox. Made of wood, it was a piece of furniture big enough to support framed sepia photographs of people in old-fashioned clothes. There was my father in an oval frame as a boy of eight in a ruffled shirt, knickers, high socks, his hair slicked down and parted in the middle. There were so many photos the top of the radio was like a gathering of ghosts. There was Uncle Norman sitting on a horse, and Uncle Donald standing as a groom with Aunt Harriet in her wedding dress. There was Grandpa Adler standing next to his horse and wagon. Each picture had a faded quality, the photo itself on its way to oblivion. Also on top of the radio was Grandma's telephone, the stand up kind with a separate earpiece that hooked on the side. None of her things were picturesque to me. They were embarrassing. I didn't want an old-fashioned grandma.

Grandma Adler was waiting for us in the kitchen. "Sit," she said, "you'll eat." She opened the door of her wood-burning stove exposing a hellish flame inside, tossed in a log, and latched the door closed. "Sit," she said, indicating a Formica table next to windows covered with gauze curtains. There were pots and pans in her deep soapstone sink, and the icebox next to her pantry dripped into a pan underneath. Sometimes during our visits an iceman holding muscular tongs arrived at the back door with a huge cube of ice. None of Grandma's supplies were behind cabinet doors but were in full display on the shelves in the pantry, cans and boxes and bottles of soda. The view from the kitchen window was the abandoned brick mill next door and the driveway full of sparrows pecking in the gravel for the crumbs Grandma threw out to them.

Grandma set before each of us a bowl of soup the size of Lake Michigan. "Eat," she said. "Eat." The spoons were the size of shovels. I chewed the cooked celery and mushy carrot coins and the pieces of chicken the size of thumbs. Grandma turned from stirring at the stove and sat in a chair next to me. She dipped her fingers into my soup, plucked out a piece of chicken and stuffed it into my mouth. Mouth full of fingers, I gagged. She did the same to Joan. Our comfort meant nothing to her compared to the sin of wasting food. She couldn't bear to throw away food any more than Grandma Greenstone could throw away a slip made of silk. The older generation echoed sadness and want. Because of their efforts and their bravery, I had escaped hunger and deprivation. I knew this and wished that I loved Grandma Adler more.

My father came into the fragrant kitchen, saw what probably looked like a cozy scene, little girls with curly hair being tended by a plump grandmother, and said, "I'm going up the store, Ma."

"Wait, Daddy! We'll come with you!" He went without us.

At last, Grandma let Joan and me get up from the table. I saw her pour what remained in our bowls back into the pot on the stove. We ran out of the house. The deserted mill next door was separated from Grandma Adler's property by a moat filled with trash, someone's shoe, a rusted fender, soggy newspapers, beer bottles. Joan and I paused at the edge of the driveway, picked up a stone, and hurled it across the moat in an attempt to break one of the mill windows. We looked around to see if anyone was watching then pitched more stones that hit the red bricks and fell to the ground. At last Joan's pitch shattered the glass, and we ran for our lives all the way down the sidewalk past the wooden Indian standing in front of a cigar store. We caught our breath and continued in a lady-like manner under the railroad bridge and up onto Main Street. Red brick on both sides of the road, stores at street level, offices above with placards in the windows announcing lawyer, dentist, insurance broker. The pharmacy window displayed trusses and bedpans. At the end of the block was a cinema so small it seemed like a toy theater. The marque announced only one film and the letters weren't straight. Not understanding film distribution, I thought the theater manager selected his obscure offerings because he had bad taste.

Next to the Gift Shoppe was Adler Furniture. The store represented the crowning achievement of my father's father, who began by selling dry goods from a wagon. My mother had nothing nice to say about any of her husband's family except Grandpa Adler. "He was a saint," she said. She told me that he gave credit to anyone in need, and that it was up to Grandma Adler to collect what was owed to them. When Grandpa died suddenly of a heart attack at sixty, the store passed on to Uncle Murray who was two years younger than my father. The store was a thriving business under Uncle Murray, customers trying out chairs and chatting with the salesmen. I loved Uncle Murray who was kind and gentle. He died suddenly from a heart attack.

The store passed on to the youngest brother Norman. Now the windows that used to be fun to look at, miniature living rooms or bedrooms, arranged so customers could see how they might decorate their own rooms, were just a jumble of chairs, tables, and lamps. Joan and I opened the front door and a bell attached to the door clattered. Inside a dimly lit cavernous space there were no customers and no salespeople. Chairs and sofas and lamps were all over the place with narrow aisles between. Mattresses wrapped in plastic were leaning against the wall. It smelled of stale cigarette smoke.

Uncle Norman emerged from his office at the far end of the store. He was a spectral figure at first then took on substance as he shuffled toward us dressed in a tan cardigan, wrinkled trousers and bedroom slippers. Stoop shouldered, he kept his chin close to his chest and looked at us from the top of his eyes. "Hi, Uncle Norman," I said and hurried toward him forgetting as I always did the Adler family's dislike of hugging. The instant my front touched his he turned rigid, put his hands on my shoulders, and set me back saying, "Hello, girls." I got a whiff of the peppermint he was sucking to camouflage the smell of whiskey.

"Norm," my father called as he came from the office at the back of the store holding a ledger book, his spectacles low on his nose, "what's this item here?" What a contrast he was with his younger brother! Seymour never slouched, his stomach was flat, shoulders squared, shirt starched, expensive shoes, and a fire inside that seemed to burn too hot. Uncle Norman was listless and sloppy. While I had nothing to say to Uncle Norman, who seemed as if he couldn't tell the difference between me and Joan, I did feel sorry for him because I knew he didn't want this job. No one had ever imagined that the store would land on Norman. The store was supposed to support his wife, their three children, Grandma Adler, and Uncle Murray's widow. "Norm," my father said noticing the mattresses, "what are those mattresses doing up here? Why don't you have the boy take them down cellar?"

"He's unwell, Seymour."

"Isn't there anyone else? Put an ad in the high school paper. There must be some kid in town wanting to earn a dime." His younger brother stood with bowed head like a shamed child. "Now what about the windows, Norm? Thought you were going to get some help arranging them." I wondered at my father scolding his brother in front of us. Didn't seem nice. But I understood his exasperation. It was Seymour who had to pick up the loose ends, Seymour's paycheck that paid for Norman's dental work, paid to get the store roof patched, paid his mother's electric, phone, and doctor bills. I was proud of my father for stepping up and confused when my mother groused about it. How could she not want a husband who looked after his family?

Uncle Norman took a crumpled pack of Lucky Strikes from his breast pocket, lit a cigarette with his lighter, inhaled and swallowed the smoke. Some of it leaked out his nose. My father pointed at the office with a raise of his chin and Uncle Norman followed him to the back of the store.

While Seymour went over the books with Uncle Norman, Joan and I tried out all the chairs and beds and whispered too hard, too soft, just right until our father finished and came out of the office with his lips pinched together in disgust. Angered by what I had heard him describe as his brother's laziness, he strode out of the store, the bell clattered behind him, and Joan and I hurried to catch up with him on the sidewalk. It was evening now and lights had come on in the bars, one on every corner.

When we came to the wooden Indian on the sidewalk, my father paused, adjusted his expression to something more pleasant, and went inside the cigar store, a small odiferous place with boxes of cigars lining the walls. "Sy!" the owner said. "I didn't know you were in town!" O'Brian came from behind the counter and clapped my father on the back. He was a thin red-faced man with freckles on his arms. I wondered if he was one of the boys in elementary school who threw stones at Seymour shouting, "Dirty Jew!" I wondered if he was part of the gang that chased Seymour shouting, "Christ killer!" We heard about this from our mother who said that the boys learned their ideas from their priest. My father could not say the word Catholic in a normal voice. He whispered it as if it was obscene. *Catholic.*

"You closing up, O'Brian?"

"No, no. Not a bit of it. Not atall. My you girls have grown. Getting to be regular young ladies." He showed my father various cigars, rolled them between his fingers, sniffed them, brought out others. "Took the wife to Worcester, Sy, saw *Pat and Mike.* Enjoyed it. That Spencer Tracy is some fine actor. You ever meet him in person?"

"Yes, a fine chap. Made a test of him."

"You discovered Spencer Tracy?"

"It's a group effort, O'Brian."

"What about Lana Turner? Oh, my goodness. When she walks across the screen, Sy, I'm telling you . . ." then he remembered Joan and me and put the lid on his lust.

"A lovely girl," my father said. "Very down to earth. Heart of gold."

"And how's the missus?"

"Fine, fine."

"I still can't believe she got her hooks into you, Sy. We all thought you'd never get married. Why get married with that life you lead? But she caught you. We couldn't believe it." He lifted another box of cigars from the shelf, set it on the counter, and said, "Zero blemishes. And look at the size of the leaf. Look at the sheen. Almost has a chocolate hue." He handed one of the cigars to my father. "Sy, I want to thank you for what you did for Darleen."

"I told her what I tell all of them," my father said sniffing the cigar then nodding approval. "It's no business for a lady."

"It's a double whammy, Sy. They tell her she needs experience then she doesn't get the part because she has no experience. What's she supposed to do?"

"If she follows my advice, she'll be all right. Start locally, amateur theater here in town."

"Should I encourage her? Do you think she has what it takes?"

"Who's to say? We don't make stars. The public does."

New cigars in his pocket, we continued on our way along the sidewalk. Coming in the other direction was the woman who rented the third floor of Grandma's house. "Seymour Adler!" she said. "As I live and breathe! I thought that was your car in the driveway." She shook his hand. "Look at you girls. Tsk! You should put them in the movies, Seymour." Then, "Tell me. Did you ever meet James Cagney in person?"

"Yes, many times. Started as a hoofer, you know. Very talented."

"And what about Hedy Lamar?"

"Yes, yes indeed. She's really something special, Mrs. O'Malley."

"Isn't she from some foreign country, Seymour?"

"She is indeed. We had to work on her accent. She's got a perfect profile."

The woman put her hand over her heart. "Holy Mary mother of God I don't know how you do it. I'd faint dead away if any of them got so much as close to me!"

Grandma's house was now full of the smells of cooking. She was standing in front of the stove on the bald patch where the linoleum had worn away over the years. Seymour went upstairs without a word, and Joan and I could hear his footsteps above us walking down the hall to the small bedroom that used to belong to his now dead brother.

First to arrive was Uncle Donald and his wife, Aunt Harriet, my father's only sister. She was carefully groomed, her hair a helmet dyed the color of pee on snow. She never hid her shapely legs under trousers but always wore skirts, and when I kissed her hello, I got a whiff of pleasant-smelling face powder. She and her husband owned a hardware store in Framingham. Uncle Donald, always chuckling like Santa Claus, round as Twiddle Dee, sat down immediately on one of the armchairs and took up his position as watcher of whatever happened. I went to the bottom of the stairs and called up, "Daddy! Aunt Harriet's here!" then heard Harriet say on the way to the kitchen, "Ma, put me to work."

"Seymour," said Uncle Donald when my father came into the front parlor from the steep staircase, "Did you take 95 or 127?" From the kitchen, Aunt Harriet called, "Did you run into that construction on 302?"

"I think that's completed, Wifey," Uncle Donald called to her. Aunt Harriet came to the kitchen door wiping her hands on a dishtowel. "Did you take route 9 through Lancaster, Seymour?" My father and his sister didn't greet each other with hugs and kisses. "You didn't get caught in that hospital construction on 302 did you, Seymour?"

Joan and I went upstairs, got our sketchpads and colored pencils, returned to the parlor, and lay down on the large braided rug that covered most of the floor. Uncle Donald was saying, "The DeSoto is a reliable vehicle. They've increased the engine size from 291 cubic inches to 330. Has enormous fins." Seymour was only half listening. He was standing in the corner turned away from Donald and practicing some sleight of hand movement with a deck of cards. Joan and I flipped our sketchpads to a blank page, selected a pencil from our extensive set, and began to draw. Seymour turned from the wall and said to Donald, "Take a look at this, Don" He fanned the deck in front of his brother-in-law. "Pick a card. Any card. Don't show it to me. No, Don, don't show it to me. Let's start again." He shuffled the deck in his expert way and fanned the cards again. "Any card. Don't show it to me." Seymour closed the fan while saying, "Did I make you choose that card?"

"No, Seymour. You did not."

"Did I influence you in any way?"

"No, you did not."

"Now I want you to put that card back in the deck. Anywhere. There? Fine. Good."

I was drawing a meadow with a red barn in the background and a yellow horse looking at the viewer as it galloped by. In a cartoon bubble coming from its mouth I wrote, Wild And Free I Will Always Be. Joan paused, lifted her pencil off her sketchpad, and said, "That's good. Maybe put some crows in the sky." I put several black Vs in the sky above the barn.

"Now, Don," my father said, "cut the cards. Good. Just like that. Now I believe your card has risen to the top of the deck. Let's see." I glanced over and saw him turn over the top card. "Here it is, the ace of spades. Was that your card?" Uncle Donald exclaimed, "No! That wasn't it at all!" My father said, "It wasn't? What was your card?" Triumphant, Uncle Donald said, "The seven of diamonds."

"The seven of diamonds?" said Seymour. "Let's see." He riffled though the deck whispering, "The seven of diamonds." Then he said, "I can't find it. Wait a minute. What's that in your pocket?" Uncle Donald reached into the breast pocket of his shirt and pulled out the seven of diamonds. His mouth hung open as Seymour put the card back in the deck, smiling in an apologetic way that I saw him practice in the mirror on the back of his bedroom door. I wondered why he couldn't just sit down and talk to his brother-in-law, why he felt he had to entertain him. I couldn't figure out why he and his fellow magicians thought people liked to be fooled. I hated being fooled and was always trying to figure out how my father did his tricks. When I asked he said, "A good magician never tells his tricks." This hurt my feelings. Shouldn't the daughter be exempt from that rule?

Aunt Harriet came from the kitchen. "Where's Violet?" No one answered. She said, "Girls, go up and get your mother. She probably doesn't know we're here."

Seymour said, "She's a bit under the weather, Harriet."

"Oh, that's too bad. I'll bring some soup up to her."

"No, no. Thought it best if she stayed home."

"In New Rochelle? All by herself? She's all alone in that big house of yours?"

"No, no. Not a bit of it. She's with the girl."

"What girl?"

"Ruby," Joan said.

"The maid?" When we didn't respond he said, "What does the maid know about taking care of someone? What starts as a cold can turn into pneumonia."

"Ruby's a natural born doctor," I said.

"She's a nurse?"

"Wifey," said Uncle Donald. "Leave it alone."

"I'm worried, all alone in that house. What if she falls down? What if she's burning up from fever?"

"Wifey," said Uncle Donald. "Leave it alone."

"She's all right, Harriet," Seymour said. "Probably just something she ate."

"Let's call her," Harriet said walking to the old-fashioned telephone. "See how's she doing."

"No, no, no," said my father. "Not at all. Best let her sleep." Aunt Harriet gave him a questioning look and went back into the kitchen.

There was a commotion in the hall, the door opened and there was Uncle Norman still in his tan cardigan, his wife Maggie, and their three children, Eddy, Claire, and Avery. Eddy, the same age as Joan, wore a Red Sox cap and Red Sox jacket. He knew the batting averages of every player even those who played at Fenway Park before he was born. A prisoner in Hebrew school four afternoons a week, his mouth was never fully closed. His lower lip hung down so he looked stupid but he was, in fact, an honor roll seventh grade student. I could not understand why Joan liked him.

Both his sisters were dressed in clothes that had once belonged to Joan and me. The younger one had to wear thrice-worn dresses because I got Joan's hand-me-down, then Claire got my hand-me-down, then Avery got the dress and by then the puffy sleeves were too tired to puff. Claire, age nine, had blond Shirley Temple ringlets but no animation in her face. She was beautiful but faded, as if her personality had been bleached right out of her. It embarrassed me to see my cousins in those used clothes. It could easily have been the other way around, me in their used up clothes. I didn't want sadness thrust in my face like this. I was disturbed by my cousin's poverty and wanted it to stop, as if someone was holding a flashlight into my eyes.

Aunt Maggie, a cigarette dangling from her lips, was yellowish and skinny, a capable woman who managed the furniture store as best she could, dealt with wholesalers and customers and a husband who stayed for hours in the bathroom doing crossword puzzles. Grandma Adler yelled from the kitchen, "Eddy come take out the gahbidge!" Eddy headed toward the kitchen with no resistance. Aunt Maggie yelled, "He's coming, Ma." Aunt Maggie lit a fresh cigarette from the butt she was holding then said to me as she ground out the stump in an ashtray, "Where's Violet?"

"Not feeling well," said Uncle Donald. "Decided it was best to remain at home."

"She didn't come?"

"Decided it was best," said Uncle Donald.

"Rats," said Aunt Maggie. "I wanted her to help me with that cable stitch." She went into the kitchen where we heard her voice mix with Aunt Harriet's and Grandma's. At these moments, when I heard my two aunts and my grandmother chatting amid the clatter of dishes, heard an occasional burst of laughter, I wondered if my mother was correct in feeling so superior to them. They were having fun together preparing dinner. My mother never helped Grandma Adler or laughed at anything my aunts said. I wondered if she misled me, had failed to see what was good about the Adlers and now here I was blind to it too.

"Wanna hear me sing a song?" said Avery. She was six, had a front tooth missing. Her sash was tied in back like an old piece of string. She stood up on one of the chairs and burst forth with, "How Much is that Doggie in the Window."

From the kitchen, Maggie yelled, "Avery! Put a sock in it!"

"I'm singing, Ma!" But she stopped and climbed down from the chair.

Aunt Maggie yelled from the kitchen, "Girls? Ya want some tawnick?" Tonic was the word for soda.

"I do!" said Avery and ran into the kitchen. I heard Aunt Maggie say, "It'll ruin your suppa." There was the sound of pots and pans, and then Grandma said something that made the other two women burst out laughing, Harriet in a delighted squeal and Maggie with the mirthless tat tat tat of a machine gun.

Eddy returned from taking out the garbage, gestured to Joan and me with a deck of cards, then sat down cross-legged on the braided rug and began to deal out Crazy Eights.

"I wanna play," Avery said. "Eddy, I wanna play."

"Get lost, pea brain."

"Ma!" Avery stamped her food. "Ma! Eddy won't let me play cahds with the girls!" No one in Woodbridge ever referred to me by name. Joan and I were a unit, the girls.

Aunt Maggie called from the kitchen, "Knock it off, Avery. Maybe the girls will play with you later."

Meanwhile, standing against the wall and saying only with her expression that she would like to play too, was Claire who gave the organdy dress that I used to wear an ethereal look, as if she were the ghost of a little girl. "Come over here, Claire, dear," said Uncle Donald. "Come sit near me." Claire crossed the room and sat at Uncle Donald's feet but said nothing. Eddy, I knew, would not let her play cards. He always wanted Joan and me to himself. This, perhaps, came from his having no friends. If he did have friends, I never saw them. In Chicago, I knew my cousins' friends, energetic and intelligent boys who were fun to be with. Wiley's house was always full of boys filling the place up with their masculine laughter and showing me how much they could lift with heavy weights.

I tore the picture I'd drawn out of my sketchbook and carried it to Claire. "Would you like to have this, Claire?" The girl looked up from her seat on the floor, took the page, and held it to her chest. She held it there too intensely with her eyes closed as if carried away by a beautiful piece of music. Then Claire opened her eyes. They were pale blue with an unsettling opaqueness behind them. She smiled weakly at me. I went back to the game of Crazy Eights but did not sit down. "I don't want to play with you," I said to Eddy. "You hit too hard." As if he hadn't heard me, he dealt out the cards and I sat down cross-legged on the rug. Every game over the years began with my complaint and included his hitting too hard. On the other hand, I loved playing cards and sometimes won.

The winner of Crazy Eights got to smack the losers' knuckles with the closed deck. The number of points left in the hand was the number of smacks the loser had to endure. Made no sense to really hurt each other. It was just a dumb game that we played sitting on the braided rug in Grandma's old-fashioned room because there was nothing else to do. When Eddy won, as he did this time, I made a soft fist and held it toward him. "Make a better fist," he said.

"No. You hit too hard."

"Make a fist. Go on. You lost. Make a fist. That's the rules." So I did and tried not to pull back or cry while he smacked my knuckles with maniacal glee until they turned red. All the fury he felt at being stymied by adults and all the nastiness that was part of his character were unleashed on my extended hand. I won the next game and paid him back, both delighting in seeing him wince and disliking seeing him wince. I didn't want to be doing this. He wasn't the sort of boy I wanted to be with. I had to be with him. He was in my family. Cousin Avery in the kitchen said, "Grandma, did you make chocolate pudding?" The reply was, "Listen to her. Why wouldn't I make chocolate pudding?"

When it was time for dinner, everyone went into the kitchen where the table was set with plates that didn't match and former jelly jars for glasses. There were two candlesticks at the head of the table. When everyone was seated, Grandma pulled a shawl over her head, struck a match, lit the candles, waved her hands over the flames in a circular motion and said the Sabbath prayer in Hebrew. Everyone, except Joan and me, said it along with her. We never lit Sabbath candles at home. It was only here that I realized my father knew the words of the prayers, and I got glimpse of how different his childhood must have been from mine. He was the child of a religious mother, which meant his boyhood had been full of constraints.

My other grandmother lit candles on Friday night, too, but she did it by herself in the corner of the kitchen with her back turned to anyone who might walk by. As if performing a secret ceremony, she struck a match and held it to each wick and whispered the prayers in English. "Blessed art thou oh Lord our God, King of the universe who has commanded us to kindle the Sabbath lights." Unaware that I was watching, she turned from the candles with a soft abruptness as if saying to some internal judge, duty done.

In Woodbridge, Grandma Adler intoned, "*Barukh atah Adonai, Eloheinu, melekh ha'olam . . .* " She and her family did not homogenize the Hebrew but spoke it with a guttural throat clearing. They said the prayers enthusiastically while my father just mouthed the words with his eyes lowered. Was he as embarrassed as I was by their unabashed Jewishness? How could that be? He was brought up with them. Here was everything Grandma Greenstone was trying to assimilate out of. Except for forbidding Violet to buy a Christmas tree like her brother and sister in Chicago, Seymour did nothing Jewish in New Rochelle. When Passover time came, he drove to Woodbridge and celebrated with his mother. Now, like the other men at the table, he had a yarmulke on his head and a prayer shawl around his shoulders and looked bizarre to me.

Instead of wine for the adults there was seltzer. The children had to drink soda, not milk. The butter was margarine. "No one makes a roast chicken like Ma," said Uncle Donald. Aunt Maggie made a joke about the carrot stew, "Ma, this tsimis looks good enough to eat."

The next day, Saturday, Joan pulled the chain on the light in the hall and Grandma Adler screamed, "What? Are you crazy? Turning on the light?" Joan forgot the Sabbath rule—no electricity. Grandma let the stove go cold. She was not allowed to ride in a car so she and Seymour walked to Temple but it wasn't called temple in Woodbridge. It was Shul. My father did not insist that Joan and I stay for the service. It was chanted entirely in Hebrew. We wouldn't understand a word. But he did insist that we accompany him to the building, go inside, and say hello to the people who greeted us. It looked to me as if there was almost no one there compared to the large congregation of reform Jews at Temple Israel in New Rochelle where Joan and I went to Sunday school, an education that was not reinforced at home.

Grandma Adler was one of the founders of the synagogue. When she first arrived in Woodbridge, she couldn't find ten Jewish men to form a *minion*. There could be no official Jewish service without ten, and there weren't ten Jews living in or near Woodbridge. I wondered how she managed to stay so observant in a place with no kosher butchers. It must have been a shock to find herself in a town where there were no Jews after being surrounded by Jews in her tenement on the Lower East Side. I wished I could ask her, but I knew she'd only answer with a shrug, say something like, "Listen to her." I couldn't ask my father either. His childhood seemed a forbidden topic so I imagined it was horrible, but this didn't square with the fact that he always wanted to visit Woodbridge and was attentive to all the members of his family, so it probably wasn't horrible. I suspected he saw Woodbridge as it used to be before the Great Depression, when the mills were going full speed, producing carpets that were sold all over the world, and the stores were full of customers and the sidewalks full of neighbors and the outskirts were farms not housing developments.

At the synagogue, people came to shake his hand, admire his daughters, and ask him for gossip about Hollywood celebrities. Some of the people were shy, star-struck. Some of the older people remembered when Seymour, in his early twenties, arrived in town with his latest girlfriend, an actress named Lucille LeSeur, who would one day turn into Joan Crawford. I heard about Joan Crawford's visit every time I went to Woodbridge. They never got over it. The story made me uneasy because it was about my father and sex. Inside the synagogue, Grandma Adler was treated with deference, guided gently to her seat at the front of the women's section.

The next day was the big outing to the Wauchusett Dam. I thought if I had to visit that stupid dam one more time I'd die of boredom. It was a massive long wall of gray stone with a promenade on top and water on one side. I had to pretend it was a thrill to walk across the top of that wall and look down on the reservoir.

Usually Aunt Maggie took Eddy, Claire, and Avery in her car and Seymour took Joan and me in the Cadillac, but this time Seymour suggested that we switch. He hadn't yet had an opportunity to talk with Eddy. He worried that his nephew would grow up and not know how to make use of the wide world because he wouldn't even know there was a wide world. Eddy, but never his sisters, stayed with us now and then in New Rochelle so that Seymour could devote himself to educating his nephew. He took him to Times Square to see the thousands of blinking lights and to the Empire State Building. He sat center orchestra with the boy and brought him backstage to meet the actors on Broadway. My mother told me that my father was disappointed when I came out a girl. I was sorry to have disappointed him. What hurt was that my mother told me this. She liked hurting my feelings, apparently. From my point of view, if Seymour wanted Eddy instead of me, he was welcome to him.

When Eddy visited us, he slept in my father's bedroom and my father slept on the other side of the house in the guest room. The first time Eddy visited, Joan and I heard a buzz as if a June bug was in the room. Joan was terrified of bugs, especially those because they were the size of a finger and encased as if in plastic. "Mommy!" she shouted out in the dark. "Mommy! There's a bug in my room!" Mother came from her bedroom wearing her bathrobe, flicked on the lights and hunted for the bug. "Find it," Joan begged. "You have to find it, Mommy." But after a few minutes' search Mother paused and went into the hall. She stood close to Eddy's door then returned to Joan's room where Joan was hiding under her covers. "It's not a bug," Mother whispered. "It's Eddy. He's humming."

"There's no bug?"

"No. It's Eddy."

"Why's he humming?"

"He's frightened."

"Of what?"

"I don't know. Could be anything, bless his heart."

In Woodbridge, Joan and I climbed into Aunt Maggie's old Plymouth. The Plymouth reeked of cigarette smoke. The ashtray was overflowing. It was a sunny day, the leaves still new on the trees, daffodils up at the side of the road, forsythia in bloom, and Magnolia trees already dropping their flowers. "My granddad died working on this dam," Maggie said as we came within sight of the landscaped park that edged the dam.

"How?"

"diphtheria."

"How'd he get diphtheria?"

"Everyone got it. No sanitation." Aunt Maggie pushed in the lighter on her dashboard, flicked her cigarette butt out the window, then lit her fresh cigarette when the car lighter popped out. "The laborers lived in sod huts. They had no floors, just dirt. When it rained or snowed, they lived in mud. Six, eight, ten people in one shack. My granny told me she couldn't even understand what the people living next to her were saying. She spoke Italian, they spoke German, the ones next to them spoke Polish. My granddad was a stonemason. Every block of granite in that dam was set in by hand. Italian stonemasons are the best in the world."

This was the first time that Joan and I had ever been alone with Aunt Maggie. Usually, she was surrounded by her children or else she was at the store. I was both happy to be alone with her and uncomfortable because I didn't really know her.

"How come you always make us look at the Wauchusett dam?" I said from the back seat.

"Me? It's not my idea. It's your father."

"Why does he do it?"

"I don't know. What does he say?"

"Nothing."

"Well, if it was me guessing, it's because he wants to show you his past." She slowed the car to a stop, let a woman walking a dog cross the street, then drove on. "Do you girls know anything about your Seymour?"

"His father," Joan said, "used to sell dry goods from a horse and wagon."

"I don't even know what dry goods is," I said. Next to me on the worn back seat was Eddy's Boy Scout sash with merit badges sewn on.

"Pots and pans," Aunt Maggie said. "Dish towels. Rolling

pins. Stuff like that. Pa Adler sold those things to the people working on the dam. All immigrants. This is the largest hand-dug dam
in the world. It was all done with pick axes and mules and pulleys.
No bulldozers, no excavators, no cranes. Just men and shovels."

"But why do we always have to come look at it?" I said.

"Maybe because he wants to show you the reason he grew up
in Woodbridge."

I turned to look at the car behind us, my father at the wheel,
Eddy riding shot gun, and Avery's arm sticking out the back-seat
window feeling the air push against it. "Pa Adler came here when the
dam was being constructed. It was just a huge hole in the ground."

"But why?"

"The way I hear it," Aunt Maggie said, "Pa Adler needed the
work, so he brought Ma and your father up here. Must not have
been any work in New York. The company building the dam found
them housing. That house was built for workers. I remember that
house from when I was a kid. Used to be a Polish family on the
second floor and a German family on the third. Ma Adler told me
she was so lonely, she thought she'd die. She had so many Jewish
girlfriends in New York. You should ask her sometime about
Delancey Street. She told me there were pushcarts full of fish and
acrobats with their hats turned over hoping for coins, and mattresses airing out on the fire escapes. She said she used to stand at
the window with her baby in her arms just looking out at all the
excitement going on. She doesn't talk about it any more but she
used to. She said the nights were the hardest part because it was so
dark. She was used to thousands of lights at thousands of windows
and music coming out of windows. She said when she first got here
and the train used to roar past without stopping she'd cry."

I had never imagined my grandmother being young. "Pa
Adler used to give credit to everyone," Aunt Maggie said. "He
was a soft touch. Ma used to throw your father into his snowsuit
and drive the wagon to the construction site and demand that
the people pay what they owed. Mostly women. The men were all
shoveling dirt and smashing stones with pick axes. Every woman
had a different hard luck story, including my own granny. She had
eight kids all stuck in that sod shack. Manure all over the place

from the mules. She told me the men got drunk, took advantage of the women left alone all day. Said there were prostitutes, gamblers, every sort of riff raff. You girls know what a prostitute is, right?" Joan and I exchanged a shocked look. Aunt Maggie said *prostitute!*

We parked next to Seymour and set out for our usual amble across the top of the dam. This time though, when we stopped in front of the sign that read Wauchusett Reservoir Dam completed in 1906, I read the description, how the dam was built to provide water for the city of Boston thirty miles away, how railroad cars carried away the dirt that the men dug. I read about how schools, cemeteries, churches, and houses were leveled in Woodbridge by the construction, how the population of the town, New Englanders whose families had been there since the days of the colonies, was changed forever by the influx of immigrants who came to work on the dam then stayed after the dam was completed. My father was surprised, I think, that I took his hand when we did our annual promenade across the top of the dam then stood looking down at the water in the reservoir.

CHAPTER FOUR

· · · · · · · · · · · · · · · · · · · ·

To make my father want a divorce, my mother abused her charge accounts. Her lawyer, a blustery bully named Saul Ruben, said she should get at her husband through his bank account. A husband was responsible for his wife's debts. Mother was out shopping every day. She returned home with boxes from Bergdorf Goodman, Bonwit Teller, and Saks. Sweaters, bathrobes, skirts, suits, blouses, shoes with high heels and shoes with low heels, shoes with straps and shoes with bows on the toes. I climbed up on her high canopy bed and watched her unwrap the new things and put them away.

He canceled her charge accounts. It was as if my father thought his wife would outgrow this combative stage of life. All he had to do was wait it out. He never complained to Joan and me or confided in us. Perhaps he thought involving us was bad form. Mother, on the other hand, pulled us into each new skirmish. I knew that her father was sending her money so she wouldn't need her husband's charge accounts. "Why don't you just grant her a divorce?" I said to my father who never replied except with an injured expression that I took to mean I didn't know what I was saying.

Home was not a sanctuary. There was no relief from the anxiety of junior high, the horror of those long corridors, the clanging bell that meant I had to find the room for the next class, those big teenage hoods slouching in the hall, the tough girls in the bathroom, a different teacher for each subject, and a weird holding cell called homeroom full of people who were not in any of my classes. Plus, my best friend from sixth grade took up with some girls who were more popular and didn't invite me to sit with them in the lunch room.

Though I had Ravel's *Pavanne for a Dead Princess* perfected enough for the junior high orchestra audition, I was almost sick with anxiety on the day of the tryout. There would be ninth graders in that orchestra. They would be better players, and I wouldn't stand a chance. I'd never get the solo, I'd never make first chair; I'd be stuck in the second violin section never playing the melody, hidden from view whenever the orchestra performed. Humiliation was waiting to attack me even in this realm of life. For all I knew, I wouldn't even get into the orchestra. By the time I'd finished lunch, sitting with a new girl who just moved to New Rochelle from Indiana, I had decided to quit violin. I would locate the music teacher, he would scan his long list of people about to audition, find my name and cross me off. Then I'd go home and be done with it.

The music room, maybe because it was noisy and needed to be far away from classrooms, was not easy to find. It was in the basement at the end of a corridor that was littered with janitor supplies. The door was closed. Violin case in one hand, I knocked. No one responded. I tried the doorknob and the door opened. I stepped into a dimly lit room with instruments all over the place, violins and clarinets and drum sets, an upright piano against the wall and cymbals lined up on a shelf. A tall man with gray hair was sitting at a small desk in a corner, writing. He looked up when I came in but said nothing. I stood where I was and said across the room, "I'm quitting."

"Excuse me?"

"I'm quitting the violin."

He got up from the desk and came toward me saying, "And you are?"

"Sonya Adler."

Standing next to a cello, he took off his glasses, huffed on them, then wiped them with a handkerchief. "From Roosevelt? Mr. Freedman?" How did he know what school I was from? How did he know the name of the orchestra conductor at my grammar school? "What do you mean you're quitting the violin?"

"I don't want to play any more."

"Do you always do whatever you want?" When I didn't answer he asked again, as if I hadn't heard him. "Do you always do whatever you want?"

He stood there, waiting for me to answer him. I had to think about that for a minute. Did I always do whatever I wanted? Sort of. Joan and I didn't have much supervision but on the other hand I was a child with whole days of school full of things I didn't want to do. That's why I looked forward to growing up. Anyway, what business was it of his? He stood there waiting for me to answer, but I knew his question wasn't really a question. He was saying something else. Heart pounding, I heard him say it more directly. "What kind of parents do you have? Do they let you do whatever you want? What kind of parents are those?" Frozen, I said nothing. "Get out of here," he said in a loud voice. "Just get out of here. Go on. Get out!"

At home, no one asked about the audition. I put my violin in a closet in the attic and my sheet music in the piano bench. After dinner, I went into my mother's room. She was sitting at her desk looking at a book entitled *Nebraska Divorce*. I noticed a brochure entitled *Where To Stay in Reno*. She looked up. "I want to quit violin," I said.

"You don't want to play anymore?"

"No."

"All right," she said. "If that's what you want. I'll cancel your lesson." Then she went back to reading her book. "Close the door all the way," she said as I went out.

I went into Joan's room. She was peering into a magnifying mirror looking for blackheads to squeeze. "I quit violin."

"What'd you do that for?"

"I don't know." I never bothered to tell my father, and he never seemed to notice.

Seventh grade eventually ended, and Joan and I went to camp. The year wasn't all bad because my English teacher encouraged my writing, gave me A's, and told me I had talent and should keep on writing. I loved him. The next year, the English teacher also encouraged me and told the class I was an "avid" reader, which was the first time I ever heard that word. Then eighth grade ended, and Joan and I went to camp again, but this time when we got home our parents were divorced. After fighting for almost three years over the house, my mother gave up. Joan and I moved with her to an apartment in Scarsdale.

CHAPTER FIVE

· · · · · · · · · · · · · · · · · · · ·

The apartment in Scarsdale was in a new building close to stores and to the commuter train. Since I had no idea how much an apartment in Scarsdale cost, I thought we'd moved not exactly to the slums but to an embarrassing part of town. My friends in New Rochelle lived in big houses framed with hedges and oak trees. They didn't get mail out of a cubby hole in a wall of brass boxes or go up to their home in an elevator and walk down a hall of closed doors. I knew only two people my age who lived in apartments. I wondered how they could stand such small places with the sounds of other people and the smells of cooking.

I saw the inside of Sydell Canter's apartment in downtown New Rochelle when I was in fifth grade. She was the reason I knew the word *prodigy*. We had the same violin teacher. She suggested that Sydell and I play a duet. Sydell was not only talented but very nice too so I always left her apartment confused about what money buys. Just being near her while she played felt like a gift though the sofa was torn and the walls dingy. Her clothes were not new but she was much more accomplished than I was and had an inner seriousness that I hoped could be acquired by someone like me even though I wasn't poor.

The other person my age who lived in an apartment was Teresa Kanopka. Her hair was dyed blond and teased into a disheveled mane, an announcement by hair that she was unsupervised. She and her gang bullied girls in the hall, wore flats and stockings instead of bobby sox and oxfords, tight straight skirts instead of full skirts. They did not consider themselves too young for eye shadow. We met the day Teresa sat behind me in assembly when I was in eighth grade. Her neck was bruised as if she'd been strangled. I didn't know anyone else who had been strangled so I turned to ask her what happened. She whispered, "What? You mean this? No, it's a hickey." She said when a boy sucks on your neck you get a mark there. I said, "Why would he suck on your neck?" She must have explained in a gentle way because I brought her home and introduced her to Ruby in the kitchen and brought her upstairs to my bedroom where she read some of the autographs on the movie star photos.

I showed Teresa my mother's bedroom with its wallpaper of roses and canopy bed and fireplace, and her separate dressing room with a wall of mirror and my father's adjoining bedroom done in masculine gray. "How come they don't sleep in the same room?" Teresa asked. "Because he snores." This was my stock answer when asked, but I knew it wasn't the whole truth. I took Teresa upstairs to the attic where there were closets full of my mother's Spanish dancing costumes, flouncy gowns the color of tomatoes and black bolero jackets and shoes with chunky heels and lace shawls. "My mother studied Flamenco in Spain," I told Teresa. "She was once on the cover of *Dance Magazine*." I was aware of Teresa's discomfort in my big house. We never repeated the visit, and I never did see the inside of her apartment above a bicycle shop. Our friendship became just a wistful smile in the hallway. When I asked her to stop picking on my friend Ellen in the girls' room, Teresa called off her gang and I got a taste of the pride that comes from having connections.

Now I was one of those pathetic people without a backyard whose front door was just like all the other front doors on a boring beige hallway.

Grandpa Greenstone financed my mother's divorce then paid for the apartment in Scarsdale. He expected her to remarry. This time she would marry a man who owned his own business, not a wage slave like Seymour. He was not impressed that my father was head of production at MGM headquarters in New York. If my father *owned* MGM, then Grandpa Greenstone would be impressed. He gave his daughter Violet an allowance out of company funds, put her on the books as a Customer Liaison Agent.

We drove a new Thunderbird convertible and charged the gas to Greenstone Enterprises. He told his daughter to spare no expense when furnishing the apartment because "money attracts money."

I had never seen my mother so happy as she was when her divorce became final. She devoted herself to decorating, immersed herself in the selection of tile, wallpaper, sofas, chairs. She studied fabric swatches and carpet samples. She was creating the splendid stage set for her new life.

Given that everyone decorating their home turns into a gigantic bore, even forgiving her being temporarily in the clutches of a cause, I felt her happiness was tactless. I wanted her to acknowledge that she'd upended my life. She didn't seem to care that I was making uncomfortable adjustments. She attributed my sullenness to my age. This infuriated me because it let her off the hook. As long as she could see me as a sulky teenager, she could absolve herself and act as if she had nothing to do with my mood.

The apartment in Scarsdale was so new the floors were still concrete and the walls raw plaster. I did my homework in a square room with one rectangular window. Not used to modern construction, it seemed a room appropriate to a motel. I was used to a bedroom that had an irregular shape, an alcove for the desk and a curved window that looked out at trees. When my mother said I would have to select wallpaper, a bed, carpet, and a bureau my reply was, "It's your room, not mine. Do what you want." Mother concentrated on the parts of the apartment that she could decorate without argument.

There were three bedrooms. Mother's would serve a dual purpose, that of sleeping quarters as well as sitting room for entertaining suitors. She didn't want men to get the wrong idea, she said. The right idea was that just because she was a divorcée it didn't mean she was desperate for sex. Instead of a regular bed, she chose a sofa bed. She had to store her comforter in the closet every morning and yank the thing out every night. Her bedroom looked like an office, all brown and beige. Though she said her goal was to remarry, her bedroom was quite off putting, downright unfriendly.

In defiance, to get back at her for making us displaced persons, Joan and I tormented her when she made us go wallpaper shopping. We were as obnoxious as possible, called her Ma, spoke to each other in a thick Brooklyn accent with lots of oy yoy yoys thrown in, and kept a disgusted look on our faces as if each turn of the page of the wallpaper book showed us something even uglier than the one we just saw. "Holy mackerel," I said. "Will you look at this? Who would put this on their walls?" Joan looked and said, "Well, you could barf on it and it wouldn't show." We were aware, of course, that our behavior made our mother look weak in front of the salesperson. Punishment by embarrassment. The worst part of this aggression, besides the shame of hurting my own mother, was how easy it was to do. She didn't fight back. She didn't take charge. She would not engage.

Then Joan found wallpaper she liked. She chose twin beds, tweed bedspreads and flecked carpet. To that room Joan fled when arriving home from school and, in that room, she stayed with the door shut.

Hunched over my books on the cot that would be replaced when I selected a bed, I heard my mother knock. The first time I saw a parent barge into a teenager's room without knocking was in a movie and the dialogue didn't mention how rude that was. The teenager in the movie seemed to expect that a parent would burst in so that's how I knew my mother had good manners. She entered with her new wary expression that sized me up so she could brace herself if necessary. Dressed in her terrycloth bathrobe, she was holding a heavy wallpaper book. She had given up dragging me to the stores and now brought home heavy sample books. "You must choose something," she said coming close to the cot and waiting for me to make room among my schoolbooks for the wallpaper book. "This cannot go on."

"I am doing my homework."

"You cannot continue living in an unfinished room."

"If you don't like how the room looks, just keep the door closed. You don't have to come in here." I moved my books. She had lost much of her authority but not all of it.

"Look at this," she said setting the open book on the cot. "It's a mural of a Paris café. It would fit on that wall there. Then we could pick up the pink and blue theme in the bedspread and curtains."

Why would I want a picture of French people on my wall? The figures in the wallpaper were carefree, breezy people sipping wine at a café with the Eifel tower in the background, the men in berets, the women with little poodles. They were more cartoonish suggestions rather than images of actual individuals. The dreaminess of the pastel mural was a painful contrast to the actual me whose belongings were in boxes on the concrete floor, the actual me who was trying to navigate Scarsdale High where I didn't know anyone. My mother was seeing the room without seeing me suffering in it, almost as if she worked at Bloomingdale's and had to design a room for display in the furniture department.

I knew that in many ways I was a lucky person, a girl who lived comfortably, a person who could choose her own bed and not have to share it at night with sisters and brothers. But try as I might, I didn't like anything that wasn't my old room at home, my real home, my home with my father and my cat Rinso and my friends who lived down the street and my bicycle in the garage. This place where I found myself, this unfinished cube meant nothing to me. I said, "Do what you want." My mother could be no comfort to me. And so my room was pink and blue with a mural on the wall of lighthearted French people.

One reason my mother moved to Scarsdale was to give Joan and me the advantage of the excellent high school. Scarsdale High was rated the best public school in the United States. High school started in tenth grade and, by the time we moved to Scarsdale, Joan had already completed tenth grade at New Rochelle high. She had the right to continue in New Rochelle because our father was a resident there. Joan did not argue or scream. She simply said, as if speaking to an office coworker rather than her mother, "I am not going to Scarsdale High, so you can forget that." She started her junior year in New Rochelle, figured out the bus schedule, and went there from Scarsdale every morning. It was an hour's commute.

Because I had never been to any high school, I decided to try Scarsdale because I too heard it was top rated. But when I entered that place I couldn't figure out what was best about it. In New Rochelle, I was with all kinds of students. Some would study cosmetology, some would learn typing and shorthand, some would study auto mechanics, some would go on to play professional football, and some would go to college.

Scarsdale High was different. It was as if the college prep level had been sheered off the top and placed in a building of its own. The rest of the school just wasn't there. No one was learning to change spark plugs or how to perm straight hair. None of the boys wore black motorcycle jackets and slumped against the corridor walls. There was one black girl in the whole place, and the football team was easy to tackle. What was better about Scarsdale High? Was it better because there were no penniless kids who had to earn a living immediately after graduating?

I knew no one there. Feeling ashamed of not living in a house, ashamed of having a messed up family, I watched in a kind of fog as everyone else hugged and jumped up and down with happiness at being reunited after summer vacation. Many of the girls were exceptionally pretty and everyone seemed well-scrubbed. One of the best looking girls parked her red MG sportscar in the school parking lot. The license plate was her name, Bonnie. I felt inferior to everyone I saw in the halls. I was from a *broken home*. All the teachers would know this. It must surely be on my "record." If I got good grades, they'd say isn't it remarkable considering she's from a *broken home*. If I failed every subject, they'd say what could you expect? She's from a *broken home*.

After two lonely weeks of walking the halls shrunken in on myself, I returned the textbooks saying to the various teachers, "I'm not coming back." I explained nothing, left the teachers confused. Their bewilderment felt like a brief victory over grownups.

My mother was furious but I didn't care. She didn't have to go there. The teachers were not better than others I'd had, especially the math teacher who didn't explain anything. Joan and I trudged up Popham Road, took one bus to Eastchester then changed to another bus that dropped us in front of New Rochelle High School, a beautiful gothic structure edged by lakes where geese and swans lived.

It was a comfort to be with friends I'd known since grammar school in that big building with its wide, steep staircases. When asked why I'd missed the opening week, I said we moved to Scarsdale and no one asked why. Life, it seemed, was somewhat back to normal.

One morning during homeroom, I was summoned to the principal's office. The principal was a terrifying woman, more male than female. Big and square with a muscular neck, she wore a belt that ended in two balls dangling below her stomach. It was embarrassing to be singled out by the homeroom teacher who said, "Take your books."

When I opened the principal's door, I saw my mother sitting in a chair, her face both frightened and defiant, her eyes swinging with apprehension. The broad-shouldered principal was not sitting at her desk but standing as if eager to end this meeting. My sister's face was drenched in tears. In our family, crying was like going to the bathroom. You never did it in front of anyone. You closed the door and hoped no one would hear the sounds. So this display of open sobbing in front of a stranger made my heart leap. Joan said, "She's unenrolled us. We can't go here anymore."

"What?"

"We can't go here anymore. She's unenrolled us."

"She can't do that."

"Yes," Joan sobbed, "she can."

"Your mother," the principal said in a way that meant it was useless to argue, "has custody. It is her wish that you both attend Scarsdale High."

"But we don't want to!" Joan said in a desperate voice.

"I'm doing this for your own good," Mother said. "It is a far better school. You will meet a much better class of people." She didn't see the principal bristle when she said Scarsdale was a better school.

"The principal of New Rochelle High," the principal said, "does not have the authority to go against a mother's wishes. Go clean out your lockers. Now, please."

Carrying our gym clothes and notebooks, we stepped out into bright September sunshine and walked to the parking lot where the Thunderbird waited. That my mother could just walk in and extract us from school meant that all accepted rules of behavior no longer applied. That very day, I'd heard the most delightfully foul curse. Someone in the hall said it. I shouted at my mother, "If shit could roll, you'd be a big wheel!"

She ignored me and we all got into the car. Sitting at the leather steering wheel, she adjusted her sunglasses, backed out of the parking space, and drove onto North Avenue. I knew people in all the neighborhoods we passed, Ellen in a brick house near the cottage where Thomas Paine wrote *Common Sense,* Donna in one of the new ranch houses on the other side of North Avenue, and Susie in a Tudor house on Trenor Drive with a boxer dog that sprang at Joan once for no reason. My mother kept herself very still, looked ahead through the windshield, but her aura was trembling.

When she came to a red light on North Avenue, I poked Joan in the shoulder and gestured to the door. She opened the door, our mother cried out in surprise and tried to grab Joan's skirt and I thrust the front seat forward and was sorry to slam into my mother's arm as I scrambled out of the cramped back seat. We ran liked pursued thieves along the sidewalk then ducked into an opening in the hedges that bordered the Wykagyl Country Club and raced across the golf course. Doubled over, we sucked in air with such urgency we squeaked. We could see the back of our house, no maid at the kitchen window watching for us with lunch waiting. It never entered our heads that we wouldn't be able to get inside. The house had never been locked against us. We tried the back door, front door, side door. "Daddy will know what to do," Joan said. We counted the change in our book bags and had just enough for two train tickets.

If we were heading into the pandemonium of Calcutta, we couldn't have been more apprehensive though we'd been to Manhattan more than any of our suburban friends. We met Grandma and Grandpa Greenstone at the Waldorf Astoria when they disembarked from the Queen Mary. We saw everything on Broadway appropriate for children, *South Pacific, Fanny, Oklahoma, Carousel, Charley's Aunt.* But we had never gone into the city alone. There were crazy people rummaging in trash barrels, dogs' doo on the sidewalks, panhandlers with anguished faces, streets going every which way, crowds coming up from the subway all at once like schools of fish, ambulances shrieking, and taxis honking.

At Grand Central Station, all corridors led to the central rotunda with a vaulted ceiling. We used up our money on the train tickets so we couldn't take a cab nor were we savvy enough to flag one down or nervy enough to tell a grown up man where to take us. We asked a policeman for directions and found, after a few block's walk, the chaos of Times Square dominated by the Camel cigarette billboard, a man's huge face with a hole for a mouth that emitted smoke rings that fell for a few beats then broke apart over the traffic below. Billboards everywhere that blinked and danced as spellbinding as fireworks. The Pepsi Cola sign had a real waterfall on top of a building. Joan and I stood gawking at the signs for Admiral television, Bond two-trouser suits, Budweiser, Chevrolet. We had seen Times Square many times but never without holding a parent's hand.

1540 Broadway, a sixteen-story office building, known as the Loews State Building was Metro Goldwyn Mayer's headquarters. Hollywood was just a pretty face; New York was the heart and lungs of the movie business. We knew that Clark Gable's paycheck was signed in the building we entered, and that every movie produced at the studio in California had to first be approved by executives in New York. It was a relief to be inside the lobby, out of reach of the chaos in Times Square. When we told the elevator man that we wanted to go to Seymour Adler's office, he let us off on a high floor that felt exclusive because of the hush. "Turn left," he said and clattered the brass gate shut with a white-gloved hand.

We entered a large waiting room with many chairs and walls covered in glossy stills from various MGM movies, Gene Kelly clicking his heels in the air from *Singing in the Rain,* Judy Garland in pigtails from the *Wizard of Oz,* Elizabeth Taylor as a child petting Lassie. A secretary typing at a desk, gray hair held severely back from her face, looked up over half glasses. We had never been to this office. "I'll be dipped," the secretary said. "You must be Joan and Sonya." We knew her name too because she had been with Seymour for twenty years and he sometimes mentioned her. "Was he expecting you?" she asked. We just stood there. "He's not here." We hadn't thought of that possibility. What would we do? Where would we go? We didn't have a dime between us. "Don't worry," Bernice said. "He'll be back. Wait for him in there." She pointed to an open door on the other side of the waiting room.

His office had the feel of a gentleman's club, Oriental rug and forest green leather. From the window I looked down on the clogged streets of Times Square, the windowsill speckled with white and gray pigeon poop. Sixteen stories up, we could hear the traffic and though it was stimulating to look out over the activity, I understood why my father fled to the country most weekends, took Joan and me walking on country roads in Connecticut, where we could pause to appreciate red barns and Holsteins grazing.

The walls of his office were decorated with autographed portraits of movie stars arranged salon-style from floor to ceiling: Couldn't have done it without you, Franchot Tone. Thank you for your confidence in me, Dean Stockwell. To Sy with gratitude, Walter Pidgeon. Lionel Barrymore's signature was across a photo with his arm around Seymour's shoulder. On a large desk were the framed school portraits of Joan and me, each of us smiling with a mouth full of steel against a watery blue background. "Why does he have this picture of me?" I said to Joan, "I look hideous."

"You? Look at the one of me!"

Compared to the celebrities framed on the wall, we were painfully real, with our poodle cuts and smiles forced by the school photographer, who had no talent for lighting. We waited then got bored waiting. "Let's borrow some money from Bernice," I whispered, "go see a movie."

Joan and I walked across Times Square just in time to see *The Bad Seed*. The credits were rolling as our eyes adjusted, and we took our seats among the few people sitting in the dark in the middle of the day. On the screen, an angelic-looking eight-year-old with blond pigtails was beating a boy to death with her toe shoes. She dumped his body off a pier into the ocean. This murder was justified because the boy won the penmanship medal that she thought she deserved. When the handyman in her building became suspicious of her, she murdered him. She pushed an old lady in a wheelchair down some stairs. I had said shit in front of my mother but Patty McCormack, the star, was bad with a capital B!

Seymour Adler strode out of his office when he heard us return to the waiting room and beckoned for us to join him. Impeccably dressed in a navy pin-striped three-piece suit, his posture straight, he flicked his eyes toward Bernice as a warning to Joan and me that we were not to let anything personal spill out in front of her. He closed the door to his office and listened to our tale of being taken out of school. Bad-mouthing someone's mother was against his rules but the effort to stifle disapproval of his ex-wife seemed to propel him across the room, where he grabbed his scarf from a coat rack, flung it around his neck, and gestured for Joan and me to follow him. "You have to pay back Bernice," I whispered running after him. "She lent us money for the movie." Coiled around his anger, he didn't even say goodbye to Bernice, just strode with us to Grand Central Station and sat reading *Variety*, or pretending to, during the thirty-minute train ride. His Pontiac was parked at the New Rochelle train station. We drove without speaking down North Avenue, then onto the leafy street where our house, dark at all the windows, stood forlorn in its emptiness.

The phone was ringing when we entered the house, a shrill blast that echoed through the hollow rooms. We knew who it was. Joan and I left the matter to our father and went to the living room to wait. The divorce had sucked the life out of the house. The furniture was still in place but there were gaps, things missing like the brass samovar on the hearth and the china plates that once were displayed in the breakfront. There were indentations in the carpet where the piano used to be. The green sofa was still there and so was Rinso, our white cat, who leapt up and settled on my lap. My father insisted upon custody of Rinso, said it was for the cat's own good but I thought it was because without Rinso the house would be just too empty. My father said an apartment was no life for a cat, especially not for one used to hunting in the woods. He had moved the television set from the den into the living room so he could watch in front of the fireplace. I winced thinking of my father sitting alone watching *The Ed Sullivan Show* on Sunday nights.

We heard Seymour slam down the phone. Almost shivering with fury, he came into the living room with his bow tie yanked loose, the top button of his shirt open. "Do we have to go home?"

"You'll stay here."

"Can we go to New Rochelle High?"

He didn't know. The court would decide. For more than a
week, we were in limbo at his house. I enjoyed the naughtiness of
missing school, but I was bored and I worried about falling behind.
I was proud of being a good student and had always liked school
better than home. My father's lawyer, Clement Monroe, thought we
did have the right to go to New Rochelle High because our father
was still a resident. However, we had now missed enough school
to be declared truants so our case had to be decided in children's
court. There was a court especially for children?

The Municipal Court House of New Rochelle was a lime-
stone fortress with Greek pillars in front and a heavy door with
iron hinges. Long monotonous corridors were lined with benches.
There were policemen in the halls and lawyers with bulging briefcases. People sat on the benches slumped and vacant.

We had become slumped and vacant by the time a young
man approached, said he was the judge's aide, and asked us to
follow him. My father said he'd wait in the corridor for his lawyer.
Joan and I were ushered into a small unimpressive office with a
wall of bookshelves, no window, and an insignificant desk. Mother
was sitting in there with her lawyer. Her face lit up when she saw
Joan and me. She sprang to her feet. She hadn't seen us for more
than a week and hurried to embrace us. We turned our backs. I
pretended to examine the books on the shelf. My mother's lawyer,
a big-chested man, six feet tall, a Bullmastiff, a champion of weak
women, rose from his chair to intimidate me with his physique.
Known for getting generous settlements out of reluctant husbands,
Saul Ruben said, "Say hello to your mother, young lady."

I was finished respecting adults. Adults were supposed to be
taking care of me but they weren't. They had dragged me into court
like a juvenile delinquent. The adults I knew were acting childishly
and here was one more of them, the schoolyard bully. "You can't
tell me what to do," I said. "You're not my father."

"You say hello to your mother. Don't you know your mother
is doing this for you? Don't you know she has your best interest at
heart? Don't you know she only wants the best for you? What's the
matter with you? You're lucky to have such a mother."

"Saul, that's enough," she whispered.

He moved in too close to me, towered over me and glared down into my face. I had never been physically threatened by a man before, had never felt the superiority of masculine strength. The men I knew, my father's friends, some of my teachers, my orthodontist, treated me in a rather courtly way as if there was something attractive about me that merited deference. Saul Ruben saw nothing appealing in me, and my heart leapt into my throat as I saw the color come into his face. "Say hello to your mother."

My mother whispered, "That's enough, Saul."

I heard Joan say, "You're not the boss of her."

Puffing up, he turned his attention from me to Joan, who was now standing next to me. "How dare you speak to me like that," he said.

My mother said, "Saul, Saul. Please," and put a steadying hand on his arm.

He seemed dying to engage with me, to do battle with the fourteen-year-old girl he saw before him whose wrists he could have snapped with one hand, but the door opened and Clement Monroe came in with my father. Clement Monroe was tall but stooped, as if he carried the world's sorrows on his shoulders. He bowed to Joan and me in an apologetic way that acknowledged our innocence in the face of these degrading proceedings. He moved with my father to the back of the office and there they stood in a corner whispering. It was disconcerting to see my parents acting like strangers, both of them needing bodyguards. They'd been married for eighteen years and now they couldn't look at each other. No outside force, no tornado, avalanche, or witch working at her cauldron had turned them into enemies. They did it themselves.

I got tired of standing so I sat in the nearest chair, the one behind the desk. I sat in it swiveling back and forth while the adults whispered to each other. We waited and waited. Then the door opened, and a nondescript middle-aged woman dressed in a rather shabby suit came in. I thought she was going to tell us how much longer we were going to have to wait for the judge. Her eyes widened when she saw me. "Young lady," she said, "when you become a judge you can sit in the judge's chair." I didn't know what she was talking about. Why was she talking to me in such a rude voice? I just sat there bewildered. "Get up!" she said. "Leave this room at once." Was she the judge? A woman judge? I didn't know there were such things. "Get out!" she said. "These are my chambers, and you are to leave at once."

On fire with embarrassment, I glanced at my mother who looked like a scared bunny. She could not protect me. I was motherless. Joan, in a show of solidarity, left the judge's chambers with me. Covered with shame, I sat on one of the corridor benches and Joan sat down next to me. I suspected that the judge, like Saul Ruben, saw herself as a person mandated tto pick up the disciplinary slack of soft parents, as if it was her job to sculpt the next generation. If the parents were too weak to do it, she'd pitch in. I sat next to my sister, fuming about the limitations of adults despite their being in charge of everything. I was not a girl who needed to be screamed at. I would never turn my back on my mother for frivolous reasons. I didn't greet her when I saw her in the judge's chambers because she had mistreated me. She was expecting too much of her daughters. Bad enough to be turned out of our house but then to force us to leave our friends, that was too much. She was working out some idea of bettering us, an idea generated by snobbishness. I thought she should just listen to us and hear what we needed at this time. Nor was I a girl who delighted in being rebellious. I didn't know it was the judge's chair. I'd never met a judge before. I'd never been in court before. The judge had been unjust. I felt some innocence drop off of me.

Many of the people who walked passed us were tough-looking boys accompanied by sad-looking women and men with briefcases. Probably the mothers and the lawyers. The judge, so it seemed, clumped me in with juvenile delinquents. "What do you suppose he did?" I whispered to Joan when one of them walked by. "Stole something," she said. "I wonder what he wanted so much." There we sat for years and years and at last the door opened and out came our parents and their lawyers. My mother's face was contorted in anger but even in her fury she had a hesitant alone quality that was heartbreaking and attractive. She noticed Joan and me sitting on the bench and her angry face turned worried. Her worried glance infuriated me because I believed she should have been able to predict that her actions would land us in Children's Court. The staccato of her high heels grew fainter as she walked away down the corridor, small next to beefy Saul Ruben.

Clement Monroe, his shoulders even more rounded, his face even more worried, raised a regretful palm in farewell to Joan and me, was kind enough not to smile, and walked away down the corridor. My father, aglow with victory, said, "Turns out the judge was a graduate of New Rochelle High, thinks it's top notch."

CHAPTER SIX

· · · · · · · · · · · · · · · · · · · ·

Every Wednesday evening, per court mandate, Seymour had the right to be with his daughters. He drove to Scarsdale in his Pontiac and parked in front of the entrance to our building. He never asked to see our apartment. I assumed it was because he wanted to avoid his ex, yet I thought it odd that he didn't want to check out where his daughters were now living. To not even know the look of your own daughter's bedroom seemed too distant. Had we said to Mother, "Daddy wants to see the apartment," she would have agreed, perhaps gone into her bedroom and closed the door until he was gone.

Each Wednesday evening, the intercom buzzed. Joan and I took the elevator down eight floors and found Seymour standing in the lobby dressed in his cashmere overcoat, his fedora at a rakish angle. His expression was mortification whitewashed with cheerfulness. He had just been required to announce himself to the doorman as if he was the plumber or a deliveryman. Seymour had to stand before Kyle stripped of all authority, waiting for his own daughters to come from a home where he was not welcome.

The Colonial Inn was a restaurant in an antique house about a half hour from our apartment. The wallpaper was a design of shepherds with their flocks, the ceiling was wooden beams, and the floor was wide floorboards from some gigantic tree that perhaps shaded the pilgrims. The Colonial Inn was pure New England though in a suburb of New York City. The patrons were mostly gray-haired people who sat across from each other eating in a cud chewing, thoughtful way. The hostess was familiar with Seymour, and that made me sad because it meant he ate there even when it wasn't Wednesday. I didn't like thinking of him sitting at one of those wooden tables all by himself. The first time the hostess met us she said, "Mr. Adler! What gorgeous granddaughters you have!" They had their little routine. He looked at her and said, "What? What's this?" and took a coin out of her elbow and she said, "Oh, you!" and bopped him on the arm with the menus.

Every Wednesday, we ordered the same things. I always had roast turkey with extra cranberry sauce, Joan had fried chicken with mashed potatoes smothered in gravy, and Seymour had New England boiled beef dinner with boiled potatoes and boiled cabbage. For dessert, Indian pudding. We never had what could be called a conversation. Seymour never asked about our friends, our studies, our hopes, our concerns. Just as he didn't want to know anything private about us, so did he not want us to know anything private about him. To prevent intimacy, he drowned us in an avalanche of words. "It's a dandy story," he said referring to a script he was reading. "The butler enters and says, 'If you don't mind, Sir,'" Seymour used a haughty British accent. "'I do mind, Jenkins,' says the Earl," and Seymour used another voice. "'How many times must I say do not bother me while I'm working on my stamp collection?'" Joan and I kept our eyes lowered. "Enter the wife. 'Murdock, you are not dressed. The party starts in an hour and here you are in your riding clothes.'" Seymour made his voice high to sound female. "The basic plot is that the wife's sister has stolen some jewels from their aunt, but not because she's a bad person. It's because her son is ill and she needs the money. When she enters she says, 'tisn't fair Madeline. Tisn't fair atall.'" I found Seymour's female voice insulting as if all there was to sounding female was pitching the voice into a shrill register. He described the scene of the two sisters sitting in the drawing room drinking sherry, and the clock ticking on the mantel, and the close up of the husband when he comes in and realizes that the sister is not the real sister but an imposter, and he wonders why his wife doesn't realize she's talking to an imposter. Then he looks at his wife and realizes it's not really his wife but also an imposter, and that the two women in his drawing room are total strangers. So he backs out and tiptoes down the hall to find the butler. "And he says, 'I say old chap, have you noticed anything peculiar?'"

How could Seymour go on and on like this? Why did this happen every time he took us out to dinner? His torrent of words stopped only long enough to pay the check.

Driving back to Scarsdale, I turned on the radio because I thought that might shut him up. I couldn't bear to hear one more meaningless word out of him. That hurt his feelings. Every Wednesday, it was the same unsatisfying encounter. Nothing was moved forward, nothing was settled, we became no closer. Every week as he turned into the entrance of our building he said, as if it was an afterthought, "Mother doing all right?"

"She's okay."

"Seeing anybody?"

He wanted us to spy on her? Did he imagine getting back together? His interest in her was not reciprocated. She never once asked about him. "I don't know," one or the other of us lied.

She was seeing someone. She met Phil Goodman at her Great Books course at the New School in Manhattan. Mother regretted not going to college, blamed her mother for insisting that she become a dancer. Now she was determined to make up for lost time. I found her reading excerpts from the *Illiad* and Alexander Pope and Socrates. She said that sometimes the teacher praised the questions she asked. She said that she planned to take the SATs and go to college. To be helpful, I suggested she get an SAT tutor and was surprised that my suggestion hurt her feelings. "But there's math," I said. "There's math questions." She turned from me. "Mommy, you can't learn math by yourself." Maybe she didn't know that hiring a tutor was common, that even the smartest kid in class sometimes needed a tutor to prepare for the SATs. In an injured voice she said, "I can take care of myself thank you."

Phil Goodman was an informal person, sprawled on the sofa in a relaxed way that I didn't understand. I was used to three-piece suits, starched shirts, cuff links, and polished shoes. His shirts were open at the neck, his shoes were scuffed loafers, and his socks weren't high enough so when he crossed his legs I saw his hairy calves. It was comforting to see my mother with a man her own age. Made her seem younger, more vivid. He was a teddy bear sort of person with brown hair and warm eyes. His masculinity was of the cuddly sort. He was a psychologist who worked at a VA hospital. He was studying the two hemispheres of the brain. One of his patients was a person who bumped into the edges of doors because he had no perception of the right side of his body. His patient didn't know what one whole side of his body was doing. Synapses that were supposed to be shooting back and forth were not. I liked Phil Goodman but wondered why Mother chose him. Her father had outfitted her so she could attract a wealthy man, yet even I knew a psychologist working at the VA did not earn a lot of money.

Mother, as it turned out, enjoyed cooking and was good at it. Often I found her in the kitchen experimenting with soufflés, omelets, and different kinds of dough. Sometimes I thought she would have been better off in her marriage with less money. Without a maid, she would have had to devote herself to the domestic skills that she enjoyed and was good at. I wondered how life in New Rochelle would have been with Mother stirring at the stove and the rest of us at the kitchen table saying, "Yum!"

When Phil Goodman came to dinner in Scarsdale, Joan felt no obligation to charm him. Sitting across from me at the new dining table, eating from the plate that used to live in New Rochelle and using the silverware that used to live there, she chewed and kept her eyes down. Phil told us about the research he was doing for the benefit of people with epilepsy. The idea was that if the two hemispheres of the brain could be separated, then maybe the flash that leapt from one side to the other triggering the seizure would be blocked. He was about to actually try this, had a patient who was about to have the two sides of his brain separated. "But what if it doesn't work?" I said. Joan finished her dinner, carried the empty plate to the kitchen, stuck it in the dishwasher, then went toward her bedroom. "Don't you want dessert?" Mother asked. Joan said, "No. I'm done," and closed the door to her bedroom.

Joan didn't seem to care that Mother was happy getting dressed to go to a movie with Phil or out for a day at the Metropolitan Museum of Art. What our mother did was of no concern to Joan unless it got in her way. It was as if we were three roommates living in an apartment together. One evening, as I was absently looking at the calendar on the wall, I realized that none of the squares were filled in with the word Phil. Then I realized she hadn't gone out in a while and he hadn't come over. "Did you break up with Phil?"

"What?"

"Did you and Phil break up?"

"He wasn't for me."

"What happened?"

"Nothing happened."

"So why'd you break up?" I wanted her to hurry up and get married. Her family in Chicago was tapping its fingers. I overheard defensive conversations on the phone. "Mama, I'm not going to marry just any old person just to be married." My mother was in a degraded position and I wanted it to stop.

"Phil wasn't for me. He had no background, no culture, no breeding. A man who has never been married by the age of forty-seven is set in his ways."

"What were his ways?" I wanted to know.

"I don't know, Sonya. What difference does it make?"

A few months later the name Jerry was in one of the calendar squares. A lawyer with an apartment in Manhattan and a summer home in Amagansett, she met him in a Modern Poetry class at the 92nd Street Y. He was a well-nourished man whose wife died of cancer. When he came for dinner or when he arrived to take my mother out for a date, he did not try to draw me out in conversation. He had children of his own and knew there was no reason to make me like him until he was sure he liked my mother. When the weather got warmer, we visited Jerry Applebaum at his summer home, a graceful place by the ocean. Then one day his name was gone from the calendar squares, and Mother told us that he was engaged to the nurse who had looked after his wife. "A mama's boy," Mother said by way of explanation.

Max Greenstone meant to bail his daughter out of a difficult situation, not support her for the rest of her life. "What job, Mama?" I heard her say on the phone. "What exactly would you have me do? Be a secretary? Yes, of course I know how to type. Do you have any idea how much a secretary makes? Be realistic, Mama. I can't live on a secretary's salary. Oh, all right. I'll go be a waitress. Would that satisfy you? I'll go get my bottom pinched and take tips." These phone calls, like music sung off key, were painful to hear. Grandma was relentless, called two or three times a week. I hoped some new man would appear to save Mother but week after week there was no one.

CHAPTER SEVEN

· ·

At first, the requirement that Joan and I sleep at Seymour's house every other weekend was not onerous because we wanted to be in our familiar bedrooms and we wanted to be with him, the other person suffering from the divorce. The three of us were struggling for equilibrium and rooting for each other though this was never expressed in words. However, the symbolic him was quite different from the actual him. Being with the actual him was a chore. Joan and I much preferred to be with our friends. He was always grouchy and seemed to expect us to take care of the house, to vacuum and scrub the toilets. I would have liked to have been a fairy tale good girl but I wasn't. My boyfriend Pete lived a few blocks away, so we took the bus to the movies Saturday night and on Sunday afternoon we did our homework together in between kissing in his bedroom still decorated with cowboys from when he was little. Often on weekends in New Rochelle, Joan and I were with Seymour less than two hours.

I wished my father would not make pancakes for us because he didn't cook them long enough so they were like mucous inside, and it was embarrassing seeing him in an apron at the stove. The kitchen was a mess and Joan and I felt put upon cleaning up after him, though we understood he meant the pancakes as a loving gesture. It was as if he was trying to show us how the weekends should be, a loving little family eating pancakes for breakfast. The visits turned into guilt fests. He complained that I didn't change all the beds. He cast me in the role of housekeeper, and I suspected it was because I was a girl. Girls were supposed to do that sort of thing. On the other hand, I believed a more loving daughter would help her father around the house. Someone good, like Cinderella, would have the patience to scrub the burn off the pancake griddle. My father seemed to blame me for not being able to make his life better. He screamed at me to get off the phone, to play my music more softly, to stop sleeping so late in the morning.

One warm spring day, my boyfriend Pete came to pick me up in jeans and a T-shirt and my father screamed at him, said he should show some respect for a young lady and dress more appropriately. Pete and I both understood that Seymour was old school but that didn't make the tirade any less offensive. Pete did not deserve to be treated scornfully. He won the national science fair in ninth grade, and MIT had already told him that he would be accepted if he applied. He had invented a computer that could recognize his voice. Had my father taken the time to talk to Pete, he would have discovered an interesting boy.

Because Joan and I were often unavailable to Seymour on our every other weekend visits, we were scrupulous about being available every Wednesday night for dinner. One Wednesday, much to our surprise, we saw that someone else was in his car. The head almost touched the ceiling and the person's width overwhelmed the front seat. Who would dare intrude on visitation night? When Joan opened the back door, the car light went on and, as we climbed into the back seat, a very beautiful very fat woman turned from the front seat to greet us. Her nose was finely chiseled with slightly flaring nostrils. Her full lips were painted the color of merlot, large brown eyes, arched eyebrows, and delicate shell-like ears. She wore a silver turban and dangling earrings. She waited for each of us to say our names then turned back to spare twisting her neck around. Everything about her, including her attractive perfume that changed the atmosphere in the car, announced that she had as much right to be there as we did, which I took to mean she was my father's lover. He said, as we drove away from the apartment building, "Miss Morrison is an opera singer." She corrected him, "Annabelle." She wasn't going to do any pretending in front of girls old enough to understand. She had a womanly voice in the alto range. She had come to his office, he explained, because he was casting an opera singer for a new MGM film. "Miss Morrison," he insisted upon that formality, "has performed at all of the finest opera houses. At the moment, she is expecting Maestro Bocabella to contact her with plans for her next world tour." We said nothing. "Miss Morrison," he continued, "mentioned that she wants to lose weight. I said to her that nothing is more effective than working outdoors in the garden."

"Let's hear you sing," I said.

She turned to see which of the girls had challenged her. Our eyes met. She was not cowed by cheeky girls. The contralto boom that came out of her vibrated the windows and almost blasted us to Mars. "Holy moly!" I cried. She laughed, a big laugh that filled the car. When we got out of the car at the restaurant, I saw she was massive as a breakfront, about a foot taller than my father and was wearing a red velvet cape.

The next time we slept at his house, she was there and after a few weekend visits we realized she had moved in. Her bedroom was in the attic, but when we snuck up there to inspect we saw it wasn't a real bedroom. It was more like a child's clubhouse, mattress on the floor, her things scattered all around. The attic bedroom was for show. Obviously, she slept downstairs in Seymour's bed except every other weekend when Joan and I were there. He began to refer to her as his housekeeper. I was sorry he didn't understand that I was happy he found a companion.

Like a dog marking its territory, Annabelle marked the furniture in the house with what amounted to her logo, a pink rose with a dew drop on one petal. She was good at painting that one particular rose. The fireplace screen got a rose. The backs of wooden chairs got a rose. One weekend, I discovered a pink rose painted on the headboard of my bed. Couldn't she tell it was an antique? How could my father let her? That bed was mine. Or was it? Most of the time, that bedroom was empty. She believed she was improving the furniture. When the toilet seat lids got a rose, I began to wonder if Annabelle had enough to do.

Her primary work was creating the wardrobe she would need for her upcoming world tour. Maestro Bocabella was biding his time waiting for the best moment to put her back on top. The sun porch, a large room with walls of windows and views of the lilac trees in the backyard, became her atelier. Gone was the ping pong table and the remains of any toys that Joan and I once used. Now the sun porch was dominated by a large sewing table heaped with cases of bobbins and thread, boxes of sequins, tape measures, dress patterns. Bolts of fabric were stacked against the walls, brocade, taffeta, suede. Dress forms, they looked thinner than the real woman, wore Annabelle's latest creations, mostly capes made from vicuna or velvet, some trimmed with chinchilla. "This," she said as she showed me a new bolt of gold Lamé, "feel the texture, this will be a dinner garment when I'm on tour in Roma. The Italian women are more chic than the French. The Italians have that *je ne sai quoi* . . . " She thought for a moment then said, "*Sprezzatura!*"

One evening, she cooked dinner for Joan and me, badgered into it by my father probably. He would not relax his prudishness, continued to insist that she was his housekeeper. Annabelle knew nothing about cooking. She was a New Yorker. She went out or she ordered in. But, good sport that she was, she boiled some chicken pieces and set them on the dining room table. The divorce was in the absence of things, the good silverware and the crystal chandelier now in a box in Scarsdale. The inexpensive fixture that replaced it sent down unflattering light. It was odd to set the table with stainless knives and forks and ugly dime store glasses. The only thing that remained of my mother in the dining room was a sterling silver tea set on the sideboard, a wedding present. Her mother was always nagging her to go retrieve the tea set, but my mother didn't want to store it.

At first, Joan and I hung back to give Annabelle space as the producer of the cozy dinner show, but soon it became apparent that she did not intend to wait on us. So we helped bring the butter and slices of Wonder Bread to the table, dumped a can of cranberry sauce into a bowl, found place mats, and at last the four of us sat down to stare at the bald chicken pieces. On her own, Annabelle ate peanut butter and banana sandwiches in the living room in front of the TV.

She wasn't the only one who gained weight. Our cat, used to stalking in the woods behind our house and pouncing on chipmunks, grew into an enormous blob, big as a beagle. Annabelle brushed him and brushed him and he closed his eyes and let this happen like a pasha being fanned by slaves. She showed him to me like a cat show judge, lifted Rinso up by his armpits, stretched him out, and held him high above her head so I could see how she had improved him.

I didn't care that she was a person adrift. I was glad she was there in the house with my father, glad to think of her sitting on the sofa next to him watching his favorite show, *The Beverly Hillbillies*. I saw home movies of visits to Woodbridge, Annabelle brushing cousin Claire's blond hair into a French twist, Claire with her eyes half shut from the pleasure of it and the result, a shy Claire obeying the instructions of her Uncle Seymour to turn right, then left, then look straight into the movie camera lens. I saw home movies of Seymour and Annabelle's road trips to see foliage in Vermont.

That Seymour Adler continued as a corporeal man came as a shock to my mother. As far as she was concerned, he vanished when she was done with him. He was an irritant she once endured, a boil that got popped. One evening, when we were eating in the kitchen of the apartment Mother said, "Who is that woman?"

"What woman?"

"The one in your father's house."

"Who, Annabelle?"

"I don't know her name. Some woman. She came to the door all gussied up in a cape."

"She's his housekeeper," Joan said.

"Does she live there?"

"She's an opera singer," Joan said.

"An opera singer? What kind of opera singer?"

"Mezzo."

"But why is she there?"

"Waiting for Maestro Bocabella."

"She lives there?" Here was a power shift she hadn't expected. She liked to say that Seymour couldn't love anyone, liked to say it takes two to tango, meaning she was blameless. Perhaps she took pleasure thinking of him punished for his bad behavior. Alone in the house that he wrenched away from her, he would wish Violet would return to give him a second chance. Their problem, as my mother saw it, was that she was lovable but he wasn't. Here was proof of the opposite. He'd replaced her. Just like that. Snap of the fingers and another woman was standing at the front door of the house, her house.

"She sleeps in the attic, supposedly," I said.

"But who is she?"

"Annabelle."

"Annabelle?"

"His housekeeper," Joan said.

"She must have been interested to meet you," I said.

"She lives there?"

"What happened?"

"She stood there."

"What do you mean?"

"She came to the door and just stood there."

"You mean she wouldn't let you in?"

"She made me stand outside."

"She didn't let you in the house?"

"She wouldn't open the door. Who is she?"

"You mean she talked to you through the closed door?"

"She opened the top of the Dutchdoor."

"You told her you just wanted to take the tea set?"

"Yes. She said she'd have to ask Seymour."

"So what'd you say?"

"I came home and called Saul Ruben."

"What did he say to do?"

"He's going to write a letter."

My mother seemed as if waking from a deep sleep, rubbing her eyes perplexed like Rip Van Winkle. She was sure she had been right. Seymour was unlovable. He was impossible to live with. "How long has she been in the house?"

"I don't know," I said. "A year maybe."

"She was there last year? Why didn't you tell me?"

"You never asked."

"You could have told me."

"Why?"

"So I wouldn't make such a fool of myself going over there and standing like the Fuller brush man at the front of the door." It didn't seem normal to me that she would imagine that Seymour would cease to be a man in trousers with a sex drive just because she no longer had any use for him. She got up from the table, dazed as if someone had punched her.

Mother had to go to court. She returned with an order saying she was allowed to enter the house to retrieve her tea set but was not allowed to touch anything else nor was she allowed to go there unless Seymour was home. I heard her crying behind her closed bedroom door, wanted to go in and comfort her but knew she'd hastily compose herself and deny that anything was the matter. She had been marginalized as nothing more than a pest. It would have been so easy for my father to invite her to come get the tea set, a wedding present from her aunt that he never used. He chose war over peace, made her appear before a judge as a supplicant. He'd made her cry over a stupid tea set that neither of them wanted.

CHAPTER EIGHT

. . . .

One evening during the winter of junior year, my mother was standing at the kitchen sink washing lettuce and I was sitting at the kitchen table taking a *Seventeen* quiz with her. "Okay," I said. "Here's the next one. 'What do I do when I make plans with a friend and they cancel on me? One. Do I ask them why? Two. Do I make fun of them then call up someone else? Three. Do I feel hurt because I was looking forward to tonight? Four. Do I say doesn't matter, I kinda wanted to stay home anyway?'" I looked at my mother as I waited for her answer. We had already discovered that her dream prom date was Clint Eastwood while mine was Roy Rogers. The evening sun was coming in the window in a way that lit Mother's profile. Her apron was bulging in front.

She said, "I say doesn't matter, I wanted to stay home anyway."

"How come you're getting so fat?"

Startled, she said, "What? Am I?"

Surely mirrors showed her what I was seeing. Her stomach was sticking out. Why didn't she say no more sticky buns? Cottage cheese and peaches from now on. Her expression wasn't scolding for my lack of tact, but alarmed. Later, when we were about to watch *Gunsmoke* she said, "Sonya, I want to talk to you about something." I expected a lecture about calling attention to a person's faults. She couldn't help having a slow metabolism. "Get Joan," she said as she sat on the sofa. "I want to talk to you both."

"What about?"

"Get Joan, please."

I went to Joan's room, knocked on the door. "Come," she said. She was on her bed with the nail polish brush poised over one toe.

"Now?" she said. She put aside her pedicure and came with me into the living room walking on her heels, toes in the air separated one from the other with wads of cotton. Mother's expression was pure distress. "What's the matter?"

"Sit down, both of you," she said. We sat at attention across from her on the matching chairs. "The doctor," she said, "has discovered a tumor."

My heart leapt. "You have cancer?" Was my mother going to die? Was I going to have to go live with my father?

"They won't know until they remove it," she said.

"They can't tell while it's in you?"

"No, they have to examine it."

"Is that why you're getting so fat?"

"Yes. It's in my stomach."

"Does it hurt?" I thought if she said she was in pain, my feelings of compassion might be stirred. So far all I could think about was myself. I didn't want to be without a mother. Not only would I be lonely, but I'd be deluged with pity. Was this shame going to be added to the shame of divorced parents? Was this why she was crying at night behind her closed bedroom door?

"No. It doesn't hurt. But it does have to be removed." She looked from Joan to me and when we didn't speak, she said, "It's growing and has to be removed. It's a very delicate surgical procedure that very few doctors know how to perform. There's only one hospital in the country where they do it."

"Mount Sinai?" Joan asked. Her friend's father was a surgeon there.

"No. It's a hospital in Louisville, Kentucky."

"In Kentucky?"

"I'll be gone three or four months," she said. "It's the sort of thing they have to monitor. Ruby will come stay with you two. You are to tell no one. Do you understand?"

"What?"

"You are to tell no one. Especially not my mother."

"But isn't your mother supposed to know if you catch cancer?"

"Don't argue with me, Sonya. You are to tell no one."

"But suppose they call up while you're gone?"

"You'll say that I'm in the tub."

"But you can't always be in the tub."

"Then say I'm at a class or at a show. It is very important that you tell no one. I want to be sure that you understand."

"Why?"

"Because. Because I don't want my mother nagging me, and I don't want them all worrying over me. It's hard enough without their interfering. Now promise. Both of you. Promise you will tell no one."

"Okay."

"No. Promise me.

"I promise," I said.

"Joan?"

"I promise."

"Bills will come for me while I'm gone. You are to forward all my mail to Frau Waldman."

"Frau Waldman?"

"Yes."

"Why can't we just forward the mail?"

"Don't argue with me, Sonya. Just listen. Frau Waldman will forward all bills and letters to me, and I'll send the necessary money and replies to Frau Waldman. That way my correspondence will have a New Rochelle postmark."

"But Joan and I go to New Rochelle every day. We can forward your bills and drop your letters in the mailbox at the bus stop." I was fifteen, I could take care of something like this. Why didn't she trust me?

My mother had no friends, but I thought that was because older women didn't have friends. Friends were something young people had because of school. But just how alone my mother was, how isolated, now dawned on me. She had to call upon her dressmaker in her time of need. Frau Waldman of all people! Joan and I also had dresses made from fabric that Grandma Greenstone brought back from Europe, so I knew the drab inside of Frau Waldman's apartment and the gray feel of the woman as she folded under the hem of the dress she was making for me and secured it with pins she took from between her lips. In downtown New

Rochelle, you entered a cramped lobby then walked up smelly stairs to her one big room, the kitchen at one end with pots and pans showing above the rim of the sink, and a long table in the middle for her sewing machine. There was always a plate of store-bought cookies on the table, hard vanilla cookies smeared with sugary icing that was so sweet it made my teeth thrill. I thought it polite to eat one and say, "Thank you, Frau Waldman." She never spoke except to say, "You vill to turn please." This woman, whose windows were so dirty you could hardly see the marquee of the Loews Theater below on Main Street, who didn't brush the dandruff off her shoulders, who reeked of despair, this was the one person on earth my mother could trust.

"Ruby will take care of you two," my mother said. "She will live here while I'm gone."

"Can we tell Daddy?"

"Absolutely not."

"Suppose he finds out?"

She looked at me in a menacing way. "Make sure that he does not." She must have thought he would use her affliction against her in some way, and I too thought he might.

The day my mother left with her largest suitcases, Ruby arrived looking like a nun or a Jehovah Witness person in her drab black coat and hat. Did Ruby know? Were we allowed to talk about the cancer with her? As my mother lugged her suitcases down the hall to the elevator, Ruby lugged her suitcase into my mother's bedroom and closed the door.

Sometimes, sitting in homeroom, or riding on the bus, or walking down the causeway that separated the two lakes in front of the high school, my heart would suddenly leap and I'd be filled with dread. They would take the tumor out and it would be crawling with maggots and my mother would die.

With Mother in Louisville, Joan and I had the use of her car to drive to school. We didn't have to worry about affording gas because all we had to do was present our Greenstone Enterprises charge card. I was too young to drive but Joan had her license. Dressed in our Loden coats, we set out after eating the breakfast Ruby prepared for us. "How come she won't sit with us?" I asked

Joan as she drove up the garage ramp and out onto a road bordered by high mounds of snow left by snow plows. Pedestrians were huddled in their coats, scarves wrapped around the lower part of their faces. "She just serves us and stands there and won't sit down. Do you think Mommy told her not to sit with us?"

"No! Mommy would never say that."

"Should we ask her? I could say, Ruby, how come you don't sit with us?"

"You could I guess," Joan said. We drove slowly by the comfortable houses of Scarsdale, swing sets decorated now with snow, front paths shoveled, a snowman in a yard with a carrot for a nose. Still a new driver, Joan drove so cautiously that cars behind us got impatient, honked, and pulled ahead of us with their snow chains clanking. "These windows keep fogging up," she said. "There's some gizmo thing you can spritz the windshield with. Wait. Here it is." Joan pressed the button and water flew up over the windshield freezing immediately, obscuring our view entirely.

"Pull over! Joan, pull over!"

"I am. I am!" She slowed the car and we skidded to a stop by the edge of the road. Ice made the windshield opaque. We should have been able to predict that the water would freeze. When we had finished laughing our heads off, we got out of the car and opened the trunk. There was only one ice scraper in the trunk next to the spare tire. With that, and a ruler from my book bag, we chipped away at the ice on the windshield. On both sides of the road the trees were coated with icicles. Joan said, "Isn't there a defroster thing?" We got back into the car and Joan searched the dashboard. She pushed a button, nothing happened. "Maybe the car has to be turned on," I suggested. She turned the key but only cold air blasted out so we continued scraping until there was a patch on the windshield big enough for Joan to peer through. Hunched forward over the steering wheel, she strained to see as we drove slowly on the icy streets. "Do you think she's going to die?" I said.

"I don't know. Maybe."

"Will we have to go live with Daddy?"

"Oh! Wait!" Joan exclaimed. "Elvis! I love this song. Turn it up!" I did and we sang "Love me Tender" together.

Joan and I collected the mail from the brass cubbyhole in the lobby and forwarded it to Frau Waldman. My boyfriend Pete now had his license so he could visit me in Scarsdale. Joan's boyfriend also had a car. On weekends, our boyfriends stayed in our rooms until midnight or later. The only person who saw them depart was the night doorman Kyle, who said suggestive things to me. "When the cat's away, huh? What Mother don't know won't hurt her, huh?" He seemed to actually expect me to engage in that conversation with him, to gloat about my freedom, but I was appalled by Kyle's lewdness. I was a virgin and intended to remain one until I got married. My mother said a girl cheapens herself if she does it before marriage.

One day I went to the door, and a handsome black man was there. At first, it was jarring to see a black person in the hall. Scarsdale didn't have black people, at least I never saw them. In a gentle manner, he asked for Ruby just as she hurried from her bedroom. He refused my invitation to come in. "No, it's okay," I said. "Come in." But he would not. There was some unwritten code that he refused to defy. Why? Why couldn't he just come in and visit Ruby? As I retreated to my room, I heard that Ruby did not invite him in though they were obviously fond of each other. She lit up when she saw him. I left her to speak privately with him at the open door. Was that her boyfriend? Was that her husband?

At first, making excuses for my mother was easy. But by the second month, Grandma Greenstone became suspicious. Calling from Chicago, she said, "Not home? She is never home when I call. I have called three times in the last week, and three times you have said the same thing."

"I know, Grandma, but she's taking all these classes in New York."

"I have called at eight, I have called at nine, and now I am calling at ten and still you say she is at a class."

"I know but she has to take the train home. She doesn't drive into the city. It's hard to park in New York, and it costs a fortune to leave the car in a garage so she takes the train, and the train only goes at certain times and if she misses it then she has to take the next one so sometimes she doesn't get home until late. And sometimes she gets a bite to eat afterward. So she doesn't always get home right after her class."

"I have called at eight, I have called at nine, and now I am calling at ten. Tell your mother to call me. I want to hear from her."

"Okay, Grandma. I'll do that."

"See that you do. I want to hear from her. Tell Violet that I want to hear from her."

Then Uncle Alan, who seldom phoned, became suspicious. "We're starting to get worried about your mother," he said. "We haven't been able to get ahold of her. Is everything all right?"

"Sure," I said sitting on my bed surrounded by my books. "Yes. Fine."

"Is your mother ill?"

"No! She's just really busy."

"Will you have her call me, honey?"

"I sure will."

"How's school going? Getting ready for the SATs?"

"No. I don't take them until next year. Joan is though."

"Does she have her college picked out?"

"I think she wants to go to Carnegie Tech."

"And what about you. Where do you want to go?"

"I don't know. I don't even care. They all seem the same to me. Probably Northwestern. Then I could visit you."

"I'd like that."

"Me too."

"How's the violin coming along?"

"I don't play anymore."

"Why?"

"I don't know. Just lost interest, I guess."

"That's a shame. You were a promising student."

"Who told you that?"

"Your mother."

"She thought I was a promising student?"

"Sure she did. She was real proud of how you played the violin."

"She never told me that."

"Well, sometimes parents don't always say the right thing."

"You're telling me!"

We both laughed. "How are your grades?"

"I'll get into some place decent probably. What's up with you, Uncle Alan? "

"Fine, honey. Just fine. You tell that mother of yours to call me."

The third month Grandpa Greenstone phoned, and this was unusual. He never chatted on the phone, left keeping in touch to his wife. Of all my relatives, I believed Grandpa saw what was good about me. What he saw, I had no idea but it felt like an honor to be respected by such a successful man. "Grandpa? Hi! How are you?"

"Fine, honey. I'm just fine. Honey, put your mother on."

"My mother?" Silence. "She isn't here." Silence. "She's just been so busy. I'll tell her to call you."

"What's she up to?"

"My mother?" He did not help me. He left me in the vibration of his silence. I forced myself to say, "She's at a class." Again he said nothing.

Just as the silence was becoming unbearable, he said, "Aw right, honey. Anything you'd like to tell Grandpa?"

"No," I said. "I . . . " A quiet click. "Grandpa?" He hung up on me. My heart ached.

My mother's sister Dovey Lee phoned again and said in her musical tinkling voice, "What's cooking?"

"Nothing much. School."

"And how's that going?"

"Good."

"Is it cold there?"

"Yes. But at least it isn't getting dark at four anymore."

"It's freezing here. We went skating yesterday, me and the kids. I'm not much of a skater." She lived in a big house a block from Lake Michigan.

"You have a distinctive style."

"Ha ha! Now that's certainly a diplomatic way of putting it."

"It's true," I said. "You push off with one foot and glide with the other."

"Yes I do, come to think of it. Never thought to call it a style."

"What do you call it?"

"Ineptness." We laughed.

"Well, if you think of it as a style, you'll be happier every time you go skating."

She laughed again. "That is certainly true. Sonya, is there something you'd like to talk to me about?"

"Like what?"

"Anything. You know you can talk to me. I'm always here for you. You know that don't you?" Should I tell her? It would be such a relief to tell someone how scared I was that my mother was going to die, that they'd take the tumor out and it would be too late. "There's no hard feelings twixt your mama and me are there? Did I do something?"

"No, Aunt Dovey Lee! No!"

"Well, you know sometimes I say too much, don't always bite my tongue."

"No, no. Not at all. Not at all."

"But, honey, it feels like she's avoiding me. I was thinking of flying there, have it out face to face."

"No, no, Aunt Dovey Lee. She's not mad at you at all. Not at all."

"Will you ask her to call me?"

"Yes, I will."

"Is she there now?"

"No, she's at a class." Silence.

"I can't help thinking something's wrong, that you're mama's sick or something. I wish you would confide in me, Sonya." I couldn't speak. At last she said, "You would confide in me, Sonya, if you could, right?" I said nothing. "Yes. I can see your heart, Sonya. Even from here in the windy city. You're a girl who keeps her word." I felt tears welling up. "Okey dokey, honeybunch. You take care." When I said bye, it came out a croak.

One evening, as I was writing a short story for English class, my mother phoned from Louisville. Thinking that she was calling to reassure me about her health, I was surprised that she immediately began to grill me about my replies to her relatives. The call was not to reassure me, but to reassure herself that Joan and I were continuing to lie about her whereabouts. It was bad enough to turn me into a liar without suggesting that I might betray her either on purpose or because I was a dope who let important information dribble out by mistake. She didn't seem to appreciate the effort it took to lie to my relatives and thus belittle my loyalty to them.

One Wednesday night during the third month of Mother's absence, we picked up the intercom expecting to hear that our father was waiting in the lobby, but the doorman said, "Mr. Adler is on his way up." This was unprecedented. "Ruby!" I shouted. "Daddy's coming up!" She was a grown-up; she'd know what to do. She opened her bedroom door dressed in a gray bathrobe, shook her head slowly saying, "Sha," then closed her door just as the doorbell rang and my sister came hurrying from her bedroom.

It was very odd to see Seymour standing at our door in his tweed coat with a navy scarf tied like an ascot. "Come in," I said as he peered around me. "She's not here." He entered, embarrassed like an uninvited guest, and darted his eyes here and there as if trying to hide that he wanted to look at everything.

"Spiffy," he said. I went to the closet to get my coat. "Your mother not home?" This was why he'd come up. How did he know? "Seems to be keeping busy," he said. Had to have been Kyle, the doorman. Maybe he felt sorry for a father who had to come calling on his own daughters. Seymour's age showed that he had waited a long time to have children. Maybe during those moments of fanning cards and asking the doorman to pick a card, any card, Seymour got information. Maybe this time Kyle said, "The missus ain't in, Mr. Adler. Go on up. She ain't been there for weeks."

I stepped into the hall, he followed, and Joan shut the door behind us, tested it to be sure it was locked. "Leaves you alone, does she?" he said. But if it wasn't Kyle, when exactly had we slipped? "Will she be here when you return?" It was one thing to lie into a telephone but quite another to lie to my father's face. Neither Joan nor I could answer except with a noncommittal shrug. "Tisn't right," he said stepping into the elevator. "Tisn't right to leave girls alone in an apartment building." The elevator door slid shut and we descended. "What do you know about the people who work here?" he said, "Do you have any idea who they are?"

Annabelle wasn't waiting in the car. "Under the weather," he said, but he said it with no warmth, so I took that to mean either she didn't want to join us or he had asked her not to. Did he know before he set out that he was going to come up to our apartment and find our mother absent? How long had he suspected that she wasn't home? Why weren't we allowed to tell him? What was so shameful about a tumor? Maybe she thought he'd try to get custody of us, though he never said he wanted custody, often said girls need their mothers.

We sat in strained silence at the Colonial Inn only long enough to give our dinner orders to the waitress. Then he began to fill up the space by telling us about a movie he was casting about juvenile delinquents. To give the film authenticity, the cast was to be mostly unknowns so a casting call had gone out. "A kid comes in," he said, "wearing a motorcycle jacket, tough, talking like he comes from the streets. I say to him Paul, just be yourself. Just be yourself and read the lines. He's got a baby face, and he's trying to sound like Al Capone! So he starts off with an Italian accent. He's a Jewish kid. I said to him do you have any experience, Paul? He says no. I said to him what are you doing to support yourself? He says bar tending. I said what will you do if you don't get this part? He said, I don't know Mr. Adler, probably cry. Sweetest kid you ever met. A good little actor too. I told him if he'd just remember to be himself he'd go far. Then in comes another one, Vic something. This one really has bad boy inside. This kid could be the next Brando. I said to him if I send you to the coast, Vic, you have to promise me you won't go Hollywood. I said to him the minute you lose your tough-guy pose and start wearing business suits you're finished."

Intending to continue, my father opened his mouth but then closed it and fell into a kind of reverie. He looked at Joan and me in a worried way. I sat with my eyes lowered, wishing with all my heart that he wouldn't make us tell on our mother. I had promised not to tell. A promise was sacred. Eyes on my plate, dividing up the cranberry sauce so the amount would come out even and I'd have some for my last bite of turkey, I peeked at my father across the table. He swiped his front teeth with his tongue then sucked some food out of his side teeth. Then he fished a quarter from his pocket and in an abstracted way, not paying much attention to it, he began to manipulate it from one finger to the next as if it had wheels and could roll across the back of his hand.

CHAPTER NINE

....

M ost nights, Pete and I talked on the phone for hours. When we moved to the apartment Mother installed two phone lines, one for her and the other for Joan and me. While she was in Louisville, we used her number so Joan and I never had to argue about the phone, could stay on as long as we wanted. I talked to Pete and she talked on the other line to her boyfriend sometimes until two or three in the morning. I was grateful to Grandpa Greenstone for giving Violet enough money to afford two different numbers, and I loved my mother for using the money in this way, for understanding the importance of the telephone to high school girls.

One evening I was sitting on my bed working on a book report about *Main Street*. The main character, Carol Kennicott, was taken from her childhood home by her new husband and thrust into a house she didn't like in a prairie town full of people she didn't like. Her task was to adjust and she couldn't. With every turn of the page, I hoped she would escape and, at last, she does. In Washington D.C., she finds what she imagines are like-minded friends. That ending would have been the easy one but Sinclair Lewis chose the more difficult. He had to show us how slowly but surely Carol Kennicott begins to miss her husband and the simple structured life of a small town. She ends up just like all the other women in town, rocking on her front porch gossiping about neighbors. The theme of my paper was that Carol Kennicott was just like all the others to begin with but she didn't know it, thought she was better than they were because of false ideas about herself that only experience could knock out of her. I ended the paper with a direct quote from the book. "She was snatched back from a dream of far countries, and found herself on Main Street." I loved Sinclair Lewis's writing. I was copying another of his sentences into my notebook when the phone rang.

"Ho, ho, ho, and a bottle of rubbish."

"Listen to this, Pete. Listen to this sentence. This is what Carol Kennicott's husband says to her. Listen to this. 'No matter even if you are cold, I like you better than anybody in the world. One time I said that you were my soul. And that still goes. You're all the things that I see in a sunset when I'm driving in from the country, the things that I like but can't make poetry of.'"

"Nice. You're my soul."

"I am?"

"If I had a soul, you'd be it."

"You don't think you have a soul?"

"No."

"What do you think you have?"

"A body."

"But your body isn't everything."

"Yes it is."

"No. What about the part that listens to music and the part that has feelings?"

"Brain functions."

"Can't be. When you swoon to music, the feeling is in your torso."

"Be that as it may. Fry that inferior frontal gyrus or the dorsolateral frontal cortex and goodbye swoons."

"Okay. What about love?"

"All of it. You can't do any of it without the brain."

"You mean you think those people who are brain damaged and drool can't love?"

"Some probably can. But the ones with damaged amygdala can't."

"Who'd you do your book report on?"

"Steinbeck."

"Which one?"

"Grapes."

"What'd you say?"

"Too many words."

"How could it be too many words? It's Steinbeck!"

"It's too many words."

"Which words were too many?"

"The scene with the grown up man nursing on her boob."

"I know. Wasn't that so disgusting? Did you mention that in your paper?"

"No. Just wrote about how *East of Eden* is better and why. Did you get the Algebra?"

"No. Did you?"

"Which problem stumped you?"

"The third one."

"You have to clear out the parenthesis on each side then simplify each side."

"Then what?"

"Add 18w and 4 to both sides to get all the w's on one side and the terms without a w on the other side."

"Then what?"

"Divide both sides of the coefficient of the w."

BANG! A sudden loud thud and clatter of broken china. "Wait a second, Pete. Hold on."

I hurried from my room into the kitchen and saw Ruby crumpled on the floor, broken dishes around her. "Ruby!" The water was running in the kitchen sink. "Ruby!" Her eyes were closed and she was inert. "Joan! Joan!" I put my hands on Ruby's shoulders to shake her softly, hoping she'd open her eyes and stand up. "Joan!" I screamed. "Joan!" I ran to Joan's room and burst in, "Joan!" From behind the closed bathroom door Joan said in an annoyed voice, "What?"

"Ruby. Something's happened to Ruby."

"What's that supposed to mean?"

"I don't know. I don't know. Come out of there."

"Can't. I'm pooping."

I ran back to the kitchen. Ruby's dark skin had become ashen. I ran back to Joan's room and screamed through the bathroom door, "Should I call an ambulance?"

The toilet flushed and Joan came out in her pajamas, her face dotted with medicated acne patches. We ran to the kitchen. "Oh my god. Ruby! What happened to her?"

"I don't know. I don't know. What are we supposed to do?"

"I don't know."

"We have to do something."

"Call an ambulance," Joan said.

"How do you call an ambulance?"

"I don't know," Joan said. "I don't know." Her chin started to tremble. "What are we going to do?"

I yanked up the receiver of the wall phone, heard no dial tone, then remembered Pete was on the line. "Pete. Hang up."

"Why. What's the matter?"

"Something's happened to Ruby."

"What happened?"

"Hang up. Just hang up."

"Where's your mother?"

Even Pete didn't know. "Just hang up. Just hang up." He did. I dialed the operator, told her we needed an ambulance. The operator connected me to an ambulance service. The man on the other end kept asking questions, wanted to know where a responsible adult was, was I sure I got the address correct, did I understand this was not a free service, and at last promised that an ambulance would arrive. Some liquid started to seep out of Ruby's mouth. I ran out of the apartment, pushed the elevator button, it didn't come and it didn't come, so I began running down flight after flight of stairs and, midway, realized I could have just picked up the intercom and alerted Kyle in the lobby, but I was already on floor three so I just kept going and finally burst out at the far end of the lobby and ran to the switchboard where Kyle in his brown uniform was sitting. "Kyle," I said. "Ruby's sick. Ruby's on the floor. Something's happened to Ruby!"

"Slow down, slow down!" he said. "Who did what?"

"Something's happened to Ruby!"

"Ruby? Your maid?"

"I don't know what to do. I don't know what to do!"

"Did you call the police?"

"Why would I call the police?"

"For an ambulance."

"The police have an ambulance?"

The switchboard buzzed. Kyle put the plug in the hole and said, "Yes, Mrs. Weiner?"

"Kyle!" I said, "I don't know what to do!"

"Yes, ma'am," he said into his headphones. "They delivered it this afternoon. Yes, ma'am. I did sign for it." He pulled out the connection and said to me, "I can't leave the switchboard, Miss Adler. I'm the only one here."

"But she could die! She could die!"

The switchboard buzzed. Kyle put a phone plug in the hole where the light was blinking and said, "Yes, Mr. Tepper. How can I help you?"

I ran to the elevator, pushed the up button, pushed it again and again. It came at last. Joan was kneeling next to Ruby patting Ruby's lips with a washcloth because more liquid was coming out. I yanked up the phone receiver, dialed the operator, said, "Get me the police," a line I'd heard in a movie.

"Is this an emergency?"

"Yes. Please get the police. Or tell me their telephone number. Oh, wait. It's here on the cover of the yellow pages. Wait. Here it is." I was so relieved to see the number that I almost burst into tears, but I steeled myself and dialed the Scarsdale Police Department. In a rush of words, I told the man my name, address, and that Ruby had collapsed.

"How old are you, Miss Adler?"

"Fifteen."

"Put your mother on the phone."

"She's not here."

"When will Mother be home?"

"She's not coming home. Please come. Please come. We don't know what to do."

"Can you put your father on the phone, Sonya?"

"No. He's not here."

"When will Father be home?"

"He doesn't live here. Please come. Please come now."

"Here's what I'm going to do. I'm going to send a patrol car. Now I want you to calm down, and I want you to call whoever is in charge of you. Aunt, uncle, cousin. There must be someone. Will you do that?"

"Okay, okay." I hung up.

Joan was picking up the pieces of broken plates. "I'm calling Daddy."

"Daddy? No!"

"We have to. Ruby could die."

"You can't call Daddy."

"But we have to. Look at her."

"You can't, Joan. You can't call Daddy. What would you tell him? What would you say about Mommy?"

"I don't know but I'm doing it." She picked up the phone and dialed his number.

"Don't do that, Joan! Don't you understand? They'll say she's unfit. They'll say she abandoned us. They'll make us go live with him."

"Sonya, shut up. Ruby could die. So just shut up." Seymour's phone rang and rang in his empty house. We hurried to our rooms and got out of our pajamas so we'd be ready when help arrived. Joan peeled the patches off her face. Sitting on chairs in the kitchen next to Ruby, we waited without talking and at last there was serious banging on the front door. Two large men wearing white shirts with badges on the sleeve stood next to a rolling stretcher in the hall. "In here, in here," I said and they pushed past me into the kitchen where one of them bent way down to listen to Ruby's heart with his ear. "She's got a pulse," he said. They maneuvered the gurney into the kitchen where they lifted Ruby up, straightened her uniform so she'd be decent and put a white sheet over her body. At the elevator one of the men said, "Who's in charge here?"

"What's the matter with her?" Joan said. "What's the matter with her?"

"How long has she been like this?"

"I don't know, I don't know," Joan said.

The other man said, "Who's in charge here?"

"Ruby," Joan said.

"Who's Ruby?"

"Her," Joan said.

"Do you know her last name?" the medic said.

"Myers."

"She lives here?"

"Not all the time." The elevator arrived, the men maneuvered the gurney in and we squeezed ourselves around it. "What's the matter with her?" Joan said.

One of the medics said, "Is your mother alive?" We didn't reply. "Where is she?"

Joan's chin started to tremble. I said to the medics, "She's out of town right now."

"She didn't leave a number?" When neither Joan nor I answered, the medic whispered to the other man, "What the hell's going on here?"

The ambulance was idling in front of the building, a red light on top whirring round and round with no sound. This was us. We were now people who had called an ambulance. The medics opened the back of the van and pushed the gurney up inside. As one of them got out of the back and went around to sit behind the wheel, the other one stuck a needle in Ruby's arm and hung a plastic bag of liquid next to her. Then he tapped on the interior window and the ambulance headed off with its siren screaming. The medic next to Ruby spoke into a pager and the reply was words coated in static. I had never been in an ambulance before.

At White Plains Hospital, Ruby was wheeled away in one direction and we were told to go in another direction to a waiting room where there were rows and rows of chairs. Injured people were rushed through the Emergency Room doors on stretchers, some of them bloody, some of them moaning. The metallic sound of female voices paging doctors came from loud speakers. Sitting across from Joan and me was a family, three adults and a boy about eleven. A man holding paper cups of coffee came into the waiting room, brought the cups to the adults, then sat down with them to wait. They were dazed. We waited and they waited. We were in the same boat, but I felt no connection to them. Nor to any of the other people in the waiting room, an elderly man with a patch over one eye, a woman with her head back sleeping.

We sat and sat, our posture slowly wilting. "Suppose she dies?" Joan said.

"Do you think we should call Frau Waldman?" I said.

"Probably."

"Are they supposed to take us home? What time is it?"

"Maybe Daddy's home now."

"Joan. We promised. You can't call Daddy."

"Then who's going to take us home?"

We sat without talking for a while. Then I said, "Did we do something to her?"

"I don't know."

A woman dressed in a blue suit with a hospital badge hanging like a necklace approached and pulled up a chair in front of us. She wore glamorous eyeglasses with cat-eye frames studded with tiny diamonds. "Girls, I'm Miss Lorenzo, the staff social worker. I'm required to ask you some questions." She looked at us in a steady way that lasted a bit longer than was comfortable. She settled her clipboard on her lap and held a pen poised above it. Name, age, phone, address. Easy. "And your mother? What is your mother's name?" When we didn't answer, she said, "What is your relation to the patient Ruby Myers?"

"She's taking care of us," I said. "While our mother's away."

"Is your mother on vacation?"

"Yes," I said. "She's in the Caribbean."

"When will she return?"

"In a few weeks."

"What's the best number for contacting her?"

"What?"

"What's the name of her hotel?"

"She's staying with friends," I said. "In a beautiful villa."

"Do you have the telephone number for that beautiful villa?" When we said nothing, the social worker said, "It's my understanding that Ruby Myers works for your mother. Is that correct?"

"Is she going to die?" Joan said.

The social worker said, "Girls. Come with me. We'll go to some place more private." We followed her down a long corridor and into an office where she sat behind a desk and motioned for Joan and me to sit in the two chairs that faced her desk.

"Joan," Miss Lorenzo said. "Am I right? You're Joan? You're the older sister, am I right?" Joan nodded. "Tell me Joan, where is your mother? The medics said that you told them she is alive." Joan nodded. "What is her name?"

"Violet."

"Is her last name the same as yours? Is it Violet Adler?"

"Yes."

"Does she have a middle name?"

"Greenstone."

"Violet Greenstone Adler. Is that correct?" Joan nodded. "Is your father alive? What is his name?" Joan told her. "Where is he tonight?" We shook our heads because we didn't know. "Do you live with him?" We shook our heads. "Are your parents separated?"

"No. Divorced."

"So I assume, and please correct me if I'm mistaken, that it would be your mother who is the responsible party in this situation? Am I correct that your mother has custody?" We nodded. "Let me ask you. Do either of you know where Ruby Myers lives when she is not with you? Do you know her address?"

"No."

"Would your mother know Miss Ruby Myer's address?" We hunched our shoulders. "Do you know if Ruby Myers is married?" We shook our heads. "Girls, I'm going to have to insist that you tell me where your mother is. Even if it's difficult to say, I'm going to have to insist. Miss Myers probably has family somewhere. We need to know who to contact. You understand that."

"We don't know where she is," Joan said.

"You don't know where your mother is?"

"No."

"And your father? Where does he live?" She sighed in an exasperated way. "Does your father know where your mother is?"

"No."

"Do you have any other relative we might call?"

"No."

"No grandparents?"

"No."

"Would you like to phone your father to see if he can come pick you up?" How would we explain this to him? He'd ask why Ruby was staying with us. He'd accuse Violet of negligence, make us appear in children's court, pounce on her at the hospital where doctors were examining her tumor and announce that he was awarded custody of us. "What is his telephone number?" We said nothing. "Girls. We must notify an adult. Do you understand that?" She held her pen poised above her clipboard.

"What happened to her?"

"They think it was a heart attack," Miss Lorenzo said. "I'm sure her family, if she has one, would like to know."

"Her mother's in Alabama." I remembered my mother telling me Ruby sent money home to her sick mother.

"Do you know where in Alabama?" We shook our heads. The social worker stood up, looked at us for an uncomfortable amount of time then said, "There's nothing more to be done here." She went out, leaving us to ourselves in the cluttered office with a diploma framed on the wall.

"We have to call Frau Waldman," I said. "She has to call Mommy and tell her what happened."

"You think she knows the name of the hospital?"

"She must. She's forwarding the mail."

"Why don't we just tell Daddy that Mommy has a tumor? Why is that such a big secret?"

"Because we promised we wouldn't. And they'll make us go live with him. They'll say she's an unfit mother. Do you want to go live with Annabelle?"

Just then the door opened and a policeman came in. He pulled the chair behind the desk around in front of the desk so he could sit closer to us. "My name is Sergeant Copp," he said. Another instance of an apt name, like Seymour's tailor Mr. Taylor. The policeman handed us each a Snickers bar and when we didn't unwrap them he said, "Go on, go on. Enjoy." We whispered thank you then peeled the wrapping off and ate the candy, first licking off the chocolate then sucking on the caramel. The officer lit a cigarette, inhaled, and sat there watching us. He said, "Young ladies.

Are you aware that the hospital isn't free?" This was news to me. I thought hospitals were supported by taxes, like schools. "Someone has to pay the medical bills. In your case, who will that be?" We both shook our heads. "Let me be blunt. We are not going to release you until you tell us who to contact. Do you want to sit here all night? Aren't you getting tired? Don't you have school tomorrow?" The words in my head were, *you can't make me talk. You can't make me talk.* My eyes prickled from tiredness. Sergeant Copp reached behind him, grabbed the phone from the desk, and handed it to Joan. "Call someone," he said standing up. "First dial nine then dial the number." He went out of the room. Joan started crying. I dialed information. Luckily there was only one Waldman on Main Street.

Frau Waldman picked up on the first ring. I told her what happened, asked if she could contact Mrs. Adler. "I vill." she said.

"Could we call her?"

"No."

"Did she give you any information about Ruby? Where she lives or anything like that?"

"Yah. Hold on." She ruffled some papers. "You call her husband." She told me a number then said, "I call your mudder now." She hung up.

I dialed the number and a man picked up. "Hello is this Ruby's husband?"

"Yes."

"This is Sonya Adler. The girl . . . "

"Has something happened, Sonya?"

"Yes." The calm inside of me threatened to melt and I had to speak to it sternly, tell it everything depended upon it's staying in place. "Ruby . . . "

"Go on."

"Ruby . . . "

"Where are you?"

"At the White Plains hospital. Ruby's had a heart attack I think."

"I will be there in twenty minutes." I recognized him right away. He was the man who had come to the door that time but wouldn't come inside the apartment. The social worker with her clip board and a doctor in green scrubs intercepted him on his way toward us and lead him away to a far corner where he received the news. Then the three of them went out of the room. Sergeant Copp came to tell us we were no longer needed at the hospital. "Is Ruby going to die?"

"No. She's resting comfortably. I'm sure she'll be very happy to see her husband." He spoke into a walkie talkie and soon another policeman arrived. We sat in the back seat of his cruiser as if we were crooks. Now and then, I saw him check on us in the rearview mirror. He drove us to Scarsdale.

I didn't want to sleep alone in my room and was grateful to Joan for letting me sleep on her other twin bed. She helped me put on sheets and blankets, and that made me think maybe she was glad I'd be with her in the dark. As a safety precaution, we took a kitchen chair and jammed it up under the front door knob, a ploy we'd seen in a movie. We had no faith in the doorman Kyle as a protector. None of the other three apartments on our floor had been sold yet. There was no one on the eighth floor except us.

Because we weren't relatives, the hospital would give us no news of Ruby when we phoned. Joan and I drove there after school, saw Ruby hooked up to tubes in her bed. It surprised and troubled both Joan and me how uncomfortable it was to visit Ruby, especially when her husband was there. If we showed up while they were chatting, he in a chair next to her bed inclined toward her so he could hear her every word, her hand limp on the sheet, his large hand over hers, the flow between them congealed. He sat up at attention and spoke in a formal way to Joan and me. Ruby kept apologizing to us, and we had to keep reassuring her that we didn't mind staying with our father (a lie meant to release her from obligation), that we understood she was too ill to fulfill the agreement she'd made with our mother. Yes of course we'd explain to Mrs. Adler, of course she wouldn't blame Ruby. Sometimes when we arrived there were four or five black people there, men and women from Ruby's church. They were overly polite to us, offered us the candy they'd brought for Ruby, asked us about school. I didn't know if we brought tension into the room because we were white or because we were the daughters of Ruby's employer or because we were teenagers, or because we had nothing in common with the others. Whatever the reason, we were relieved when we heard that Ruby went home to Mount Vernon where she lived with her husband.

Joan and I felt like lost lambs alone in our apartment, and we felt like grownup women alone in our apartment. Ours was not a mother who believed money should be a problem for children. Joan and I both had charge cards for the major department stores and were allowed to sign for goods at the local grocer, dry cleaner, hardware store, and pharmacy. It wouldn't have occurred to us to abuse Mother's trust. We bought what we needed, mostly prepared food that didn't need cooking. We took for granted that I'd sleep in Joan's room rather than in my own. After finishing the last TV show of the evening, I went to the bathroom at my end of the apartment then returned to her end and got into the "guest" bed in her room. She complained that I made noise moving around and I complained that she made noise sniffling. "Will you lie still!" she scolded. I'd try. Then I'd drift off and be pulled awake by sniff! Sniff! "Stop sniffling!" But neither of us suggested that we sleep in separate rooms.

One day, there was a fat letter in the box addressed to Joan. She had been accepted at Carnegie Tech. That was her first choice so we shrieked and jumped around the lobby together. We carried the mail upstairs and sorted through the catalogues and flyers. There was a letter addressed to us in Mother's almost illegible handwriting. "Darlings, I return Saturday, May 16, at 3:00 p.m." She wrote the flight details. "Pick me up at La Guardia. I can't wait to see you both. Love, love, love you tons, Mommy." We had been living alone for two weeks.

Why wasn't I glad she was returning? Joan rattled the letter as if shaking a child. "How am I supposed to know how to get to La Guardia?" I wondered the same thing. "The day after tomorrow?" Joan said giving the letter a dirty look. "No way. I'm supposed to go to the Cloisters with Tommy." She went to the refrigerator, peered inside, and said, "Did you finish the barbecued chicken?" I nodded. "There's nothing to eat in here," she said. Then she leaned in closer. "Oh, good. There's still some potato salad." Eating from the cardboard container, she said, "Let her take a taxi."

Joan had no experience driving on highways. The demand that she ratchet up her driving nerve was an example of my mother's philosophy of child rearing. Her goal, she often said, was to make us independent. Joan was to get in the car, steer it onto the highway, follow the signs, and get to Queens. How could she ever learn to drive on highways if she didn't drive on highways? She stayed way over to the right almost hugging the railing and barked, "Oh, shut up stupid!" to all the cars that honked at her.

We missed the parking lot and had to exit the airport. "You were supposed to be watching!"

"I was watching!"

"Well, watch harder stupid!"

"Oh, shut up."

"You shut up. Just keep your eyes out for the sign. I can't be looking for the signs and driving at the same time. That's your job. Just do it."

"Oh, shut up. I am doing it."

"Well, if you were doing it I wouldn't have to be driving around this stupid place ten times. You think I like doing this? You think this is easy?"

"There it is!" I said. "Turn there! Joan! Turn there!"

"Where?"

"Where it said American!"

"Where did it say American?"

"Back there where I said."

"But you said it too late! I was already a million miles away from it."

"No you weren't. You could have turned."

"How could I have turned? I was way over in the left lane!"

"So we have to go all the way around again?"

"Yes, stupid. We do." I felt miserable. We were already a half hour late.

Amid the rivers of people hurrying along the corridors and the loud speakers announcing departures, arrivals, gate changes, she was standing by the gate searching for us with a mixture of worry and impatience. Expecting that I'd run to her with open arms, be relieved that she was still alive and home, I was astonished by the loathing that welled up at the sight of her. My revulsion was involuntary. It was in my body, and I didn't know why. When she caught sight of us, her face lit up with joy. She pushed through the crowd blind to everyone else, rushed to me with open arms, "Darling! Oh, my darling! It's so good to see you! I missed you so much!" and clasped me hard, then let go quickly when she felt how rigid I was. She shrank into herself like an injured turtle. Joan allowed herself to be clasped but didn't hug back. Mother's surprise at being thus greeted infuriated me. How did she think we would feel? She'd turned us into liars, trusted her dressmaker more than she trusted us, and only contacted us twice in the four months she was gone just to reassure herself that we were not betraying her secret. She seemed to have expected the excited chatter of a reunion but we said nothing. She didn't ask about Ruby. Instead, walking as a group toward baggage claim, Joan and I stood close to each other in an exclusive way and hurried along the corridor as if Mother was a tag-along. This was not planned. I was as surprised by our chilly reunion as my mother was. What exactly had she done wrong? We stood at baggage claim watching suitcases plop onto the conveyor belt then go around until someone yanked them up. We watched without speaking. After a few minutes, I glanced at my mother and at that exact second, she glanced at me and our eyes locked, both of us drenched in confusion.

"What do they do with tumors?" I asked from the back seat as Violet drove toward home. "Throw them away?"

Joan said. "Don't be gross."

"Did they show it to you?" My friend Ellen told me they showed her her appendix.

"No," Mother said.

"Didn't you want to see it?"

She glanced at me in the rearview mirror with a look that was too penetrating for what I thought was a frivolous question. "No," she said. "No, I didn't."

Joan and I helped lug our mother's bags from the elevator into our front hall. "Where's Ruby?" Without waiting for an answer, she strode into her bedroom. We heard her pulling up the shades. At her door she said to us as we stood in the hall, "What's going on?"

Joan said, "As if you care."

"Where's Ruby?"

"Home," I said.

"What are you talking about? Where's Ruby?"

Joan carried one of the suitcases into Mother's bedroom and heaved it up on the sofa bed. Then she went out of the room and into her own bedroom and closed the door, leaving a trail of chill.

"What's going on? Where's Ruby?"

"She had a heart attack."

"Ruby?"

"In the kitchen."

"When?"

"I don't know. A while ago."

"Have you been here by yourselves?"

"Yes."

"For how long?"

"I don't know."

"Is Ruby in the hospital?"

"No."

"Well where is she? You're making me pull teeth. Why don't you just tell me? Where's Ruby? What happened? Why didn't you go stay with your father?"

"And tell him what?"

"I don't know. You could have thought of something."

"Like what?"

"Oh, you're impossible, Sonya. You're just impossible. Tell me what happened to Ruby."

No. I would not tell her. I left her standing in her room and went to my room and closed the door. I was ashamed of being so cold. Feeling miserable, I put on Rachmaninoff's second piano concerto, turned the volume up to huge, and felt comforted being enveloped in the sound.

Later, when we all got hungry, we came out of our rooms and met in the kitchen. "Shall we go out?" Mother said. "Get Chinese?" We nodded and went back to our rooms to get a jacket. "Come in here a minute," Mother called from her room. "I've brought you a present." She handed me a package. I pulled the wrapping off and saw a light blue cashmere sweater. How could I ever wear that thing? It would be like buttoning myself inside the trauma of the last few months. It reeked of lies and hospital and worry. "They call that color robin's egg," my mother said. I just stood there with it in my hand. Joan's present was a sweater but not the same color. "They call that one toffee." Joan said nothing, just set the sweater down on Mother's bureau and went out of the room and back across the living room to her room. Apparently, Frau Waldman never told Mother about Ruby. I was sure that if Mother had known, she would have returned to continue her cancer treatment at a hospital in New York. I said, "Thank you," and carried the sweater to my room and closed the door.

CHAPTER ELEVEN

. . . .

Like a dust storm, the SATs rolled toward me and my classmates. We were helpless to avoid them. We believed our lives would be ruined if our scores were low. Getting into a good college was vital to existence. It was impossible to complain about the pressure to my mother because to her everything about college was touched with glamour. Her daughters would go to that shimmering, elusive place and never suffer the humiliation that she did. "Oh, you'll do all right," she said. She was proud that I was smart enough to take the SATs, had no idea how it felt to be made to choose a college without knowing one from the other and without wanting to go to any of them. My father said everything there is to learn is learned after college.

My boyfriend Pete's future was clear to him. He would major in physics and that would lead to a career in science. I would major in English because that was the subject I found easiest. That major would lead exactly nowhere, and it wasn't even supposed to. College was supposed to lead to a husband and marriage. I was supposed to meet him during those four years and marry him when I graduated. Pete couldn't decide between MIT and Cornell. "Opportunity keeps knocking," he said. "It's banging and banging! Shut up, opportunity! Leave me in peace!"

I had to write application essays saying why a particular school was right for me. Who was me? Which me did they want to hear from, the one who got A's on her English papers, the one who was a good swimmer at camp, or the me who sat in front of a full-length mirror with legs apart hunting for the hole where the Tampax was supposed to go? How many holes were down there?

Three? One for pee, one for poop and one for babies? Is that how it worked?

University of Chicago was right down the street from Grandpa Greenstone. Being close to relatives seemed a good reason for choosing a school. I made an appointment for an interview and got myself from Scarsdale to the Sheraton Hotel in Manhattan. A gilded ballroom with high ceilings was full of long tables with young supplicants on one side and their interviewers across from them each pair leaning toward each other in an effort to shut out the discussions on either side. I'd never seen so many people my same age gathered in one place. There were hundreds of them sitting in chairs next to the walls waiting for their name to be called. I was the only one dressed up in heels and basic black. The other girls looked like they knew how to do orienteering. The boys were scruffy, in jeans and plaid shirts. The interviewers were men young enough to have been recent graduates. They set themselves apart by wearing suits and ties. I didn't want to be interviewed by someone who could be my boyfriend. I wanted an older man who would ask me easy questions in a tender way and be smitten by my clear complexion and sparkly eyes, a man so old I'd be free to pour out my entire personality on him.

After I waited quite some time in one of the chairs lined up against the wall, my name was called out. It was humbling that I was so real to myself, so important to myself, yet the usher had no idea which person was Sonya Adler and looked from one girl to the next to see which one would stand up and identify herself. I'd never been so anonymous before. The wide world had no idea who I was and couldn't have cared less. I followed the usher to an empty chair at one of the long tables. Across from me was a dark-haired young man with sideburns, steel-rimmed glasses, tweed jacket, and a bow tie. On my right the applicant and the interviewer were laughing about something and on my left the applicant was saying sentences that sounded brainy. My interviewer glanced at my application then asked a most reasonable question because he'd just seen that this candidate intended to be an English major. Who was my favorite author? Blank. Author? Nothing. A blizzard of snow in my mind. "Who is my favorite author?" I couldn't think of one name. Not one. Then, "Hemingway!" I'd never read one word of Hemingway. Not one word.

The interviewer said, "Do you think Nick Adams is kble ystobblu, or more mskdlek sleifjkdls when he flaidhen and the taldkure gjakdles?"

I had no idea what the man was saying, had never heard such big words. He waited for my answer. I said, "No."

He said, "No what?"

"No, I don't think so."

As surprised by my answer as I was by his question, we were done. He had nothing more to say to me. We were supposed to converse for ten minutes and during that time he was supposed to discover if I would be a credit to the University of Chicago, but he'd discovered upon his first question that I would not be. While others around us talked, bantered, laughed, I sat there in silence because the interviewer didn't ask me anything else. When our ten minutes was finished, he blushed when he stood up and shook my hand.

On the train back to Scarsdale, I told myself that being pretty or smart or clever or talented is not what matters. What matters is how a person handles herself under pressure and I'd failed. I was weak, useless, an idiot. And this wasn't the only interview. There would be others, each one more humiliating than the last. No one was in the apartment when I got there. Joan was in Pittsburgh at college.

Fall turned into winter, the college essays were done, the application fees sent in, and now all we had to do was wait. My mother and I had lived in that Scarsdale apartment alone together for about six months. We had dinner together most nights and watched TV together, but we never spoke about anything important. One night she came into my room while I was blasting the Scheherazade Suite. "Turn that down," she said.

"You."

She fiddled with the knobs, made it go all treble, then all bass, but found the right button at last and muted the music. She sat on the edge of my bed. "Aunt Dovey Lee is moving to Rome."

"I know."

"She has to sell her house."

"I know. Wiley's mad."

"It won't matter to Wiley. He's in college."

"Where's he going to go on school breaks?"

Dovey Lee and Jack were moving to Italy because Grandpa Greenstone had selected his son Alan to be the next president of Greenstone Enterprises even though his son-in-law Jack was a better businessman. Furious, Jack quit. It was Jack who opened up foreign markets. He was energetic and risk-taking. Uncle Alan was conservative, believed a penny saved is a penny earned. Dovey Lee owned twenty-five percent of Greenstones and demanded that her father buy her out. With that money, she and Jack bought into an international poultry company, Agricola Lazio, with headquarters in Rome.

"Dovey Lee is afraid that if she leaves her house empty vandals will break in. I've agreed to stay in the house until it's sold."

"What?"

"There's nothing for me here. You have your whole life ahead of you."

"But how long will it take to sell?"

"Dovey Lee has arranged a membership for me at Highland Acres Country Club."

"What?"

"You know that house. It would cost a fortune to leave the lights on in every room every night. Someone needs to be there when the brokers show it, someone has to keep it looking lived in. I'm flying out on Tuesday. I've asked Ruby to come stay in the apartment with you. I was lucky to get her. Would you prefer to stay with your father?"

"You're leaving me here by myself?"

"No. I just told you. Ruby will cook your dinner and make breakfast for you. You have your boyfriend Pete, you have your school work."

"But suppose she gets sick again?"

"She won't. She's in good health."

"But suppose she does."

"If anything like that happens, I'll come right home."

I got up from my bed and turned the volume on my record

player up to earsplitting. On the one hand I was angry, but on the other I could see my mother's point of view. There really was nothing for her in Scarsdale and she wasn't getting any younger. She *had* to get re-married. A grown woman without a husband was a disgrace, so we all thought. The suburbs of Chicago would be fresh hunting grounds.

My concern was getting into college. My first choice was Connecticut College for Women. My guidance counselor suggested it. She said I should apply to the University of Wisconsin as my safe school. I dreaded going there. I'd be lost. Also, it was taken for granted that I'd meet my husband at college. The joke was that girls went to college to earn their MRS degree. I thought this was insulting but believed it. I figured that if I went to the University of Wisconsin and got engaged, I'd end up living in Wisconsin, and I didn't want to live in Wisconsin though I'd never been there. My boyfriend Pete was immune to the worry about college. He'd been accepted early at Cornell so all he wanted to do was get drunk on the weekends. His father told him that if he learned how to fix a car, he'd buy him one. We drove in Pete's old Ford, whose every shake and rattle Pete understood, to the Candlelight Inn in Scarsdale where the waitress examined my driver's license doctored by me to say that I was not sixteen but eighteen, the legal age for alcohol. We ordered screwdrivers because we liked the taste of orange juice better than the taste of whiskey. We couldn't taste the vodka in our drinks and drank them down like soda. There was a jukebox, and Pete and I danced close. I loved feeling how excited he was. He whispered that I smelled delicious and I could hear him breathing in my ear on that small wooden dance floor surrounded by couples at small round tables each with a candle lit in the middle of it. We were both plastered when he drove me home. We arrived safely only by the grace of the invisible guardian who watches over drunk teenagers. Pete believed as I did that it was forbidden to have sex before marriage so this was never an argument. We just kissed and rolled around on my bed and then he went home. Getting into my pajamas, I wondered at the slimy stuff in my underpants, touched it then gave it a sniff. Yes, it did have an odor unlike any other. I wondered why Mother Nature made sexual smells so much less pleasant than the smell of lilacs or ripe melon or mowed lawn. Tigers, for all their majestic symmetry, smelled horrible up close at the zoo. When I took the lid off of my mother's hamper, a pungent female smell came up from the clothes inside.

Joan had not waited for marriage, she told me on the phone. "You did it? You went all the way?" That she would break this rule, that the rule *could* be broken and by a nice girl who wasn't the least bit cheap, gave me a teetering feeling. "With Freddy Rosenthal?"

"No. Buddy Wingate."

"Who's Buddy Wingate?"

"A communist."

"What did it feel like?"

"I don't know."

"Did it hurt?"

"Yes, sort of. You have to get used to it. Is Mommy still in Evanston?"

"She doesn't call you?"

"Never."

"Why?"

"She says she doesn't want to bother me."

"How'd you meet a communist?"

"In the bookstore."

"Where'd you do it?"

"He has an apartment off campus."

"Do you love him?"

"Yes."

"Are you going to marry him?"

"Are you kidding? I'm never getting married."

"You aren't?"

"Not if I can help it. Did you hear from Connecticut?"

"No."

"Why on earth would you apply to a girls' school? You must be out of your mind."

A skinny letter from a college was bad news, and a fat letter with forms inside meant acceptance. All we talked about at school was who got in where, who was on the wait list. Some of the girls in my class received rejection or acceptance letters from Connecticut College, so I knew such a letter would be waiting for me, yet when I went to the mailbox it was empty. "Wasn't the mail delivered today?" I asked Kyle.

Kyle showed me a wicked smile. "Yes. It was delivered."

"Wasn't there any for Adler?"

"Might have been."

"But was there?"

"Maybe yes, maybe no."

"What are you talking about? Was there or wasn't there?"

"Could be, couldn't be."

"What do you mean? What are you talking about?"

"What would your mother say if she knew what time your beau left the apartment?"

"What? What are you talking about?"

"Must be kinda fun having Mother away."

I hurried to the elevator, my heart pounding from anger. The next day, I opened the mailbox and it was empty again. On the third day of an empty mailbox, I phoned my mother in Evanston. No answer. She was often not there. I phoned much later that night. "Kyle won't give me the mail."

"What do you mean Kyle won't give you the mail?"

"He won't."

"What do you mean? You have a key don't you?"

"Yes."

"Just open the mailbox."

"I did. There was nothing in it."

"Then there was no mail."

"But there was none yesterday either."

"That's not Kyle's fault."

"He won't give me the mail."

"Don't be silly, Sonya. If there's mail, Kyle will put it in the box. That's his job."

Was there some federal law against interfering mail? I had no idea. I was appalled to find myself the victim of an adult bully. I knew there was some board that governed the apartment building but I had no idea where the board met or who the people were who sat on that board or even if my sort of problem mattered to them. If I told my father, he'd know my boyfriend stayed past midnight.

"How much do you want that mail?" Kyle asked in a suggestive way the next time I opened the empty mailbox. He ran his eyes down my body and my heart leapt up. I was just home from my friend Ellen's where we'd experimented with eye shadow and bright red lipstick. My hair was up on top of my head in the hairdo she'd given me. "I'm going to tell on you," I said and cursed the trembles in my voice.

Kyle laughed. "You do that."

To outsmart Kyle, I pretended to have no interest in the mail and each day walked past the wall of brass boxes. The problem was that if I got accepted I had to let the school know right away or else I'd lose my place, according to the grapevine. All my friends had received their letters. Everyone felt sorry for Ellen not being accepted anywhere and we wondered how she would go on living, especially because her sister was at Smith. This would probably happen to me. Kids at school would say, "What are you going to do now? Take a year off?" Off from what? From life? Behind my back they'd whisper, "Did you hear about Sonya? She didn't get in anywhere. Not even her safe school!"

Probably Kyle didn't know what to do with all the accumulated junk mail because one day I opened the box and it was crammed full. I thumbed through the flyers from Sears and Gristedes and found two fat letters, one from the University of Wisconsin and the other from Connecticut College. They were both happy to inform me . . . I burst into tears then realized I had no one to tell. I couldn't share my relief with my friend Ellen. She was hiding in her bedroom from the shame of not getting in anywhere. Pete never suffered from college pressure so he'd say, "Of course you got in." I couldn't call Joan because she'd say, "You'd choose Connecticut over Wisconsin? You must be nuts." She chose Carnegie Tech because there were four boys to every one girl.

It was a sunny day when I drove to New Rochelle to tell my father that I'd been accepted and that the tuition at Connecticut College was twice that of Carnegie Tech. He was supposed to pay for college as per the divorce decree and it was my understanding, based on some fluffy idea of his career, that he could easily afford to. He was a Jewish man and Jewish men, unless they were my Uncle Norman, sent their children to college and paid for it.

Behind the wheel of my mother's new Buick, two-toned blue with giant fins in the back, a sensible choice according to Grandpa Greenstone who paid for it, my heart began to thump in anticipation of fighting with my father. He was pushing a lawn mower when I arrived, a task once performed by a gardener. I parked in front of the house because once when I parked in the driveway he complained that I was boxing him in. "But if you needed to leave couldn't you just ask me to move my car?"

"I shouldn't need to. You should know tisn't polite to block a person's driveway."

Dressed in a sleeveless undershirt that showed his gray chest hair, he adjusted his old Yankees cap, leaned on his rake and said, "New car is it?" I went forward and gave him a dutiful peck on the cheek. Why hadn't he shaved? Usually he was fastidious.

"A Buick," I said.

"Spiffy," he said. He continued mowing, the sound of the blades turning announcing that he wasn't going to stop what he was doing, because he didn't care if I visited him or not. He thought I was neglectful and was sour about it each time I visited.

"Annabelle here?" I said.

"Inside," he said and flicked his chin impatiently toward the living room window, which I took to mean she was watching television instead of helping him with yard work.

"Daddy," I said. "I got into Connecticut College where I want to go. It's my first choice."

"Zat so?"

"Do you have a moment to sit and talk? Have tea maybe?"

I left him standing there in the garden. From the kitchen, the television in the living room sounded like a distant crowd cheering. I turned on the flame under the kettle and went into the living room. "Hey, Annabelle," I said.

Dressed in a red caftan, she was stroking Rinso on her lap. She turned and said, "Hello."

"How's everything?"

"Oh, everything's just fine."

"That's good."

I retreated to the kitchen, put some cookies on a plate, filled two mugs with hot water and put a tea bag next to each one and carried the tray out to the yard. My father indicated I should set the tray on the wrought iron table under the apple tree, and we both sat down on lawn chairs. "One tea bag is enough," he said. "You don't need two." He dunked the bag in his mug then handed the spoon with the soggy tea bag to me. I dunked it in my cup. "It's a waste to use two," he said. I took a sip of weak tea. "In fact," he said. "You can use this tea bag a third time. Tisn't any reason to throw it out."

"Daddy," I said. "I have to send in a deposit."

"Zat so?"

"Otherwise, I lose my spot. We have to send the first semester tuition by June."

"What's the cost?" I told him. He opened his eyes wide. "That's twice what I pay for Joan!"

"I know."

"Why should I pay double? That's ridiculous! Go some other place. Didn't you get in any other place?"

"University of Wisconsin."

"How much does that one cost?" I told him. "Then you'll go there."

"But I don't want to. Connecticut is a much better school."

"Nonsense. Everything there is to learn is learned after college." A robin bounced on the lawn, inclined its head to listen for worms beneath the grass, then bounced to another spot. My father stirred his tea nervously, clinking the spoon against the side of the cup. "I'll give you what I give Joan. Not a penny more."

I couldn't tell him that I was afraid to go to Wisconsin because it was so far from home and there would be so many students there and the teachers wouldn't pay any attention to me sitting way in the back in huge lecture halls, and none of them would make a fuss over me the way the English teachers did in high school and I was afraid of sororities, of being rejected by other girls, afraid of fraternities where there were kegs of beer and boys got drunk and said lewd things, afraid of big football games and people in raccoon coats leaping to their feet to bellow forth, and pretty blond cheerleaders waving pom poms and showing their crotches as they leapt in the air with their legs wide apart. That school was too big and loud. I wasn't up to it. Quite unexpectedly, the sting of tears prickled my eyes and sent the taste of salt into my throat. This was not part of the plan. I never cried in front of my father. Whine and nag, yes, but a display of actual distress, never. My father had been on earth many years longer than I, so if he said everything there is to learn is learned after college then it probably was true. He was telling me that it didn't matter which school I went to. The University of Wisconsin was easy to get into. I could never be proud to say I went there. Anybody could get in there and everybody knew anybody could get in there. Tears were rolling in fast like a tsunami. I wailed, "But it's my future!" and put my head down on my arms so he wouldn't see my weeping face. Part of me was sobbing and part of me was saying get a grip. But I couldn't find the turn off button. I was so tired of nobody taking care of me and now I'd have to go be all alone at a huge university full of cheerful blond coeds. I felt him tapping my arm with impatient, rigid fingers. "Tut tut," he said. "Don't be so dramatic."

Everything in me clamped shut. I stood up, left the tea things for him to clean up, and walked across the lawn vowing to never see him again plus if I ever had children I'd never let him near them. I got into the Buick and drove home to Scarsdale.

"I'll ask Dad," my mother said on the phone. "There's no reason on earth that Dovey Lee and Alan's children can go to the schools of their choice and you can't. Why should my children have less than theirs?"

CHAPTER TWELVE

....

C onnecticut College was in New London, a seedy place with lots of bars, one small movie house, and an elderly hotel that seemed slightly ashamed of itself. In a taxi from the train station driving toward the college, I saw the Coast Guard Academy, a conglomeration of red brick buildings that seemed to shine with orderliness. Young men in navy blue uniforms were marching in formation while the biggest American flag I'd ever seen in my life waved high above them. Across the street was Connecticut College, a series of modest gray stone buildings that seemed like mousy librarians. They faced a grassy quadrangle where girls in short skirts and shin guards whacked a field hockey ball.

Everywhere there were parents unloading station wagons, girls saying goodbye to their dogs, fathers carrying lamps and typewriter cases. I lugged my suitcase up some wide stairs, down a hall, and into the room designated on my housing form. I expected to find the other girl assigned to that room. I knew nothing about her except that she was from Atlanta, Georgia, and her name was Elaine. That she was from so far away gave me post purchase reassurance. This college, apparently, was highly regarded all across the nation.

The room was empty but the roommate had been there. She'd made up the bed near the window. I saw her perfume and lotion bottles on top of one of the bureaus and her dictionary and expensive electric typewriter on one of the desks. I unpacked, hung some clothes in the closet, put my sweaters neatly folded in the empty bureau, made the bed up and sat on it to wait for Elaine to return. We would go together to the required orientation meeting, maybe get lost together trying to find the auditorium.

The dorm was full of girls moving in, the voices of mothers and fathers and the squeals of girls being reunited with girls they knew from before. How did they know each other? I didn't know anyone. When my roommate did not return, I found my own way to the auditorium, and took a seat surrounded entirely, front, back, sides, by girls my age. I'd never seen so many girls gathered in one place. Many of them were knitting.

Above the click, click of knitting needles, the school president introduced herself. She was a middle-aged woman with gray hair and sensible shoes. Standing at a podium, she said into the microphone, "Girls, you are the privileged few." I didn't know what she meant. Did she mean we were better than everyone else? How could she say such a thing? I had never felt so lonely in my life. What was privileged about feeling so bereft? She went on to say that because we were different from everyone else, set apart, the world expected us to contribute. Was she talking about money? Did she mean I was privileged compared to my Woodbridge cousins, Claire and Avery, who would go to work right after high school? I understood that college was an advantage that was handed to me. All I had to do was get good grades. I didn't feel privileged to be among that roomful of scrubbed and polished girls. I was on the conveyor belt of life.

I'd been plunked down amid a tribe of immaculately groomed young women, no rough edges, nothing fly away, nothing slouchy. Many were blond with small noses and coiffed hair. They wore blouses tucked into plaid kilt-like skirts. It seemed they all had a circle pin on the round collar of their blouses. It was an announcement in gold of something I couldn't translate, a badge of some sort.

Assembly over, groups of three or four of them walked together across the quad back to the dorms, chatting in the rapid way of girls catching up. How did they all know each other on the very first day of school? I hoped my roommate would be waiting for me. She was probably feeling just as lost as I was. Maybe we'd unpack our records and discover we had the same taste in music. Maybe she'd be an English major too. Maybe we'd have the same sense of humor and laugh our heads off about something.

A startling sight awaited in my dorm room, twin girls. They were identical, both with frizzy dark hair and thick glasses. They were busy unpacking books and did not greet me. They seemed a self-sufficient unit, two beings wrapped in a kind of obliviousness, almost like insects who don't care if you stand there and watch them. Chatting in a southern accent, they glanced at me as I sat on my bed. "Elaine?" I said and looked from one to the other. "I'm your roommate, Sonya." She nodded in a way that meant obviously I was the roommate otherwise I wouldn't be sitting on the roommate's bed. After several minutes of arranging and chatting, they got up and without saying goodbye went out of the room. This was a blow. I'd been assigned a roommate who didn't need a friend.

I went next door to introduce myself. There were four or five girls in the room, some sitting on the beds and others cross-legged on the floor. It seemed I'd stepped into a meeting so I was going to retreat but a lanky fawn of a girl standing in front of a mirror picking something out of the edge of her eye said, "And who do we have here? I'm Inky." She made me feel welcome just by turning her gaze on me. "My last name's Blackwell." She gave a helpless shrug and said, "Thus the Inky. They gave it to me at Miss Porter's." The other girls paused their conversation when I entered and each one told me her name and then when I'd taken a seat at the end of one of the twin beds, they went back to what they were talking about.

Teed said, "You can't ask Todd Coddington."

Elizabeth said, "Why not?"

Blanche said, "Who is he?"

Elizabeth said, "He's a Walcott on his mother's side."

Anne shook her head. "Your grandmother will not be pleased. His mother had him in the public schools until grade six."

Elizabeth said, "What about George Farrington?"

"Can't," Teed said. "He's escorting Suzi Howe the weekend before."

"She's coming out this season? Isn't she still in Switzerland?"

Were these the privileged few? I learned that they knew each other from boarding school, had been away from their parents since they were very young. There was a ranking among them, highest being girls whose coming out parties were at the Waldorf

Astoria, lowest were the girls who would "come out" at their country clubs. They all had to choose two male escorts. Some boys would do, others would not depending not on the boy's personality but on his family, best being a family that included politicians, preferably state governors. All of the girls were afraid of disgracing their parents. They all had the same way of speaking, with a tinge of an English accent, and they all dressed alike and seemed to announce by their very presence that there is nothing more important than conforming. Their struggle to please others was endless. Imposing that struggle upon others was inconsiderate. Thus, the inexpressive faces, the erect posture, the correct smile at the correct time.

To express personality through dress was in poor taste. To express personality at all was in poor taste. The debutantes set the standard at Connecticut College. We knew which one was the wealthiest. Her father worked for the government for a dollar a year. Her grandmother took her to Paris over Christmas vacation, and she came back with clothes designed by Pierre Cardin. She opened her closet and showed them to me. "You are so lucky," I said. She said, "You jest. Well maybe your fittings don't take as long as mine do." Was my father right? Should I have gone to Wisconsin?

By the end of freshman year, a gold circle pin was on my round collar. My blouse was tucked into a tartan kilt. On my feet, blue and white saddle shoes and on my wrist a single gold bangle. My sister Joan, in Pittsburgh, was wearing black knee-high boots, a leather jacket with fringe on the sleeves, tight jeans, dangling earrings, Bakelite bangles up to her elbows, and a black velvet ribbon choker. Her curly black hair was down to the middle of her back. She changed the shape of her eyes with a thick line of black like Nefertiti. Her design teacher called her Beauty right in front of the whole class.

Television in my dorm lobby showed white adults screaming at small black children and protesters being pushed back by fire hoses. Pete, at Cornell, was inhaling weed while at my school we were expelled if caught with wine in our room. During second semester, via telephone, Pete and I decided to break up. We were so far away from each other and we wanted to try out other people. It did occur to me that *other people* were more available to him than to me. They were in his classes and living in a room next door, while I had to be in my dorm by ten every night. He guffawed when I told him. "You have a curfew? You?" He could stay out as late as he wanted. During the week before exams, *reading week*, I would be expelled if I left the campus for any reason. Pete laughed when I told him this. "Sonya. You're in a nunnery!"

On Fridays, the bathrooms in the dorm were crowded with girls taking showers and shaving their armpits and leaning in close to the mirror with tweezers. We took the train every weekend to service the boys at Harvard, Yale, and Wesleyan. While just last year those boys sat next to us in high school, now they were considered adult enough to make their own rules while we, being girls, had to be cloistered. The boys never came to our dry campus where there was nothing to do. We always went to them with freshly shaved legs and silky hair perfumed by our youth and shampoo. They were expected to pay for the motels where we slept, but we paid for the train tickets. While America was erupting, my biggest concern was getting a date for the Harvard/Yale game and finding a husband to pay the bills after graduation. I became fluent in shapes of diamond rings—emerald, pear, marquise—and knew how to describe the jewel thrust into my face for inspection by the latest lucky duck who just got engaged.

CHAPTER THIRTEEN

·····························

All students at Connecticut College were required to go to chapel every Sunday morning. The church, next to the library, was one of those white clapboard structures with a steeple, so charming in New England town centers. If we skipped going in to hear a sermon about the power of Good, we were supposed to tattle on ourselves. If we decided not to sit in the pew and sing about saints marching in, it was our obligation to report ourselves to Honor Court. We were not to be policed by adult authorities but by our fellow students, the judges on Honor Court. We elected them mostly based on their academic achievement and their talent for being cordial to everyone. *Admonish* was a word I first heard when the Honor Code was explained to the freshman class. It meant that we were not only supposed to tattle on ourselves but we were supposed to remind others who might be doing wrong to report themselves. Did that apply to the girl across the hall who was sleeping with her English professor? We were especially supposed to admonish a girl we caught cheating on an exam. The first time I skipped chapel and did not report myself I lived in fear for several days. After that, I skipped chapel and didn't worry about it.

We had two ways of meeting boys. We could be fixed up or we could meet at mixers. The most important date of the year was the Harvard/Yale football game. If you didn't have a date, you might as well kill yourself. You were pathetic. We all knew who had a date for the game and who did not. Those who had been invited took a train from New London to New Haven and slept in a motel. The boarding school girls had an advantage because they arrived knowing boys at the Ivy League schools. One of those girls fixed me up with a boy named Bob White. I thought it odd his parents would give him a bird's name. He met me at the New Haven train station. I didn't like his face. But there we were.

We left my suitcase at the motel he'd booked for me then went to the Yale Bowl where spectators wore raccoon coats and drank beer and smoked cigars and shrieked when there was a touchdown. It was raw November, white sky, no leaves on the trees. Some of the people in the stadium had blankets over their legs but we didn't. I was icy cold and couldn't have cared less whether the Harvard Crimson or the Yale Bulldogs won. I understood football, had been going to professional games since grammar school because my friend Betsy's father was Marty Glickman, the announcer for the New York Giants. Here I was watching college boys and, when one of them ran the wrong way and made a touchdown for the rival team and everyone was going crazy from anger, I thought it was funny.

After the game, there was a dance at a fraternity house. It was awful to be there in my basic black sheath and string of pearls with someone I didn't like and who didn't like me. When the party ended, Bob White drove me to the motel and without asking came inside where he insisted that I sleep with him. I said no, he said yes, I said no and after a while I became afraid because even though he was short, he was beefy, a real Yale bulldog. The motel room was big enough for only a twin sized bed, a cheap room in a cheap place, but I didn't blame him for this because he was just a student. Girls were not allowed to stay in the Yale dorms. "What do you mean no?" he said and he came at me and we wrestled as he tried to force his lips onto my neck and face. I said, "Stop it, get off me!" He shoved me onto the bed, and I twisted away from him and stood up. He said, "I'm not paying for this room for nothing," and lunged at me. "Take that damn dress off." I smacked him, shoved him, kicked him, and at last he left the room slamming the door behind him. I locked it and lay trembling in the motel bed my eyes wide open. I was full of beer that I didn't want but drank just to be polite and to fit in. He was supposed to pick me up in the morning and drive me to the New Haven train station but he didn't. I had never been to New Haven before, had no idea where I was in relation to the train station. Maybe it was around the corner and I could walk or maybe it was a fifty-dollar cab ride. I'd never-called a taxi by myself. In Manhattan, my father just held up his hand and a cab pulled up and we got in. Never having stayed in a motel before I didn't know there was an office where there was probably someone in charge. Added to the worry of the train station was the worry about finishing my term paper on the origins of the King Lear legend, which I was discovering had something to do with salt. I had assumed that I'd take a morning train from New Haven to New London and work on the paper for the rest of the afternoon and into the night. At last, I noticed yellow pages on the bedside table. I phoned a cab. It took about forty minutes for it to show up. When we got to the station, the meter read $15.82. I only had seven dollars with me. "I don't have that much money," I said.

"Well, darling, you're going to have to call somebody and get it."

"I don't know anybody."

"Then why did you call a taxi?"

"I didn't know how much it would cost."

"So you're saying you want me to pay for your taxi ride."

"No."

"Yes. That's what you're saying. I have to turn in as much money as the meter says."

"I don't know what to do."

"You don't?"

"No."

"You can't think of anything?"

"No."

"You think all you gotta do is turn those big brown peepers on a guy. Can't blame you. It works. Do I look like an old man to you?"

"Yes."

"How old do you think I am?"

"Seventy?"

He guffawed. "I'm forty-six." He was talking to me in the rear view mirror. "What were you doing in that motel?"

"Sleeping."

"All by your lonesome?"

"Yes."

I took seven dollars out of my wallet. He grabbed it out of my hand and said, "Christ, I hate college girls."

I already had my return ticket but now didn't have enough for a taxi back to campus. So I walked with my suitcase back to school under freezing November skies. I had achieved one of the great feats of freshman year. I'd had a date with a Yaley for the Harvard/Yale game.

We ranked our dates according to their college. Best was Harvard, then Yale, then Brown. Wesleyan and Trinity were lumped together as merely okay. Coast Guard Academy cadets were the lowest. I saw them in their uniforms, walking around our campus with their girlfriends, and winced for the girl who couldn't get anybody better. Nevertheless, with a bunch of other girls, as the weather was warming in late April, I walked across the street to the Coast Guard Academy for their spring mixer.

In a ballroom decorated with swags of American flags, there was a sea of young men in white uniforms and a band made up of Coast Guard musicians in blue uniforms, and a table of tea sandwiches, cookies, and soda. I stood there waiting for someone to ask me to dance and was grateful when someone did. After a while, the music stopped and the officer in charge announced a Sadie Hawkins dance meaning the girls asked the boys. Usually I handled my shyness by asking whatever boy was standing next to me. What difference did it make? It was just a stupid dance. This time I decided to find the handsomest boy in the room and ask him. I took my time. I walked among the spotless white uniforms selecting, not him, not him, not him and, just as I was deciding I'd sit this one out if the music started up before I could find someone, I spotted the handsomest boy in the room. He looked like Paul Newman. He said, "I was hoping someone would ask me." I was seventeen and had never before felt the power of chemistry. While I liked my high school boyfriend Pete, enjoyed his company and respected him, smelling him never made me feel like fainting.

Dick Boyce took me in his arms and my knees buckled. I

actually had to hold on to him while we danced or I would have fallen to the floor. He walked me back to my dorm and came to visit me every day. I helped him write his essays and term papers. He helped me with physics, taught me about momentum, vectors, inertia, and critical mass.

It was during one of our frequent discussions about being virgins that I learned he believed in hell. "As a concept," I said the first time he told me. "As another way of describing being uncomfortable."

Sitting on our favorite boulder in the woods behind campus he said, "No. Not as a concept."

"You mean you really believe there's a fiery place under the earth where you go if you're bad?"

"Yes."

"You're kidding."

"No."

"You're telling me you believe there's literally a place with flames and devils where you'll go if you're bad?"

"Yes."

"So does that mean you believe there's heaven some place above the clouds?"

"Yes."

"You're kidding."

"No."

"But Dick. That's so dumb."

"Not to me."

"But you believe it because you were taught that. If they didn't teach it to you like they didn't teach it to me, you wouldn't believe it. I mean it's not an actual fact."

"You could say that about everything."

"No you can't. If they didn't teach me about gravity it wouldn't mean this pebble would float up instead dropping down."

"Have they proven there's no hell?"

"I think so. I mean wouldn't they know by now?"

"How deep do you think scientists can explore? How deep down do you think they can go? How do you know there aren't souls suffering in the deepest magma?" He saw me shrug. "See?

Don't be so sure of yourself, Miss Big Brown Eyes. You don't know everything, Miss Soft Skin, Miss Smell So Delicious."

I lived at my father's that summer, got a job as a day camp counselor. Dick Boyce went home for the summer to a small town in Minnesota where he lived with his Lutheran parents. His junior year started a week before my sophomore year so he invited me to New London to visit.

Girls were not allowed in the Academy dorms so Dick got a room for me at the Mohican Hotel. I think we both suspected what was going to happen. For me, having sex before marriage meant I'd ruin my reputation. I'd turn into a cheap girl. For him it meant he'd burn in hell, a consequence that should have seemed more dire than mine but instead seemed equal.

Mother Nature prodded me, "What reputation are you protecting? You don't have any reputation." Just as I believed I had a *record* and the bad things I did would *go on my record*, I believed that I had a *reputation*. Mother Nature said, "You don't live in a small town. No one's standing around the pump talking about you. If you don't tell, no one will know."

Mother Nature must have somehow made Dick Boyce wonder if hell might be a pretend place. We decided together that the time had come. It was a decision. We were both tired of being excluded from the In-The-Know club. I knew he would never tell, and he knew I wouldn't either. We didn't pretend that sex might lead to marriage. I had no intention of being the wife of a Coast Guard officer. I couldn't imagine anything more confining. I never said that to him just as he never said to me that he couldn't marry someone who didn't celebrate Christmas or Easter.

From the window in our room at the Mohican Hotel, we only saw the brick wall of the airshaft. No sunlight came in to brighten the faded upholstery or the dowdy bedspread. I liked the run-down quality of the place. It was just an old room and anyone, even us, could be comfortable in it. We were both modest. I made him turn around while I took off my clothes and hurried under the covers. He made me turn my head while he took off his clothes and got into the bed next to me. I pulled the covers up to my chin. We embraced and it began. I think we both thought the act just happened, that there was some magnetic force down there that would attach him to me. But he had to find the place. I didn't exactly know where it was. Somewhere down there. Was I supposed to guide him to it? Was he supposed to find it himself? We rolled around and he did find it and then it was over and I thought, what was so great about that? Why does everyone go on and on about that? Dick said, "I think we have to practice." When he got up to go to the bathroom he wrapped himself in a sheet so I wouldn't see him naked.

I floated back to the train station, floated onto the train, floated back to my father's house and treated him with great tenderness because I was a woman at last and he, poor dear soul, didn't know I had drifted into another realm.

When I returned to college for sophomore year, Dick Boyce was waiting for me. One day when we were walking in the woods, the trees ablaze with color, we came upon a discarded refrigerator carton. This became our hideaway. We put pillows in there and blankets and made love over and over again then lay next to each other talking about God and our studies. The bright leaves fell off the trees and made a crunchy sound when we walked to our hideaway. Then the winds came and blew the last remaining leaves off the branches and high above us geese flew in a V to a warmer place. Then it rained. One day it snowed. Our hideaway collapsed, became a soggy mess of cardboard. Now we had no privacy at all. With snow on the ground and freezing temperatures there was no place where we could be alone together.

There was an athletic facility across from my dorm that housed a small café, the college swimming pool, a bowling alley, and the gym teachers' offices. At night, the only lights in the building came from the café. Dick and I had an ice cream soda then wandered upstairs where all the corridors were dark and empty. We kissed for a while then I absently tried the doorknob on one of the closed doors. It opened and we found ourselves in the office of one of the gym teachers. The streetlight outside illuminated a desk, bookshelves, and some trophies. We were alone at last. We fell to the floor, ripped off our clothes, madly embraced, began the rhythmic motions that would lead to ecstasy and the light flicked on and there was the gym teacher. We grabbed our underpants and tried to hide ourselves as the gym teacher, a woman in her fifties, stood there with her mouth open and her eyes wide. We scrambled for our clothes as she retreated and closed the door. "Oh my god. Oh my god," was all I could say. I was torn between feeling embarrassed and feeling angry. Where were we supposed to go? We were young people. Sex happens to young people. Both his school and my school were set up in a way that pretended we were not normal eighteen-year-old people. Mortified, Dick walked back across the street to the Coast Guard Academy.

Now I had to face reporting myself to the Honor Court. Were they kidding? Did they, girls my own age, really think I'd write a note detailing my infraction and asking their forgiveness? When I got a note in my mailbox from the dean asking to see me in her office, I realized there really was no such thing as an Honor Code. It didn't matter if you reported yourself or not. You got in trouble anyway. Okay, I'd go to her office. But I wouldn't say one word. She could heap scorn upon me for as long as she wanted. Not one word would I say.

Hers was a large, sunny office with an impressive desk and bookshelves around all the walls. She was a tall, gracious, gray-haired lady with pink cheeks and a graceful manner. I entered, closed the door, took a few steps to the center of the room, and stood there looking down at the oriental carpet as she sat erect behind her desk. I said nothing, just waited for the lecture to begin. From outside came the sounds of snow plows clearing the paths between the gray stone buildings. I examined the design of triangles and squares on the carpet, how the design was repeated again and again, how harmonious the colors were, wine, blue, white, and orange. Then I examined the tassels on my loafers. Still she said nothing. Outside I could hear girls chatting as they passed by her window. At last I couldn't stand it another minute. I looked up and saw she was blushing. She didn't know what to say anymore than I did. I'd put this blameless woman in an awkward position. Because of me, through no fault of her own, she was uncomfortable. My actions had consequences beyond myself. "Well," she said in a tender voice, "I guess you won't do *that* again."

CHAPTER FOURTEEN

....

Before departing for Rome, Aunt Dovey Lee introduced my mother to some friends at the Highland Acres Country Club. Here was the beautiful daughter of Greenstone Enterprises in need of a husband. While Greenstone Enterprises meant nothing to New Yorkers, it was famous in Chicago. Mother was invited to dinner parties where there was sure to be a divorced man or a widower.

We spoke once a month. Sitting at the phone in my dorm hall, I reversed the charges. For the first time in her life, Mother had friends. One was an artist, did oil paintings in her studio on the grounds of her large house in Glencoe. She and my mother visited the Art Institute in Chicago and had lunch at a nearby café. Another had a subscription to the Chicago symphony and invited my mother to concerts. Another loved to bake and invited her to sign up for cooking classes.

When the house in Evanston sold, Grandpa Greenstone bought my mother an apartment in Chicago a block from Lake Michigan. He felt renewed optimism about her future, as I did. Surely with all these good-hearted women on the hunt, a match would be made.

Marv Bernstein was a widower who lived on Lake Shore Drive. "He has an excellent Dunn and Bradstreet rating," Mother told me on the phone.

"Well that's good, I guess."

"Yes, that is very good."

"So he's rich?"

"Don't say rich. He's wealthy."

"What does he do?"

"Imports baskets." I imagined wicker hampers filled with treats and wrapped in a big red bow at Christmas time. "Sells them at all the finest stores, Neiman Marcus, Marshall Fields."

On Spring break, I flew to Chicago and stayed for the first time at the apartment Grandpa bought for my mother. It was odd seeing our modern Scarsdale furniture bravely trying to fit in to this new home in an older building. It was a sunless apartment with a kitchen so narrow a table couldn't fit, so we ate at a counter that separated the kitchen from the small living room. Across the street was Huge Hefner's Playboy mansion, a brick structure that took up almost one city block. I had to pass it walking to Old Town. Usually there were no people visible either outside or inside. One day the sidewalk was enlivened by a group of centerfold hopefuls clustered near the front gate. They were gorgeous in spike heels and tight skirts. When I got half way down the block, I realized they were men and when I whirled around for another look they curtseyed to me in a sassy way. That was the first time I ever saw men dressed as women and it confused me because I wasn't sure I agreed with what they thought represented women. Were spike heels shorthand for women? Did gobs of lipstick, fluorescent eye shadow, and tight skirts, a woman make? Why did they broadcast maleness despite themselves? Did I broadcast femaleness? How far out did my female emanations project?

Marv Bernstein invited Mother and me to dinner. Meeting *the children* was a serious step in the advancement of second marriages. My mother, nervous in her silk dress and high heels, looked at me with her critical eye, appraised my value. I understood the importance of this meeting and resented that she doubted my ability to charm Marv Bernstein. Middle-aged men were invariably delighted by young women. I was being enlisted to close the deal, and I had yet to hear her say she loved him, admired him, or even liked him. By the time the cab dropped us in front of his building, I had a headache.

We were not the only ones in the marble and chrome lobby of his building waiting for the elevator. There were several men. "It's so strange," my mother said wistfully in the elevator after the other passengers got out, "having men look at your daughter rather than at you."

Marv opened his door and I saw a modest, nondescript man whose face brightened at the sight of my mother and who brought me close for a chaste kiss on my cheek telling me how much he was looking forward to meeting me. He invited us into an apartment that was exactly my taste. A wall of windows high above Lake Shore Drive showed small rectangles of light from windows all over Chicago. His airy apartment was furnished in Danish modern with abstract paintings on the wall and a Jean Arp bronze sculpture on a pedestal in one corner. When my mother said on the phone that he imported baskets, I imagined a practical person who made sure homemakers had containers for their potpourri. I never imagined that baskets could be works of art. His collection from Africa, Cambodia, Japan, and India was arranged in a pleasing way around the room, some flat like plates, some tall enough to hold umbrellas, some with lids, most with geometric designs and exciting colors.

He asked if I would like something to drink, wine or soda, and my mother said she'd get it in a voice that was so fawning I hardly recognized it. Was she playing the role of the step-and-fetch-it wife? Is that what she thought he wanted?

My head hurt so much I wasn't sure how I'd make it through the evening. The pain made me squint. Soon I'd have to sit through a meal at a fancy restaurant so I said, "Do you have Bufferin or anything like that?" He said, "Sit next to me. I can get rid of your headache." He had the calm quality of a domestic man, one meant to live with the same wife forever.

I sat down next to Marv and he put his thumbs on my temples and pressed hard. "This usually does it," he said. There was no sexual energy in his touch but I found it uncomfortable to be so close to a stranger, our thighs almost touching. He pressed hard on the sides of my head, a method that must have worked for someone else, maybe his dead wife. Were there months of trying to relieve her pain? After a few minutes, I lied and said, "Thank you, that really helped. Thank you so much." He moved from me, was not a man who insisted. But before we went out, he disappeared for a minute, then returned with a bottle of Bufferin and a glass of water. He held them toward me in a questioning way, asking if relief was still needed. I put my palm out flat. He gave me two pills, waited while I tossed them back with a gulp of water, then carried the medicine away without a word.

Now I noticed the framed photograph of Marv and a woman I assumed was his wife. They had their arms around each other and were smiling at the camera in a relaxed way that suggested they were intimate with the photographer, maybe their daughter. The wife had a pleasant face but was overweight. I wondered if Violet was the most beautiful woman he'd ever been with.

At an expensive restaurant, I sat across from him and my mother and had to keep seeing myself in the mirror behind them. It had become reflexive for me to primp in front of mirrors, to find faults to correct in what was supposed to be a flawless presentation. I allowed myself a few peeks and saw eyelids half closed from the pain of the headache and strands of hair that had come loose from my ponytail. I could see not only the fronts of Marv and Mother but the back of their heads too. Marv was bald on top, had gray hair cut very short above his white shirt collar. My mother's hair was pulled back into a Spanish-style bun. She seemed on tip toe, straining to be lighthearted and attractive. I'd been taught that there was nothing more attractive to a man than a good listener, so I asked Marv questions about himself. I was only mildly interested in who he was. He could have been anybody so long as he had enough funds to get my mother out from under the humiliation of depending upon her father. I said, "Really?" and, "That's so interesting." Marv told me that his daughter Amy was out of school and working as a buyer at Marshall Field. "A buyer?" I said.

"She buys jewelry," Marv said, "works closely with jewelry designers, some of them exclusive to Marshall Fields, and she goes to trade fairs and wholesale showrooms to select merchandize that she thinks her customers will like."

"What a great job!" I said while thinking, poor girl her mother's dead.

"Yes, very competitive. They had a lot of applicants."

"How do you get a job like that?"

"It requires a genuine passion for the product," Marv said. "She always loved jewelry even when she was a little girl."

"But what do you have to study?"

"She majored in economics."

"That's a requirement at my school. I had to take it freshman year. I didn't know what the teacher was talking about half the time."

"That probably wasn't your fault," Marv said. "If you didn't understand, then the teacher wasn't doing a very good job."

"That's what I thought, but everyone kept telling me about how much stuff she's published."

"She wasn't so great for you."

"That's what I thought. She only paid attention to the girls who understood immediately. Your daughter must be really smart to understand Keynesian fiscal policy."

"Yes. She is." He said this so sweetly I felt off balance for a second. Some lucky girls, apparently, had fathers who were proud of them.

I held up my wine glass and said, "To Amy." He smiled and we clicked goblets. Ping!

My mother said, "It's just costume."

"What?"

"It's not valuable jewelry. It's just costume, plastic and rhinestone, that sort of thing. She doesn't buy fine jewelry," Mother said. "Now my father, he's the one who knows jewelry."

"Costume jewelry is popular now," I said.

"Oh, it's always been popular. If you can't afford real, you buy costume."

"And what about you," Marv said to me. "What do you plan to do after college?"

"Me? I don't know. I think I'm supposed to be married."

"That shouldn't be any problem," he said.

"But it is a problem. I don't want to get married."

"Why is that?"

"Don't be silly," my mother said. "Of course, you'll get married."

"I know," I said. "It's inevitable."

"When you meet the right person," Marv said looking adoringly at Violet, showering her with light, "you'll change your mind."

My mother responded by saying in a coy voice, "Well, thank you kind sir."

Several weeks later, when I was back at school delighting in Trollope, the intercom buzzed, which meant I had a phone call. I assumed it was Dick Boyce but it was my mother phoning to say Marv proposed. She was engaged. "The wedding will be at the end of August at the Drake Hotel." I was so happy, I told everyone. "My mother's engaged! My mother's engaged!"

The weather grew warm, sophomore year ended, Dick Boyce returned to Minnesota to work in his father's hardware store, and I flew to Chicago to work as a switchboard operator at Greenstone Enterprises. Through plate glass windows, I watched chemists in white lab coats peer at gauges on steel vats. There was a steady hum of machinery. Grandpa's office was a wood-paneled room dominated by his portrait, an oil painting of him in a three-piece suit holding a cigar. Though he had retired and now Uncle Alan was president, Grandpa still went to work every day. The limo parked at the entrance, Jordan opened the back door, Grandpa got out, and the two old men, stiff from sitting, went into the building.

I was trained at the switchboard by Lois who could recognize a person's voice after hearing it once. I clamped earphones on my head and stuck plugs in appropriate console holes. When a light blinked, I stuck a plug in the hole and said, "Good Morning, Greenstone Enterprises," if it was before noon. If another light blinked at the same time I said, "Good morning, Greenstone Enterprises, thank you for holding," never wasting time by asking if it was okay to put them on hold. Then I stuck the latest plug in and said the same thing and went back to the first one and said, "Thank you," and "May I ask who's calling?" Lights popped on continually and I had to manage three, four plugs at once. Lois never had to ask who's calling. She said, "Thank you Mr. so and so," and was never wrong and could do that if the person had called only once. It was as if she heard the whole person in the voice. Sometimes, her husband phoned and she chatted with him. Other times she yanked out my plug so I couldn't hear the call. Then she spoke in a dramatically formal way and hinted that she wasn't alone, so that's how I knew she was cheating on her husband.

At noon I ate in the lunchroom with the secretaries, women in their forties and fifties who told such lewd stories I couldn't believe my ears, how they screamed when their husbands made them come. They mimicked the noises they made and everyone laughed except me. I'd never heard older women talk like that. I didn't even know sex could be a topic of conversation. At school we seldom talked about sex except to describe someone as a good kisser. We all knew about Dr. Adams in Pennsylvania. Girls returned by bus to the dorm after their appointment, hemorrhaged, and hurried to the college infirmary. I was one of the only girls on my hall who hadn't had an abortion. My guardian angel must have been looking out for me because Dick Boyce and I were not always careful.

At her apartment in Chicago, my mother was on the phone with the florist and chef. She selected table linen and place cards. She listened to musicians' tapes and chose a harp player. The event had to be subdued because his family and friends would necessarily be thinking of his dead wife. Mother bought clothes for the honeymoon cruise. Sometimes she complained about Marv's daughter. "I don't know why he takes her side all the time," she said. "We come to a decision, she objects, and that's the end of it."

"Like what?"

"Everything."

"Like what?"

"I wanted roses, she says why spend so much money when tulips are just as pretty and he says tulips really are just as pretty and that's the end of the discussion."

"Do you like her?"

"I don't care one way or the other about her. I'm not marrying *her*."

"You're going to be her step mother. Do you think she likes you?"

"She wouldn't like anyone her father marries."

"And it's not as if she's going to live with you."

"Exactly. She doesn't have anything to do with anything."

Joan's summer job was in New York. She was marking the price on underwear at Alexander's, a discount department store.

A new shipment came in and she made a mistake, marked the underpants ten cents rather than $1.10. "Can you believe it," she laughed on the phone to me. "I didn't set the stamp thing correctly. The whole shipment of underpants went out to the table marked ten cents! It was like locusts descended. The customers cleaned off the table in a second."

"Did you get fired?"

"Of course!"

Both of us were in the wedding and so was Marv's daughter. We could choose our own dresses so long as they were the color of the swatch Mother sent us. My sister, with her excellent color sense, matched her outfit to the swatch exactly, saw the matching as the most important part of the assignment. She showed us her wedding outfit, pale blue pantaloons with a low crotch like a Turkish pasha might wear, a soft yellow blouse with pale blue embroidery on peasant sleeves and a brown leather vest. She was especially proud of this outfit because she got all the pieces at a second-hand store for almost no money. Mother insisted that Joan buy a proper dress. "She wants me to look like some suburban moron," Joan said.

"Just wear whatever she wants then throw it out later."

"But that's such a waste of money!"

"What do you care? You're not paying for it."

"It's still a waste of money."

"No, it isn't. The point isn't the garment. The point is to make Mommy happy."

"Well, it's pretty dumb to get happy over throwing away perfectly good pasha pants and that blouse happens to be beautiful, for your information. That's an ancient Aztec design."

Neither of us had ever met Marv's daughter. "I thought it would be fun to get pizza together one night," Mother said, "but his daughter can't be bothered to find the time."

"Why not?"

"I don't know. Every time Marv asks her to join us, she makes some excuse."

"Do you think maybe she doesn't like you?" I thought this question was straightforward but saw by my mother's startled face that it was tactless. I tried again. "Did she ever say she doesn't want him to marry you?"

"Oh, yes. All the time."

"Why?"

"What difference does it make?"

"What did she say?"

"Oh, I don't know. Thinks I'm after his money." I wanted to say, "But you are, aren't you?" She was almost fifty and was used to cashmere and Egyptian cotton sheets. She was accustomed to living in spacious well-furnished rooms. How easy for Marv's daughter to feel superior, a girl with a college education. On the other hand, if his daughter was anything like him, warm and down to earth, she would want a more doting person than Mother was able to be.

By the end of the summer, the wedding was off. "I'm not going to marry a man who's under the thumb of his daughter. She bosses him around. He can't stand up to her. When you marry a man, you marry his family."

"You broke your engagement?"

"He's just an overgrown baby."

"So you aren't going to marry him?"

"I certainly am not. I don't need a girl like that in my life."

I was disappointed but was also impressed that she felt optimistic enough to reject a bird in the hand. She would begin again, meet someone else, maybe a tycoon of industry, maybe a famous surgeon, maybe a man with a yacht. Her friends at Highland Acres Country Club were probably already on the hunt.

But instead of waiting to be introduced to someone else, she announced that she intended to go around the world. She wanted to see the pyramids in Egypt, the temples in Kyoto, the heather in Scotland. She sold her apartment in Chicago and put all of her belongings into storage.

The airmail letters I took out of my college mailbox as the snow fell, as the snow melted, as the crocus stuck up their caps too soon, as I studied for exams then rested then studied for more exams, then wrote papers, handed them in, and wrote more papers, had postmarks from Cairo, Sydney, Casablanca, Tel Aviv, Paris.

The letters might as well have been written in Chinese. I couldn't read a word of the scribble. Her brain had been scrambled when her kindergarten teacher tied her left hand behind her back so she would become a righty. Her unintelligible handwriting was not her fault, but that didn't make it less frustrating. I took the letters personally, understood them as teases, each one saying here I am but you can't have me. I crumpled them and did angry slam-dunks. My letters to various American Express offices complained that I couldn't read her letters. By the end of my senior year, I received a letter I could read, typed on my mother's new portable Olivetti.

She was in Florence, Italy, living in a tower on the estate of an elderly Contessa. Mother introduced herself as an American sculptor who needed a quiet place to work. At the top of a narrow stone staircase was her studio and bedroom that overlooked topiary gardens. From large sacks of clay my mother dug out wet wads and smacked them on a board and punched out the air bubbles. She twisted wire armatures into human forms and set them on pedestals with swivel tops. She loved the feel of her wooden tools used for carving, smoothing, digging. She had pliers and hammers. When she finished a piece of sculpture, she carried it to a foundry near the Ponte Vecchio where it was cast in bronze. She wrote that she liked her single bed because there wasn't room in it for anyone else.

The Contessa befriended her, invited her for tea and they sat in the villa surrounded by furnishings that had been in the Contessa's family for generations, a dark wood coffee table with fat ankles, a floor lamp with a shade made of fringes, an Empire sofa upholstered in velvet, a large armoire so antique the silver had come off the edges of the mirror. The peacock blue velvet drapery with heavy swags could not keep out the cold so the Contessa was always swathed in shawls.

My mother knew nothing about my life except what I wrote in letters, and I knew nothing about hers except what she wrote, how the man who cast her sculptures praised her work and gave her a good price, how she hoped "one fine day" to show her work at galleries in Chicago and New York. I imagined her strolling through the streets of Florence, happy that she could now justify her life. Art critics would praise her and collectors would line up to buy her work. Her friends from Highland Acres Country Club and her parents and her sister and brother would understand at last why she couldn't become a leisure lady hosting gracious dinner parties. She was an artist.

It had never occurred to me to plan for life after college. I was supposed to graduate with an engagement ring on my finger. But no one had asked me, so I had to think up what to do next. Where were the most eligible men? Harvard. I applied and was accepted. It was like going from famine to feast. One week, I had eight different dates. And the biggest surprise was how the work was easier at Harvard. It seemed that Connecticut College was always trying to prove it was as good as any Ivy League school and Harvard had nothing to prove so didn't need to make its students jump through ridiculous hoops. There was plenty of time to enjoy my cousin Wiley when he came to visit. He was working at Merrill Lynch in New York.

We went to Hayes Bickford, a cafeteria in Harvard Square and instead of sitting down after he'd gone through the line and paid for his dinner, Wiley carried his tray right out the door onto the sidewalk. Still laughing, we sat at a table and ate our chocolate pudding and mac and cheese. "I don't blame her for running away," he said.

"Who?"

"Aunt Violet."

"You mean because she was so ashamed of hurting Marv Bernstein?"

"He might have been disappointed but he wasn't hurt."

"How could he not be hurt?"

"Why would he be hurt?"

"Because she jilted him."

"Who told you that?"

"She did."

"You mean you think she dumped him?"

"Yes. He was under the thumb of the daughter."

"Amy? She told you Amy bossed him around? Did you ever meet Amy?"

"No. Did you?"

"Of course. She was in the grade ahead of me. She used to go out with my brother's friend." He picked up his ramekin and licked out the remaining chocolate pudding. "She's like Marv. A lamb."

"But she didn't like my mother, right?"

"I don't know. She never told me she didn't like her. She'd never talk trash about someone's aunt."

"Was she sorry that my mother broke up with him?"

"Your mother didn't break up with him."

"Yes she did."

"No. She didn't. He broke up with her. You never heard about the ring fight?"

"No."

"Did you ever see that diamond ring?"

"Yes. It was bigger than my thumb nail."

"Didn't you wonder what happened to it?"

"I figured she just didn't want to wear it anymore."

"No. He demanded it back. She wasn't going to return it, said he'd given it to her and it belonged to her." Wiley tapped a Kent out of his pack and lit it with his lighter made of white enamel with a Playboy bunny in the center. He inhaled and blew out a perfect smoke ring. "Dovey Lee convinced her to give it back."

"Are you saying Marv Bernstein broke up with my mother and not the other way around?"

"Yes, Cuz. That is what I am saying." He offered me a cigarette then lit it with his lighter. He was the only person I knew who had a key to the Playboy Club. "My Dad played golf with Marv Bernstein," he said, "and my mother played bridge with his wife who died. Everyone at Highland Acres knew Marv just couldn't go through with it."

"You mean those women she played bridge with knew he broke up with her?"

"Of course they did. They were the ones who fixed him up. Sally Tepper was his late wife's best friend."

"But why did he wait so long? Why did he let my mother send out invitations?"

"Inertia?"

"Inertia! You don't have inertia about something like that."

"Well, from what I gather he thought your mom was after his money."

"So it was Marv, not my mother?"

"You didn't wonder why she ran away?"

CHAPTER FIFTEEN

....

At first, it seemed reasonable and even frugal that Annabelle would make a wardrobe for her return to the stage but as the years went by and Maestro did not phone and the dress forms wore a continual parade of garments that were never actually finished, Annabelle lost her luster and her pose as a diva began to sag though she continued to practice, booming up and down the scale until the house shook.

Seymour's complaints about Annabelle escalated year after year. It was as if he was helpless in the face of an inexorable force. "What does she need all that fabric for?" he said. "I told her do not buy any more fabric but she buys it anyway. Spends a fortune. Clutters the place up. Bobbins and whatnot. It's everywhere. She doesn't cook. She doesn't take care of the garden."

"Tell her to move out."

"Can't have an intelligent conversation. She's a master of trivia." He used me as a go-between. "Go ask Annabelle to join us."

"Why should I ask her? You ask her."

"Go on. Ask her. She's upstairs. Go ask her."

I stood at the foot of the stairs and screamed up, "ANNA-BELLE! Wanna go out for dinner?"

My father said, "Tsk!" and made a disgusted face at me as she called down, "NO!"

I dreaded going there. Annabelle was angry because now when he complained about money it was justified. He'd lost his job. The federal government agreed with independent film producers and independent theater owners that the five major studios formed a monopoly. MGM, RKO, Warner Brothers, Paramount, and 20th Century Fox were all owned by theater corporations that produced movies for their own theaters so a small place like the Strand in Woodbridge could never show a first run picture staring Clark Gable or Ava Gardner. MGM movies were shown in Loews theaters, Paramount in Paramount Theaters. The government demanded that the theater corporations divorce from the Hollywood studios so Loews was forced to cut MGM adrift. Now the Hollywood studios were on their own without the flow of money from their parent organizations. When I asked my father why he lost his job he said, "Because Metro is going to buy pictures rather than make them." He meant that MGM could not afford to produce movies any longer and had decided to buy films from independent producers. It was the end of the studio system. My father's job had become obsolete.

The double humiliation of losing his wife and losing his job made it impossible for him to be with his pals at the Society of American Magicians, all of them prominent in their professions as doctors, architects, and lawyers. They loved the glamour he exuded and liked to imagine him bedding the lovely young creatures who came into his office. For the annual magic show, he was able to persuade famous actors to participate. Jimmy Durante one year and Joan Crawford the next came up on stage to volunteer to be fooled. Seymour never told any of his fellow magicians that he was divorced or that he lost his job. It was easier to stay home and avoid those hearty extroverts.

He became active in local politics. When a developer threatened to build apartments close to his house, he circulated petitions, wrote opinion pieces for the *Standard Star* about how the rural quality of New Rochelle kept house prices up, how people moved there precisely because there were no apartment buildings. Neighbors got together to plan resistance strategy. I went with Seymour to a neighborhood meeting. He didn't know any of the people. His was a downtown life, Times Square, Broadway, and Sardi's. Now life had brought him to this meeting where he had to ingratiate himself without the aid of card tricks. He couldn't think up one word to say to the people standing near us. None of them knew he was a friend of famous movie stars. Perhaps all they saw was an elderly man with pink New England cheeks, a fringe of gray hair, and uneasy hazel eyes, standing with a young woman who was probably his granddaughter. The people who did pause to introduce themselves moved on quickly. It hurt to see my father so awkward. We walked home without speaking. Several months later, earth moving machines arrived, trees were felled, foundations laid and ugly apartment buildings came out of the ground and changed forever the bucolic quality of the Wykagyl section of the city. The woods behind his house where there was once a brook became a housing development with fake colonials on a grid of new streets named for the murdered trees, Elm, Maple, Beech.

He puttered around the house dressed in plaid flannel shirts and old shoes, stubble on his cheeks. He raked up leaves in the yard and neighborhood children, who called him Uncle Sy, jumped in the leaf piles.

CHAPTER SIXTEEN

········· · · · · · · · · · · · · · · · · · · ·

When Lyndon Johnson became President after Kennedy was shot, he started "a war on poverty." Johnson made money available for the "culturally disadvantaged," a veiled way of referring to black people. The city of Cambridge wanted some of that federal money and hired me to write grant proposals.

In order to qualify, we had to include in our planning the local people who would use the new services. They were to sit on the board and voice an opinion. My boss and I went looking for suitable candidates in the housing projects. I had never been anywhere near a housing project. Ugly brick buildings with trash strewn everywhere and iron bars on the lower windows, I would have held Mr. Sarkisian's hand if I'd had the nerve. We pushed open the graffiti smudged entrance door, saw the *out of order* sign on the elevator, and headed up narrow stairs to the third floor. Mr. Sarkisian was a small man with rashes on the backs of his hands and edging his scalp. He intimidated no one and was therefore excellent at his job. He was in charge of distributing United Fund money to the various non-profit agencies in the city of Cambridge.

When a stout black woman opened her door, I was surprised to see a well-furnished tidy apartment. I ignorantly thought people who lived in housing projects had nothing, like people who live in refrigerator cartons. The woman welcomed us into her living room where eight other cheerful women were waiting to meet us. Mr. Sarkisian knew a few of them because they were active in Cambridge politics. I was afraid of black women because of the maids who preceded Ruby. From preschool to grade five, Joan and I were tended by women who tore branches off the maple tree and switched our bare legs, washed our mouths out with soap, and dug the ends of combs into our scalps when they yanked our hair into pigtails. I felt apprehensive in this housing project meeting. There was a television, a new sofa, nice carpet, lamps, a separate kitchen, window shades that went up and down, an air-conditioner, and a bathroom with a toilet that flushed. Far from wearing rags, the well-fed women who greeted us wore good clothes. I was confused about what poor meant. The hostess gave us coffee and cookies. Maybe they noticed that I was frozen with fear, because they didn't put me on the spot. The few times they spoke to me, it was with kindness.

They took us for a tour of the building and spoke about how difficult it was to keep glass off the playground. Now I realized what poor meant. It didn't mean the children didn't have swings, it meant the city didn't bother to sweep glass from under the swings. All of the women had four, five, six children. I'd expected shame and cringing but found the opposite. They were outgoing, big-hearted, and confident. They patrolled the hallways to shoo away the drug users; they fixed the plumbing, they nailed broken doors. For the first time I understood the word *sheltered*. It meant the kind of ignorance that I had. At the same time I resented having to pretend that these women were poor compared to the world's poor and even compared to Hazel Greenstone, my own grandma, when she was young and living in a shack in New Mexico and had to ride for miles to get the Cavalry vet to fix her sister's broken arm.

In an effort to qualify for Headstart money, I did a survey of available daycare in Cambridge and discovered that there wasn't any. I had to explain what daycare was and often the response was, "You mean women would leave their little children all day?" It was assumed that some of the women on welfare did not work because they couldn't find child care. If they had child care and if they had training they would be able to support themselves. That was the idea behind the Title V money that poured in on us after we submitted our proposal. We started a sliding fee daycare center. Welfare mothers paid nothing, Harvard professors paid a fair price. The daycare center was in a large basement in Central Square. About twenty children enrolled, black and white, between the ages of three and five. My office was a room at the back. Except for chutzpah, I had no qualifications whatsoever for being the director of a daycare center. Nonetheless, I hired two teachers, consulted with dietitians, arranged food service, scheduled visits from social workers, interviewed parents, and gave interviews to reporters who came to see what it was all about.

Title V was a training program for women on welfare. In exchange for teaching them workplace skills, employers could use their services. A Title V woman was assigned to me. I was supposed to teach Franny to be a secretary. She was about my age, twenty-two, and already had four children. She wore bright red lipstick and fuzzy angora sweaters and pulled her hair back into a ponytail that looked like a shaving brush. When I pointed to her desk and told her to sit there, she was surprised. She thought it would take her years to merit a desk. "No. It's yours. That's where you sit." She sat down at the desk and patted it. "It's your job, Franny, to answer the phone. There's a way of answering the phone when you work in an office. You don't say hello. You say, 'Good morning,' if it's morning, or 'Good afternoon,' if it's after noon." About answering the phone, I had some real knowledge thanks to Lois at Greenstone Enterprises. I really could help a person learn a practical skill. Maybe I could save Franny from a life with no salary. Because of me, she'd stride the world with her head held high. "Then you say, 'Cambridge Community Daycare.' That's all you say. 'Good morning, Cambridge Community Daycare.' Nothing more. Then the person on the other end will say who they want to talk to and mostly it will be me. Then you say, 'Thank you. May I ask who's calling?' After they say their name you say, 'Thank you' and transfer the call to my phone by pressing this button here on your phone. Then I'll pick up and you'll say the name of the person, and I'll say whether or not I want to talk to them and if I do, then you'll press this button and I'll be connected and then you hang up. I know this is sort of silly because I'm sitting right over there, and all you have to do is put your hand over the mouthpiece and tell me who's on the phone. But when you go work for someone else, you might be in a separate office so I'm teaching you something that will be useful later on. Let's practice."

I went to my end of the office, sat at my desk and said, "Okay. When your phone rings pick it up and say, 'Good morning, Cambridge Community Daycare.' Okay? We'll practice the rest later. Here goes." I phoned our number. Our phones rang, and Franny looked at hers as if it were an alligator. "Franny! Pick up the phone!" She couldn't. So I said, "Okay. Here's what we'll do. All you have to say is good morning. None of the other stuff. Just pick up the phone and say good morning." I phoned again. Franny picked up the phone and said, "Hullo."

"No! Franny, don't say hello! Let's try again." All day long we practiced just picking up the phone and saying good morning and by the end of the day she still couldn't do it. We were girls playing a game and both of us laughed until we had to gasp for air. I was sure she'd get it right eventually, and she probably thought she would too. But the next day was no better than the first and by week two, we weren't laughing anymore. Franny kept forgetting which button to press so most of the callers got cut off. It was frustrating because sometimes the callers who got cut off were the mothers of kids who were in my care, and that did not inspire them with confidence.

I tried to teach Franny filing but the concept of alphabetizing things seemed beyond her. Of course, she knew the alphabet, certainly knew A came before G but she just couldn't connect how that translated into putting files in order. She told me that if she knew there was such a thing as daycare she'd have more children.

One day, Franny picked up the phone, said, "Hullo," listened, then put her hand over the mouthpiece and said, "It's for you."

"Can you say may I ask who's calling please?"

Franny said, "Who's this?" then said across the room, "It's your sister."

I said, "Thanks, Franny. Push the last button." She did.

"Who on earth was that?" Joan said.

"Yes, thank you," I said.

"She's in the room?"

"Yes. And how are you?"

"Listen, Sonya. Daddy's in the hospital."

My heart turned over. "Why?"

"Because he can't feel his feet."

"What?"

"He can't feel them. If he tries to walk, he can't. And his hands are numb. And he's lost his appetite. He says nothing has any taste."

"But what's the matter with him?"

"They don't know. They're doing tests on him."

"How long does he have to stay there?"

"They don't know."

"What hospital?"

"New Rochelle."

"How long has he been there?"

"Three days. I go there every day after work."

"Three days? How come you didn't tell me before?"

"They kept saying he could go home. Then he'd have another test, and they'd say he can't go home."

"Should I come home?"

"Can you?"

"I'll take the shuttle tonight. Can you pick me up at LaGuardia?"

When I hung up, I burst out crying and put my head down on my arms. I didn't expect this to happen but it did. I heard Franny's chair slide back. Then she was next to me saying, "Sugar, it's all right."

"It's my father," I said snuffling and trying to control myself. "He's in the hospital."

This was the first time I felt how work concerns fall away when personal concerns take over. The daycare center that filled my thoughts morning, noon, and night suddenly meant nothing to me. It would have to get along as best it could. I knew my boss would fill in for me.

Joan was at the wheel of our father's car outside of the Eastern Airlines shuttle terminal. As she pulled into traffic, she said, "Daddy said he'd be able to walk better if he had new slippers. So I bought him some new slippers. When he opened the box, he screamed that they were the wrong kind and he threw them at me."

"He threw them at you?"

"Yes."

"How awful!"

"I know. Right in front of the guy in the next bed. Some guy all hooked up to tubes. He pretended he didn't see."

"So what did you do?"

"Nothing. Took them back to the store. He's really skinny."

"Skinnier than when I saw him last?"

"Much." She flicked her brights a few times. "Look at that! Dim your lights you moron!" she yelled into her closed window. "Oh, want to hear the most embarrassing thing in the world?"

"Yes."

"Well, these executives from Schumacher came into the studio and asked me to go out for lunch with them because they're featuring one of my designs in their ad campaign, and they want me—"

"Wow! Congrats!"

"Doesn't mean a thing. They don't pay me a penny more. Anyway, we go down Seventh Avenue to that expensive place on the corner and guess who the hostess is."

"Who?"

"Guess."

"Can't."

"Annabelle."

"Annabelle?"

"Yes. Annabelle. She's working as a hostess at Three Penny!"

"No."

"It was horrible."

"Did she say hello?"

"No. We pretended we didn't know each other."

"Oh, my god. How'd she look?"

"The same."

"They hired a fat hostess? Isn't that unusual?"

"But she's glamorous."

"So she just showed you to the table and handed you a menu like nothing?"

"Sort of. I hung back and let the reps take the lead so she was next to them most of the time."

"But when she handed you a menu?"

"She was really good at being invisible."

The house was black at all the windows when we pulled into the driveway. I still expected our cat Rinso to run into the kitchen and Yow! at us, but he died of old age and now the house was entirely without life. It was depressing to think of my father living in all those rooms by himself, ghosts of his former life in all the corners. All traces of Annabelle were gone except for the pink roses she painted on the furniture, ridiculous at first, now annoying like stains.

Joan and I had breakfast at Schrafft's in downtown New Rochelle then drove to the hospital where Seymour was in a room with one other patient. My stomach dropped when I saw a flesh-covered skeleton, his rosy New England complexion now the color of putty. His head was a skull, his forehead oddly prominent. He turned his head to see who had come in and smiled weakly. "Hi, Daddy," I said and felt tears well up. Limp in a loose hospital gown, he took my hand in his for the first time since I was a child. I'd always admired his hands because they were athletic from all his shuffling, cutting, and palming cards. Now his hands were bony and the blue veins stuck out too far. Crying in front of a sick person was supposed to increase their feeling of depression, so I'd heard. A cheerful demeanor was appropriate to the bedside so I said, "How are you?" His answer was a squeeze of my hand. "It snowed last night," I said. "Did you see? It was so beautiful. Now it's mostly slush." He turned his gaze to his feet sticking up under the blankets.

"Daddy," Joan said in a forced voice louder than her usual, "do you want anything from the store? Want me to get you more licorice?"

Wires were attached to the man in the next bed and transparent liquid was dripping into tubes. His back was toward us. He was unaware that his smock had parted and his ass was showing. Would this be me one day? Was loss of dignity inevitable? A nurse came in and pulled the curtain around the man and said something to him in an exasperated voice.

A young doctor in a white lab coat wearing a stethoscope necklace came in, nodded to Joan and me, said to my father, "Good morning, Mr. Adler. I see your granddaughters are visiting." He unhooked a chart from the end of the bed, scanned it, then replaced it, and went out. I followed him to the corridor where food carts were clattering down the hall and someone in one of the rooms yelled for attention and the smell was that hospital smell that exists nowhere else, thank goodness. "What's the matter with him?" I whispered.

The doctor shook his head. "His vital signs are good. Heart rate, blood pressure. Blood work doesn't show anything."

"You mean you don't know?"

"Not yet."

"So what's the matter with him?"

He looked at me with too much sympathy and I didn't like that. It scared me. "We've scheduled him for another test tomorrow and that might show us something." He walked away from me and into another room.

Joan and I, alone in the house, sat next to each other on one of the love seats in the living room and watched television. The house felt hollow around us. We went to bed at last, she in her room, me in mine. The phone jangled me awake at three in the morning. I was still telling myself to get up and answer it when Joan came into my room and said in a trembling voice, "Daddy's dead."

"What?"

"Daddy's dead. We have to go to the hospital."

"Daddy's dead?"

I could only see her vaguely in the darkness, well enough to see her face collapse and that was enough to make me cry too. We dressed and went out to the garage, our breath puffs of cloud. Snow sprinkled down on the withered gardens at the edge of the driveway, gardens once full of roses and daffodils and tulips and my mother in her overalls digging in the dirt with her hair tied back in a bandana.

We hurried down the long entrance path to the hospital and went inside that terrifying structure that contained disease, death, worry, and misery. We were the only ones in the elevator at that time of night. The corridor was empty as we hurried to his room, and there he was in his bed covered with a sheet. The bed next to his was no longer in use, the mattress rolled up. We stood there looking down at our father's outline under the sheet. I had never seen a dead person before and was afraid but only seeing his outline didn't seem enough. "Should we look?" I pulled the sheet down off his face and there was our father, a weird yellow color, his eyelids closed and purple, his blue lips pulled back in a sort of grin, his top teeth showing. Someone had crossed his hands over his chest. He was still wearing a hospital gown and his arms were flesh-covered bones. "Put it back! Put it back!" Joan said so I pulled the sheet over his face. When she started crying, I said, "I'll call Uncle Norman," and hurried out of the room down the empty corridor to the pay phone. I went into the booth, closed the door, dropped a quarter into the phone, dialed the operator, and reversed the charges. Would I start crying when I said it? Why wasn't I crying now? What was the matter with me? Woken from sleep, Aunt Maggie croaked, "Hullo?"

"Aunt Maggie? It's Sonya. I have some bad news. My father died." Silence on the other end. Why didn't she say anything? "Well I just wanted to tell you," I said after what seemed centuries.

At last she said, "Hold on. Here's Norm." I heard her say to him in her raspy cigarette ruined voice, "Seymour's dead. It's Sonya." Uncle Norman said, "Sonya, dear? Are you there? When did it happen?" I told him about the telephone call then didn't want to talk anymore. I just wanted to get off the phone and go back to Joan. "So will you tell everyone else?" He didn't answer. "Okay," I said at last. "Okay?" He said nothing. "Okay, Uncle Norman?" At last he said, "Yes, dear." I hurried down the empty corridor, all the patients' rooms dark on either side.

Joan was standing next to the bed making an odd mixture of sob sounds and groans. "What are we supposed to do now?" I said.

She sniffled hard, stopped crying, and said, "I don't know."

I felt steely. I would not cry. There were things to be done. "Should we go home?" I said.

"You mean just leave him like this?" She started sobbing again. "Leave him here?"

Now we heard footsteps in the corridor and the young doctor of that afternoon came in wearing his stethoscope necklace. He suggested we go with him to his office. His attitude was solicitous, and I wished he wouldn't be like that. No need to act so kindly. We just needed to know what to do next. The doctor sat behind his desk. Joan and I sat in the two chairs on the other side. "Why didn't you cure him?" I said. "You should have given him something that would make him better. But you didn't. You didn't do anything." He received these slaps, thought to reply then didn't, just sat there watching me with a look in his eyes that lumped me in with suffering mankind.

"I suggest," he said, "that we do an autopsy to discover just why your dad died. We need your permission. Please sign here, and we'll send the results to you. I'm sure you both want to know what happened." We signed.

"Do you throw Dad away after that?" I asked. It was meant as a slap, but also I was curious. I really didn't know what happened to bodies that had been cut up.

"No! He'll either be cremated or buried. That's up to you."

"How will he be buried?" I said. "The cemetery is in Worcester."

"We can have the body transported. You need to find out the name of a funeral parlor, let me know and I'll make the arrangements." Now I saw a tired young man doing what his job required, new at it but struggling to do it as best he could.

"Do you always have to stay up so late?" I asked by way of apologizing for blaming him.

"Often," he said.

"So you're used to it?"

"No," he said. "You never get used to it."

Our house, with its charming clapboards and ample yard, the gnarled apple tree near the front path, seemed changed when we went inside. Now it was just a three-floor container of stuff Joan and I had to get rid of. Your father's dead, I kept telling myself. Why don't you cry? Your father is dead. You are now a girl with a dead father. We went into the living room and sat across from each other on the love seats that still wore the quilted upholstery my mother once defended as necessary when my father screamed at her about the price.

We climbed the stairs to our bedrooms. I expected to stay awake until morning, but I fell asleep immediately. I woke up and didn't remember, and then I did and felt as if now nothing was the same. This was a new me waking up, a me who had no father. Did it matter? We spoke only when I phoned him and it was unpleasant.

I wasn't sure he even knew what I was doing to support myself. It wasn't as if I lost a friend. I never confided in him nor him in me. So what did it mean for me to have a dead father? All I knew was that something momentous had happened and it would keep on happening in various forms for a long, long time, spreading like ripples when a stone is tossed in the lake.

The doorbell was ringing. The sound didn't wake Joan. I could hear her snores. I grabbed my bathrobe and ran downstairs. There was a man on the front porch. Dressed in a hat speckled with snow and an overcoat, he stamped his feet to keep warm. When I opened the door, a raw winter chill rushed in as the man thrust his right hand toward me depositing a business card in my palm while announcing his name. As he put his glove back on and tried to peer around me into the house, he told me he heard the house was for sale and he was sure he could get us a good price. "What?"

"Is it four bedrooms or five?"

"What?"

"This is a destination neighborhood," the man said, "and the house seems in good condition."

"What? How did you—"

"I won't take up any more of your time," he said. "We've been in the real estate business in New Rochelle for forty years. Guaranteed to get you the best price possible." Then he turned and stepped carefully down the icy front path that no one had shoveled, got into his car, and drove away. I closed the door and stood there stunned. How did he know?

Joan came to her door rubbing her eyes. "Did someone come over?" I showed her the card. We were speechless for a while. Then Joan said, "They must check the hospitals. See who died." I tore the man's card to pieces. Joan lit a cigarette, something she would never do if our father was there.

When we finished eating corn flakes in the kitchen and were sitting in the living room looking at all the stuff we were now responsible for, Joan pointed to the wall near the breakfront and said, "The only thing I want is that painting." It was a landscape of New York City in the snow, pedestrians on the sidewalk ducking their heads, the buildings blurred by white flakes, a painting that my father owned before he was married, a painting that was so him and so full of the all the fights that happened in that house I never wanted to see it again.

"You can have it," I said.

"Is there anything you want?"

"Yes. The car. I need a car."

"Okay. What are we going to do with all this furniture?"

"Do you think Mommy would want any of it?"

"Mommy? Why would she want any of it?"

"I don't know. She picked it out."

We went through the books. I selected an old book titled *Masterpieces of American Literature*, Washington Irving, Benjamin Franklin, Ralph Waldo Emerson, Edgar Allan Poe, Henry Wadsworth Longfellow, with biographical sketches and a portrait of each author. It was the property of Woodbridge High School. My father must have taken it when he graduated. I packed up Oliver Wendell Holmes, *The Autocrat of the Breakfast-Table*, Horatio Alger's *Helping Himself*, a biography of General Ulysses S. Grant called *Our Standard Bearer*, *Tales from Shakespeare* by Charles and Mary Lamb, Dale Carnegie's *How to Win Friends and Influence People*, and *The Power of Positive Thinking*. I took *Modern Magic* by Professor Hoffman, *Thurston the Great Magician*, *Fun with Magic*, and *The Art of Conjuring*.

Joan wanted the art books, Degas, Cezanne, Fra Angelico. Mother bought those and was pleased when Joan and I sat cross-legged on the floor or sprawled on her wide canopy bed thumbing through the pages in *Michelangelo*. She encouraged us to look at those pictures and perhaps knew the reason we never opened *Cezanne* or *Degas*. We didn't want to look at ballerinas or vases of flowers. We wanted to see Adam's uncircumcised penis laying on his thigh so unselfconsciously on the ceiling of the Sistine Chapel and the statue of David with its prominent penis that had the hair surrounding it lovingly chiseled. The naked women in *Michelangelo* were not interesting because they didn't look like women. Their breasts were little hard mounds too close to their armpits.

In a small leather-bound edition of Dante's *Inferno*, a photograph fell out. "Hey! Look at this!" It was a sepia-toned wallet-sized snapshot of my mother naked from the waist up. She must have been about twenty-two, proud of her well-formed breasts. "Do you think Daddy took that?" I asked. "Sure," Joan said. "Probably so he could look at her whenever he wanted." I thought it touching that he wanted a picture of his wife when there were probably dozens of young women willing to take off their blouses right in his office.

That afternoon, we phoned Clement Monroe. When I saw him standing in his snow sprinkled coat at the front door, tears welled up so I swallowed hard and kept them down. He knew just how to look at me without too much sympathy or too much dramatic sorrow. I wondered if it was possible to learn to navigate the world as he did or if diplomatic skill was innate. He came in and greeted us both by name, something few dared to do because most people couldn't tell us apart. Sitting with us in the living room, he said that the will had to be probated but that our father, except for small gifts to his nieces and nephew, left everything to us. He said that probating the will would take several months. I thought now the truth will be revealed. Was he a miser as Mother claimed or did he, in fact, have to pinch pennies? "Do you know where he's to be buried?"

"Worcester. His family's buried in Worcester."

"His brother, Norman, can take care of that for you. He'll know the name of the place. Tell your uncle to have the funeral director phone me and I'll make arrangements with the hospital to have the body transferred." He stayed with us for a long time, talking only of practical matters, how to find a furniture dealer, how to find a real estate agent, what to do with the clothes. When there was a pause in the conversation, he looked at us with a rueful and pensive expression that told me that I was too young to lose a father. Since I had yet to be any age older than the one I was right then, I didn't know what consequences he was thinking of.

"He's so nice," Joan said after he drove away in his black Oldsmobile.

"Do you think we should try to phone Mommy?"

"Why?"

"I don't know."

"Does that countess person have a telephone?"

"I don't know."

"Do you know her name?"

"Contessa."

There was a lot of medical jargon in the autopsy report, but basically it said no one could see any reason that the patient died. The doctor wrote that the patient lost his appetite and complained of feeling numb. Then the doctor revealed his poetic nature by adding, "And so he languished." He should have asked me. My father lost his wife and his job and died of a broken heart.

Joan and I drove four hours to Worcester to meet up with the Adlers. I didn't want hugs and sad faces. I wanted to remain steely. They were all waiting outside the funeral home, Uncle Norman, Aunt Maggie, Aunt Hattie, Uncle Donald, my cousin Claire with her faded, ghostly presence, Avery now grown into a tough teenager, and Eddy, a grown man in an Army uniform but still with that loose lower lip and a sly expression. Grandma Adler was in a nursing home and everyone thought it best not to tell her that her firstborn died. The aunts and uncles greeted Joan and me with intense solemnity. We went into the funeral home, a white colonial house that edged a busy highway. I had never been to a funeral parlor before, so I expected a more commercial structure, something less personal than a renovated house. I did not want to go inside that place but had no choice. Inside it lost its residential charm. The atmosphere was hushed, weighty, and dark. A guest book lay open on a pedestal in the foyer where there were photos of men in prayer shawls on the walls, Jewish stars on framed certificates, a stack of yarmulkes for anyone who might have forgotten to bring one. The men who worked there wore dark suits and black ties and were impeccably correct as they ushered us into a small auditorium with wooden pews all facing a coffin draped in black cloth. My stomach turned over. Was my father inside that box? Had they sewn him back together or had they left him a pile of feet and arms and ropes of intestines?

The funeral director whispered that there was a private room and ushered Joan, me, and our two uncles out of the main auditorium. He guided us with the authority that comes from experience. His professional manner was supposed to be reassuring but it wasn't. It trivialized my father's death. That man in his somber suit had escorted dozens of mourners to the private room, and this particular death was no more momentous than the one yesterday. He closed the door with a practiced tenderness and left us to seat ourselves on a wooden pew that faced a one-way window. We could see the congregation but they couldn't see us. What was wrong with seeing us? Why not wail to the skies like Greek women in black shawls do in the movies? Why did everything have to be so tidy? A brief knock on the door, and a small man dressed in a black suit and wearing a yarmulke came in and introduced himself as the rabbi. We stood up and he gave each of us a piece of black ribbon with a pin on the back and told us to attach it to our clothes. We did.

It seemed odd that suddenly now that my father was dead, Jewishness was flooding over us. It was almost as if he wasn't there anymore to protect us from it. A rabbi was suddenly in charge of everything. He stood right in front of me and said some Hebrew words. He said the words mechanically, recited them in a rote way that made me think they didn't mean much, so it came as a shock that he reached toward me with a razor and slashed the black ribbon I had pinned to my shirt. His invasion of my space and the abruptness with which he did it felt so violent my mouth dropped open and I took a step back, torn between wanting to smack him and appreciating the symbolism of being severed from my father. Yes, it was abrupt, yes it was painful, yes it was death. It was Jewish, he was doing something Jewish to me whether I wanted him to or not and I realized Jewish was much bigger than me. I was part of it even though I never went to temple and didn't know the prayers and ate spare ribs and shrimp.

Through the one-way window, we saw people coming into the funeral parlor. Some of the people went up to the coffin and crossed themselves. When everyone was seated, the rabbi said prayers in Hebrew then changed to English to speak of Seymour Adler, a man he never met. Seymour Adler, he intoned, was a movie producer, devoted father, brother, son, he blah blah blah. Here was a strange job, having to praise a total stranger in front of those who knew him well.

When we went outside after the service to join the others, a hearse waited by the curb. Now I understood why we had to stay so long in the hidden room. They didn't want us to see them putting the coffin in the hearse. I could see it in there through the back window. Everything was designed to remove us from our feelings. Joan and I didn't know whose car we were supposed to go in for the ride to the cemetery so we just stood there until the funeral director ushered us to a black limousine, opened the door for us, and waited while we climbed in next to Uncle Norman and Uncle Donald. We were the celebrities of this event. Our driver, dark suit, dark tie, pulled away from the curb and a line of cars followed us. Uncle Norman took out a pack of cigarettes and lit one, so I did too and we flicked the ash into a little silver cup on the car door. Someone would have to give it a good scrub before the next family rode in the limousine. How jarring it would be to open the little metal flap and see someone else's cigarette butt in there!

The trees at the cemetery were decorated with icicles. We were ushered to a rectangular hole in the ground. Dirt was piled up next to the hole and there was some pulley contraption there. I was amazed to see Aunt Dovey Lee and Uncle Jack standing next to the hole. They were from the other side of my family, had nothing to do with Adler people. "You came all this way?" I said.

"Of course we did, honey bunch," Aunt Dovey Lee said. "Of course, we did."

But if they came from Rome, why didn't my mother come from Florence? Do divorced people go to each other's funerals? Aunt Dovey Lee and Uncle Jack stood out among the twelve or so mourners because their clothes were so chic. Whispers among the Adlers identified them as Violet's sister and brother-in-law. There was nothing haughty about Dovey Lee or Jack, but they did look expensive in their sleek Italian coats that were long to their ankles, an elegant couple who didn't try to mingle, just stood quietly together, apart from the others.

I turned and saw the hearse, saw it come to a stop, saw the driver get out. Then the coffin came toward us carried by my uncles and men I didn't know, probably from the funeral home. All of them had the same expression of intense concentration as if they were afraid they might stumble. No one spoke as they came toward us, a timeless scene, the coffin and the pallbearers. My heart leapt to my throat. This was scary. This I hadn't imagined. This was death and it was coming toward me, a colossus coming toward a speck. The workmen waiting by the rectangular hole came to attention. My heart was thudding as the men lowered the coffin onto the pulley contraption. The pallbearers stepped back and the rabbi started saying Hebrew words and the workmen lowered the coffin into the hole slowly and the pulleys made a metallic squeal, and I couldn't believe my eyes, they were lowering my father into a hole, a dirt hole all dressed up like it wasn't a dirt hole with green blankets around the edges but it was a dirt hole and into that pit they were putting my father. I was paralyzed, heard my sister crying, heard the other relatives crying. Someone handed me a shovel, a heavy shovel not a ceremonial toy. I had no idea why. They pointed to the coffin at the bottom of the hole and it dawned on me that they meant I was supposed to shovel some dirt onto the coffin. They wanted me to shovel dirt onto my father. Were they crazy? Why would I shovel dirt on my father? It was my father! Then someone took the shovel out of my hand. It was Dovey Lee. She took the shovel out of my hand and passed it to someone else then put her hand in mine and just stood there with me, not looking at me, not hugging me, just with me.

She wasn't there anymore when we arrived at Uncle Norman's home in Woodbridge. As Joan and I walked up the path to Uncle Norman's small stucco house, Joan said to me, "Daddy kissed me."

"What?"

"Daddy kissed me. I felt him kiss me at the cemetery."

"He did?"

"He kissed me on my cheek. I felt it." We made our way up the icy front walk and went inside the house. He didn't kiss me. He was still hurting my feelings.

The house was the size of a cottage, kitchen divided from living room by a short wall so everyone in the living room could see into the kitchen but it wasn't like a loft. It was just small, and you couldn't escape the sound of the television that was always on, nor the clutter of the newspapers piled up next to Uncle Norman's armchair, all the pages folded back to the crossword puzzles, nor the ashtrays everywhere full of cigarettes, nor the piles of Readers Digests.

Some thoughtful person had put food out on a folding table set up in the living room, coleslaw, cold cuts, Kaiser rolls. Woodbridge people came through the front door cautiously, looked around in hopes of discovering the proper protocol because they were used to wakes. Some brought bottles of whiskey and looked around for the bar to set the bottle down, but there was no bar and no one was drinking. I had to greet them and shake their hands and receive their looks of solicitude and listen to their tales of when they did such and such with Seymour, what a great guy, how he helped them that time they were having trouble with their insurance company, how he volunteered to judge the talent contest at the Knights of Columbus that time thirty years ago, how once he brought Joan Crawford to Woodbridge but her name was Lucille LeSeur then. Midway through their story, they remembered they were talking to the daughter of a dead man and a cloud passed across their faces as they realized their story would soon come to an end and then they'd just be face to face with a stunned young person. I heard anecdotes from the man who owned the cigar store, the fire chief, the local newspaper editor, the manager of the Strand cinema, stories that all ended with a sympathetic look that was supposed to mean they understood my sorrow. But I didn't have sorrow. I had numbness.

Joan and I had to remain at Uncle Norman's for three days, sleeping all that time on the pullout sofa bed in the living room, Joan on one side, me on the other, her whispering into the dark, "Stop wiggling," and me trying to lie still, something impossible for a wiggly person. But Joan wasn't easy to sleep with either. She sniffled. She wasn't crying. She just always sniffled before she fell asleep. It was infuriating.

Barely rested, I woke up thinking, *My father's dead,* as I heard Aunt Maggie early in the kitchen, clanking pots and pans and opening and closing the refrigerator door. Sitting at her kitchen table eating the eggs she made for us, I marveled that of all people it was Aunt Maggie who was taking care of us. Here was an adult woman stepping up when needed. Try as I might, I couldn't imagine my mother helping like this, filling the role of the female head of the family. Someone organized the funeral and the reception after it, and the food required for the three days of Shiva, and it certainly was not Uncle Norman. It had to have been Aunt Maggie who was now an example for me.

Joan and I returned to the house in New Rochelle with no idea how to get rid of all the stuff or how to choose a real estate broker. There were tax receipts, bank statements, unused checks, files full of paid bills and letters from the insurance company and the hospital. "Hey, look at this," I said. "It's a letter from our mother." It was typed on Barbizon Hotel stationery so Mother must have written it when she was twenty and living at that all-women residence while trying to launch a career as a Spanish dancer. She wrote that she intended to move to Chicago if Seymour didn't marry her. "You mean he didn't want to marry her?" Joan said. "Apparently."

"I wonder why he did?"

He had saved the playbill from the Apollo Theater where she gave a concert and he had saved a copy of *Dance Magazine* with her on the cover, adorable in a gypsy costume. Joan said, "Because he was forty."

The letter helped to explain why my parents never spoke of their courtship, why my father never mentioned the first sight of my mother, or why neither of them ever spoke of dates they went on or parties they attended or mishaps that only proved how much they were in love. They never spoke of their wedding. It was as if they had no past together. He was an aging bachelor who had a housekeeper/cook who came in every day to his apartment on Central Park West and, suddenly, so it seemed, Violet got attached to him and babies came out and they moved to New Rochelle. The union was wrong right from the start and this was a consolation because it meant that marriages didn't necessarily have to sour, that divorce didn't strike suddenly like lightening but was there from the start so if I paid attention, if I was careful, I might not get divorced. I dreaded nothing more than getting divorced. My goal in life was to raise my children in a peaceful home.

Joan and I contacted an appraiser, who told us none of the stuff in the house was worth very much. He gave us a price, we said okay, and he took much of it away. We knew he cheated us. He could hardly look at us as he left with the contract we signed.

Maybe it was guilt that made him leave his expensive Mont Blanc pen on the kitchen table. He told us there were men in trucks who would take away all the rest of the furniture, like the bureau in our father's bedroom, but we had to clear out all the drawers. We did not want to deal with Seymour's clothes, were not ready to acknowledge that he'd never wear any of them again.

The Salvation Army said no, they would not come to the house. We had to pack it all up and bring it to them. We started with the bureau, opened plastic garbage bags and dropped his socks in and then we had to see his underpants, white cotton briefs all stacked neatly one on top of the other. This was too much for Joan, the underpants so abandoned. She started crying and saying, "Daddy, oh, Daddy," and this annoyed me so much that I glared at her and scooped up the cotton underwear, the underpants and the sleeveless undershirts that always showed his gray chest hair at the neckline, and dumped it all furiously in the garbage bag and said, "Are you going to help or not? If you're not going to help, go away. Just go away."

She said, "But it's Daddy. It's Daddy."

I said, "Oh, shut up. Just shut up," and I slammed the empty bureau drawer so hard a piece of the veneer fell off. "Darn. Look what I did."

Joan said, "Doesn't matter. Isn't worth anything anyway."

I opened the next drawer and saw his folded starched shirts in neat piles. "You want any of these?" I said. Joan wiped her nose on the back of her hand, looked into the drawer and whispered, "His shirts."

"So what," I said. "Do you want them or not?" She shook her head and I dumped them in the garbage bags and hoped that some poor person would find them at the Salvation Army, because they were expensive shirts. He kept his ties in a drawer, each one curled up into a little circle. Joan said, "I want this one," and selected the one that was the most him and my stomach roiled for a second with jealously. I wanted that one. I didn't want it before she wanted it, but the second she said she wanted it I wanted it. Why should she get everything good? Why couldn't I have something for once in my life? I didn't dare tell her I wanted it too because she would give it to me and I only wanted it because she wanted it so it wasn't fair that the person who didn't really want it should end up with it. So I hunted among the ties for the next best one and chose one not because it was so him but because it had colors that would go with a jacket I owned, and I thought it might be chic to wear a man's tie. I was sick with jealousy. It was as if that tie she selected was the most precious thing in the world. We uncurled all the ties and examined them. "Look at the design on this one," Joan said. "Would you mind if I keep this one? I'm going to copy this design at work." How did she do that? How did she always home in on the best thing? I shrugged then selected another tie, but knew I'd never use it. "Oh, look at this one," Joan said. "This would make a really good sash." She tied it around her waist. "You could put a buckle on it or maybe a loop with a leather strap. Don't you think that would be cool? Do you want it?"

"No."

"Are you sure?" At last, all the bureau drawers were empty and we set about tackling the closets, but my insides were aching from jealousy though I knew the items my sister had taken were worthless to me.

His suits were on hangers lined up perfectly. "What are we supposed to do with all this?" Joan whispered. We stood there looking into his tidy closet, everything precise, the wingtip shoes on the floor, the shoulders of each jacket precisely in line with the shoulders of the jacket next to it, the cartons of playing cards on the shelf above. Joan patted the shoulder of one of the pinstriped jackets and cooed, "Daddy. Hello, Daddy." I felt tears welling up, and I didn't have time for them, and I didn't want to face being sad. I hated being sad. There was a chore to do and we had to do it, so I lifted the suit from the closet, jacket plus trousers, and was surprised by its weight. It felt almost human in my hands, so I dropped it on the bed. "Are you going to help or just stand there?" I said. "I have to get back to work. I've been gone almost two weeks." We took all the suits out of the closet then mashed them into plastic bags. It felt obscene to discard such expensive clothes. When we came to the tuxedos, Joan said, "Look at this," and fastened one of the cummerbunds around her waist. "Does that look weird?" She looked at herself in the mirror. "Do you mind if I take this?" I hadn't even noticed that cummerbund. Now I wanted it. Just because she had a better eye it didn't mean she should get everything. Now that she pointed it out to me, I could see that the cummerbund was the most extraordinary thing in the world.

At the bottom of the closet was my father's shoe polishing kit. It was a wicker basket with a lid that folded back, exposing a piece of metal shaped like a shoe. Inside the basket were polish, rags, and brushes. Often I watched my father shine his shoes on that basket. "I want that," I said embarrassed because my voice was so harsh and urgent. Nothing in any of the closets said Seymour to me as much as his shoe polishing kit. I was sure Joan would object. Here was the most Seymourish thing in the whole house. There wasn't a trace of screaming or door slamming lodged among the tins of cordovan and black shoe polish. Even the distinctive aroma of the contents was peaceful. Of course Joan would want it. She'd say it wasn't fair, a couple of ties didn't equal a whole shoe polishing kit, the symbol of how fastidious he was, the emblem of one of his favorite sayings, "If you look like a million dollars, you'll feel like a million dollars." Joan said, "What do you want that old thing for?" I was so relieved that I had to turn away and bite the insides of my cheeks. When I could speak I said, "I don't know."

We went to the lawyer's office to hear the reading of Seymour's will. I believed we'd discover that Seymour left everything to Joan and nothing to me, despite what Clement Monroe said. We would also discover whether it was justified to ask him to pay for my expensive college and whether he was right during the divorce to demand the mortgage-free house. Was he a miser as my mother claimed or just a man living within his means?

The answer was ambiguous. Yes, he could have been more generous and yes he was right to squirrel away his savings. He was going to have to live on his portfolio for a long time. He certainly didn't expect to die at sixty-four. His estate was equally divided between Joan and me. I tortured myself by wondering if I would rather have Daddy or his money. It wasn't a lot of money. I would still have to work for a living, but it was a cushion that afforded me the bliss of feeling independent even though, in reality, that independence would have only lasted a year or two.

Joan and I had to come up with words to put on his headstone. We couldn't say beloved husband. Could we say beloved father? Some of the girls at school had beloved fathers. I saw them walking around the campus comfortably chatting, the energy between them relaxed. I heard them on the phone in the dorm speaking with no strain. Their fathers figured into their conversation, seemed to know just what their daughters were doing. I was always surprised when a friend's father knew my name. My father didn't know the names of any of my friends. Beloved brother? But beloved brother alone sounded as if he was never married and had no children. Having just graduated and still being full of Shakespeare sonnets I suggested: *Who can say more than this rich praise, that you alone are you.*

Uncle Norman was supposed to be in charge of getting those words etched into the gravestone but he phoned and said he didn't want to be the one who chose the stone, that it was too important and Seymour's daughters should do it. "You mean you want us to come to Worcester?" I heard Joan say on the phone. When she hung up she said, "Can't he do anything? I've got a whole backlog of color combinations and repeats. I can't drive five hours to Worcester and five hours back to New York." We agreed that I'd go by myself once we put the house on the market, because Worcester was only an hour from my apartment in Cambridge. Clement Monroe said he'd deal with the real estate broker so Joan and I left the house forever and went back to our apartments. I wasn't sorry to say goodbye to that house, though it was a charming house on an ample lot in a leafy neighborhood full of robins and antique stone walls.

On a street in Worcester, I parked my father's Pontiac. The front yard of the gravestone place was full of gravestones carved in various ways to show customers what was possible: garlands, angels, hearts, Jewish stars, crosses. Uncle Norman was waiting for me inside and said, "Hello, dear," as I came toward him for the ritual hug that wasn't a hug. He smelled of peppermint gum which I took to mean he'd had a few before arriving. The salesman, a man in his fifties, told us his family had owned the Monument Company for eighty-five years, that granite needed no maintenance, and that he would stand behind anything we chose to buy. Then he told us the prices, and I chose one that wasn't cheap and wasn't expensive. "Have you decided on an epitaph?" he asked Uncle Norman, who looked at me so I handed Uncle Norman the quotation from Shakespeare written on a piece of note paper. He read it, then fished his glasses from his breast pocket and read it again. He stood there with the notepaper in his hand unable to respond, unable to say one word. He seemed dumbfounded. He did not like our choice at all. We hadn't said *beloved*, we hadn't said anything that sounded as if we loved his brother. How could daughters be so cold? Uncle Norman probably thought Seymour was a wonderful father because he gave Joan and me so much, a nice house to grow up in, summer camp where we learned to swim, braces on our teeth, a college education. Seymour had provided us with so much more than he had enjoyed as a child. Nothing was given to Seymour. Everything he had he earned. And everything he earned went toward providing a comfortable life for his daughters. Uncle Norman stood there baffled because he'd just heard from Seymour's daughters that they thought *beloved* didn't apply. Chin on chest, he looked at me from the top of his eyes. "If that's what you girls want."

CHAPTER SEVENTEEN

······························

M y mother's letters from Florence didn't mention Seymour's death. She couldn't imagine, so it seemed, that anyone would need consolation for the death of man she found so unlikable. Nor did she seem to understand the difficulties Joan and I faced clearing out his house while somehow not getting fired from our jobs. She wrote about casting her pieces in bronze, how she stood before Michelangelo's *Lamentation over the Dead Christ* at the Museo del Opera del Duomo and marveled at how he made marble look like fabric. Each time she went to the Uffizi and saw Botticelli's *Primavera* it was as if she'd never seen it before. The paint colors were so vibrant after so many years! As for Fra Angelico's *Annunciation* at the Convent of San Marco, she didn't think there could ever be a more delicate work of art. New paragraph. The Contessa had become frail and was starting to rely on my mother. The housekeeper, also an elderly woman, had gone to Bulgaria to visit her daughter and the Contessa seemed to think Violet should fill in for her. My mother was a tenant, not a servant. Love you so muchy muchy muchy, Mother.

I was surprised that she came home for Joan's wedding, and she was offended that I was surprised. When I asked why she came home, she said, "It's the thing to do," and frowned at me. A mother plans her daughter's wedding, that's the rule. I was sorry she had to express her love for Joan in that way instead of just saying she wouldn't miss her daughter's wedding for anything in the world. It was her darling daughter whose baby dresses had smocking and who, around the age of six, had changed Violet into a tip toeing tooth fairy.

Joan was engaged to Raf. He'd been married before, to a Macedonian woman who wanted a green card. He was handsome and well-built, taught riding at summer camps when he was younger. I enjoyed riding with him because he was fearless and when we went to a stable outside of the city we galloped flat out. He seemed an odd choice for Joan because they had nothing in common. The love of horses is built in and it wasn't built into her. What she liked was his blacksmith muscles. She listened to Beethoven, he liked Willy Nelson. She admired Fellini, he loved John Wayne. He had to be outdoors, she liked being indoors at art museums. He was gregarious, she was introverted. They didn't even laugh at the same jokes. Nor did she share her feelings with him. She told me that she was making dinner and sliced her finger with the knife and ran into the bathroom and closed the door so he wouldn't hear her crying.

Raf couldn't keep his hands off of her. Sometimes it was embarrassing how much he hugged and kissed her in public. He just loved her!

I assumed Mother would stay for several months then return to Florence but instead, she rented an apartment on the Upper East Side and got her things out of storage. When I asked why she wasn't going back she said, "It was time." I wondered if that meant she was tired of looking after the old Contessa. Or did it mean the Contessa asked her to leave for some reason? Something must have happened because she never mentioned sending her a gift or calling her on the phone or mailing a letter or receiving a letter. She didn't say one word about the Contessa, though she'd lived on her estate for more than three years.

My mother had changed. Before she went abroad there was a pliable quality about her. Now she exuded a defiant self-assurance. It wasn't exactly confidence. There was a foot-stamping quality about it, like a child who's been scolded and stands glaring at you. Whereas before I might look up and hook eyes with her, now it was impossible. Her gaze was sealed, no admittance, doors locked.

Joan was oddly passive about her wedding. It was our mother's event and it was going to be a smash hit in a room drenched in flowers at the Plaza Hotel. When I asked Joan if she wanted a fancy wedding, she answered, "I don't care."

"You mean big or small doesn't matter, because Daddy can't walk you down the aisle?"

"No. I mean I don't care. Let her do what she wants." Age twenty-six, she stood still for dress fittings, was patient during menu discussions and guest list decisions. Should Joan invite Stevie Barash who lived next door to us in New Rochelle even though Joan hadn't seen Stevie since high school? Maybe he would never hear about the wedding but if he did would he be hurt? Grandpa Greenstone was paying so might as well include Stevie Barash. "It's only fair," Mother said. "Why should Dovey Lee's children have fancy weddings and mine get skimpy little nothings? Why should Alan's children have lavish ceremonies? Alan isn't Dad's only child." Grandpa Greenstone paid for a room full of white orchids and a prenuptial dinner of lobster and champagne. Joan's dress was studded with seed pearls and had a train that bustled out like a flow of white lava.

Joan told me that the night before the wedding, at two in the morning, Uncle Alan phoned her. They were both in rooms at the Plaza. He seemed to know she'd be awake. He said that if her father were alive he would be the one to reassure her. The jitters were normal. She really had nothing to worry about. He said that he could tell that Raf loved Joan by the way he looked at her. The wedding really had nothing to do with marriage. It was a performance and would soon be over, and then she and Raf could be together with no one interfering. Joan said she did have the jitters and couldn't believe Uncle Alan knew that.

Uncle Norman in a tuxedo, chin on his black bow tie, was chewing gum to freshen his breath. I imagined he was thinking of his brother's loss, Seymour unable to see how beautiful Joan looked in her wedding dress, tiny waist, a tiara on her head holding a lace veil, her feet encased in white satin shoes. Uncle Norman's daughters Claire and Avery were bridesmaids. Claire had graduated high school and was doing office work in one of the Woodbridge factories. She came, step pause, step pause, down the aisle with my cousin Wiley, who, despite his courtly way of escorting her was so full of natural exuberance the contrast was painful. Claire seemed like a blown dandelion puff, lots of little pieces drifting in the air.

As maid of honor, I had a job. I had to lift Joan's veil up from her face so she could take a sip of wine when the time came. I wanted to get an A+ in veil lifting. Maybe the gauzy thing would get stuck on a bobby pin, or I'd pull too hard and it would come off entirely and she'd have to shove it back on and it wouldn't be centered. The groom was already there standing in his tux, big and handsome.

His elderly parents walked down the aisle together arm in arm, step pause, step pause, then sat in the front row. Uncle Alan walked down the aisle with Grandma Greenstone, who seemed to be getting smaller every year and whose cheeks were bright pink from the ice she'd held to them in front of her mirror. My mother came down the aisle with Grandpa Greenstone, who refused to step pause but walked at his own pace, my mother next to him bravely matching his steps as he surveyed what his money had wrought. He was pleased. This was a shindig to beat all shindigs! They took their seats in the front row on our family's side of the audience. Long pause, just long enough for us to start getting fidgety, then out it came, the wedding march played by violin, piano, cello, and viola, a quartet from Julliard.

There stood Joan, a vision of loveliness, as they say, standing next to Uncle Norman who seemed a bit greenish but at least had spit out his gum. Visible under Joan's translucent veil was a smile that others might have thought endearing but I knew to be a grimace. It was horrible having everyone's eyes on her. They stepped onto the aisle, step pause step pause, then jerked to a standstill. Violet had warned Norman in a stern voice to be careful not to step on Joan's train. Uncle Norman, in the habit of doing a bad job at everything, did step on Joan's dress which brought her to an abrupt stop so they had to start all over again matching their pace as they step paused to the altar. Uncle Norman forgot to give his niece a fatherly kiss, hurried to his seat next to my mother who gave him a stony look.

Officiating was Rabbi Slarsky from the Sunday school in New Rochelle where Joan and I learned that Moses said, "Let my people go," and the Pharaoh said, "No." Did Rabbi Slarsky remember me? Though my mother was nonobservant, she insisted that Joan and I continue Sunday School until we were confirmed. There was a window in the bathroom on the first floor of the Sunday school. After the teacher took attendance, I excused myself to go to the bathroom and crawled out the window and roamed around the neighborhood. I didn't know anyone in that part of town. I returned in time to come out the Sunday School door to meet my mother waiting in the car. At the confirmation ceremony, Rabbi Slarsky called my name. I thought he was going to announce that I didn't deserve to be there. He announced to the congregation that I won the award for perfect attendance.

We came to the part of the wedding ceremony where I had to perform my task. The rabbi said some words about sharing life and declared that the time had come for the couple to seal their contract by each taking a sip from the same goblet. It was a silver goblet with Hebrew letters on it. Joan turned toward me and I lifted the veil and set it back on her head. She turned and faced the rabbi again. The rabbi said that now the bride would take a sip of wine and pass the cup to the groom. He nodded to Joan who put her hand on the goblet stem. That's all. She didn't lift the cup. She just stood there with her hand on the cup. Maybe she didn't hear the rabbi's instructions. The rabbi whispered it again, but Joan just stood there with her hand on the goblet. Inside my head I said, "Joan, pick up the goblet. Didn't you hear him? You're supposed to pick it up." But she didn't. She just stood there. Should I give her a poke? The whole room was waiting for the ceremony to continue, for the groom to take a sip then smash a glass under his foot. With the bang of his heel and the sound of the glass crunching to bits everyone would yell, "Mazel tov!" But Joan just stood there with her hand around the stem of the silver goblet. At last, the rabbi put his hand around hers and lifted the goblet and directed it toward her lips. She took a sip and passed it to Raf.

The chairs were cleared away and tables set up for dinner with space for a dance floor. A band started playing. Raf took Joan in his arms and danced her around. He was a good dancer, twirled her around with exuberance despite her extreme self-consciousness. She seemed relieved when the guests stopped watching and started dancing. Now began the interrogating of the younger sister. When was I going to get married? Any prospects? "You'll be the first to know," which meant mind your own business. I was embarrassed being single, and worried. Even my roommate was now engaged, which meant I was going to have to find an apartment I could afford on my own or advertise for another roommate and live with a stranger. What if I never found a husband? What if The Great Unknown had chosen me to be barren? I loved children and wanted a baby. But I didn't envy any of my married friends. It was appalling to me to watch my friend from college stopping her day to cook dinner for her law school husband who sat at the table waiting to be served then commented on how close she had come to pleasing him. "Could be hotter," he said the night I visited.

After the wedding dinner, when the band was on break and Raf was talking to some friends across the ballroom, I sat down next to Joan. "How come you didn't pick up the goblet?"

"I couldn't."

"What do you mean?"

"It wouldn't budge. It was like asking me to pick up a car."

"Why? Why did it feel like that?"

"Because Daddy was holding it down. He didn't want me to seal the contract."

"Why?"

"He doesn't like Raf."

"But he never met Raf."

"He did tonight."

CHAPTER EIGHTEEN

....

When I came from Cambridge to visit, Mother made dinner for Joan and me, and it was always a relief when Raf wasn't there. His was a big presence. He loved to talk about the Vietnam War, how we shouldn't have bombed Haiphong, about corruption in Albany, about how Albert DeSalvo was not really the Boston Strangler but just some nut who wanted publicity. He talked about the wonders of Wilt Chamberlain setting an NBA record of forty-one rebounds. He didn't believe the Warren Commission's conclusion that Lee Harvey Oswald was the only one who fired at President Kennedy. Raf believed there was a second gunman, that the mafia was involved and so was Fidel Castro.

It was troubling how quiet Joan became around him. Was that true when she was alone with him? She told me that she'd done a painting in her night class and brought it home and put it on the kitchen table. When Raf got home, he set his briefcase right on top of it, didn't even notice. I was torn between blaming Raf for being so oblivious and wondering why Joan didn't say anything. Why, instead of wilting and hurrying into the bedroom, didn't she say get your briefcase off my painting! They were living in a small apartment near the George Washington bridge close to the school where Raf was principal. He was out at meetings two or three evenings a week. As the principal's wife, Joan had to go to PTA picnics and basketball games. Raf wanted her to change her style, stop looking like such a hippie, cut her hair, wear high heels.

"I have to go to Stockbridge again," Joan said reaching for the porcelain gravy boat we hadn't seen since it went into storage when Mother moved from Chicago.

"Don't you like going?"

"Are you kidding? For what they're paying me, they could at least put me up at the Lion's Inn. I have to stay in some dinky motel next to the factory. It's torture. You deliver the design, the guy looks at it, says no problem, then you wait for the printer to come out with the sample and he shows it to you and you have to say are you blind? You think this yellow is the same as that yellow? Open your eyes! Then he goes back to print it again and you sit there forever. He comes out at last, shows you the sample, and it's like he doesn't have eyes in his head. Can't you see there's too much green in the blue flower? He argues. I say can't you see that? You can't see there's too much green? Where do they get these people?" She poured gravy into a dent in her mashed potatoes.

"Aren't you flattered that they send you?"

"No. They have to. I'm the only one in the whole place with any color sense."

Joan's chair faced a mirror on the wall. "I hate this haircut," she said. "I'm never going to Remio again. I can't believe I went back to him. I said to him, just a trim, Remio. Don't make it too short. He says he knows exactly what I mean. Next thing I know, I'm sitting there with a crew cut. I said, Remio! Look what you've done to me! He says with the first washing it'll curl right up again. So I go home. I'm telling you, I was walking along Seventh Avenue like some kind of criminal. I thought if I meet anyone I know I'll drop dead. I go down into Penn Station and guess who's there. Every day I take the train and never see a living soul, and just the day I look like an army recruit who do I see but that Linda Sud-halter person from Carnegie Tech who's having that one-woman show." Joan took a spoonful of cranberry sauce. "You know what she told me? She said going to Yale graduate school made all the difference to her. She said she never really took herself seriously as an artist until she went there. She said I should go. I felt like saying, oh, yeah, with what." Joan paused to nibble the inside of her cheek for a beat or two. "Anyway, there I am talking to her like nothing's the matter. After a while, I couldn't help bursting out with, Linda, don't you notice anything strange? She said, what. I said, my hair!

Hasn't it occurred to you that you're talking to a person with a weird crew cut? She didn't even notice. Some artist, huh? I never liked her work anyway."

I said, "Your hair doesn't look bad."

"Not now. I went back to him the next day. I said, Remio, I washed my hair and it still looks too spikey. Fix it. Meanwhile, I have to sit there and listen to him tell me all the movies he's ever seen. Takes hours."

"They don't pay you anything extra for going to Stockbridge?"

"Yeah, they do. A little. And I don't mind getting out of town. It's so pretty there. Trees, birds, it's New England."

"Raf doesn't mind your going away?" Mother said.

"Raf? I don't know."

"He lets you go?"

"Let's me?"

"He doesn't object to your being away?"

"I don't know."

"Surely they could send someone who isn't married."

"Why?"

"Why? No husband likes to be alone. And certainly not one as good looking as Raf. I've seen the way women look at him."

"You mean you think Raf is going to find someone else while I'm gone for four days?"

"I mean no husband likes to be alone. Men are men."

"What's that supposed to mean?" I butted in. In Cambridge, I was a member of Bread & Roses. I went to "cell" meetings where we talked about not getting equal pay, and whether or not to have children, and how marriage was a capitalistic institution meant to enslave women, and how we were barraged with images of infantile women with their index finger on their pouting lower lip, and how the men at work called us honey and slapped our bottoms, and how the men on the street shouted lewd things at us, and now it was time to join together, strength in numbers, let them all know we were not going to stand for it.

"You can say what you like about equality and men being the same as women and all that feminism talk," Mother said. "Women are not doing themselves any favors with this feminism business.

They're going to end up taking care of the children and the house-work *and* having to bring in a paycheck."

"Men can do housework. Nothing says the woman has to do all the housework."

"Men are men," my mother said.

"But don't you think if the husband and wife are friends the husband will want to help out?" I said.

"Friends? No. Impossible."

"What's impossible about it?"

"Men and women cannot be friends. There's always that spark."

I would have liked to argue that the days of the servile wife were finished but I didn't know if ideas translated into action. I was too young to know how life really worked. Secretly, I was sometimes appalled by the women I met at the Bread & Roses meetings because they said awful things about being a mother, about how children ruin a woman's life, keep her from her true creative self. At the same time, there were attractive women at the meetings, especially one named Ginger who lived in a basement apartment in Central Square. One evening as I sprawled on her sisal rug listening to her talk about how capitalism created the suburbs in order to isolate women and sap our confidence, I realized with a start that she was a lesbian. Here was Ginger with her abundant auburn hair and her nipples sticking out under her T-shirt and while I was not drawn to her in a sexual way, because everything below her belt did not interest me, I could certainly see her appeal. If a woman didn't need to attract a man, then she enjoyed a kind of freedom the rest of us didn't have. Ginger and I were in separate orbits.

The women who were in the other feminist group in Boston, the National Organization of Women, also seemed foreign to me because they were so comfortable. I went to one of their meetings in the posh living room of a house in Newton. The women there, with big diamond engagement rings, talked about changing the status quo but I couldn't see why. The status quo had done them good. They said daycare was the most pressing feminist issue.

Joan licked mashed potato off her fork. "How's your job? How's that Franny person?" She didn't want to argue about wom-en's rights with our mother. It wasn't that long ago that we were glaring at our mother in children's court. Now here we were eating her delicious meal.

"Quit. She got pregnant."

"I thought you said she has five children."

"Now she'll have six."

"And we'll have to support them," Mother said.

I couldn't argue with this begrudging attitude. Franny didn't deserve any help and Franny deserved all the help she could get. Both. The only solution was for Franny to be dead and anyone who met her would never want that. "There's a welfare mother in my daycare center," I said. "Her daughter is four and she's a model. The woman showed me her daughter's head shots, all dressed up in bonnets and little outfits. I saw pictures of her walking down the catwalk carrying a little parasol."

"They let black children be models?" Mother wondered.

"This one's white. A little blond girl. So I said to the mother, how do you make her do that? How do you make her get all dressed up and walk in that stylish way down the catwalk? The mother said, How? I tell her I'll fucking kill her if she don't."

"Lovely," Joan said. We cleared our plates then set out dessert dishes and sat down to sample the pecan pie Mother made.

"I had to kick out one of the kids," I said.

My mother took a bite of pie and said to herself, "Came out all right."

"He was what they call anti-social. Did you ever hear of that? You know what it means? It means he pinned down other kids and smacked their heads on the concrete playground. He would have killed them if the teachers didn't pull him away. He's four. He's a criminally insane four year old."

"Really?"

"Yes. He'd wait until the teachers weren't watching then he'd attack one of the smaller kids, sit on the kid's chest, and take his head in his hands and smash it against the concrete. He's big for a four-year-old."

"Oh, my god."

"Yes. Luckily no one was seriously hurt. But I had to call in the parents and expel him. The father is a deacon in the African

Episcopal Church and the mother is a leader in their community and they're from an old Cambridge family that's been there for generations. So in they come, the father and the mother and I tell them that I'm sorry but James can't attend the daycare center any more, and I describe his behavior and suggest that they take him to the Judge Baker clinic for evaluation. The mother tells me this will be very inconvenient for them because she works, and I say I understand but I have to consider the safety of the other twenty children at the daycare center. So next thing, the mother goes out of my office and into the play area and comes back with James and she says to him, 'You apologize to Miss Adler and tell her you will behave yourself.' James climbs up into my lap and says, 'I'm sorry.' 'You're sorry who?' says the mother. 'I'm sorry, Miss Adler.' 'And what else do you say,' says the mother. He's already forgotten what else. 'What else did I tell you to say?' He can't remember. So I say, 'James, I'm going to set you down, now. And your parents are going to take you home.' 'You should have given us more warning,' the mother says. So I remind her that I'd been phoning her for several weeks and she never bothered to return my call. And the daycare social worker tried phoning and they never returned her call either. So the parents get up and James is standing there and the father grabs him by his ear and they drag him shrieking out of the daycare center."

"I don't like you being around such people," my mother said.

"My job is such people."

"Delicious," Joan said about the pie. "Did your sculptures arrive?" We knew Mother was worried because the shipment from Italy was taking so long.

"Yes. Do you want to see?"

"Of course!"

"I don't know. I don't know if they're ready."

"But aren't they cast?"

"Yes."

"Then they're ready," Joan said pushing back her chair and standing up. "I mean you can't fix them now, right?"

Mother had stage fright. She had experienced the toil and delight of artistic work and now it would be judged. I was a member of the undiscerning public, but Joan's opinion would matter. Joan's whole life was either producing art or looking at art or thinking about art.

We followed Mother into her studio where there were a few pedestals, some bags of clay, and a smock hanging on a hook. She was nervous. She had gone to Europe for the privacy required to turn into a different person, a person closer to her conception of herself. She was an artist, not the entitled and useless wife of a rich man. In Florence, the elderly Contessa was willing to believe whatever version of herself Violet presented but in New York she might be evaluated in a harsher light. She had hoped to escape what she had been and now she would see if she'd managed that. "You haven't unpacked them?" Joan said. Mother went to one of the cartons and from the sawdust lifted out something encased in bubble wrap. It would be magnificent. Here was her calling, here was what she was meant to be, not a wife in the suburbs worrying about canapés. For years she'd been an artist trapped inside a conventional woman's body. Now she was out. Now she would shed her married name and the real Violet Greenstone would emerge, an independent person able to make her own living, needing no one. She would never marry. Why should she? She pulled at the tape and bubble wrap fell to the floor. She lifted a bronze statue about a foot tall and set it on a pedestal. "There," she said in a tremulous voice.

It was the figure of a nude woman cradling a tiny grown man in her arms, holding him as she might a nursing infant. The tiny man had a tiny erection. Everything about the piece was repulsive, including the brown surface that had not been smoothed but looked like turds patched together. The female had sinewy biceps, calf muscles, and the chest of a body builder with little breasts stuck on. She seemed copied from an anatomy book. Her face was devoid of expression but couldn't be mistaken for a mask because there was no one behind the face, no spark in the eyes. Here was the lifeless representation of an idea, an angry idea. Men are big babies and women are forced to take care of them. "Whoa," Joan said.

"What do you think?"

"Powerful," Joan said.

"That's what I was striving for." Mother turned to me. "Sonya, you're very quiet."

I was struck mute by this glimpse of the bitterness that was inside my mother. She hated men and was afraid of them. The work was furious, ugly the way an angry face is ugly. Not knowing what to say, disappointed because I wanted my mother to have success, wanted the burden of her unhappiness to be lifted from me, I said, "What's it supposed to mean, that men are big babies?"

"If that's what it means to you, then that's what it means. It's open to interpretation."

"You mean it's symbolic?"

"I mean it has an abstract quality that can be interpreted several different ways." This was exactly what it wasn't. I nodded and hummed a sound that was supposed to mean I stood corrected.

"Are there any more?" Joan said. "Let's see some more."

Mother unwrapped three more, all of them variations on the theme of big women, emaciated men, except for one other that was a horse on its back as if it had been felled by a trip wire, its legs thrust out in panic, the focal point being the horse's penis and balls that were exposed while it lay flailing on its back. All the dignity of Horse gone, it was a heap of clumsy parts. Just as disturbing as the sculptures was how few of them there were. Four. "So," she said, obviously unnerved by our response, "there you have it." Joan said something about a strong point of view. We stood in the room without speaking, keeping our eyes lowered, wishing things were different. After a few minutes, Mother stopped drooping, gathered herself together perhaps believing that she misunderstood our response. Maybe our silence was the result of being moved. "So do you think I should start looking for a gallery?"

Joan, the champion feeling hider, said without hesitation, "Sure! Why not?"

"What's the protocol? Do you send photographs? How's it done?"

"Slides."

"Could you do it for me, Joanie?"

"Me? No. You need a large format camera. You have to hire a photographer. They have to be professional photographs."

"Won't that be expensive?"

"I'll ask around at work. Has to be someone who's good at lighting."

We returned to the kitchen, cleared the table, wrapped up the remaining pie, put it in the refrigerator, scraped mashed potatoes into a Tupperware bowl, snapped down the lid, rinsed the dishes, fitted them into the dishwasher, stuffed the cork back into the wine, dumped the wilted salad into the garbage pail, lugged the trash out to the incinerator down the hall, shoved the heavy green plastic bag into the shoot, heard it whoosh on its way down to becoming someone else's concern.

Under a cloud of chagrin, we re-assembled in the living room amid the furniture from Scarsdale now in its third home. Bought at the beginning of the dream, sunlight once glinted off the glass coffee table. Here, twelve stories above the traffic, it looked tired. I could see my mother's heart aching. It was on her face and the way she sat on the sofa, with her chin lifted, as she twisted the wedding band she still wore on her finger, a symbol perhaps of how she was unavailable to suitors or perhaps an announcement to the world that someone had once loved her.

CHAPTER NINETEEN

· ·

One of the men at work said that he had to get home to talk to his wife about something, and I asked him what he meant. He meant he wanted to discuss a work problem with her. I was still perplexed. Why would he talk to his wife about something that was troubling him? It was his surprise that gave me pause. "Don't you think married people talk to each other?" he said. "Who do you think they talk to if not each other?" He looked at me with such intense concern that I felt all my attitudes wobbling.

Age twenty-six marked a turning point. Married men began to pursue me. I'd rounded some unsavory corner. Too vulnerable before, now I was fair game. It was as if my front door got a new smell and a different breed of dog was scratching there. At first, I was full of sympathy for the lonely husband so misunderstood by his wife but when I'd heard the same story three or four times and realized none of the men intended to get divorced, that they were bored at home, I made an appointment with Dr. Goldfarb and lay down on his couch.

His office was on the first floor of a brick building in Brookline. I sat on the edge of a chair in his waiting room. When his office door opened, it was always the same young man who came out, the one with the appointment before mine, the one who, as etiquette required, did not glance at me. Seeing a psychiatrist was a private matter. No one was supposed to know. Dr. Goldfarb stood in his doorway and nodded at me as I entered. In his late forties, old to me, compact and formal, wearing a dark suit, tie, and dark shoes, our eye contact was a quick tap. I knew nothing about him except that he was obviously shy. Perhaps at school he was the smartest boy in the class but nobody asked him to the prom.

His office seemed to be intentionally unrevealing. Nothing coordinated with anything else. Behind a nondescript narrow couch was a black leather Charles Eames chair, a modern chair that contrasted with his curlicue carved Victorian desk. The Van Gogh print of *Sunflowers*, available at the Harvard Coop for students furnishing their dorm room, was too commonplace to mean Dr. Goldfarb preferred the impressionists or even cared about art. Maybe he liked modern furniture or maybe the Eames chair was just the most comfortable for sitting all day. Maybe he liked Victorian desks or maybe the person who had the office before him left it there. Yet he was not a shadowy person. By the end of our very first fifty minutes together, I understood that he was not my friend and had no intention of being my friend. He was impervious to the charms I used on others. He did not laugh at my turn of phrase or my humorous observations. On the rare occasion when he did laugh, a sound came out devoid of merriment, a snuffle. He was the most serious person I'd ever met.

I visited him four times a week and lay on the couch and said whatever came into my head, narrated my dreams, described incidents from my childhood, and learned that when I was boring myself to death it was because there was something I didn't want to talk about. He seldom spoke, but when he did it meant I was supposed to pause and examine what I'd just said. His silences were just as forceful as his few words. "You were fifteen," he said repeating what I'd just said.

"Yes. She went to Louisville."

"Louisville?"

"That's where the best tumor hospital was." Silence. Then more silence. "Isn't it?" Silence. "Isn't that where the best tumor hospital is?"

Dr. Goldfarb said nothing.

"You know," I said, "I've always wondered about that. I mean to go to Louisville when you live in New York. I always wondered how Louisville could have better hospitals than New York." Silence. "Did you ever hear of a famous cancer hospital in Louisville?"

"No."

He spoke!

"You mean there isn't one?" I asked. His "no" was steering me in a direction I didn't want to go. "Did there used to be? They didn't used to have some special treatment there in Louisville?"

Dr. Goldfarb said nothing. Just let his silence do its job. "So why'd she go there?" I asked. Flat on my back, I twisted my head to find his face but could only twist far enough to see his shoes and trouser cuffs so I turned back and continued looking at the venetian blinds at half-mast shielding the view of the street and telling me by their closed slats that everything I said was private, for his ears only and in this room only. "She said it was a very delicate operation and Louisville was the only place where the surgeons knew how to do it."

He said nothing, just let the silence vibrate.

"She looked pregnant." If a wind storm can be silent, then that's what his silence was inside of me, trees blown sideways, waves rising, debris from the sidewalk swirling. "You think she was pregnant?" Bracing myself as if outside in a storm I said, "You mean you think she was pregnant but told me she had a tumor? How could someone tell their daughter they have cancer when they don't? What a mean thing to do!"

Silence. Then silence on top of silence.

"So you think she was pregnant?" Silence. He was making me work this out for myself. "Who from?" So that's what that time was all about! "Maybe Jerry Applebaum. I came in one time and she was on top of him in her bedroom and she leapt up. It was so disgusting to think about old people even touching each other. They weren't undressed or anything. I'd just caught her making out. He was a nice guy." Silence. "I think she would have married him but he never asked. He ended up marrying the nurse who took care of his wife when she was dying. So do you think he knew? You think she told him? No, wait. He was long gone by the time she got that tumor." Silence. "She wasn't seeing anybody when that happened."

"Why don't you ask her?"

He spoke! I understood him to be shoving me, almost as if saying I should grow up already. "Ask her? Are you kidding? I'd never ask her. Oh, my god. I'd never dare ask her."

"Why not?"

"Ask my mother? Are you kidding? Ask my mother if she was pregnant that time? Are you kidding? I'd never ask her." Silence. More silence. "You think I should ask her?" Silence. "She'd never tell me the truth. How could she do that? How could she think it was better to tell me she had cancer and make me think she was going to die than tell me she was pregnant? Anyway, why didn't she get an abortion? They had abortion back then. I know they did. My grandmother was always paying for her maid's abortions. Or did once. Someone said something about it, used some euphemism like how Grandma "took care" of Willa. Gee. So you think she was pregnant? You think my mother had a baby? I wonder what happened to it?" Silence. "She gave her baby away?" What had been a blur was now clear. "I wonder what it was." Is that what happened that time? Could that have happened? "You mean you think I have a brother or sister out there some place?" Would the secret linger in the form of a stranger lurking somewhere? "Maybe it died. It probably died." Silence.

I reviewed that time for my doctor. "She made me lie to everybody. I had to tell her mother she was in the tub, tell her sister she was at a class, had to lie to my grandfather. I wasn't allowed to tell anyone she wasn't home. She sent all her letters to her dressmaker and the dressmaker forwarded them so they'd have a New Rochelle postmark and not a Louisville postmark. I was hurt she trusted the dressmaker more than me. But also, I thought it was pathetic she had no one to trust except her dressmaker. Not one friend. No one. We had to stay with Ruby. It was horrible. She had a heart attack right in the kitchen. Joan and I didn't know what to do." Silence. "What a jerk. Can you imagine telling your daughter you have cancer when you don't? So mean. She'd rather tell me she was going to die than tell me she's pregnant." Silence. "She never said she was going to die. I don't think she ever said she had cancer. She said she had a tumor and she was going to a hospital in Louisville that specialized in taking tumors out. It was a special kind of tumor. I remember wondering if she was going to die but not really worrying about it. She wasn't even there when I got my college acceptance letter. No, wait. That was a different time."

For almost an hour the revelation of what really happened had been swirling around the office almost like clothes in a dryer, some clunking against the side, all of them in motion. "You mean my mother had a baby?"

Later, back in my apartment, thinking about the session, I decided that Dr. Goldfarb could not possibly know every clinic that was ever in Louisville. Maybe there did used to be one that specialized in taking out tumors. Just because it wasn't there now and just because he never heard of it in medical school or during his years in practice, didn't mean there wasn't such a place. How would he know what's in Kentucky? His accent was New York. He graduated from Harvard and did his residency at Columbia, so how could such an East Coast person know anything about the South?

I phoned Joan at the apartment she rented after her divorce from Raf. "Joan. Do you think our mother was pregnant that time?"

"What time?"

"The tumor time."

"Pregnant? Why would you think that?"

"Because don't you think it's weird a person would go to Kentucky instead of to Sloane Kettering?"

"No. She explained that. There was only one doctor who knew how to do it. Wait a minute." She put her palm over the phone as she shouted at her four-year-old daughter who was again bullying her two-year-old son. "Jenny! If you do that to him one more time . . . Stop it! Just stop hitting him. Give that back to him. Give it back! I'm going to count . . . One . . . two . . . " She took her palm off the receiver. "I'm going bonkers. Guess how much child support Raf owes?"

"I don't know."

"Guess."

"I don't know."

"Fifteen thousand dollars. I have to go to court again. Stupid moron. Always dragging me into court. Oh you should have seen him the last time. The girlfriend dresses him in leisure suits. Looked like he just came from a game of pinochle at the golf club."

"So do you think she might have had a baby that time?"

"No. Don't be ridiculous."

"But why would she go to Kentucky?"

"She told us. There was only one surgeon who could remove that kind of tumor."

"What kind of tumor?"

"The kind she had," Joan said.

"She never told us the kind she had."

"She told me. She told me it had to be removed vaginally."

"What? She never told me that."

"She told me."

"What kind of tumor comes out of your twat?"

"I don't know. Her kind, I guess."

"Joan. She had a baby. Our mother had a baby."

Silence. Then, "What'd she do with it?"

"I don't know."

"Poor Mother."

"Poor us."

"Poor everybody in the whole fucking world. Jenny, put that down. I told you not to play with that."

CHAPTER TWENTY

U nlike his father, Uncle Alan's goal was not to grow Greenstone
Enterprises. It was just the right size, from his point of view.
He admired no one more than his own father but understood himself to be a different kind of soul. While Max Greenstone loved
taking risks, Alan Greenstone preferred safety. He was a domestic
man, liked walking the dog on suburban streets at night with no
flashlight, going on cruises with another couple, eating breakfast
with his wife on the patio in warm weather. His father traveled on
luxurious ocean liners, combined business with pleasure when
he went to inspect his manufacturing plants in Greece, France,
England, India, and Japan. But times had changed and travel was
a chore. Alan waited in lines at crowded airports, hurried down
endless corridors, and waited for suitcases in foreign hubs where
baggage claim was slip shod. Was it necessary for Greenstones to
be international? The domestic branch alone would keep Alan and
his family secure.

Grandpa Greenstone, tired of going into the office and enduring freezing winters, moved with his wife to Miami. He wanted
Jordan to move with him but Jordan wouldn't. The chauffeur said
he would never live in Miami, the place was too racist. Willa was
not invited because Grandma had fired her. She said Willa was a
thief. "What did she steal?" I asked Grandma on the phone. "Never
mind. That is not important. She cannot be trusted."

Grandpa let it be known that he no longer wished to be
consulted. He was done. He was happiest wearing his pajamas
and watching Perry Mason on TV. If his son Alan thought selling
the foreign companies was the right thing to do, then it was.

In order to attract buyers, Alan had to purge excess from the books. His accountants eliminated the salary paid each year to a Customer Liaison Agent. "He can't do that!" My mother yelled to her mother on the phone. "That's not what Dad wanted. Who does Alan think he is? What does he expect me to live on?" Grandma did not come to her defense. "She so much as called me a parasite," Mother told me.

No longer able to afford Manhattan, my mother moved to an apartment in Mount Vernon. She noticed cigarette butts pushed into the dirt of the potted plants in the lobby and cigarette holes in the rubber plant leaves. But she didn't take those tiny brutalities as a sign that she might not like her neighbors. She never factored in neighbors. She never had anything to do with neighbors, not in New Rochelle, Scarsdale, Chicago, or the Upper East Side. In Mount Vernon, the neighbors forced her to pay attention. From behind locked doors, dogs cried piteously all day until their owners returned from work. Rock music blasted out into the halls. She could hear other people's televisions through the walls, and the tenants above her were always scraping furniture across floors with no carpet.

She had no interest in men even as occasional escorts. She had no interest in women either, never mentioned wanting to make friends. She was devoting herself to the study of Zen, which she understood to be a philosophy that justified a desire to be alone. She was *letting go*. Having no interaction with other people was not a fault but a virtue. One had to detach from all worldly things. Almost every time I phoned she was meditating. She responded to what I said in a distracted way as if she couldn't wait to hang up.

The creative energy that had been focused on sculpture now turned to other pursuits. She bought calligraphy brushes and practiced forming Chinese characters. She knit coats with patterns that required the interweaving of six or seven colors. She joined the Paranormal Society where people took seriously visitations from the dead and having a college degree meant nothing, as if it was the least important ingredient to knowledge. But all her activities, including her practice of meditation, could not erase the humiliation of being a poor relation. Her sister Dovey Lee in Rome frequented the famous designer who dressed Audrey Hepburn, sat on a comfortable loveseat while models paraded for her alone. Her brother installed a swimming pool in his backyard, the water always welcoming. Neither of them got off an elevator and stepped over a dog pee stain on the hall carpet.

Grandpa Greenstone was dead for three days before I heard about it. Joan told me. She wondered what time I was getting to Miami. "How could you not tell me Grandpa died?" I spoke to Mother as if shaking a child who played with matches.

"Why? There was nothing you could do about it."

"But it was Grandpa! He was my grandfather! You could have told me. Now Grandma thinks I don't care about her because I didn't call her."

"Whatever you say."

"What time are you getting into Miami?"

"I'm not going to Miami."

"What do you mean? You're not going to your father's funeral?"

"No. All that mumbo jumbo. Means nothing."

"But won't your mother be hurt?"

"My mother? What's she got to do with it?"

"He was her husband!"

"I know he was her husband, Sonya. You're always so superior all the time."

Joan didn't go either. "He says he can't take the kids so I can go to Grandpa's funeral, because that's the weekend he's going to Cancun with his girlfriend. I said, 'You think going to Cancun with whore brain is as important as me going to Grandpa's funeral?' He says that I never liked Grandpa anyway so why go to his funeral and pretend I'm bereaved."

Wiley met me at the airport with the top down in his rented convertible. He grabbed me and hugged me and carried my suitcase out to the car. We pulled out into traffic and sped off onto the highway lined with palm trees. Wiley's attractiveness never failed to enchant me. "So how are you?" I shouted. He shouted back, "I'm leaving Price Waterhouse. Going to Fidelity."

"Why?"

"They wouldn't let me keep my parrot in the office."

"Your parrot? What parrot?"

"Conchita."

"You brought your parrot to work?"

"My clients didn't care. They liked her. She can say stock market and Dow Jones."

"But people don't bring their pets to work, Wiley."

"I do."

"Is Fidelity letting you bring your bird to work?"

"I told them if they want me, they get Conchita too."

"You must have some pretty good clients, Wiley."

"Yeah, I do. All the old ladies love me."

"Can't you just leave your bird at home?"

"No. I can't. She gets lonely. She needs someone to talk to."

"Wiley, you are a weird person. You know that, right?" He glanced at me to see if I'd said that in a mean way, saw I said it fondly, and patted my hand. "I wish I'd visited Grandpa. I didn't know it was so bad. I should have come down here the first time he went to the hospital."

Word had it that Grandpa's stomach cancer was caused by all the aspirins he took.

Grandma Greenstone's apartment had a wide view of the Atlantic and was the same height off the ground as pelicans fly. Standing on her terrace, they were at eye level as they glided out over the waves and dive bombed into the water. Grandma was shrunken, as if her substance was sucked out. I'd seen other widows and knew she'd inflate again after some time. Now she was as fragile as a spider web. No one hugged her. No one kissed her. No one put an arm around her shoulder. She didn't cry. She didn't speak. She seemed surrounded by a force field that repelled others. At first, I thought she was particularly rejecting of me. I said, "Grandma, I didn't know Grandpa died. My mother didn't even tell me." She did not reply, just turned her head and endured the next person who stood before her and said some words. Uncle Alan was there and Aunt Dolly and their now grown children, but Aunt Dovey Lee and Uncle Jack were not there. They had never forgiven Grandpa for choosing Alan above Jack to run Greenstones. I wished I could have consoled Grandma about this, said something like it must have been difficult to not have either daughter at the funeral but it was impossible to console her. She was aloof.

When I saw the coffin at the chapel, I started crying but quickly hid my face because no one else was crying. It seemed bad manners. We were supposed to just sit there in the pews, stony, while the rabbi said words about a man he'd never met. I knew the body inside was not the grandfather I remembered, because Wiley had seen him before he died and told me Grandpa weighed about ninety pounds. I was glad the coffin was closed. I was sorry I'd never taken time off from work to visit him in the hospital. I should have learned from my father's death but I didn't, was still amazed when someone actually died.

We gathered at Grandma's apartment where it was disturbing to see Grandpa's recliner orphaned in front of the TV. Sandwiches, potato salad, coleslaw and various breads, cookies and cakes, had been set out on the counter in the kitchen by Lester the chauffeur meant to replace Jordan. Lester thought he was too good for the job and had every right to use Grandma's Cadillac whenever he felt like it. Sometimes she called down to the garage and the car was gone. Lester was afraid of Grandpa but had nothing but contempt for Grandma. He wasn't going to let some old white lady tell him what to do. Grandpa was the one who hired the chauffeurs so in a way Grandma never had a chauffeur, which is perhaps why she didn't understand the boundaries of the job. She wanted Lester to mop the kitchen floor and clean the bathrooms and go to the grocery store. She was trying to turn him into Willa.

Cousin Wiley and I escaped the reception and took a walk on the boardwalk. The people enjoying the beach were an odd combination of men in thongs, orthodox Jews covered head to toe, and elderly women walking in pairs on the wet part of the sand near the waves. "Poor little Grandma," I said. "I wish she had Willa. At least that would be some continuity with the past. Wow! Did you see that? A dive-bomber! How does it see the fish so clearly from up in the sky?"

"Polarized vision. To pelicans the ocean is clear glass. They don't see the sparkles on the waves."

"So I don't need to admire?"

"Go head. Admire." We paused to watch a cruise ship make its slow progress near the horizon. "Don't mention Willa."

"Why?"

"Just don't, Sonya. Never mention her to me again. And don't ask me why."

"Why?"

"I can't tell you."

"You can too."

We sat down on a bench. I had stopped smoking but Wiley still did, lit his cigarette with his Playboy lighter, exhaled smoke, and said, "But you swear upon the children you'll have when you get married that you'll never tell?"

"Yes." We watched the waves that came in one after the other perpetually forever. I wondered if they could suddenly swell and turn tidal with no warning. I didn't trust the ocean. Nor did I like sitting in the sun. There was a spot on top of my head that received sunrays as if they were daggers. It actually hurt to be in the sun. But Wiley was loving it. He was basking with his face turned up.

"But you'll hate me."

"Tell me anyway."

"It was my fault Willa got fired." He glanced sideways at me on the bench next to him to see my reaction and when I didn't react he continued. "I was visiting Grandma and Grandpa in Chicago. My parents were in Rome, and I had to stay with them during Thanksgiving break. I was really bored so I was wandering around one evening and went into Grandpa's room and looked in his bureau."

"Why?"

"I just told you. I was bored. You know how his socks were in the top drawer?"

"No. I didn't know that."

"You did too."

"Why do you say that?"

"Because I know you."

"You mean you think I looked in Grandpa's bureau?"

"Yes. You did. Don't lie."

"Okay. I did."

"Right. So you know how his socks were all neatly paired in the top drawer? I wanted the brown ones with the stripes on them so I took them."

"But what does this have to do with Willa?"

"That's when Grandma fired her. That was just the sort of thing Grandma would fire her about."

"You mean you think Grandma knew every pair of Grandpa's socks?"

"Absolutely. That's why she's never said exactly why she fired her because even Grandma knows it was petty. She could never tell us she fired Willa over a pair of missing socks but that's what she did."

"But why didn't you just ask Grandpa if you could have those socks?"

"How could I ask him? He'd know I was poking around in his bureau."

"But why didn't you confess when you found out Willa got fired?"

"Too embarrassed. I've never told anyone. Ever."

"You mean you let Willa get fired? You just let her get fired? What about her children?"

"See. I knew you'd judge me." Here was a guile he must have used with his mother when she scolded him. Shrinking into himself and looking very miserable must have worked.

"How could I not judge you? That was a terrible thing you did. You should tell Grandma. You should tell her now. She's probably still disappointed that her beloved Willa turned out to be a thief. How could you do that?"

"See. I knew I shouldn't have told you." He increased his injured child posture by pushing his lower lip forward.

"I mean I could sort of understand if you were a child. But you weren't a child. You were a grown man."

"Well, not exactly."

"Grown enough." We sat without speaking for a while, watching the waves roll in, roll in, roll in. A man walked at the water's edge with a little boy then paused to wait for the child to dig some treasure out of the sand. The dad put the little treasure in his bathing suit pocket then they continued hand in hand. I tried to imagine Wiley in college with parents living in Italy and his childhood house sold out from under him. He must have greeted every college break with anxiety instead of joy. He had to make do with friends' houses. My mother was in Italy too but at least I had my father's house. I might not have liked being there with Annabelle but at least it was mine and I had a right to it. Maybe Wiley felt the world owed him something. "You must have liked those socks."

"I did."

"Do you wear them for dress up?"

"No."

"You mean you just keep them like your little wad of secret shame?"

"Not exactly."

"Wiley, you have to wear those socks. That way it won't be an entire waste."

"I can't."

"But you should. You should wear them. Grandpa would be sorry you stole them but he'd be glad you're enjoying them."

"I threw them away."

"What? When?"

"At the time."

"Why? Why did you throw them away?"

"Couldn't stand to look at them."

"So Willa got fired for no reason whatsoever?"

"Yes."

"Wiley! You're a coward."

"Yes."

"But I don't want you to be a coward."

"I don't want to be either."

"Then tell Grandma. You have to tell Grandma. Then she can write to Willa or call her or something. I'm sure she still feels terrible about Willa."

"I was an idiot to tell you."

"Do you want me to forgive you?"

"Yes."

"But it's not up to me. It's not my forgiveness that you need."

"So do you hate me?"

"I hate that you did that."

"So do you hate me?"

"I can't stand the sun on me anymore." I stood up and walked to some shade under a palm tree. Wiley stayed on the bench with his hurt expression. Maybe this was what Dr. Goldfarb meant by relationship. He kept telling me it didn't matter how many college degrees, how handsome, how rich, the person was, it was my relationship with the person that mattered. You can add a person up on paper and the total might be impressive, but it didn't mean you got along. The men I dated all went to Ivy League schools and had professions. My boyfriend was the youngest doctor ever accepted onto the Harvard faculty at Mass General. He graduated from Yale undergraduate then Harvard Medical School. My mother met him and called him "a prize."

I went back to the bench and stood before Wiley. "You're a total moron," I said. So this was how women could stay married to drunks and crooks. Their heads said one thing and their hearts said another. He stood up and we hugged. "You won't tell?" he asked.

"No. I want to, but I won't. What you should do is try to find Willa. Tell her you know she did nothing wrong. Can you imagine how injured she felt when Grandma fired her?"

"Stop. Just stop talking, please. She would have lost her job anyway. She wasn't going to move to Florida with all her kids."

"But she wouldn't have lost her job shamed."

"Sonya. *Basta! Stai zitta!*" He spent summers in Rome and was fluent in Italian.

My estimation of Wiley had gone down, but I still loved him. His presence was dear to me, his body and his face and his hair and the gap between his front teeth and his physical warmth. This was perhaps the first time I ever felt that head/heart divide, that cliché of song lyrics that the head says one thing and the heart another. For a second I felt like I was Titania in *Midsummer Night's Dream* and woke up loving Bottom.

It wasn't long before we all learned the contents of Grandpa Greenstone's will. He left everything to his wife. When she died,

DIANA ALTMAN • 215

it would go to their children. He left nothing to his grandchildren, believing the money would trickle down to us eventually. The only gift Grandpa left to Violet was half of a warehouse in Oklahoma City. He bestowed the other half on Alan with the stipulation that when Alan sold the warehouse, Violet's share would be put in trust with Alan as trustee. Grandpa did not believe his daughter capable of taking care of her own affairs. This was a terrible blow to my mother. I think she saw herself as her father's favorite. She was "the pretty one." Now she realized that her father thought her so stupid she couldn't even take care of her own money. The warehouse was worth about a million dollars, and when it was sold she would get five hundred thousand that she couldn't spend without asking her brother, who was only one year older. It was as if the last words her father said to her were, "I don't respect you. You are incapable of acting like an adult." On the phone she said, "Well, that's that," which I took to mean she had no intention of sharing her pain with me and that some decision was forming inside of her.

CHAPTER TWENTY-ONE

....

My boyfriend Stewart Weintraub was the youngest man ever accepted to the Harvard Medical School faculty. His goal was nothing less than to cure blindness, especially that caused by *retinitis pigmentosa*, a hereditary malady passed from mother to son. Stewart was a medium-sized man with brown hair, a large nose, and very clean fingernails. His eyes were blue and sad. There was an injured quality about him that was appealing. From him, I learned that there was a machine that could actually measure the amount of electricity generated by the eye. The feeling of having someone looking at you came from actual beams shooting out of the person's eyes. The intensity of that beam could be measured. This deepened the meaning of the words *ogle* and *leer*. It wasn't only in a woman's head, after all, that she felt sullied by such looks. Something actually got on her when men looked at her that way. Even if the person was behind her, she could feel the penetration of that look. People with *retinitis pigmentosa* gradually lost the electricity in their eyes until there was none. I admired Stewart's obsession with his work, his dedication to helping people. He was five years older than I, believed in "spheres of influence." Mine would be the home and his the outside world. It was the husband's duty to bring the outside world inside to his wife. "You mean I have to stay inside all the time?" I said.

"No. I mean the wife is in charge of the home."

"But suppose I don't want to be in charge of the home."

"Then you hire somebody."

"Thank you."

"The wife organizes the home. That's her sphere of influence."

"Well, I'm glad I don't have to mop the floors all the time."

"Don't be silly. You know what I mean."

"Can I ever go out of the house?"

"Yes. You can go out of the house."

"Thank you."

"You're welcome. Now let me work. I'm almost done with this."

If I complained to my mother about Stewart's preoccupation with his work, she said, "A man who only has you on his mind, doesn't have much on his mind." I never suspected that the opposite might be true. Stewart was the sort of person I was supposed to marry. He published papers in the *New England Journal of Medicine*. He graduated from Yale then Harvard Medical School. He took me to expensive restaurants where I sipped wine and admired him as he spoke about himself. He believed he would die young and had no time to waste. We never just hung out and took walks or sat in a coffee house but always had dates, either for dinner, the symphony, or a play. Though Stewart was preoccupied, it was in the cause of others. There was nothing conceited about him.

If we had nothing scheduled, I went to his apartment and listened to his expensive stereo with headphones on while he worked at his kitchen table. We slept at his apartment but never at mine. He was an indifferent lover, not particularly interested in sex, often too tired to even bother. Nor was he one of my friends. He was never one of the group sitting around in my apartment, passing a joint and convulsed with laughter. Yet I was hoping we would get married.

Jewish mothers all over Boston tried to fix him up. He was the catch of all catches. Sometimes he went out on blind dates but mostly he didn't. We were a couple. I was the one he brought home to meet his parents in their dark house in Boston, where Stewart sat at the table with his eyes lowered not saying a word and slumping in his chair like a child of eight. His father was a doctor and his mother was a snob. It was illuminating and horrible to see him with them, silent and sheepish despite being the winner of several prizes. I was the date who went with him to family weddings where we didn't dance because he didn't know how. He didn't approve of my clothes, wished I would dress in a more conservative manner, *a la* the Junior League. In particular, he didn't like my leather jacket with the curly sheepskin lining and the embroidery on the front, my favorite jacket. We spent a lot of time wishing that the other would change. He was allergic to my cat.

One evening when I was alone in my apartment in Cambridge, I tried to draw my cat sleeping with a paw over her face. As a child and even as a teenager I could have done this but my skill had atrophied. I had forgotten how much I enjoyed drawing and regretted losing this skill so I signed up for a night art class at the Boston Museum School. When I went to register, there was a young man ahead of me in line, a teddy bear cuddly person with curly hair, funny, easy to talk to.

The class was in a large room with a ceiling of exposed pipes, the veins that carried the life blood of the building. I admired that the architect didn't hide the pipes, how they made a pleasing design though that wasn't their purpose. We sat in chairs designed for drawing. One arm flared out into a flat desk big enough to hold our oversized newsprint sketchpads. The teddy bear man and I selected chairs next to each other in front of a raised platform. At the back of the platform was a screen. From behind the screen a woman in her thirties walked to the front of the platform absolutely naked and sat on a chair with her legs slightly apart. She had small triangular breasts, exactly the kind I don't like to see, a roll of fat around her stomach and a bush of black hair that came part way down her thighs. She put her hand behind her neck and slouched and everyone in the room began to sketch, so that's how I knew the class had begun. A little while later, a young woman dressed in a long skirt and a silky blouse, with brown hair down to her waist stood in front of the raised platform and said, "Twenty second sketches," so I figured she was the teacher. The model changed her pose every twenty seconds and the room was filled with the sound of sketchpad pages flipping up and charcoal scraping over paper. I was happy when the poses lasted longer, because then I could concentrate on making the fingers exact and getting the nose the right distance from the eyes. At break time, the model put on a robe, a strange gesture of modesty seeing as how she'd already showed a roomful of strangers her privates. Maybe she thought the robe-covered person was the real her.

A week later, the night before my second drawing class, I was at Stewart's apartment. He was sitting at his kitchen table working on a paper. I was sitting on his sofa with big headphones on listening to the Brahms clarinet quintet and feeling lucky to have a boyfriend with such expensive stereo equipment. Just as I was getting up to turn the record over, the phone rang. Stewart got up from the kitchen table and went into the bedroom to answer his phone. I did not turn the record over but stood still so I could hear what he was saying in the next room. I heard him making plans to see another woman. I could tell by the formality in his voice that he was making a date with a person he didn't know. I was sitting right there in his apartment and he was making a date with someone else. He came out of the bedroom, sat down again at the kitchen table where there were papers and books strewn about, picked up his pen, and returned to writing.

I flew at him with my fists and smacked him again and again. He tried to contain me, tried to grab my hands but my rage was so intense, fury made me strong. Papers blew all over the place as I slapped him and punched him and smacked him all the while hearing a voice inside my head saying, "This is the most uncomfortable feeling I've ever had." I was out of my mind. At last the storm passed and there I stood, spent. He said, "That shows you love me."

The following night, I went to my second drawing class full of gloom. That was the worst fight I'd ever had with anyone in my life. Now I knew what blind rage was. I sat at my desk sketching the nude model and feeling as if my heart weighed a ton. During the break, I went to the school store to buy a gummy eraser. Maybe if I had one of those erasers I'd draw better and get happier.

Worrying about the fight, new eraser in my pocket, I headed back to class down a corridor under a ceiling of exposed pipes. Suddenly, I had an epiphany. It was as if the skies opened up and bright rays were shooting down from heaven carrying a voice that said, *That's how you felt as a child. This man makes you angry, jealous, and disappointed. You were angry at your father, jealous of your sister, disappointed by your mother. You're in the habit of being jealous, angry, and disappointed and that's why this man feels like home. It's a habit. Those feelings are a habit, and you can break the habit just like you broke the fingernail biting habit in second grade.*

I stood there, rooted, as other students walked by me unaware that I was in the middle of a life-changing event. Being single wasn't the worst thing in the world. It was much better than being with a person who provoked such rage. I didn't need to change myself so Stewart would find me more acceptable as a mate. What I had to change was allowing myself to be with people who made me feel bad. Myself was okay as is. What I had to avoid was being with people who made me unhappy. There was only one criteria for the next man. Does he make me happy? Being happy is a choice. Stunned, slightly trembling, I went back to class.

The drawing teacher stood at the front of the room advising us to see the model as a combination of shapes, negative spaces, and shadows. We should view the model as we might an eggplant. Then she went from chair to chair offering suggestions in a soft voice. Looking at the squeezed down little figure in the corner of my paper, she suggested I fill up the whole page. I understood her to be saying, take a chance. Be bold. Dare to fill up your life. It seemed a prophetic coincidence that she said this to me immediately after my visitation. Yes, I would flip the paper over and use big strokes.

I was so dazed, I just sat there absently watching the teacher go from student to student. Across the room she leaned down to speak to a man who was too tall to fit neatly in his drawing chair. His long legs stuck out in the aisle. As the teacher leaned down to offer suggestions, her silky hair fell forward and I was stabbed by a dagger of jealousy. The words in my head were *Stop it! Stop taking advantage of your position as teacher to flirt with him. Get away from him!* This was strange. I had never seen that man before.

At the break, when the room was empty, I went from chair to chair pretending to be looking at everyone's drawing but really I wanted to see his. Now I saw what the teacher meant by big gestures. All the other sketchpad pages were full of sweeping lines, suggestions of a female form. Mine was the only tiny squeezed up literal representation of the model. This, apparently, was a class of art students who had sketched models hundreds of times. Walking as nonchalantly as possible, I paused at the lanky man's sketchpad. His was the best. The figure on the page was full of personality. He'd captured the slovenly posture and the anxiety in the unkempt hairdo. He'd drawn the nipples like little structures.

I went out to the hall as he was coming back, maybe from the bathroom. His walk was unusual, as distinctive as his drawing. He undulated, graceful as a giraffe. His hair was brown, straight, shiny, combed over to the side so it fell over one eyebrow. He came right over to me, stood fearlessly in front of me, maybe even a bit too close, and said down into my face, "Hello."

There was something familiar about him, like I was with a cousin or someone I'd known since kindergarten. I said, "Do you see the model as shapes?"

"I'm trying to," he replied without stepping back, still right in front of me looking down into my upturned face.

"You're a good artist." I felt surrounded by calm.

"Thank you."

"Are you an artist?"

"Yes. I'm an architect." Architect? (Wow! That would do. That would do nicely.)

He asked, "What do you do?"

"I'm a writer." Where did that come from? I was the director of a daycare center in Cambridge who, besides writing grants and newsletters and press releases, also wrote stories at night, sent them out, then got happy if an editor wrote encouraging words on the rejection letter.

"Ever have anything published?"

"No," I said. "Boo hoo." I put my forehead on his chest. I touched my forehead to the chest of a total stranger and in that second I got a whiff of that male odor that cannot be bottled. My knees buckled. He said his name was Leo and I told him mine was Sonya but neither of us said our last names.

That night I phoned Stewart and told him we were finished. He said I shouldn't take our fight so seriously. He had to go on those blind dates. The mothers were friends with his mother. He wasn't going to take that girl out again. But I was now a different person.

If a surgeon opened my head, he would confirm that everything in there had been rearranged. (Thank you, Dr. Goldfarb!)

I couldn't wait for my next art class. When Leo saw me his face brightened. We stood in the hall talking during class breaks. I discovered that he didn't have a job and lived at home. No job and living with mother were deal breakers. Yet all I could do was smile when we were together, and my insides felt in a continuous riot of giddiness. I just couldn't stop smiling when we were together. "How come you live at home?"

"Because I just got home from Vietnam."

"You were in Vietnam?" Everyone I knew tried to escape going to Vietnam. They got notes from their shrinks saying they were too crazy.

"Yes. I was an officer in the Navy."

"You got drafted?"

"No. I wanted to serve. I was an officer on a destroyer."

"You were in the Vietnam War?"

"Yes."

"You couldn't get out of it?"

"I didn't want to get out of it."

"You didn't? Why not?"

"I wanted to serve my country."

"But the war is all wrong."

"Maybe. Time will tell whether that's true or not."

"You got drafted?"

"No. I was in ROTC during college."

"What?"

"I believe men should serve their country."

"Did you shoot anybody?"

"Not directly. But I was the gunnery officer. The Admiral came aboard once, and said I had the best guns in the Atlantic fleet."

"What does the best guns mean?"

"Here's what I did. There's a strict hierarchy in the Navy. The lowest is the seaman. It's important for the guns on a ship to be clean and ready to fire at all times. They need to be oiled and polished. This is not easy to do. They're huge. On my ship, the petty officer third class in charge of the guns was lazy. He was a bad influence on the seamen whose job it was to keep the guns in good order. The seamen were hard working men, and I could see that they could take no pride in their work. So I fired the petty officer and put one of the seamen in charge of the guns. This was unheard of. I promoted a lower rank above the higher rank. The petty officer complained. I said he was more than welcome to request a transfer. He complained to the Captain. The Captain was my friend not only because we played bridge at night but also because I redesigned the ward room. The result was the seamen were so happy to be given the chance to show what they were capable of and our guns were polished and oiled and ship shape all the time. That's how I did that."

Who was this person? "What's the ward room?"

"Where the officers eat. It was cramped and ugly when I came aboard, so I redesigned it."

"They knew you were an architect?"

"Sure."

Nothing was more unfashionable in Cambridge than participating in the Vietnam War. I could hardly believe I was meeting a person who went voluntarily. "I wanted to see the world," Leo said, "and I did."

"But you could have just strapped on a backpack and hitch hiked across Europe."

"No. I wanted to see the world aboard a ship. It was my dream since age ten."

"Why?"

"I don't know. I like boats."

"How come you don't have a job?"

"Because I just got home."

"When?"

"About a week before this class started."

"Are you going to get a job?"

"Of course. By the way, when we were in line registering for this class, I saw you with that guy you're sitting next to. He's not for you."

Sitting in the passenger seat of Leo's Saab, being so near him in that small car as he dominated the space behind the wheel, his head almost touching the roof, he seemed intensely other. He did nothing exceptional yet everything he did was fascinating, how he handled the gear shift, his jacket sleeve moving to reveal a thin wrist, how he flicked the blinker, how his hands looked on the wheel, beautiful large graceful hands, how he sat slightly slouched looking out the windshield. He was entirely not me, another species altogether.

We went to a bar called My Father's Moustache and sat at a table across from each other. I found myself leaning forward to inhale his smell. It took me a while to figure out what was odd about his gaze. He did not keep his eyes on my eyes but more on the area under my eyes so that our pupils never really connected. It was the Catholic priest gaze. I couldn't see into him nor did he look into me. One of his eyes was blue and the other was hazel. They did not align exactly. One was slightly turned in and that kept his gaze from being straight forward. This physical defect made it very easy to be with him. Perhaps because my mother was so critical, I did not like being looked at. When anyone looked at me I thought they were finding fault. So Leo's gaze was restful. At the same time, I did enjoy the sexual pleasure of looking deeply into a man's eyes. This could never happen with Leo not only because his eyes did not focus in that way, but also because he was too shy to burrow into anyone. This would be a loss for me. Now I realized that being with someone was a matter of agreeing to a series of losses. Him too. With me.

I worried that his being in Vietnam was just an excuse, that maybe he was a chronic unemployed person. As for living at home, maybe he was a mama's boy and couldn't leave home. But none of that seemed to matter. We laughed so much, we liked the same movies, we closed our eyes and listened to Brahms. Friends who had yet to meet him asked, what's he like? What could I say? He makes funny gentle jokes? Like when we went to Sanders Theater to listen to chamber music, Leo turned in his seat and pretended to shout, "Is there a doctor in the house?" Everyone was a doctor! Or when we went to the opera to see Verdi's *Ottelo* and he called out softly as we were applauding, "Author! Author!" When I told him I was worried about always writing about the same thing he said,

"That's like telling Cezanne enough with the apples already!" He touched me all the time, stood close to me, held my hand, played with me by flinging me around. He wasn't *like* anything. We just got along. Still, we didn't tell each other our last names. Perhaps we both felt that our last names would reveal our backgrounds and our backgrounds might not be compatible. I thought he was a Wasp. His hair was brown and straight like the boys at Yale, he wore preppy clothes, and Christian boys seemed to be the ones who liked the military. I didn't want him to know I was Jewish. I thought that would ruin everything.

After two months, we decided to tell. "You go first," I said.

"No. Ladies first."

"You."

"You."

"You, Brownie."

"Brownie?"

"You have big brown eyes."

"Okay. Adler. Sonya Adler."

"You're a Jewish girl?" he said with a Yiddish accent.

"Is that bad?"

"Better I should marry an Italian girl? I thought you were Italian. I thought I'd have to bring home a Catholic girl."

"They wouldn't like a Catholic girl?"

"No, they would not. They're kosher."

"You're Jewish?"

"Yes."

"You mean you're a suburban Jewish kid just like me?"

"Yes."

"Are you kosher?"

"No."

"Why?"

"I wanted to try lobster."

"Did you like it?"

"Yes. But I don't like ham."

"Did you ever try it?"

"Yes. I don't like it."

"What about bacon?"

"I like bacon."

"So, you mean you're the boy next door?"

"Yes, Brownie. Seems to be turning out that way." When he told me he loved me, something inside of me relaxed, as if an armistice was signed and I could go home.

Leo's father was a dignified, affable man who swept Grandma Greenstone right off her little pumps, sat her down, and shared family history with her. He was accustomed to Lower East Side Jews, never knew there were Jewish pioneers in Texas and New Mexico, Jews like Grandma's cousin who set up mercantile stores in dusty towns where the population was 350 and cowboys came into town after moving cattle to the freight cars. Leo's father possessed the attribute Grandma prized above all others: he was tall. It was in her reverence for height that her immigrant past leaked out. At four years old, she probably couldn't see that the men were small on the ship from Lithuania but she certainly could see as time went by that her father and uncles and even her chubby husband had to tip their heads back to look into the faces of the other Texans. When she met Leo, she said, "My, my, my. He is tall." The children of our union, if all went well, would be tall Americans.

We were at Leo's parents' house in Brookline, a huge stone place built by a railroad tycoon with a carriage house in the back, a mansion on two acres that had been on the market for years because no one wanted to maintain it. Leo's father bought it for almost nothing and was continually fixing it up in ways that the *Old House Journal* would have described as the "remuddling of the month." The grand staircase was ripped out and never replaced. Guests sat at a kitchen counter like at a drug store soda fountain. The house maintained its grand quality despite the paintings on the wall that Leo's father got at an auction, a bargain because one price got him about ten of them. My mother was sitting on a sofa talking to Leo's mother, or rather smiling politely as Leo's mother did her rapid-fire talk, talk, talk. We discovered at dinner that Leo's family and mine were from the same village in Lithuania and that perhaps Leo and I were distant cousins.

I could tell my mother felt superior to everyone in the room. While she wore cashmere, Leo's mother wore polyester. While she perhaps could lose a couple of pounds, Leo's mother was downright fat. My mother was sitting there with her patient expression, now and then darting her eyes around the living room where she saw nothing beautiful and nothing of value. It was a painful contrast, the impressive exterior of the house with its porte couchere and massive front door, and the rather shabby furnishings bought by Leo's father at the auctions that followed bankruptcies. He was proud of how little he spent on things. At that moment, for instance, he was trying to get rid of twelve barometers he bought when a nautical store in his shopping center went out of business. "Why did you buy all these?" Leo said when his father opened the bag and showed us.

"To give as presents."

"You mean I can expect one of these for my birthday?"

"Sure. Tells you the weather. Guess how much I paid."

"Can't."

"Guess."

"A hundred dollars each."

"No. Three dollars each."

"Oh," said Leo laughing, "no wonder you bought them!"

My mother said that I'd be bored with Leo in a year. All she saw was a lanky young man who did not try to charm her. Perhaps he made her feel old in the way that he didn't respond at all when she said something cute, or turned her head in what she thought was an attractive way, or said coyly, "Thank you kind, sir," when he held the door. He was more interested in the inside of things. Even I had no idea whether he thought I was pretty or not. "You were so lively," he said about his first sight of me. If anything, Leo was suspicious of beautiful people because they were often conceited and conceit was a fault he abhorred. "Everyone," he said, "has something to contribute."

"Everyone?"

"Yes. Everyone."

Joan's fancy wedding was just a big show of nothing. Leo and I got married at a Justice of the Peace then jumped on a boat for Nantucket. When we landed, we realized we'd been too hasty, the result of being in a state of bliss. We'd forgotten to bring money. We found a motel and begged the owner to let us have a room for the measly amount we could pay. I told her we were just married and she took pity on us. As the sun was setting, we rode bikes into town and could see diners through the windows of a fancy restaurant that looked out at the ocean. We would go in and just order a salad. Next to us was a large table of robust vacationers enjoying lobsters, steamers, platters of vegetables, and baskets of rolls. When they left, their table was strewn with shells and crumpled white napkins and the remains of desserts. They did not finish their bottle of wine. Leo leaned back, grabbed the wine and put it on our table. Then we hid behind our menus. From the edge of our eyes we saw that a waiter had arrived and was standing next to our table in a formal uniform with a white napkin over his forearm. He waited for us to look up then said, "May I interest you in some wine . . . glasses?" He placed goblets in front of us and poured the wine.

We pedaled back to the motel. There was no door on the bathroom, just a curtain so I could hear Leo in there, could hear him pooping. This seemed more intimate than fucking. I didn't know if hearing that would ruin everything. We had known each other six months, did have sex at my apartment. There was always an edge of shyness about it both for him and for me. Now he came out of the bathroom and smiled in a way that told me he wasn't embarrassed at all about bathroom functions. "Your turn," he said. I went in and turned on the water so he wouldn't hear me peeing. Then I came out while he was cutting his toenails. "Done?" he said.

"We're married," I said.

"I know."

"I'm married."

"Yes, you are, Brownie. To me. You're married to me and you can't get out of it."

"I could get out of it if I wanted to."

"No, you couldn't."

"Why?"

"Because I wouldn't let you."

"How could you stop me?"

He got up from the edge of the bed and took me in his arms. "Now try to get out of it." I struggled briefly. "See? Can't be done. You're mine and I'm yours. That's all there is to it."

....

CHAPTER TWENTY-TWO

I couldn't figure out why I should give up my surname just because I was married. My mother-in-law said, "You take everything else from your husband, why not take his name?" I didn't like to think of myself that way. It didn't seem equal. My mother said I was lucky to be married and should take my husband's name as a sign of respect for his family. Why? Why didn't he take my surname as a sign of respect for my family? I imagined myself in fifth grade sitting next to Leo or some other boy and suddenly when we grew up I had to change my name to his when once we were working on a project together with magic markers and Play-Doh.

Leo and I moved into the second floor of a two-family house on Crescent Street in Newton near the Mass Pike. When I went to register to vote, the matronly woman behind the counter said I had to register in my husband's surname. I said that I wasn't intending to use my husband's surname and she said I had to. "It's the law, dear."

"What law?"

"Massachusetts law. A woman's name changes automatically when she gets married."

"Mine didn't."

"Were you married overseas?"

"In Massachusetts.

"And your husband's name?"

"Doesn't matter. I'm not going to use his name."

"Don't you want to vote, dear?"

"Yes. But in my own name."

"My goodness me. This is interesting. Would you like to talk to the voting commissioner?"

I went into the small office of a pleasant man who smiled at me from behind his desk. When I told him what I wanted he said, "That's not possible. A woman's name changes automatically upon marriage."

"Who says?"

"The law, I believe. Custom, anyway."

"Mine didn't change."

"Yes, the bride's surname automatically changes."

"When? When does her own name drop off? When he puts the ring on her finger? When they sign the marriage license? When they say I Do and kiss? At what exact moment does she lose her name?"

"Ha! Ha! I never thought of it that way. Won't you have a seat, Mrs . . .?

I sat down opposite him. "Sonya."

"Here's what you have to do, Sonya. If you want to use your maiden name, you have to go to probate court and change your married name back to your maiden name."

"I have to go to court to change my name back to my name?"

"It's not a complicated procedure. I can give you the address of the court house."

"What law says my name changes automatically upon marriage?"

He opened a thick book and showed me the law cases that he thought proved my name had automatically changed. I copied the names of the cases and went to the law library at the State House in Boston to see what the cases were about. I thought it was wonderful that the law library was public, that I didn't have to be enrolled at law school to find out what I needed to know. It was a large room with bookshelves floor to ceiling, a room that seemed to have been there since the Revolution. The librarian found the books I needed. I read the cases the commissioner had sited. They were entirely irrelevant. One was the case of a woman who crashed a car with expired registration and the other was about some woman who got on the wrong bus.

The night before I returned to City Hall to register, I was up all night worrying. I would blast in there, stamp my foot, and tell them if they wanted to disenfranchise me I'd sue them. The same matronly woman came to the counter and smiled. "Hello, dear," she said. "Back again?"

"Yes. I want to register to vote."

"Yes, dear. Of course." Why did she have to be so nice? She was a peacemaker incarnate, everyone's favorite grandma! She held her pen poised above the registration form. "What street do you live on, dear?"

"Cresnut."

"Cresnut?"

"No! Chestnut."

"Chestnut?"

"No! No!" I couldn't remember my street! I stood there with my mouth open. Where did I live? There was only static in my head.

"Take your time, dear."

"I can't remember my own street!"

"Perhaps you'd like to come back tomorrow. We're here every day."

"No. No. Wait. It's near the Pike. Do you have a list? Do you have a list of all the streets?" Another person came into the office, the woman excused herself, helped that other person by getting some forms and giving them to him. As he was departing I blurted out, "Crescent! Crescent Street!"

She held her pen over the forms. "Tell me your name again, dear."

"Sonya Adler."

She filled that in. "And your husband's first name?"

"Leo." She filled in Leo Adler. "No. It's Leo Cohen."

"Oh. Yes. Yes. Now I remember. You want to register in your maiden name. I can't do that, dear. It's against the law."

"So you mean Newton is going to disenfranchise me?"

"No, no. Heavens sakes no."

"But I'm not going to register using my husband's name." She nodded to me, excused herself, and went into the commissioner's office. When she came out, she gestured for me to go in.

"Sonya," he said. "I see you're a very determined young lady."

"The cases have nothing to do with me," I said. "I'm going to sue the city if you don't let me vote in my own name."

"Sue the city?"

"Yes."

"Have you ever sued a city before?"

"No."

"Do you know how to sue the city?"

"No. But I can find out."

"So, you're going to do battle with the city of Newton? That's a rather lengthy procedure, Sonya."

"So let's just agree to let me register in my own name. Will save both of us a lot of trouble."

"I would do that if I could. I'm going to refer this to the City Solicitor, Sonya. We'll see what he says. How's that?"

"Main thing is to make sure he figures it out before the election because I want to vote for George McGovern. I don't want Richard Nixon to be president again. Okay?"

About two weeks later, the voting commissioner phoned me. He said that the City Solicitor enjoyed researching this case and had come to the conclusion that if we went to court Newton would lose. The city had no compelling reason to make me use my husband's surname. If I wanted to register to vote in my maiden name, I was free to do so.

If I could vote without going to probate court to change my name back to my name, then every married woman in the state could do the same thing. It was just a matter of alerting them and telling them to simply refuse to go to probate court. I wrote an article for the *Boston Phoenix* describing my argument with Newton. While I was impatient with the women who just did what they were told by their local election officials, absurdly trotted off to court to plead to keep their own names, I also wanted to help them. There was no reason for them to listen to me. Obviously they were women who respected authority. If there was an organization that told them what to do, they might listen. So at the bottom of the Phoenix article I wrote that any woman who needed advice about this issue should call Name Change. "What?" Leo said. "That's my telephone number too!"

I was so much in the grip of a cause that I hadn't even considered that Leo might be bothered by strangers calling our home. Leo now had a job with an architecture firm that built hyperbolic paraboloid structures, cavernous spaces used by universities for indoor stadiums. He went off to work each morning and came home for dinner with the latest alert about the boss, who was having an affair with the secretary, and how the other men at their drawing boards said each secretary lasted about six months. This one's time was up and a parade of applicants came out of the boss's office, and Leo's colleagues did secret thumbs up or down depending on if they thought she was pretty and vulnerable enough to get the job. My daycare center closed because of lack of funding and the *Boston Phoenix* suggested that I work freelance for them, so I was home much of the day doing research or writing. Dozens of women called asking what to do in order to keep their maiden names. It was as if the idea of maiden names was a cloud that was hanging over all of us, and we just happened to look up and see it, all at the same time. "Just don't go to probate court," I said to all of them. "Your name is whatever you say it is so long as you have no intention to defraud anyone." The callers thought they were listening to an expert because they'd called an organization. Then lawyers began to call and ask my advice. Then people who worked at the State House, and soon we realized this was a movement of some sort and it was happening in every state. Married woman all across the country were demanding to use their maiden names. I wrote about this for *Ms. Magazine*. Then my phone really began to ring. The callers had no idea that the person on the other end had morning sickness.

Now I understood that what made me female wasn't only those exciting parts on the outside but the hidden treasure inside. True, every month blood came out to remind me that things were going on in there but this was different. This was the first time I felt it all to be connected. The outside paraphernalia was simply the flappy odiferous door to the inside. It was the inside that really mattered. As my clothes got smaller and even Leo's sweat pants got tight, I felt perfectly self-contained. Nothing mattered or even really existed except me as vessel of magic happenings. I became everyone's darling. Strangers spoke to me tenderly. Everyone loved me! I was apart from the swirl and swarm of the world. I was in a spiritual category that strangers thought holy. In department stores, I came down to earth with a thud. The maternity clothes were hidden way in the back on the top floor, all of them designed to hide my belly as if it was shameful. They were leftovers from the days when the word pregnant was too fraught and people whispered, "She's with child." Most of the sleeves were puffy such as a little girl might wear. They were insulting clothes and I tried to avoid them by wearing caftans.

While the baby kicked, I listened on the phone to a woman in Tennessee who asked how to go back to her maiden name now that she'd used her husband's name for years. His last name was Bug and she wanted to return to Anderson. She was tired of being Mrs. Bug. She said the judge at probate court said she had to get permission from her son who was twelve. I said I'd do some research and get back to her. I went back to the article I was writing for the *Phoenix*. The phone rang. "Name Change," I said.

"Sonya. Listen. Our mother's had an accident. Some moron in the subway shot a slingshot into the crowd on the platform and hit her in the eye."

"What?"

"They took her to the emergency room."

"What? Is she blind?"

"No. They don't really know. The hospital called me, said I should bring some fresh clothes for her. I said I didn't have a key to her apartment. The woman says you are the daughter aren't you, like it's abnormal not to have a key to your mother's apartment."

"What? Is she okay?"

"She has a big patch on her eye."

"Is she at the hospital?"

"No. She's home. They released her."

"Why did they want you to go in her apartment?"

"Her clothes were all bloody. So I ended up going to the Towne Shoppe on Broadway to buy her a housecoat. Then I had to agonize about whether she'd be hurt because I bought a large. But lucky I did. They're making things so small nowadays. Have you noticed that?"

I heard Joan inhale then say in a choked voice, "This stuff is great. No seeds." She exhaled. "So you know what she said when she saw me? She says, 'What are you doing here?' You should have seen her. First of all, those emergency rooms are the most disgusting places on earth. Took the moron at the desk forever to find out where our mother was and to get me permission to see her. Meanwhile you're waiting with a room full of bleeding people and crying children, and somebody who's been shot comes in on a stretcher with cops all around. Then I go back and there she is in one of those rooms, which is really just a space closed off with a curtain and not everyone closes their curtain so you see all these people in beds all hooked up to tubes." Joan sucked smoke. "I'm telling you I almost threw up." She exhaled. "Mother was lying in one of the beds with the curtains pulled all around, and she was really surprised to see me. She had this bandage all around the top of her head. She had on one of those hospital smock things. She said, 'What are you doing here?' I said they called me. She said, 'Why?' I said because you had an accident. They said someone shot you in the eye with a slingshot. She says, 'But why did they call you?' I said because I'm your daughter. She said, 'I know you're my daughter but why did they call you?'"

"Gosh."

"Exactly. Gosh. I felt like saying who the fuck else are they going to call? Anyway they patched her up and sent her home."

"Does she need someone to stay with her?"

"They send a visiting nurse."

"Did they catch the guy?"

"No. He was on the subway and it just pulled out and away he went and there was our mother on the platform bleeding all over the place."

"Oh, my god. Who helped her?"

"I don't know."

"She wouldn't say?"

"She said she didn't know. I think she was probably in shock."

"She's home now?"

"Yes. I'll go over there tomorrow and bring her some food and things. Not to mention what I had to do to get Raf to come over and stay with the kids."

"Thanks, Joan."

"He's getting married. To Latest Girl."

"Good luck to her. Is she pregnant?"

"I don't think so."

"Does she like Josh and Jenny?"

"She likes Josh but she treats Jenny like shit. Told her she has chunky thighs. Can you imagine? She tells a six-year-old she has chunky thighs! She's a big believer in manners. So Josh comes home last weekend and holds my chair for me at the table. It was so cute. You should see how they sit up and hold their forks and everything. She's really teaching them that crap. It's great."

"Has she ever been married before?"

"Are you kidding? She's like two years old."

"Did you ever see her?"

"Yes. Blond."

"Pretty?"

"In that boring way. Everything's where it's supposed to be but nothing exudes."

"Are you jealous?"

Her silence was articulate. I'd pressed on a bruise and regretted it. Her husband had abandoned her, saw their two children only every other weekend, and even then, he sometimes had better things to do. So she had no cause to be jealous. He wasn't worth her love. Why should she care about a jerk? But she did care about him, couldn't hide the spark in her eyes when he entered the room. "Are you kidding?" Joan said, recovering her mask. "I feel sorry for her. She's about to find out she's married to the biggest dope on the face of the earth. You should see him. He's transformed. His hair's really short, and he wears leisure suits. Remember those socks Grandpa used to wear?"

"The silk ones?"

"With all those hideous designs on them?"

"Raf wears silk socks?"

"Yes. He's wearing silk socks."

It was tempting to tell her about Wiley. That seemed a proper punishment to tell his other favorite cousin. But I couldn't. "Do you want me to come down there to help with our mother?"

"You don't need to."

Violet's reaction when I phoned her in Mount Vernon was belligerent. "Who told you?" She said this with a lot of feeling as if she'd been betrayed.

"Joan."

"Well, it's nothing. It's absolutely nothing."

"Joan said you got hit in the eye."

"There's no reason to make a big fuss about it."

"I'm not making a fuss. I'm just calling you up."

"You have that tone in your voice."

"What tone?"

"That pity tone, like poor Stupid got herself into another fix."

"It wasn't your fault. I don't blame you. How could I blame you? You were just standing there."

"Some black kid."

"You saw him?"

"Yes I saw him. You know how they never move to the back of the subway car but always just stand in the door, blocking everyone getting on and off? He was in the doorway and as everyone was shoving past him our eyes met and he shot me. Looked right at me."

"You were still on the platform?"

"Yes."

"That, Mother, was not a good day."

"No. It was not."

"Are you going to be blind in that eye?"

"They don't know."

"Is your other eye okay?"

"Yes. I can see out of the other eye." The baby inside of me moved its little foot or its little elbow, and I put my palm on my belly to feel it better. It was reassuring to feel its activity. My mother said, "I want to move out of the city. I don't want to be here anymore."

"Where do you want to go?"

"I don't know."

"Would you like me to come visit and we can talk about it?"

"I don't know. I just don't know."

"Mother, listen. I'm going to get in my car tomorrow, and I'll be at your place by late afternoon."

"No, no. You can't travel."

"Actually, I feel great. Energetic, healthy."

I heard her sigh. "I just hate it here, Sonya. I don't know what to do. The people next door play that horrible rock and roll all the time. They leave their dog howling while they're at work. It cries like a baby. But there's some good news. I'm a finalist in the Publishers Clearing House sweepstakes."

"But isn't everyone a finalist?" Silence. "Mother. Those things are fake."

"Some of them are fake. But this one isn't. I've been selected."

"For what?"

"As a finalist." Had she become dotty living alone so long? Was the sting of being poor getting to be too much for her? What had become of haughty Violet Greenstone? "Maybe you can drive down, and we can watch the sweepstakes drawing on television."

"I'll be there."

CHAPTER TWENTY-THREE

....

The warehouse that Grandpa Greenstone left to Alan and Violet sold for a million dollars. Alan, as trustee, doled out Violet's half in what he probably thought was a responsible way. He required that she itemize her expenses: rent, transportation, telephone, insurance. Then she had to endure his questioning her; was that really the least expensive insurance on the market? Couldn't she renegotiate her apartment lease? Was her telephone service really the most economical? If she needed more money, she had to beg him, like the time she wanted to buy a new television. She had to detail everything that was wrong with her current television and send invoices from the repair man to prove she'd tried to fix it.

All his life, Alan had been doing what his father asked and when he looked around he was pleased with the results. He admired his father's judgment. If Max Greenstone thought Alan's sister incapable of handling her own affairs, then she was.

I drove to New York, the car seat pushed way back from the steering wheel to accommodate my belly, which made touching the pedals more difficult. I cursed the stick shift, banged into myself every time I changed gears. I cursed the seat belt that was stretched as long as it would go but still felt too tight. My breasts had become wonderfully gigantic.

It saddened me to enter the lobby of my mother's building. It was so beneath her, the ragged rubber plant with cigarette burn holes in its leaves, the useless front desk where there was never a doorman. She opened her apartment door. The whole side of her face was black and blue. She had a patch over her right eye, a raised cup made of some beige fabric. It was so seriously surgical that it made whatever was hidden underneath seem ghastly. My stomach flipped over. Her other eye was so bloodshot the white was red. "Mother!" I said. "Oh, my goodness."

"I must look hideous," she said turning away from me. "Don't look at me."

"No you don't. No you don't."

"Well, this too shall pass."

We went to a local diner for dinner where everyone tried not to stare at the injured woman. Then we returned to watch the Publishers Clearing House sweepstakes, and I had to feign sympathy when she didn't win. Later I pulled out the sleep sofa in the living room and brushed my teeth in her one bathroom, where there were pills she was supposed to take and ointments with prescription labels on the tubes.

A real estate broker had said he had a house for Violet to see, so in the morning we got into my car and I started the ignition. "Put your seat belt on, Mother."

"Oh, those silly things."

"Put it on."

"I don't need that."

"Yes, you do. Put on your seat belt." She yanked it across her chest, made exaggerated jabs at the latch then let it snap back. "I don't need that silly thing, Sonya."

"Well, I'm not driving until you put it on."

"Don't be silly."

"Mother. Put your seat belt on. First of all, it's the law. Second of all you're not safe without it." Who was this child I was with? She screwed up her face, yanked the seat belt down, jabbed again at the connection, acted as if making it work was as difficult as wiring a satellite, glanced to see if I would relent, saw that I wasn't impressed by her mild tantrum, and pushed hard enough for us to hear the required click.

The broker tried to hide his dismay when he saw a woman with a blue bruised face and a patch over her eye come through the door of his office with a pregnant woman who was in that joint loosened stage when the walk is a waddle. He showed us his book of listings and neither of us made any outward show of surprise when we saw that the house where we used to live was now on the market. It was selling for much more than Mother could afford, but we wanted to see it so the broker took us there unaware that we were wasting his time. The gardens were gone, replaced by lawn. The hedges in front were no longer there so the front yard melted into the street. The apple tree was gone and the shutters, instead of being black, were now green. The sunporch windows, once a charming wall of small panes, had been replaced by a plate glass window too modern for the house. A slender young woman and a little girl holding a doll came to the door.

We entered a living room with the kind of comfy old furniture that feet were allowed on. The little girl said, "Mommy what happened to lady?" The mother whispered, "Shh."

"She have blue face."

The mother smiled an apology to Mother, picked up the little girl and said, "Let's go play with your dollhouse, okay?" and carried the child out of the room.

Mother said, "I must look a fright."

"Unlike me," I said, "who looks absolutely gorgeous."

We followed the broker to the dining room, and I had to catch myself before blurting out, "I remember this as so much bigger!" We stood gaping at the change, the different wallpaper, the different table, chairs, lights. The room was totally drained of us. The carpet was gone. It was a surprise to see that under the carpet there were hardwood floors.

The current owner returned without her child and stood next to us. "I don't know what that hole is for," she said pointing to a hole in the floor where my father's chair used to be. "I can't imagine why anyone would drill a hole in oak floors." Mother and I were careful not to look at each other. We knew what that hole was for. We knew she was responsible for putting it there. It was what remained of the electric bell Mother installed so Seymour could summon the maid from the kitchen. My mother must have thought that this way of calling the maid was more discreet than tinkling a bell. The buzzer made a bump under the carpet next to Seymour's chair. He had trouble finding it with his foot. He pressed here, he pressed there and when his exasperation was about to explode,

Joan and I dropped under the table and hunted for the bump with our palms. The sister who found the mound pressed her palm on it and because the kitchen was not far from the dining room we could hear a rude raspberry blast forth from a speaker above the silverware drawer. To further rebel against pretension, and to get back at my mother for slights real or imagined, I came out from under the table and called, "Ruby! We're ready!" thereby announcing that the unnecessary bell was silly and my mother was a fool.

Sometimes, when Ruby retreated to the kitchen after setting a serving tray on the table in front of my mother, my father looked at the meat and said, "Is that pork?" Pork nights were something visited upon us by Seymour at least once every few months. They began when Ruby was back in the kitchen. "Oh, Seymour," Mother said, her shoulders already drooping, "You know it isn't pork."

"No. I do not know it isn't pork. Nor do you. You give her the money and she goes out and buys whatever she wants. How do you know it isn't pork?"

"Ruby doesn't buy pork."

"How do you know? How do you know what she buys? Are you there with her? Are you? Are you?"

"It is not pork."

"But you don't know that. You can't know that. Look at her. All she eats is pork."

"Seymour, be quiet."

"No. I will not be quiet. I do not eat pork." Then he stood up and slammed his napkin on the table and shouted, "I do not eat pork!" and stomped upstairs to change out of his velvet smoking jacket. Wearing his flannel shirt, he stomped out of the house slamming the back door. Next, we heard the crunch of the gravel driveway and saw the dining room shades illuminated by the car headlights as he drove away to the deli on Main Street leaving his wife shamed over nothing and his daughters frightened.

I knew what pork nights were about. My father wanted a wife stirring at the stove while he sat at the kitchen table surrounded by delicious aromas. He didn't want a maid to cook for him and he especially didn't want to pay for one. The wife/mother was supposed to keep the home fires burning, not an unknown woman from Alabama who was afraid of him. Why should he have that presence in his house? He didn't want it!

We followed the broker into the kitchen. The butler's pantry had been removed and now the room seemed bigger. The broker said, "And here we have the kitchen."

"I can see it's the kitchen," my mother said. "You don't have to tell me it's the kitchen. Any fool can see it's the kitchen."

We went upstairs. The little girl was in my bedroom, and I remembered when I too had sides on my bed so I wouldn't fall out. Here was a different child looking out those windows at those same maple trees and, before drifting to sleep, tracing the cracks on the ceiling though they were probably different lines now. It all seemed to have shrunk, my mother's former bedroom no longer a gigantic ballroom and my father's big room now just a small office where there was a cluttered desk.

At the front door, which was not as heavy and wide as I remembered, we thanked the young woman and Mother said, "You know, everyone who's lived in this house has gotten divorced." The woman gasped. My mother's lack of tact was mythic! The broker escorted us quickly to his car.

That night, instead of going out, we put Swanson frozen turkey dinners in the oven and took a Sarabeth's cheesecake out of the freezer. Sitting at the kitchen table, I pulled the cover off the turkey dinner and steam rose up. Everything in the aluminum dish was neatly divided into separate little beds, the beans, the potato, the turkey mounded over the stuffing. I had just finished the last bite of stuffing when out of my mouth came, "Mother, remember that time you said you had a tumor? Were you pregnant?" The question just rose up and came out, almost like something my body had to expel.

"Yes," she said.

"You were?"

"Yes."

"What was it?"

"A boy."

"What happened to him?"

"I don't know."

"Did you give him away?"

"Yes."

"Who was the father?"

"I don't remember."

"You don't remember? How can you not remember?"

"I don't remember."

Her tone warned that I was not to ask again. "Did he get adopted?"

"Yes."

"You said you had a tumor." I didn't want the conversation to turn to blame. But there it was. She said nothing. Her cat Midnight, sleeping on his cushion, woke up then rose, stretched elaborately, and trotted away to the bathroom where his pan was. "How come you didn't get an abortion?"

"I did."

"You did?"

"Yes. But it didn't take."

"What do you mean?"

"It didn't take. And then it was too late."

"You mean you thought you were rid of it but then you weren't?"

"Yes."

I remembered hearing her sobbing behind her bedroom door. I thought she was crying because she was going to die of cancer. "So you went through all of that by yourself?" What I meant was how come you didn't consider Joan and me?

"Oh, I've been through a lot of things by myself."

"Do you ever think about finding him?"

"Who?"

"Your son."

"My what?"

"Your son."

"What?" Now she sat up straight and glared fire at me. "No! Never. That's ridiculous."

"You aren't curious about him?"

"Don't talk nonsense." She got up and went to her bedroom where she turned on the television. She was done with me.

The next day when we looked at houses she was short with the broker. "Why show me such rinky dink houses? Don't waste my time." That evening at dinner, we talked about nothing—whether Marlon Brando would win best actor for the *Godfather*, how we couldn't stand looking at Lisa Minnelli's giant mouth, how the lawyer who was prosecuting Vice President Spiro Agnew was one of the smart boys in Joan's class at New Rochelle High, how Uncle Alan was trying to sell the foreign holdings of Greenstone Enterprises. "He's not half the man Dad was," Violet said. "He'll run Greenstones right into the ground."

I drove home the next day, waited until I knew Joan's children would be asleep, and phoned. "Are you sitting down?"

She inhaled, held down smoke, and said in a choked voice, "Alone, at last."

"You will never guess. I asked her about Louisville."

"Who?"

"Who do you think?"

"You mean that time she had a tumor?"

"She didn't have a tumor!"

"Yes, she did."

"Joan! She didn't have a tumor."

"Then why'd she say she did?"

"Joan! She was pregnant!"

Dead silence. Then a small voice, "She was pregnant?"

"I figured you knew."

"How come she told you and not me? Nobody ever tells me anything."

"I asked her."

"She was pregnant?"

"I assumed you and your therapist talked about it."

"No."

"You never talked to her about that time Mother left us alone in high school?"

"Yes. I said she went to Louisville to have a tumor taken out."

"And what did Joyce say?"

"Nothing."

"Your therapist said nothing when you told her your mother

went to Louisville to have a tumor taken out?"

"What should she say?"

I couldn't reply because all I could think was that Joan's therapist wasn't very astute.

"What was it?"

"A boy."

"A boy? You mean we have a brother?"

"I guess so."

"What'd she do with it?"

"Gave it away."

"Who to?"

"I don't know."

"I always wanted a brother," Joan said. I heard her inhale, hold the smoke, then exhale.

"Me too."

"A baby brother."

"Well, not such a baby. In his teens now."

"Do you think I should ask her?"

"If you want to."

"Do you think I should?"

"Sure. Why not?"

"What should I say?"

"I don't know."

"I mean I can't just say did you have a baby."

"That's sort of what I said."

"Anyway I can't ask her. I'm so mad at her."

"Why?"

"Because they've raised my rent and, instead of helping me out by babysitting or letting the kids stay with her for a weekend so I can have some peace and quiet, our mother tells me I should be more careful with my money. My money! What money?"

"She was so adamant about not wanting to see him. Her whole body changed. She really doesn't want to see him."

"Who do you suppose the father is?"

"Maybe it was a one night stand."

"Do you think maybe she was raped?"

"Raped?" Why did Joan think such a violent thought? How could Joan think of our little mother being attacked and violated and left to lie broken and bruised? Was Joan more realistic than I because she lived in New York City and I lived in peaceful Newton? "That would account for her not wanting to see him," Joan said. "Should we try to find him?"

"Without telling her? Suppose he's a criminal. Suppose he's a psychopath. He could stalk our kids. Or maybe he's some homeless person, and he'd ask us for money."

"Rots a ruck with that, buddy," Joan said. "You know how much Raf owes me in child support? Sixteen thousand dollars."

"No!"

"Yes. So the lawyer tells me I can take him to court and the judge will garnish his wages."

"Garnish his wages?"

"They take the money out of his paycheck. Or they sell his car."

"Right. Then your kids say Mommy took away Daddy's car."

"Exactly."

We were quiet for a while. Then I said, "How would we do it?"

"I could ask Celia. She went looking for her mother. Celia said her mother didn't want to be found but then she changed her mind. Celia said it wasn't worth the effort. She liked the woman who raised her much better. You think it was that Applebaum guy?" Joan was quiet then I heard a loud fart. "Ahh," she said, "what a relief. We have to wait til she's dead." She sniffed in an exaggerated way. "Doesn't smell. I am so bloated. Every day at work someone brings in cookies or popcorn or something. I said would you please not bring this crap into the studio? Do they listen to me? Celia's the size of a house."

"I mean maybe there's a way of finding out about him before we contact him, so if he's in prison or something we can just stop pursuing it."

"I think we should wait until she's dead."

"But he could be dead by then."

"Or we could be."

"But how would you even begin to know where to look?" The baby inside of me kicked, and I could see the outline of its foot. "Joan! I can see its foot! It has a little foot!"

"Little cutie head."

I stroked the tiny foot outline. "There are probably birth records in Louisville," I said. "How do we even know she went to Louisville? She was probably lying about that too."

"Oh, my god," Joan said. "I can't believe we have a brother. I love him already."

Just as the ghost of the dead baby Sebastian hovered around Grandma Greenstone so did the presence of Violet's secret baby hover around her, a constant low hum, irritating like the sound of air conditioners. Sebastian had a name, age, personality, regret, and love attached to him. My mother's baby, once amorphous like mist, now took shape in my imagination, sometimes Oliver Twist holding up his bowl for more, sometimes a faceless felon unrepentant in his prison cell, sometimes a playboy laughing on his yacht.

CHAPTER TWENTY-FOUR

Tossed by hurricane winds, slammed against boulders, my intellect useless, my self reduced to nothing, I howled like a beast in the jaws of a trap. Then rested. Leo, next to me, watched my face and said, "Here comes another one." I can't stand this anymore, I thought, I can't stand this wave rolling toward me again, drowning me in agony as I huff and puff and huff and puff as taught in birth preparation class where the word pain was not spoken. Leo next to me saying, "Now it's receding, now it's going away, now it's gone." He said he could see it in my face. I was on our bed where the mattress was protected with newspaper and plastic sheeting. The midwife said, "Now push." I was pushing. Couldn't she see I was pushing? "Push!" But if I pushed, I'd break apart. The thing inside was too big to get out. It would rip me apart. "Push goddammit, Sonya!" and she slapped me on the thigh and that brought me back and I pushed and pushed while animal growls and shrieks burst out of me until what felt like a boulder was dislodged at last and I sank back against the pillows. "It's a girl," the midwife said. I sat forward and saw a baby on the bed between my bloody thighs, a bluish pinkish baby with white goo on her scalp and a nose flattened by the effort of squeezing out of me. "Oh, she's so beautiful!" In my arms, she stared up at me and I'd never felt such overwhelming love in my life. Leo and I examined her fingers, toes, little knees, little elbows, teeny ears.

My breasts were swollen udders. Push up bras, low cut dresses, tight sweaters, Playboy centerfolds, how absurd! This was what they were for! I could feed her from my own body. I was a perfectly designed mammal. Hannah kneaded them like kittens do on their mothers, and for her sake, I endured the pain as she sucked. I was grateful to Mother Nature when nursing stopped hurting so much.

Hannah's closet began to fill up with tiny dresses that Grandma Greenstone sent from Florida. She went to the baby clothes outlets with her friends. Grandpa's death released Grandma from a kind of imprisonment, and we saw that she was not a person incapable of friendship but the opposite. She played canasta, had luncheons, enjoyed going to the movies with friends who lived in her building.

Nothing existed except my baby. When friends came to visit, I listened to them at first then fell to staring at Hannah as she slept wrapped in her baby blanket, a little cap on her head. Lost in her, I'd remember there was company and snap to attention and apologize. I felt sorry for Leo because he lost his importance. I needed nothing but my baby. Sometimes I wished he'd just drop his paycheck in the mail slot. At the same time, I loved those moments when Leo and I stood by her cradle and watched her sleeping, and I was grateful for those times he carried her around, so I could pass out from exhaustion. He took care of both of us for a week then got in his car and drove away to his office. This was when I felt the terrible difference between male and female. He could go, and I had to stay. The one with the milk was the one who stayed. College be damned! My head was just an accessary stuck on top. I phoned a friend, "But what do you *do* all day?" She replied, "I don't know. Do the laundry?" Panic erupted as it dawned on me that I was totally isolated in a house in the suburbs and couldn't go out when I felt like it. If the baby was asleep, I had to stay there.

My mother arrived. The patch was off her eye, the bruise was gone, and her vision was restored. Though Leo told me I was glowing, I saw how I really looked when my mother caught sight of me. Her gaze turned shallow as she appraised the disheveled fatso, groggy from lack of sleep, who stood before her in a shapeless nightgown. "You know," she said, "it's very important not to let yourself go after you have a baby. This is the time when a man's eyes stray." That too? I was supposed to be earth mother and glamor puss all at the same time?

I brought her upstairs to see Hannah sleeping in her cradle. I whispered, "Isn't she so beautiful?"

Mother hesitated then said, "Now, *you* were a pretty baby."

"So is she!" Anger roiled my middle at the same time a warning voice said don't get upset, you're not strong enough right now. How could she not think Hannah was beautiful? Didn't she have eyes in her head?

She did cook for Leo and me but she didn't make the decisions about the menu and deciding what to have was, for me, the hardest part of making dinner. I seldom thought about food and didn't want to think about food. "Well," she said as I sat nursing Hannah, "we could have lamb chops. Does Leo like lamp chops? Is there a good butcher around here? Or I could make a lasagna. Should I make lasagna? Do you have the right kind of noodles? Or maybe I should try to make a chicken stew from that leftover chicken. Should you be nursing her again so soon? Didn't you just nurse her? You know the breasts sag after you have a baby and nursing certainly doesn't help that." She left after four days.

Much of the time, she spoke about the houses she'd seen, how none of them appealed to her. Only one real estate agent stuck with Mother long enough to understand that what she really wanted was the opposite of what she said she wanted. Mrs. Adler did NOT want to live near her daughter Joan and did NOT want to babysit her grandchildren. The broker began to show Violet houses forty minutes from Manhattan—Bedford, Rye Brook, Harrison. Then an hour away, Rhinebeck, Kingston, New Paltz. Then two and three hours away in the Catskill Mountains where there were dairy farms and the closest entertainment was the grange hall.

After transferring the car seat from my car to the broker's car, an ordeal that almost snapped me in two with impatience, I drove with Nancy and my mother to see the house that my mother loved. "It needs a lot of work," Nancy said from behind the wheel, giving me a look in the rearview mirror that seemed to mean don't faint when you see it. She was a beige person in her fifties who tuned her car radio to the easy listening station. It was late summer, a warm day, and the meadows were full of cows grazing. Horses standing in mud in paddocks next to red barns turned their heads to watch us drive by as they swatted flies with their tails.

The road didn't even have a name and was so obscure that

we passed it, turned around, passed it again even though Nancy and my mother had been there before. We stopped at a general store so Nancy could phone the local broker for directions then retraced our path until we came to an antique lamppost next to a stone wall. We turned from a road of well-kept farms to a dirt road that Nancy said was once used for logging. Canopied by ancient oaks that kept the surface in eerie shadows, the bumpy road went on and on through thick woods then stopped, a dead end. As if out of a fairy tale, there appeared an entrance gate made of wrought iron spears, sentinels standing vertically. Intruders would be gored trying to climb over. Nancy got out of the car, unlocked the gate, got back behind the wheel, and drove us up a winding overgrown driveway. The house was a grand Italianate villa with a roof of red clay tile and balconies on the second floor. Invisible from the road, it sat on ten acres of what used to be cleared forest but was now a tangle of vines and new growth. Though the house had been empty for years, it wasn't easy to vandalize because the entire ten acres was enclosed by a tall fence topped with barbed wire. Nancy explained that the previous owner, a railroad magnate named Huntington, encircled the property with barbed wire because his children were young at the time that Charles Lindberg's baby was kidnapped.

"What do you think?" my mother said breathless with excitement. I was speechless. "I know," she said. "It's breathtaking." I strapped Hannah to the front of me and we explored the house.

On the wall next to a grand marble staircase were hunting trophies, mounted heads of stags with huge antlers laced with cobwebs, a tiger head covered in dust, a brown bear with a missing eye. "I'll get rid of those, of course," Mother said.

"But isn't it sort of big?" We walked along the dusty upstairs hall and went in and out of six abandoned rooms with the remains of broken chandeliers hung from the cracked ceilings.

"No, not at all. There's a room for you and Leo, Hannah can have her own room, Joan can have a room, Josh and Jenny can each have their own room. Here, let me show you my room." We entered a corner room with large windows made of antique glass that wasn't flat like modern glass but wavy. The view was thick forest.

"Of course you can't see it now," my mother said, "but eventually the view will be an orchard. I'm going to grow apples and pears."

In the old-fashioned kitchen, with linoleum curling up from the floor and pellets of mouse poop in the corners, was a leftover bottle of Aunt Jemima syrup with a rusted cap. Outside, we stood on a flagstone patio with tall weeds between each of the stones. "Now here is where I'm going to have the rose garden," Mother said. "What do you think? Isn't it magnificent?"

"It seems sort of big and out of the way. You'll be all alone in the woods."

"You and Joan will always be welcome. You two can spend the summers here. The children will have plenty of space for running around. Leo could set up an archery range over there."

"An archery range?"

"Yes. He was in the navy, wasn't he?" Then she said in a whisper, "You won't believe how cheap this place is. I don't think Nancy has any idea what she's selling."

"How much is it?"

"The bank owns it. They tried to auction it off but no one bid on it. Not one person! I can get it for a song."

The town center was miles away, a bank, pharmacy, general store, post office, and tack shop that sold saddles, bridles, horse blankets, and feed buckets. There was no mailman, just post office boxes so in winter my mother would have to drive on icy roads to fetch letters and bills.

Uncle Alan said it was an absurd purchase, a woman alone in the middle of the woods with no neighbors. He could understand her wanting to get out of New York but the only sensible thing, she wasn't getting any younger, would be to buy a house close to me in Newton. An old mansion in the middle of nowhere was not a sound investment. Had it been inspected? It was probably riddled with termites. Bats were probably living under the roof. No, he would not release the funds.

Then Alan sold the foreign branches of Greenstone Enterprises and Mother's share was two million dollars. That money, he said, had to last the rest of her life. He intended to be very careful with it. He would invest in mutual funds. Their father put him in charge, and he intended to protect his sister from once again making a wrong decision.

She consulted a lawyer, he consulted a lawyer, and soon the lawyers were talking and Violet and Alan were not. Grandma, in Florida, heard about Violet's choice and wanted me to talk some sense into my mother. "A woman all alone in the middle of the woods," Grandma said, "is a woman in danger. Not only from an intruder but what if something happens to her? Who will find her if she falls down?"

Alan flew from Chicago to New York for their day in court. Joan had dinner with Uncle Alan one evening at Tavern on the Green. She said that he did not mention the lawsuit but the distress rash on his face was the color of a baboon's bottom. The next day, hearing both sides, the judge determined that Mrs. Adler was competent, indeed intelligent, and the trust was dissolved. Alan had no authority over her money.

Her sister Dovey Lee was now living in Florida on the edge of a golf course with her husband Jack who was blissfully retired after selling his poultry business to Agricolo Lazlo for several million. My mother expected Dovey Lee to take her side against Alan. Dovey Lee thought Alan had no right to control Violet's money, no right to insist that his sister itemize all her expenses and submit them for approval, but she did not think that Violet should move so far from her children and live like a hermit in the woods. "Like a hermit!" my mother said to me on the phone. "Who does she think I am? I have no intention whatsoever of living like a hermit." Misunderstanding that hermit to Dovey Lee probably meant an isolated person, Mother said, "If anything I am going to live like a queen in that house." Nor did Dovey Lee agree to demean Alan by belittling him in the role of financial expert. "He can be full of himself sometimes," was all she said. "No," my mother said when I asked if she'd spoken lately to Dovey Lee. "I don't have anything to say to Dovey Lee." She was no longer speaking to Alan, either.

Masons, carpenters, plumbers, electricians, roofers, pavers, and landscapers set to work. Violet never phoned to ask about Hannah but did phone Leo at his architecture office several times a week for advice—were the bills her contractor presented fair, was flagstone the best material for a front path, should she put in electric heat or leave in the oil furnace, would he mind talking to the carpenter about trusses in the garage? She rented a room in a roadside motel several miles away and drove to her property every day to supervise the workers. She bought a tractor, a rototiller, and a pickup truck. She took down trees with a chainsaw and made sawdust in her own wood chipper. She planted apple trees, and pear trees. She germinated seeds in cold frames. She planted a rose garden and a perennial garden and a vegetable garden. She bought a greenhouse and delighted in the possum that had babies under there then she felt sad when her cat caught one of the babies and dropped it proudly at Violet's feet.

When she wasn't busy outdoors, she was learning how to invest. She did not sink her money into mutual funds but bought stock. She read books by Peter Lynch and Warren Buffet, watched the *Nightly Business Report* and *Wall Street Week*. She subscribed to *ValueLine*, *Barrons*, and the *Wall Street Journal*. She had a formula for investing: the company's PE ratio had to be fourteen, the company had to be debt free, and it had to show growth for the last five years. She thought computers might turn out to be popular so she bought two unknown start-ups, Microsoft and Apple. She entered the management of her money in a ferocious and private way. "Dad treated me like I was stupid," she said, "because I acted like I was stupid." Now she would show her father that she was as sharp as he was. When a stock price rose she turned her eyes up to her father who was always hovering above her and said, "Ha!" in a gloating way as if he'd advised against it.

The news spread among the six hundred residents of the village of Gideon that someone bought the dilapidated mansion at the end of the logging road. Probably they saw her at the post office and the grocery store. Maybe they noticed her in her new truck. The first intrepid visitor was the local minister.

He pressed the intercom on the entrance gate. "I didn't know what that sound was at first," Mother told me. "I thought maybe it was the toaster." Her visitor was man in his late forties who invited her to a church supper. "He suggested I join the Episcopal church."

"What'd you say?"

"I said I didn't really believe in religion. He said why? I said I thought it was the root of everything wrong with the world, the cause of wars and the cause of ignorance and priests were in it just to line their own pockets."

"You said that?"

"I certainly did."

"So what'd the poor guy do?"

"He said I would be pleasantly surprised by how congenial the people in his congregation are. There are many interesting groups to belong to. For instance I might like to join the local history group. They have quite a bit of information about my house."

"What'd you say?"

"I said like what? He said the granddaughter of the original Huntington who built the house was an eccentric who died here and they didn't find her for three days."

"What a horrible thing to say!"

"Oh, it didn't bother me. He was proving a point. If she'd gone to church, Jesus would have saved her."

"What a creep!"

"Then he started talking all kinds of mumbo jumbo about how helpful Jesus was to him personally when he had a crises."

"Why didn't you just tell him you're Jewish?"

"None of his business."

The next person to venture down the rutted logging road was a woman from the Welcome Committee. Her welcome basket included a map of the area, a list of the activities at the grange hall, the church, and the 4H Club, and a pie made almost entirely of Cool Whip. Violet perhaps made a strong impression on the welcome woman because no one else rang the buzzer until several months later, when a man soliciting votes for school committee approached the gate and heard a staticky voice respond, "Thank you, I'm not interested." The residents of Gideon got the idea

Gone were her high heels, fur coats, cashmere sweater sets. Her wardrobe was overalls, flannel shirts, and clumpy waterproof boots. She stopped dying her hair, and we saw she'd gone past gray to pure white. She was up at dawn planting, transplanting, shoveling, lugging bags of manure, peat moss, fertilizer. At night, she sewed curtains for all of the rooms from fabric she bought in Oneonta, the closest city. On Sundays, so she told me on the phone, she stayed in bed all day first reading the financial pages of major newspapers then enjoying one of her Clint Eastwood movies. He was her ideal man. Never an unnecessary word out of his skinny lips, he needed no one.

Chipping away day after day at the work that had to be done, Mother's orchard grew, flourished, and dropped fruit in the fall that the deer shared. She made applesauce. Her basement shelves were lined with canned tomatoes from her garden and her freezer was stocked with soups made from vegetables she grew. In the summer, vases on every window sill were full of flowers from her annual garden. I stood awed, watching her back her tractor out of its shed, then drive to a space she had cleared with her chainsaw for a potato patch. Using the backhoe attachment, she dug boulders out of the ground then drove them in the lifted bucket to the place where she was creating a stone patio. Once lowered, the stones had to be adjusted. This pushing and twisting and leveling required muscle. The softness in her body, the rounded belly and ample hips, melted away. It was startling to see a buff white-haired woman with toned arms, and capable shoulders. Her eyes changed, too. That filmy quality was replaced by an attractive clearness that probably came from large doses of fresh air.

When she wasn't outside, she was in her office following the stock market. After keeping careful notebooks of her buys and sells, she decided record keeping might be easier with a spreadsheet so she bought herself an IBM computer and set about trying to learn to use it. "You can't learn that by yourself," I said. "You should sign up for a class at the local high school."

"I'll get it eventually."

"No. You won't. There are all kinds of keystrokes you have to learn to make the thing work. One combination makes the word repeat, another erases the word. It'll take you til the twelfth of never to learn all that by yourself." But she did learn it. Probably if I'd watched her using her computer, I would have gone mad with impatience but she got the job done, had spreadsheets itemizing the rise or fall of every stock she bought. "You know," she said to me, "when I was married I never knew how much anything cost. I didn't care. I wanted steak, I bought steak. Now I know how much everything costs." There was no apology to Seymour in this announcement, no acknowledgement that he was perhaps not a miser but a man with a ceiling on his income.

There wasn't a trace of me or Joan or our children in any room and when Joan, in a display of how oblivious she could be, presented our mother with framed 8x10 school portraits of Josh and Jenny smiling against watery blue backgrounds, I wondered what Mother would do. She stood the frames on her bedroom bureau until Joan drove back to Manhattan, then put them in a drawer in the basement where she left them until Joan, looking for a screwdriver on her next visit, found them in the tool cabinet, brought them upstairs and said, "What were these doing in the basement?" and stood them again on Mother's bedroom bureau.

Mother hired a handyman named Carl, a taciturn old geezer who helped with mulching and spring clean up and in the winter plowed her driveway. The third winter she was there, she fell off her stepladder while trying to put up storm windows and broke her wrist. "Why didn't you call Carl?" I asked when I saw her arm in a sling. "I don't know," she said. "Never thought of it."

Watching her property change from a tangle of weeds into an estate with abundant gardens, and birds flitting their wings in birdbaths and pecking at feeders, and chipmunks scurrying across the deck, and deer peering cautiously from behind trees, and crows filling the air with their language, and troops of turkeys hunched in dark clothes like nuns walking across the snow, I was filled with admiration and confused at the same time. Her determination to be independent was understandable but, at the same time, it hurt because I was included in those she didn't need. "I am letting go," she said with pride, thinking that disengagement with the world was an enlightened position. At the same time, she often quoted Barbra Streisand's song saying, "People who need people are the luckiest people in the world."

"Everybody needs people."

"I don't." Did she think I didn't see the book on her bedside table? It was *What to Say After you Say Hello*, a book written to help awkward people make a good impression and feel more comfortable in social situations. It advised her to make eye contact.

"I'm lucky," she said "I like my own company."

When her cat had kittens, she couldn't bear to part with them so five cats prowled her house and kept it free from rodents, slept on her bed at night and cuddled with her when she watched television, and were the recipients of much stroking and fond baby talk.

CHAPTER TWENTY-THREE

··

The house Leo and I bought in Newton, Massachusetts, was a thirteen-room Victorian with a wrap-around porch, a wall of stained glass, three fireplaces, and original oak woodwork. Yes, it was old but we would modernize it, paint the walls white. How come the old lady who gleefully sold it to us kept a blanket over the stained-glass window? Why would anyone want to hide such beauty? We found out when the weather changed. The lead that held together the Tiffany panes had shrunk over the years so freezing air leaked in. We wondered why someone would put up wallpaper instead of just painting the walls. We found out when we peeled off the paper and plaster billowed to the floor. By mid-winter, we wore heavy socks and long underwear under our pajamas. We joked about buying bed caps. Our house, we discovered, was famous for its beautiful stained-glass window so we often saw pedestrians pause to admire it and cars slow down for a second look. It was just like a person—it seemed one way but was quite another when you got to know it.

We now had two daughters, Hannah and Chloe. They had a playroom and each had her own bedroom, and I had an office of my own. They had a clubhouse in the attic and swings in the backyard. I wanted to take care of my daughters, did not want them to come home to a maid in the kitchen. I did not want them to have to stay at school all day in the after school program and not get home to their own things until it was dark. I did not think I could endure the panic of rushing home from some office when the phone rang telling me one of my children was ill. Leo and his partner had a thriving architecture business, so I was lucky that I didn't have to go out to work. I liked being a freelance writer and now had contacts at various publications. I was proud of the title "Contributing Editor." We were able to send the girls to camp, give them piano and dance lessons.

Massachusetts was on its way to becoming an East Coast Silicon Valley. Digital Equipment, Data General, Wang, and Apollo Computer transformed the abandoned textile mills in Lowell into hives of activity. Leo designed new buildings on Route 128 for high tech corporations that were the happy recipients of defense contracts, favorable tax credits, and federal grants. Leo's firm designed condos for the expected influx of high-tech employees. He renovated office towers in Boston and redesigned banks. We modernized our kitchen, shocked purists by getting rid of the pantry.

Then Wang Laboratories, employer of more than 33,000 people, went bankrupt. The *Massachusetts Miracle* collapsed and Massachusetts suffered the worst real estate recession in state history. Condos languished on the market. New office buildings became ghosts. The bank called Leo's loans. Each morning, with no bounce in his step, he went to his office where the phones were dead quiet.

At night, sitting at the kitchen table, we still dunked Milano cookies in milk but now Leo looked up from the Sports section to bark, "Get that damn cat away from the table!" I took Pillow off my lap and set him on the floor. Leo's worries were needles, his melancholy stung me. His moods set up a vibration that filled the house. His agitation was my agitation. Optimism sapped, he kept getting colds, honking his nose, sniffling. Sitting upstairs at my desk, writing, I'd hear his car pull into the driveway, hear the back door open then shut, and think, "Damn. He's home."

I suffered a gnawing envy of my mother's wealth. I became a glowering infant. Even if she didn't share her money, I wanted her to acknowledge that it was a struggle to pay the mortgage, heating oil, telephone, gas, electric bills. She bragged about her stock market victories. "I bought Duggy Chemical for ten and now it's up to twenty. I made a hundred thousand dollars!" She thought I'd say, "Atta boy!" I clamped my lips shut so I wouldn't say, "Then give some of it to me."

She plowed her profits back into her portfolio. It wasn't money to her. It was a game she was playing with her dead father. She bragged that she had more than doubled her inheritance, now owned a portfolio worth five million dollars. If Joan or I suggested that Mother spend some of her profits, meaning share some with us, she became confused, as if we suggested she maim her cat. She couldn't understand why I thought I had any right to her money and of course I didn't. I embarrassed myself. But I did think that grown children did have some right to ask a parent for help in an emergency. Leo was a victim of circumstances. He had done nothing to merit the collapse of his practice. He had no clients because there were no clients. No one was building anything, at least not in Boston. Mother was puzzled by my resentment because money to her was not the stocks in her portfolio but the money in her checking account at the bank. There was just enough in there to pay the household bills. The companies represented in her portfolio were game pieces that she moved around and had nothing to do with money. Since each month she used up the funds in her checking account, she believed she was living close to the bone. When we went out to dinner she either let Leo pay or else said, "Shall we split it?" I felt like shouting, "No! You pay! You're loaded and Leo can't meet payroll!" Leo broached the subject of estate planning. Violet said, "*Apre moi, le deluge!*" Leo persisted, "But you don't want the government to get it all."

"I don't mind," she said. "I love America. The government does good things."

Never myself having been the victim of current events, I sometimes thought Leo's plight was his own fault. If he were more ambitious, smarter, more talented, better connected, we wouldn't be in such a fix. This, I knew, was unreasonable. All Leo saw when he looked at me was Demand and all I saw when I looked at him was Worry.

Meanwhile our children were growing up and, the next thing we knew, we were nagging Hannah about finishing her admission essays for college. Grandma Greenstone had started a college fund for the girls when they were born so there was enough money for tuition. We were in that stage of parenting when all conversation was about this school being better than that school, who applied where, who got in, who was waitlisted. Then Hannah was gone and there was no one in her room at night, and when she came home during vacations, she seemed a stranger.

Then it was Chloe's turn to leave and our big house was empty, and I saw myself as cliché empty nester and cursed myself for not having a career, for believing that mothering was enough of a job. At the same time, I didn't want a job because I was writing a book but how could I write a book when we needed some income? From my window, I watched neighbors get out of their Volvo station wagons and trudge with heavy briefcases into their houses. As lights came on in windows, I wondered if I too looked that old. Our children had tied us together but now nothing did. We didn't bother with neighborhood parties anymore. Gone was the slap, slap of dribbling on the street outside and the shout, "Car alert!" as the children ran to the sidewalk. The basketball hoop on the telephone pole was drooping. The boy who used to fly off the curb on his skateboard was now married and in Seattle. Gone was the child doing pirouettes on his bike.

Gone were the amps attached to electric guitars that shook our whole house and the posters for Chloe's band, *Daredevil Nurse*. Both girls were working in New York and living in their own apartments. We kept their rooms like shrines, the empty gerbil cage next to the abandoned dollhouse. "I don't want any of it," Hannah said from her office in New York. "I told you that, Mom. Throw it all away. You and Dad are like the caretakers in the museum of my youth."

Chloe, from her office, said on the phone, "Can't you keep it?"

"Where?"

"In the basement?"

"Are you ever going to use that dollhouse again?"

"I don't know. It's my dollhouse."

"But your dollhouse is taking up room, and Dad wants this room as a study."

"But it's my dollhouse."

"Then take it."

"Come on, Mama. It's my dollhouse."

"Okay. We'll keep it."

Both girls agreed to humor their grandmother and stay at her house when the year 1999 turned into 2000. All of us knew so little about computers that a rumor about their intrinsic maliciousness took on the weight of fact and appeared as headlines in the newspapers. Pundits told us that as the clock struck midnight, computers would explode with the Y2K bug. At the dawning of the millennium, all our vital records, bank accounts, medical histories, real estate transactions, would be erased and we would be as naked as baby mice. There would be no telephone, electricity, or heat.

My mother believed this and insisted that on New Year's Eve we be together, Joan and her children, Leo and me and our children. This, she thought, would be the last time we would ever see each other. Driving up the driveway in the eerie stillness of night, I turned the corner and came upon a huge house with lights in only two windows, the living room and upstairs in her bedroom. The rest of the house seemed dead. I was used to how Mother's high standards of house keeping had relaxed but my daughters were surprised by the dust on the bureaus, the torn shades, the green in the bathroom sink, and the unmade beds. As Violet aged, the work her gardens required became overwhelming. No one raked up the leaves in the fall or took the flower boxes in at the end of summer. She refused to hire a housekeeper, said she didn't want anyone hanging around. She never replaced her handyman, Carl, after he had a stroke. Sometimes she admitted on the phone that she hadn't been out of her house for two or three weeks. "Oh, I don't mind," she said. "I keep busy."

That New Year's Eve we searched in the linen closet for sheets. In the old days, when I opened the linen closet, I had the satisfaction of precision, like looking at the Rockettes lined up. Now sheets and towels were stuffed in every which way. We spent some time unfolding and sorting. "Wait. Here's a queen flat."

"That looks like a king to me."

"What does the label say?"

"Where's the label?"

"I don't know. There must be a label."

"Wait. Here's the label. But it doesn't say."

"Yes, it does."

"No, it doesn't."

"Yes, it does, Mama, put on your glasses."

We wore New Year's Eve hats and blew horns and ate bagels, cream cheese, and lox that Joan brought from Zabar's. We drank good champagne and watched the clock in Times Square on mute so we wouldn't have to listen to the hysterical emcees. When the ball came down, we hugged and kissed, looked around, heard no explosions, and relaxed in front of the fire. "Mother," I said, "should we try your computer?"

"What for?"

"To see if it works."

"I'm not turning that thing on," she said.

"What's the password," I said. "I'll go do it."

"I'm not giving you my password."

"Why not?"

"I don't want you snooping around my business."

"Snooping around your business? What's that supposed to mean?"

"You know very well what that means."

It was now five after midnight and officially the year 2000. "Mother," I said getting up from the sofa, "what's your password? Let's see if all the computers crashed."

"That's just an excuse."

"For what?"

"You know very well for what. For looking at my accounts."

"Why would I look at your accounts?"

"To see how much money I have. You're always doing that. You can't wait for me to die so you can get your hands on my money."

Everyone fell silent, the sizzles and crackles of the fire the only sound. "Grandma," Chloe said, "Mama only—"

"Don't call me Grandma."

"Why?"

"I hate that word. I may be a grandmother but I'm not grandma. Ma. Ma. Sounds so common."

"But I've always called you Grandma."

"Well, stop doing it."

"Mother," Joan said. "What's the matter?"

"Maybe it's time to go to sleep," Leo offered.

But I couldn't let the matter rest. "What do I do every time I come here?"

"Snoop around. You go into my desk drawers, read my investment reports, look at my bank statements."

"I do?"

"Don't think I haven't caught you in my office looking at my things. Don't think I didn't see you sitting at my computer looking at my accounts."

"When did I sit at your computer and look at your accounts?"

"Let's go to sleep," Leo said. "The whole Y2K bug was a false alarm, we're perfectly fine, everyone's fine. Let's call it a day."

"Grandma," Hannah said, "should we call you Violet?"

"That's my name."

"You want us to call you Violet, Grandma?" Joan's daughter Jenny said.

"You're certainly old enough. You don't have to go around calling me grandma like some little child. Why, you're old enough to be married for heavens sakes. You should be married instead of running around being promiscuous."

"Mother!" barked Joan. "How dare you say that?"

Violet raised her eyebrows and made wry lips as if to say I'm the only one here who will tell you the truth. Hannah said, "I'm going up. I'm tired." Chloe said, "Me too." Josh said, "Me too." His sister Jenny, hurt, stared at Violet as if waiting for an apology. But Mother was in some other world, lost in a darkness that drained all animation. "Time for bed," I said, going over to her as she sat on the sofa in front of the fireplace. "Come on, Mother. Time for bed. It's late."

"You go on," she said.

In the morning, I found her dressed in her tattered bathrobe, sitting slumped in a chair looking out at the bleak sky. "Will it ever get warm?" she said to the windowpane.

"Why don't you take a little trip to Florida," I said filling the coffee pot with water. "Or some other warm place."

"No. I'd miss the January thaw."

When we suggested gardeners, handymen, housekeepers, she flinched as if we were asking her to welcome snarling hyenas. She no longer went to the beauty salon, and her hair was just long white strings with pink scalp showing.

"I think she's depressed," Joan said when we were alone packing up to go home.

"I wonder if she's thinking about her baby," I whispered. "Do you think she thinks about him?" My question really meant, do you think about him?

"I think she just pushes everything out of her mind."

"I think about him all the time. I wonder if we should try to find him and if we did what we'd tell our mother. Do you think about him?"

"Sometimes."

It was one of those endless New England winters, white sky every day, fierce chill that froze the nose hairs, mounds of snow covered in soot pushed to the sides of the roads taking up parking spaces. We counted the months until relief. April wasn't spring, it only had a spring-like name. May would have its darling buds but not until it was half over. My first book was about to come out. It was a nonfiction book about the Hollywood studio system, the story of how that system came into being and how its collapse was good for some people but ruinous for others like my father. Pillow was on my desk batting at my hand with his paw every time I moved my pen. Then he stood up and pushed his nose into my chin. "I love you too," I said. "But not now, please." He shivered, stepped back, then dove into my chin again, almost bursting with ecstatic purrs. I thought, love is a many splendored thing, and lifted him off my desk and set him on the floor where he sat with his back to me saying with his posture that I'd hurt his feelings. The phone rang.

"Sonya? Our mother's had an accident."

"What?"

"She's in the hospital. Some nurse just called me. The tractor turned over on her."

"The tractor? What was she doing on the tractor?"

"Just come." Joan told me the name of the hospital.

I marveled at how scared I got thinking my mother was in danger even though I often didn't even like her. My head didn't always love her but my body did. It was visceral. My heart was pounding and little moans were coming out of my throat. How could the tractor turn over on her? How could she even *be* on the tractor? It was the middle of winter. How could she even get to the shed where the tractor was kept? The snow was higher than her boots.

Leo wasn't home. He had realized, midway through the recession, that maybe it was just Boston that wasn't building anything. In North Carolina, construction of new buildings and houses was booming. The attitude in Boston had always been whatever is old is best. The people of North Carolina welcomed the new, wanted to grow bigger. Leo was in Durham negotiating the purchase of some land. He intended to put up an apartment complex near Duke University. This would have been entirely wonderful except I had to rush to New York and Leo wouldn't be home to feed Pillow. How long does a cat last without food? I poured dried food into two bowls, opened three cans of wet food and hoped they wouldn't rot, filled two bowls with water, got into my Volvo, listened to it rev then stop, rev then stop then at last catch, buck, and get its stupid self into gear. Never again would I buy a foreign car! I drove slowly in the slushy wake of snowplows on the Mass Pike, windshield wipers sweeping an arc of heavy snow that accumulated at the bottom of the window.

Before she noticed me standing stunned in the doorway, I saw my mother propped up in the hospital bed, her head bandaged, her arm in traction, a cast up to her neck. When she turned, I saw her face was swollen and purple, both eyes black. "Mother!" I hurried to her side. "What happened?" Drugged, listless, she turned her head to see where the voice was coming from.

"Sonya," she said, then turned her eyes away as if focusing took too much energy.

"What happened?"

She closed her eyes. A nurse came in, a young brisk person who took a pile of bloody clothes out of the closet and handed them to me, saying she was sure I'd like to take them home to launder. She beckoned me to follow her into the hall. The hospital, the pride of the Catskills, was once a farmhouse. There were modern additions on both sides with photographs on the walls of farmers loading cauliflower onto horse drawn wagons and pictures of old-fashioned ambulances and people in wooden wheelchairs. "Come," the nurse said. She led me to a waiting room where we sat down. "Your mother's a lucky woman," she said. "She wouldn't have survived if that boy hadn't come along." She said that a teenage boy was snowmobiling on the old logging road. There, behind the entrance gate, he saw a woman lying in the snow next to a turned over tractor. The boy sped back to his farm. His mother called the ambulance then drove their truck to the gate to wait for it to arrive. "That's all I know," the nurse said. She said my sister had been there the day before. "She looks just like you. I thought you were her.

I went back into my mother's room. Again she turned to see who came in and again she said, "Sonya," and turned her eyes away.

"Mother. What happened?"

"I thought those tires had better traction."

"But why were you on the tractor? Where were you going?"

"To get the mail."

"You were going to drive the tractor to town?"

"One thing about Carl. He used to do a good job plowing the driveway."

"Did it skid? Is that what happened?"

"It hit that sugar maple."

"Did you break anything?"

"Probably the axle. That's expensive to fix."

"I meant you."

"Oh. Me. I think my collarbone, shoulder, I don't know. I don't know, Sonya. I tried to get back to the house. I crawled up the driveway. Next thing I knew, here I was." She held her breath to endure a spasm of pain.

"How did the ambulance people get inside the gate?"

"Smashed it, damn fools. Those iron pickets are antiques. Irreplaceable."

"Maybe an iron worker can replicate the old ones."

"Thank you for coming, Sonya. Is it still snowing?"

"Yes."

"Then that was a hard trip. That must have been difficult driving." She closed her eyes and I went out to the hall and sat in a chair and cried into my palms.

She was there for three weeks before they sent her to a nursing home. I had meetings with my publisher in New York so I stayed with Joan on West 87th, and we drove together upstate to the nursing home in Margaretville. We arrived when Violet was enduring physical therapy. She was supposed to learn how to transfer herself from the bed to the wheelchair, but she was too weak and the therapist was impatient. She said, "You should be able to do this by now." One of the doctors told us he wasn't sure Violet would ever be able to walk again. The gash on her thigh was so deep there was nerve damage. Exhausted from her physical therapy efforts, she lay back on her bed and greeted Joan and me with a weak smile. We gave her the candy we'd brought, dark chocolate covered almonds, and the bouquet of roses, and sat down next to her bed. "Girls," she said, "if you bury me, I'll come back to haunt you."

"What?"

"Cemeteries are a waste of a space. They're an abomination. All that land used for that ridiculous purpose. Think of all the playgrounds, public swimming pools, parks."

"So you mean you want to be cremated?"

"You're not supposed to get cremated if you're Jewish," Joan said.

"Poppycock," Violet said.

"What do you want us to do with the ashes?"

"Plant them under some delphinium."

"Which ones are those?"

"The blue ones. I've got them staked near the Shasta daisies."

"Are those your favorite flowers?"

"Yes. I love delphinium. And they like ashes."

She couldn't stay at the nursing home forever so a few weeks later they sent her home. After the contract with the visiting nurses expired, we hired aides. Violet didn't like any of them, said each one was a thief and lazy. She endured three days of physical therapy then somehow hauled herself from bed into her wheelchair and rolled to the front door to tell the man standing there with his satchel of exercise balls, stretch bands, and weights that she no longer needed him. She closed the door in his face.

Then Shanice appeared. She was about six feet tall with the broad shoulders of a football player. Instead of scolding and nagging Violet to eat nutritious food, Shanice brought bags of Pepperidge Farm cookies to the bedside table and accepted one when Violet offered. They sat together munching on sweets. The other aides that the agency sent had been Violet's size so she felt insecure when they helped her to the bathroom or held her up to change her nightie. Shanice picked her up as if she were a child and carried her tenderly. Besides loving sweets, they had something else in common. "Meh fav'rite flim star Clint Eastwood; he a ral badjohn in trut, y'know!"

"I don't understand a word she says," Mother complained. She was rude to Shanice, told her to go sit in the living room, told her she wasn't going to pay someone she didn't need, told her the food she cooked was inedible. "How does someone get so fat eating food you can't even swallow?" my mother said.

But by the time the cast came off Mother's shoulder, she was laughing with Shanice, telling her about her marriage. Shanice had no use for men, was married once but never again. Shanice thought Violet was hilarious and encouraged her to speak more, say more funny things. My mother regained the use of her arms and hands but could not walk. She was completely dependent upon Shanice for the most basic things, going to the bathroom and getting fed. She had nightmares and called out. Shanice, sleeping in the next room, rushed to her and held her against her ample bosom and stroked her hair saying, "Doux-doux," which I learned meant darling. Mother said to me, "I have friends who are shocked when they see a colored person kissing me. I don't think it's so bad, do you?" I said no that it wasn't bad at all. I was surprised by this mention of friends. She had no friends. Mother said. "I think it's charming."

Shanice went to her own home on the weekends, an apartment she shared with her daughter and grandson in Oneonta. At Christmas she went to visit her father, a policeman, in Trinidad.

She replaced herself with one of her cousins. Leo called it Shanice Incorporated. The substitutes spoke to Violet with such hearty friendliness they sometimes bowled her over, but she was polite to them and if they laughed she laughed even though she didn't understand their English. There was Myrtle, Angela, and Calister. At first, they came one at a time but soon two would come at once and as the months went by they came to visit when Shanice was there. The women spoke with a musical lilt. Mother couldn't tell them apart, called them all Shanice or else "the maid" but each of them was affectionate and attributed every insult to the insanity of the aged. Sometimes I'd enter a house full of chatty black women, my formerly bigoted mother in her wheelchair sitting easily among them in her living room. Sometimes the women were playing cards with Mother, Old Maid and Gin. Shanice said when I arrived. "I ax she but why you like being Old Maid? Hear she, you is meh mudder?" The other women laughed as if the joke was new and Violet joined in, but I was pretty sure she didn't understand the English any more than I did. Shanice did the shopping and Mother's tops changed from autumn tones selected from Neiman Marcus catalogs to polyester pink hearts on a yellow background purchased by Shanice at J.C. Penney. And with this change on the outside came a change on the inside, a newly emerging sweetness which must have always been there. When I arrived she said, "Sonya! Tell me, how's the book? Where are you lecturing next? Shanice, did you know Sonya wrote a book?" My mother now slept downstairs so she couldn't see how the upstairs rooms were sagging from lack of use. There were cobwebs in the corners of the ceilings. Her cats, the older one half-blind and rickety, stepped into their cat pan but left their hind quarters hanging out. With toilet paper, I picked up hard cat turds and dropped them in the toilet. "Hear me," Shanice said. "I love she." Another time Shanice said, "She hallucinate. All old people hallucinate. You didn't know that?" Most elderly people had violent and frightening hallucinations, Shanice told me. Violet's hallucinations were gentle, flowers and hummingbirds. She said that one time Violet was talking to her brother Alan, asking him why there were so many babies on the wall.

CHAPTER TWENTY-SIX

· ·

Would she know her secret baby if he appeared? If I brought him to her house and introduced him as a friend of mine, would she suspect? Shouldn't I introduce him to his mother before it was too late? Maybe I could release some of the pain he must suffer knowing his mother didn't want him. I'd be his big sister, his protector. I would turn the pages of the family album, show him pictures of his uncles, aunts, cousins, grandparents. Here's one of Violet in her gypsy costume, age twenty, when she was a Spanish dancer. Look how pretty your mother was! Here's Joan and me dressed as twins in pinafores, and that's Ruby who used to take care of us. Oh, and here's your grandfather, Max Greenstone. You would have loved him. This person? That's Wiley, our cousin. See that gap between his front teeth? His father, our Uncle Jack, had the same gap. Uncle Jack couldn't sit straight in his chair. He always tilted back and balanced on the two hind legs.

I was tired of keeping Violet's secret. I didn't want it in me anymore. I was like a cat with a hairball in its throat.

Joan would object. She'd say I was betraying our mother. So I phoned city hall in Louisville without telling her and asked how a person starts such a search. I was given the telephone of Children's Services. "Ma'am, you'll have to fill out a form saying you do want contact," a caseworker said. "But there's a snaggle. You don't have the exact birthday. And y'all don't know the adoptee's name."

"I was hoping you could help me get around that because the mother is elderly now."

"Yes, ma'am, that's what they all say."

"They do?"

"Yes, ma'am."

When I told Leo I was searching for my brother, he said, "What do you expect from this guy? He probably has a perfectly fine life. What makes you think he wants to dig up the past?"

"You mean he doesn't want to meet his sisters?"

"I don't know. But you don't know either. What is it exactly that you want from him?"

"He's my brother. I always wanted a brother."

"Well, let me warn you, Brownie. He may not be the brother you always wanted."

Months later, I phoned to see if there was any way around knowing the exact birthday. Would it work if I just knew the month? The caseworker I'd spoken to was now replaced by someone else. Couldn't she just see if someone was searching for Violet Adler? Couldn't she just look it up that way? No, she couldn't. If I had his name, that might help. Did I have his name?

"What you need," Leo said, "is a change of scene."

Leo's new work in North Carolina and royalties from my book paid for our second honeymoon. For two months we explored Europe. We sat outdoors at cafes and strolled by shops with enticing windows and figured out how to convert our dollars and slept on feather beds in Switzerland.

At the same time that we were gone, Joan wasn't home either. One of her designs caught the eye of a location scout who arranged to fly her to Hollywood as a consultant. The film plot involved smuggling money in cleverly designed textiles. Sometimes the money was attached to the textiles and sometimes the pattern of the textiles was a code the smugglers used.

A neighborhood boy took care of Pillow while Leo and I were gone. When we returned, tanned and relaxed, I went across the street to get my house keys back and to pay him. I didn't really know this child or his parents, a sign that Leo and I were turning into the old folks in the neighborhood. I used to know almost every child who walked by our house. Now I didn't know any of them. This child was living in what used to be the Johnsons' house. From my window one day, I saw an ambulance arrive and carry old Mr. Johnson out on a stretcher. Several months later, an ambulance arrived and carried Mrs. Johnson out and a few weeks later a For Sale sign was on their lawn. Now I walked across the street, rang the bell, and the boy came to the door. He was in fifth grade at the school where my daughters went. The boy handed me the keys, and I gave him twenty-five dollars. "Oh, no!" he said. "That's way too much." He stood small in the frame of his front door and I stood on the welcome mat.

"How much do you think you should earn?" I asked.

"Oh, I don't know. Three dollars? A dollar fifty?"

"No, Zach, that's way too little. Here. Take ten dollars."

"No!" He accepted the bill I thrust at him and stood there watching me cross the street. When I got to my door, I turned and we waved.

A light was flashing on my answering machine. A police officer from my mother's town asked me to phone. He said he had some sad news and suggested I sit down. It was necessary for me to claim the body at the hospital morgue. I phoned Joan at her hotel in Hollywood.

As we stood in a windowless foyer under harsh fluorescent light near the closed morgue door in the basement of the Delaware County hospital, a police officer told us that two female Jehovah Witnesses ventured down the logging road hoping to find converts. Joan took my hand. We were two little girls facing trouble. The Jehovah witnesses found the entrance gate open, walked up the driveway and rang the bell. When no one answered, they peered through the windows. There they saw a woman slumped in her wheelchair and it worried them because they couldn't see anyone else.

"I don't want to," Joan said when he opened the morgue door and gestured for us to enter a room glaringly lit, with a wall of stainless steel doors and medical devices and a young woman in a white lab coat who nodded to Joan and me as we stood hesitating at the door. "No," Joan said in a small voice, "I don't want to." Under a circular lamp dangling from the ceiling, was a gurney with a body on it covered by a white sheet. "I don't want to," Joan said. She increased her grip on my hand, and I could feel her trembling. I wanted to scream well I don't want to either! You think I want to do this? You think I want to see our mother on a slab in the smelly morgue under a sheet with her foot exposed and a tag on her toe? You don't have any right to not want to! You have to! And I am not going to say that I alone will identify her. I will not save you from this so buck up. But I only said, "You don't have to. I'll do it." I tried to disengage my hand from hers, but she held on tight. So, together, we approached the body.

The woman in the lab coat pulled the sheet down and there was Mother, the color of plaster, her cheeks sunken and her forehead lifeless as a skull. Joan stood on one side and I stood on the other, looking down at our dead mother while the lab technician, perhaps out of tact, busied herself on the other side of the floor. Something made me poke the body. It was like jabbing a stone. Joan didn't see me and I was ashamed of doing it, but the feel of it did help me understand what dead meant. Joan said, "It's my fault, it's my fault. She wouldn't be like this if I'd paid more attention to her." Instead of wanting to cry, all I wanted was to get out of there. I needed to figure out what to do next. She had wanted to be cremated, but I didn't know how to arrange for that. I couldn't imagine anything worse than having my body burned up. Did they have an oven in this place? Did we have to transport the body to some other place? Mother said she wanted her ashes planted under delphinium. I didn't have any delphinium. Joan didn't have delphinium. How was I going to find some? I said to the lab technician, "Yes, it's her." I pulled the sheet over my mother's face, which startled Joan out of her misery and made her look at me with very clear eyes. "How are we going to find delphinium?" she said.

From the grisly view of our dead mother, we came out into the gorgeous scenery of the Catskill Mountains. Why this made me cry, I don't know. Black and white cows were in a meadow, their heads lowered to the grass, their tails flicking while a red cardinal in the tree next to us called, "Wheet! Wheet! Wheet!" We got in Joan's car and sat in the front seat crying. Joan sobbed, "She was all alone. I wasn't here. I was doing those stupid things in stupid Hollywood with that moron who thought bluish green was the same as turquoise. I didn't even call her. I mean I called her, but when no one answered, I didn't even think something might be the matter. I figured Shanice took her out in the car. Where's Shanice? Why isn't Shanice here?"

"I don't know. I don't know."

Then, much to my amazement, my sister said, "Do you think she left us any money?"

"How will we ever know?"

"What's the name of her lawyer?"

"I have no idea."

"Did she have a lawyer?"

"No idea."

"So how are we ever going to find out?"

"Go through her files, I guess."

"I don't have time to go through her files, Sonya. They're putting together that display at Macy's. I have so much work. I . . . if I don't . . . I have . . . if I don't . . . I'm the . . . I can take work home but—"

"Joan. I'll do it. Just stop. I'll do it."

"I can't dump all that on you."

"Shouldn't we call everybody?"

"Do you think her cats are dead?"

Instead of driving back to Manhattan with Joan, I rented a car and drove to my mother's house. Vines had choked the gardens and, as I got out of the car, some creature darted away into the woods. The house seemed to be reverting to the self it was when Mother bought it. Maybe its fate was to be a hopeless wreck. The front door was open. Vandals had ransacked the place, took her television, the computer, the stereo, the coffee table. Her cats were walking skeletons but kept themselves alive by eating mice. There were tiny bones on the floor. The most disgusting thing was someone's shit in the downstairs toilet. I flung up the windows, the cats raced outside, and I went into the study to begin the tedious search for documents that might help us locate her assets.

It was haunting to see her handwriting still on this earth though she wasn't. Her spidery scrawl appeared in a collection of ledger books, Large Cap, Mid Cap, Market Value, Fixed Income, PG, XOM, CVX, MSFT. I found birthday cards from Joan and me, and there was a poem I wrote in second grade, all the letters painstakingly drawn, some well-balanced on blue lines and some hanging down underneath: *Once there was a tree, now it is my desk*, by Sonya Adler.

278 • WE NEVER TOLD

Then I came upon a letter from a case worker at Children's Services in Louisville, Kentucky. Its tone was tender but firm. Of course the caseworker could understand Mrs. Adler's reluctance to admit to the birth of a son she gave up for adoption, but the birth records showed that she was, in fact, the mother of a baby boy given up for adoption . . .

The letter was dated a few days before we arrived at Mother's and sat in her living room anticipating the Y2K bug on New Year's Eve. Here was the reason she didn't want me to sit at her desk, here was what she didn't want me to see.

CHAPTER TWENTY-SEVEN

....

I phoned Children's Services in Louisville. The caseworker who wrote the letter wasn't working there any more. I was given the new caseworker's number but she never picked up. I left messages. Then one day a woman picked up and told me what to do. I had to fill out a form saying I did want contact, sign it, send twenty-five dollars, and she would write to the adopted person. "Does he know about me?"

"He knows you exist."

"Does he know my name?"

"Yes, ma'am. That information is in the birth records."

"So you mean he can find out where I live?"

"I suppose he can."

"But what about him? Can't you tell me anything about him?"

"No, ma'am. I can't do that."

"But suppose he's some serial killer or something. Are you saying I just have to take a chance?"

"Yes, ma'am."

"But that doesn't seem fair."

"No, ma'am."

"So, you mean he might be stalking me right this minute?"

"Where do you live?"

"In Massachusetts."

"I can tell you he doesn't live anywhere near you."

"So, do you think I should do this?"

"I can't advise you, ma'am."

When the forms arrived in the mail, I sent a copy to Joan. She had to request contact in her own name. "Does he have any right to our money? I don't feel like sharing. Do you?"

"No."

"Then maybe we shouldn't do this."

"But shouldn't he know his mother's dead?"

"Can't the caseworker just tell him?"

"I don't know. Don't you want to meet him?"

"Not if he wants my money."

"Maybe he's rich in his own right."

"We should find that out first."

"I don't think adopted people have any rights to the property of the person who gave them up," I said.

"*You* don't think? Who are you, Clarence Darrow? Perry Mason?"

When cleaning out my mother's desk, I came upon careful records of her financial transactions and her meetings with various lawyers. I also found her will, phoned the lawyer who signed it, and went to visit his office. Violet left everything to Joan and me. She had more than doubled the money her father left her and had turned Joan and me into wealthy women. The will had to be probated, so I wouldn't know for quite a while how it felt to be free and easy with the monthly bills. I felt so lucky to have this inheritance and so sad that my mother waited until she was dead to share with me.

I phoned Children's Services again. The woman I spoke to before didn't work there any more. Her cases were being handled by a different woman. I left message after message on her machine. One day I tried and there she was. "You have to understand," she said, "we get hundreds of requests like this. I have a whole pile on my desk."

"So what's the next step?"

"I write him a letter informing him you want contact."

"You mean, he doesn't know?"

"No, ma'am."

I wondered if my mother had confided in Shanice. It didn't seem as if she did because Shanice didn't mention the baby when we got together shortly after Joan and I buried Violet's ashes in one of the overgrown gardens on her neglected property. Shanice had been in Trinidad at her father's funeral. Her cousins had gone with her so Shanice had to hire a woman she didn't know very well. She was distraught, blamed herself, said she should have known that woman was irresponsible. It was alarming to see Shanice cry not only because she was such a large person but because she cried in a way that wasn't American. It was as if her sobs were indoors then burst outdoors then ran indoors. We vowed to stay in touch.

About five months later, while working on a new book at my desk upstairs in my house, I took a break and clicked on my email. The subject line was, "Hello, I am your brother." If my eyes had been on springs, they would have boinged in and out.

"Hello, Sonya. I hope this email finds you well. The reason for my delay in responding to your request for contact is that I've been conflicted about whether to respond at all. It's not that I don't want to know you or our sister, but I appreciate how Violet handled the matter of my adoption so much that I didn't want to violate any trust she may have placed in me to leave things alone. It may well be that she was so afraid of losing your love and respect that she continued to deny my existence when I originally attempted to make contact some years ago. At that time, I was more interested in my family medical history than in establishing some kind of relationship, but I didn't get the chance to let her know.

"If you wonder when she had the time to have another child, I want you to think back to when you and your sister were seventeen and fifteen. As I get the story, she told you that she had to have surgery in Louisville to have an ovarian tumor (or other such gynecological problem) removed. I was the 'tumor' in question. I hold no ill will against Violet because I recognize that, during the 1950s, having a child out of wedlock was a social disgrace, and I'm sure she did not want to lose her social standing or the love and respect of her family up in New York. Also, I was adopted by a couple who raised me and made my life a complete joy. So if Violet had any doubts about raising me, she did the right thing by giving me up for adoption.

"Our mother named me Sebastian upon my birth. The name was later changed on my new birth certificate. Today, I am fifty-three years old and have been married for thirty years to the love of my life. We have two children. Both boys are businessmen. I am a partner in Baroff and Holder, a real estate business founded by my father's father. I am also Jewish. My daughter-in-law just gave birth to my first grandchild, so I'm in Chicago enjoying him for a while. That's about it for me. If you are so inclined, a note about you and our sister would be appreciated. Take care. Franklin Baroff."

I read the letter again and again. How did he know that "our" mother said she had a tumor? What made him think that I didn't know he existed? What did he mean that he appreciated how "our" mother handled his adoption? "Our" mother? I bristled at his claiming her. He had no idea who she was. The mother in his mind was entirely different from the mother I knew. Joan was "our" sister? He had every right to that pronoun but it made me feel invaded nonetheless.

"He thinks you don't know about him," Leo said.

"But how can I not know about him?"

"Maybe his mother told him he must never contact his birth family because that would be betraying his beleaguered birth mother who was only trying to protect her teenage children? Maybe he thinks it's his duty to keep Violet's secret?"

Much as I was excited to be in contact, much as knowing his name brought me down to earth with a satisfying jolt, his letter made me angry. His life was a complete joy while I was telling lies to my grandfather and sitting in the waiting room of the hospital where Ruby was rushed with a heart attack. "I'm writing to him," I said to Leo. "I'm going to tell him I've known about him my whole life."

"Not the best plan."

"I'm going to ask him how come Violet went to Louisville. What's in Louisville?"

"Wouldn't do that either."

"Then what should I do?"

"Don't challenge him at all. I wonder if he was adopted right away."

This seemed an odd thing to say. I never wondered if he was adopted right away. Of course he was. Wasn't he? I didn't like having Leo's thought in my head. That secret baby was mine, and Leo didn't have the right to color my ideas of him.

"What are you expecting from this guy?"

"I don't know. That he'll be my brother?"

"Meaning?"

"I don't know. We'll be all snuggly and he'll be my brother."

"It was nice of him to write to you."

Nice of him? What did Leo mean by that? Of course he wrote to me. What was nice about it? I didn't like thinking that my brother had an existence outside of my head. I didn't like thinking that he had a choice, that it was in his power to ignore me.

He wasn't on Facebook. There were a few articles in the Louisville newspaper about Baroff and Holder, a real estate development company. I waited a week until all of my impulsive responses had cooled then wrote, "Dear Franklin, Thank you for taking a chance. I was hesitant to contact you too. The woman at Children's Services in Louisville said you knew about me but wouldn't tell me anything about you. It made me so happy to learn that you are a kind and intelligent person with a life that is full of love. I've been married for a long time too. My husband is an architect, and we have two daughters. Congratulations on your new grandbaby. You mention wanting information about your medical history. I'd be glad to answer any questions you may have. I'm so happy everything turned out well for you, and I know Violet would be too. Unfortunately, she recently passed away. I hope you'll write back to me. Your sister, Sonya."

I visited Joan in New York so I could tell her in person. She was furious. "I'd never do that!" she yelled. "I'd never contact him behind your back! Never!" I explained that it wasn't behind her back. I'd sent her the contact forms, and she didn't sign them. Just because she didn't want contact with him didn't mean I didn't. I intended to contact him even if I *was* opening a can of worms, and I intended to never tell her about him or him about her if there was danger. She yelled and yelled and I was just about to pack up my suitcase and drive back to Boston when she said, "You just wanted him all to yourself."

How could that idea enter her head if the reverse weren't true, she wanted him all to herself? I'd never thought of that, competing for his friendship. When I imagined a meeting, it involved three people. Joan and I were somehow attached in that blurry vision, The Sisters. I sat down again and said, "No, Joan. I don't want him all to myself."

She said, "She named him Sebastian. I just can't believe it."

I handed her my cell phone so she could read the email I'd sent. "Leo said I shouldn't challenge him at all."

"This is a good letter," Joan said and handed the phone back to me. "I mean really what are we to him? From his point of view we're just two old ladies."

He wrote back to me, sent me pictures of his children and his new grandson. I sent him pictures of my family, asked if he'd like a photo of Violet, and when he said yes, I sent him a photo of her dressed in a black bolero jacket arms above her head clicking castanets. He replied, "Thank you!!! She was quite the looker. I see where we get our good looks, right?" Hoping for something more personal, I sent him a photo of her when she turned sixty-five, but he didn't respond to that, just told me how busy he was at work and how he and his wife bought a new house and how he was about to go get a colonoscopy. I decided to defy Leo's advice.

"Dear Franklin, I've known about you all my life. Your birth has been my most sacred secret. My children don't know and neither do my cousins. When I was fifteen, my (our) mother left Joan and me alone for four months. When relatives called from Chicago, we had to lie and say that Violet was in the tub, or at a class, or asleep. By the second month, her parents began to worry. By the fourth month, they were frantic with worry. Even my grandfather, who never chatted on the phone, called and I had to lie to him. We had to lie to our father. I worried that my mother might die. I also knew she wasn't in the least bit sick. In my twenties, I figured it out. She would not tell me the name of your father. Most surprising was the news that Violet named you Sebastian. That was the name of her baby brother who died age two when she was four. Sebastian was a little ghost who hovered over our family. I keep wondering why Violet went to Louisville to give birth to you. Do you have any idea?"

He wrote back that Violet's doctor in Scarsdale was friends with the doctor in Louisville. They were in medical school together. I imagined my mother and her doctor in Scarsdale, imagined her in his office weeping when he told her the abortion had not been successful and now it was too late. Perhaps it was his idea that she leave town.

Franklin sent the hospital records to me. All I had to do was click on the attachment. I read: "Telephone call from Dr. Jerome Levanthal advising that a baby boy had been born to the mother Violet Adler. Dr. Levanthal advised that it would be all right for a worker to interview Mrs. Adler.

"Visited Mrs. Alder. She is a charming, attractive woman with brown hair and brown eyes. She is of medium height and a little on the plump side. I advised that I had come to talk with her, as I understood she was placing her son for adoption. She welcomed my visit and had many intelligent questions to ask me. She was not curious and did not want to know details of the placement but wanted to make sure that the adoptive parents would allow him to grow up independently and not try to mold him into their set pattern. She also wanted to be sure that they would be financially able to enable the child to have higher education. At this point, I asked about her education. She advised that she only completed high school. She studied dancing in Spain and later gave concerts. She brought out that she comes from a creative family. Her father, Max Greenstone, is an inventor. Her mother, Hazel Greenstone, is an authoress. Her uncle is Maurice Ravel, the author of Bolero. Her father was born in this country, and her mother came from Lithuania when she was three years old. Violet is forty-two years old. She was born in El Paso, Texas, where her parents still live. She was the middle child. She has a brother and a sister. She married and has two children, aged fifteen and sixteen. They are both attending school. She is divorced. She hopes to return to her home in Scarsdale, New York by May 10th, as her maid wants to leave on that date. She spoke of what wonderful daughters she had, and she wanted me to know that she had been a good mother to them. In fact, they said that when they had children they were going to rear them just as she had done. She has always enjoyed good health.

She came to Louisville under the arrangement of her physician, who is a friend of Dr. Jerome Levanthal. Her family thinks that she is being operated on for a tumor. She asked me several times whether this information was confidential, bringing out that she had the responsibility of rearing two teenage daughters and, if they ever found out about this, she might lose their love and respect. I assured her of the confidentiality of our office. When I asked about the baby's father, she asked if it would be possible not to give identifying information. She pointed up that he does not know of her pregnancy and she does not want to hurt him. All she would say is that he is also Jewish, in good health, has had a high school education, is forty-three years old, and has brunette coloring and is of average size. I told her that I thought this information would suffice. I described the necessity of signing a surrender at the Chancellor's office. She was most accepting of this and asked if I would check with the doctor to see when she could leave the hospital. She does not know the name or anything about the adoptive parents. When she asked whether these were people were of a high cultural level, I told her merely that they were professional people and she seemed pleased at this. She brought out that by the law of averages her child would be creative. She has been doing interior decorating independently. For a while, she taught Spanish dancing but did not care for the teaching phase and gave it up. When I started to leave, she said that she would like to discuss her plans with me. She is thinking of marrying another man who has three sons. She spoke longingly of always wanting to have a son. She could not allow herself to see this baby as she knew that if she saw him she would love him and then would be unable to give him up. We talked for a while about the difference of middle-age marriages and marriages of youth and what one looked for in this type of marriage. She felt that companionship and security and having a big family was now what she wanted. She said that she had time to think about this and would make up her mind on her return home whether the man would fulfill her expectations.

"I asked if there was anything I could do for her. She said that she could not think of anything but would like to have my name and address so that if she thought of something later she could call me. I told her that I would be in touch with her baby for a year after the interlocutory decree and that we would use the same measure in appraising the adoptive home as we had done in appraising her. She seemed pleased to hear of this. Told her that I would call her before she left to again wish her good luck. She seemed pleased at this. On my return to the office, spoke with Dr. Jerome Levanthal, who felt that she could leave the hospital on Monday. He was quite surprised that I had no difficulty in getting the information I needed."

Four days later, the social worker wrote: "Secured Mrs. Adler's signature on a release form executed by hospital. Dr. Jerome Levanthal was the person to pick up the baby and deliver it to the Baroffs. Mrs. Adler was most emotional at this point. She said that she had prepared herself for it, but it was hard to face. We had quite a bit of time before we were due at the chancellor's office so stopped at the drug store where she talked at length about herself. She mentioned again her unhappy marriage. Her ex-husband is sixty-two years old. She mentioned that she apparently was looking for a father person. When I exhibited curiosity about this term, she told me that she had read many books about psychoanalysis and at last understood herself. Her husband tried to make her over. She brought out that her family were very busy people They gave her all the money she needed but not love. When she asked her father for a dollar, she got five dollars, when she asked her husband for a dollar, she got twenty-five cents. He lives close by the children, but they have no fondness for him. She wanted them to stay with him while she was gone but they refused to do so, so he does not know of her absence. She said that this love affair was a neurotic one, and she would not consider marrying the father. She told me at this point that she met a man in Florida, who was quite interested in her. She told him that she was going to Louisville for an ovarian operation. Just recently, he called her and told her that he knew it was not an ovarian operation but that she was pregnant. He loved her and could understand this and wanted to come and see her. He flew down for a day, even though she did not want him to come because of her looks. They reached a determination to marry in a year, as her divorce decree impels her to remain in Scarsdale for another year. Mrs. Adler brought out that money had never been one of her problems.

"She bought out a great many fears at this point about using her own name. She said that she had to do this to receive mail from her family and children. She spoke of what she did to keep occupied during this waiting period. She purchased two birds, she did some knitting, and was doing some fabric painting. Again she asked many questions about the adoption and our agency. We then took a cab to the Court House. Mrs. Adler again brought out her dread of the chancellor being a moralist, and I assured her that this was not so. She went into his chamber and came out very much relieved. She thanked me for my help and expressed a great deal of regret she had not had the benefit of our service earlier.

"Telephone call from Mrs. Baroff advising that the baby had arrived, and that he was a gorgeous baby."

I sat for a long time at my desk, heart aching for my mother so young and all alone in Kentucky, so full of shame. Most touching were the fibs she told the social worker. By placing her parents in El Paso, the hospital could never find them. Her father was an inventor, if looked at in a certain way. He was one of the first to invent not only the idea of feeding vitamins to livestock but the way to do it. As for her mother being an "authoress," Grandma Greenstone did write a lot of letters to her sisters and her grandchildren. As for Maurice Ravel being Violet's uncle, I knew she liked *Bolero* but I didn't know she liked it *that* much. She probably thought Maurice Ravel was Jewish.

The part about a suitor from Florida was baffling. She never went to Florida and didn't know anybody there. Was the suitor with the three sons the same man as the one in Florida? She wanted to appear lovable to the social worker not knowing that even without the fibs the social worker found her lovable.

The social worker was not the sort of person who liked Violet because she liked everybody. There were plenty of people the social worker didn't like and the new mother was one of them. "Visited the Baroff family. Franklin was propped up in a stroller watching television. He watches television for hours. He especially enjoys animated cartoons and Arlene Francis. He is a very beautiful child, who looks exactly like his natural mother. Mrs. Baroff is very smug about the way she cares for the baby. She told long tales of how friends observe her care. Mrs. Baroff brought out that she was with him so much that he refused to go to his father. She had many questions, which were mostly rhetorical to receive reassurance that she was doing the right thing."

I phoned Joan to tell her that I had the hospital records. "Those files are private!" Joan said. "First of all, how did he get them, and second of all what's he doing passing them around all over the place?"

"I'm hanging up, Joan. I can't stand talking to you." I was hurt that she did not appreciate the skill it took to get those records, how careful I had to be not to scare Franklin away, and how precious the records were for shedding light on that time in our lives.

"You have no respect for our mother. None." This was her most strident big sister voice.

"What are you afraid of?"

"Afraid? I'm not afraid. I just think it's wrong to go prying into our mother's life. Just because she's dead it doesn't mean she doesn't have a right to privacy."

"How come you don't email him? Don't you think it hurts his feelings to be ignored by you?"

"It's none of your business. If I want to email him, I will. If I don't, it's got nothing to do with you. You're being so mean."

"I'm being mean? You're being mean. You don't appreciate how much work I've put into finding our brother. Now all you do is blame me. That's all you do."

"I don't understand why you're being so mean. You're making such a big deal out of this, making it so unpleasant and horrible."

We hung up, and I thought how strange it would be to gain a brother and lose a sister. A perfect example of unintended consequences. How strong was the bond between Joan and me? Could I get used to not having a sister? Would I trade Franklin for Joan? Didn't her heart go out to him, rejected at birth then again when he tried to find his mother as an adult? Even though he could never actually meet his birth mother now that she was dead, didn't Joan think it was time to end whatever suffering remained?

CHAPTER TWENTY-EIGHT

....

At first there was a kind of ecstasy in my email exchange with Franklin, as if we were girlfriends at camp meeting up after a winter's absence and were hugging while jumping up and down. Then the tone became flatter and we exchanged information about ourselves, his being mostly about his health. He reported having a cold, getting an EKG, having a stomach ache. He never described his parents or his childhood home or his feelings about being adopted. He never asked any questions about our grandparents or cousins or aunts or uncles. I wanted him to know some of our history, so I inserted a few items unasked in the emails. I mentioned that our grandmother knew Pancho Villa but even that dramatic little tidbit seemed to go unnoticed. Our emails became fewer, from once a week to once a month to only now and then. The honeymoon lasted more than a year. When I sought the answer, Lord Google told me this was typical of adopted sibling reunions. Big flurry, then nothing. I didn't have a brother, after all. I had imagined that I was rescuing him, easing his sorrow but I'd misplaced my sympathy. He was not seeking a connection to me. Not once in our email exchanges had he asked about my children or my husband or my life as a writer. He had not asked about his cousins or grandparents. Now he had vaporized.

So it was a surprise, three years later, to receive an email from Franklin saying that he was going to attend a housing conference in Boston. Would I be in town and could we meet? He would be staying at the Copley Plaza for three days. "Don't expect too much," Leo said.

I phoned Joan. "He's coming to town, and I'm going to meet him. Do you want to come too?"

"You're going to meet him? Without me?"

"What do you mean? I just told you."

"You arranged to meet him without me?"

"No! He's coming to a conference. I didn't arrange anything."

"But you know I can't come. You know I have to be in Stockbridge that day. You know those morons there need supervision."

"How am I supposed to know you're going to Stockbridge? Did you tell me? No you did not. Not to mention that the day isn't up to me. It's up to him."

"Well, I can't come. So that should make you happy."

I agonized about what to wear. Would someone brought up in Kentucky prefer the tucked-in cowgirl look, the polished corporate executive look, the beehive hair country singer look? Dressed just like myself in loose writer's clothes, nothing binding, soft fabrics, autumn colors, I walked under the red awning of the Copley Plaza Hotel and into the glittery gold lobby, maneuvered around people waiting at the reception desk, and entered the dim old-world gentleman's club atmosphere of the hotel bar. At night, the red curtains were closed but now, in the middle of the day, they were open with a view of the street and jaywalking pedestrians gingerly stepping over snow mounds.

Only two of the little round tables were taken, one by an elderly couple and the other by my cousin Wiley. What was Wiley doing here? How did Wiley know about Franklin Baroff? I walked over to the table intending to say, "Not funny, Wiley. Not funny at all," but as I approached the man stood up and I saw it wasn't Wiley. Wiley, though in his seventies, stayed trim by playing racquetball every day. This man, dressed in a plaid shirt and fleece vest, had the round belly of the sedentary and the slight sag of middle age. He had Wiley's green eyes, full lips, cleft chin, and curly gray hair. The man said, "Sonya? I'm Franklin Baroff." Was I supposed to kiss him? Were we supposed to clasp like long lost siblings in a movie? He didn't know what to do either. A handshake seemed too cold, a kiss too intimate. We just stood there while I gawked at how familiar he looked. He extended his hand to me and smiled and that's when I saw the gap between his teeth and I had to sit down because my stomach flipped over. It was Uncle Jack's gap, the right tooth slightly turned in. The baby wasn't the secret. The father was.

My mother's secret that I so wanted to cough up would now be stuck in my throat for as long as Wiley was my cousin, which was forever. Should I spare him? Or should I just put my own comfort above his and say your father slept with my mother and they had a child. Your father slept with his sister-in-law and my mother slept with her brother-in-law and the resulting son is as much your brother as he is my brother.

"What'll you have?" Franklin said, sitting down opposite me in the dim bar of the hotel. I ordered a Manhattan thinking that would give him permission to order a drink in the middle of a sunny day but he ordered iced tea. "I'm sorry, sir," the waiter said. "We don't have iced tea."

"What do you mean you don't have ice tea?" He pronounced it ahs tea.

"We don't serve iced tea in the winter, sir."

"The winter? What does the winter have to do with it? It's ahs tea, not watermelon."

"I'm sorry, sir."

"I never heard of a place that doesn't serve ahs tea."

"I'm sorry, sir."

"Okay, okay. Bring me a Coke." When the waiter left, Franklin said to me, "What kind of place doesn't serve ahs tea? Don't y'all drink ahs tea?"

My impulse was to say, listen baby bro, you're in Yankee territory now, so man up. "In the summer mostly," I said. My gaze must have burned because he lowered his eyes and indulged in what must have been a childhood habit. He chewed on his tongue. The edge of his tongue. This nervous habit was so reflexive he probably didn't know he was doing it. He sat opposite me with lowered eyes while he rotated his tongue around in his mouth and clamped down on it here, then here, then here. It lasted less than a minute. Then he said, "We drink it all year round."

I wanted the Manhattan to hurry up. "I wish I still smoked," I said.

"Not good for you," he said and he wagged his finger at me in a scolding way. "You should quit."

"I don't smoke," I said.

"But you just said you wanted a cigarette."

"No, I said . . . How long will you be in town?"

"Just 'til tomorrow."

"Are you finding the conference useful?"

"I didn't know it was going to be so cold. Is it always this cold here?"

"No. Sometimes it's much colder." I wanted to say your father was the son of a farmer in Colorado, and by the time the acreage was sold, Denver had sprawled to the edge of the farm so your father sold it for a fortune. You not only have two half-sisters, Joan and me, but you have three half-brothers, one of whom is Wiley who nowadays is taking his fashion cues from the Hells Angels, wearing a black leather motorcycle jacket and black boots, and his colleagues at Merrill Lynch allow for that violation of the dress code because he sells so many mutual funds to elderly widows who love his courtly attentions and don't question him too closely about the fees. "Are you interested in hearing about your family?" I said. The waiter arrived. "Ah," I said with relief as he set the drinks down on the table.

"My wife," Franklin said, "is active in looking up genealogy on the Internet. She wondered about our connection to Maurice Ravel." He put the accent on the first syllable, as in unravel. Maurice ravel up the yarn.

Should I continue the fib? Tell him he was from a musical family, that our family had original manuscripts with Ravel's own notations on them and that Grandma Greenstone had Ravel's same chin? Or should I blurt out, how could we be related to him, he was Catholic! I raised my martini glass toward him, he raised his tumbler of Coke, we lightly knocked the glasses together but I couldn't say a word because now I remembered.

It was that time Uncle Jack came to New York without Dovey Lee and my mother came home late. I knew what train she had to catch at Grand Central in order to be home by eleven and also what train she had to catch to be home by midnight. I heard her key in the front door of the apartment in Scarsdale at three in the morning, then heard her bedroom door close. Next day she reported that she took her brother-in-law to Gallagher's Steakhouse. "How come you came home so late?" Now her startled reply, which for years had been standing on tiptoe in my memory, settled into context. "Oh, you know Jack. Talk, talk, talk."

Franklin said, "L'Chaim," and took a sip of Coke. When I took a sip of Manhattan, he said, "Careful there. That's a strong one."

I had no idea what to say to him. "How are your children?"

"All I wanted," he said, "was medical history. My son was going to have a baby. I needed to know if there was Tay-Sachs, Gaucher, maybe Bloom Syndrome. I would have cleared this up on the phone, but she didn't give me a chance to tell her."

"I'm sorry."

"Turned out all right. The child's healthy."

"Thank goodness for that." I took another sip of alcohol, felt my insides loosen. Then what he just said sunk in. "On the phone? You spoke to her on the phone?"

Franklin chewed on his tongue while he stirred the ice around in his Coke with his index finger, then looked at me across the table. "The reason I wanted to meet with you, Sonya," he said, "is to tell you I met our mother."

"What? When?"

"She did not sign the contact veto form so I was free to search on my own. Took me years, but I finally traced her to a village in New York State incorporated in 1875 and located in a valley on the east branch of the Delaware River, population about six hundred. Used to produce most of the cauliflower consumed in the United States. Now seems like the farmers are selling out to retired folks moving up from New York City."

"You found her?"

"She didn't mention it?"

"No. Never."

"Well, she was, I don't know how to say this, but she was sort of out of it."

"Did she tell you the name of your father?"

"No, she did not."

"Did you ask?"

"No, I did not."

"Why?"

"Because she didn't know who I was."

"How could she not know who you were?"

"Because she never learned the name of the family who adopted me. My name meant nothing to her."

"Who did you tell her you were?"

"Friend of yours."

"Of mine?"

"I phoned up and spoke to a Chantelle, some name like that."

"Shanice."

"Told her I was a friend of yours from college and wanted to stop by to say howdy."

"But I went to a girls' school!"

"She told me to come right along."

"But why would Shanice let some strange man come into the house?"

"Violet thought she remembered me from when y'all lived in New Rochelle. Thought I was the neighbor boy."

"Oh my god! She got you mixed up with Stevie Barash!"

"Maybe could be. The folks at the general store called her place the old Huntington place. Knew just where it was."

"And they knew her?"

"They knew she lived there. Called her the Queen of the Alone People."

"No!"

"Just a harmless way of saying she stuck to herself mostly." We both took a sip of our drinks. Outside a siren was faint in the distance then screamed by then faded. "That was some entrance gate! Very nearly scared me off when I saw that thing. Didn't know what to do at first, then saw that gizmo attached to it and spoke into it and the gate opened up. Creaky like. Opened a little, then stopped, then opened some more. Needed oiling I reckon." Franklin signaled the waiter. "Bring me more ice."

"What did she do when she met you?"

"She was sitting on a chaise lounge with a throw over her legs. Started talking about New Rochelle, the house there. Said her husband was in the movie business and made a screen test of her. Said all she was to him was a flower in his lapel. Then she says, I'm the luckiest person in the world. I have two of the loveliest daughters. Both so talented. One is an artist and the other is a writer. I'm so proud of both of them. And who are you, Sir? I tell her I'm Franklin Baroff, and we shake hands. She says I see you brought me some chocolates. I said yes I did. She says then let's open them right up and have some. What d'ya say? So the maid takes the box from me, tears off the wrapping, and presents the assortment to Violet. She says, I hope I get a caramel. Shanice says not that one, Vye Vye. That's going to be a cherry. You don't like the cherries. Shanice plucks out a square one and says choose this one, Vye Vye, and she puts the candy into Violet's mouth. Violet says, Umm. Delicious. Thank you, Franklin Baroff."

"So she never knew."

"No, ma'am. Never suspected."

"Are you glad you did it?"

"Yes and no."

"You mean sometimes day dreaming is superior to real life?"

He looked at his watch. "Well, that's about it for me, Sonya. Have to get back to the conference. Signed up for a panel discussion about controlling mold." He stood up, I stood up. Then we had a brief embarrassed hug and he walked out of the bar and I couldn't tell if he meant to leave me the check or if he just forgot because he was frazzled. Maybe he thought I was the older sister so I should pay for the drinks. I didn't mind. I paid and went out into the lobby and sat on one of the upholstered benches and fished out my phone. "Hey, Siri. Call Leo." Then when I finished telling my husband, I called Joan and said, "Are you sitting down?"

ACKNOWLEDGMENTS

. . . .

The Author wishes to thank the following people for their help: Beena Kamlani, Carol Rial, Claudia Goldyne, Jane Murphy, Katharine Davis, Kathryn Bild, Liam Everett, Nancy Newman, Richard Siegel, Vanessa Altman-Siegel, and Barbara Newman.

ABOUT THE AUTHOR

Diana Altman is the author of two books: *Hollywood East, Louis B. Mayer and the origins of the studio system* (Carol Publishing, '92) and *In Theda Bara's Tent* (Tapley Cove Press, 2010). Her short stories appeared in the *Notre Dame Review, Trampset, StoryQuarterly,* and *The Sea Letter*. Her articles are published in the *New York Times, Yankee, Boston Herald, Forbes, American Heritage, Boston Phoenix*, and other places. She is past president of the Boston chapter of the Women's National Book Association and current member of the New York City Chapter, as well as a member of PEN and the Author's Guild. She lives with her husband in Manhattan in the winter and Maine in the summer, where she teaches writing workshops. A graduate of Connecticut College and Harvard University, she sings in the 92nd St Y chorus and plays squash at the Harvard Club. She can be contacted at www. DianaAltman.com and dianaaltman3@gmail.com.

Author photo © Diana Altman

SELECTED TITLES FROM SHE WRITES PRESS

She Writes Press is an independent publishing company founded to serve women writers everywhere. Visit us at www.shewritespress.com.

Eden by Jeanne Blasberg. $16.95, 978-1-63152-188-1. As her children and grandchildren assemble for Fourth of July weekend at Eden, the Meister family's grand summer cottage on the Rhode Island shore, Becca decides it's time to introduce the daughter she gave up for adoption fifty years ago.

A Cup of Redemption by Carole Bumpus. $16.95, 978-1-938314-90-2. Three women, each with their own secrets and shames, seek to make peace with their pasts and carve out new identities for themselves.

Arboria Park by Kate Tyler Wall. $16.95, 978-1631521676. Stacy Halloran's life has always been centered around her beloved neighborhood, a 1950s-era housing development called Arboria Park—so when a massive highway project threaten the Park in the 2000s, she steps up to the task of trying to save it.

The Belief in Angels by J. Dylan Yates. $16.95, 978-1-938314-64-3. From the Majdonek death camp to a volatile hippie household on the East Coast, this narrative of tragedy, survival, and hope spans more than fifty years, from the 1920s to the 1970s.

Magic Flute by Patricia Minger. $16.95, 978-1-63152-093-8. When a car accident puts an end to ambitious flutist Liz Morgan's dreams, she returns to her childhood hometown in Wales in an effort to reinvent her path

All the Light There Was by Nancy Kricorian. $16.95, 978-1-63152-905-4. A lyrical, finely wrought tale of loyalty, love, and the many faces of resistance, told from the perspective of an Armenian girl living in Paris during the Nazi occupation of the 1940s.